HEARTLESS VILLAIN

K. LORAINE

USA TODAY BESTSELLING AUTHORS

MEG ANNE

Edited by Mo Sytsma of Comma Sutra Editorial

Cover Design by CReya-tive Book Design

To Kat, our chancla queen,
This is all your fault.

HEARTLESS
VILLAIN

AUTHORS' NOTE

Heartless Villain contains mature and graphic content that is not suitable for all audiences. Such content includes scenes of CNC, torture, ritual sacrifice, mentions of mental illness and more. **Reader discretion is advised.**

As always, a detailed list of content and trigger warnings is available on our website.

PART ONE
CHECK

"I SUPPOSE IT'S LIKE THE TICKING CROCODILE, ISN'T IT? DEATH IS
CHASING AFTER ALL OF US."*

J. M. BARRIE, *PETER PAN*,
*IMPROVED BY CASPIAN HOOK

"OH, THE CLEVERNESS OF ME!"

POST-SESSION TRANSCRIPT: KAI

Dr. Masterson: This is Dr. Elizabeth Masterson. Today marked my first session with new resident, Malakai Nash. These are my observations.

<<pacing footsteps>>

Dr. Masterson: Subject name, Malakai Nash—goes by Kai—hereinafter referred to as D174. Species, fae dragon shifter, affiliated with the Shadow Court. Age, thirty years. Height, six foot four. Weight unknown, but he's powerfully built, as is expected with his kind. Notable markings, sentient tattoo containing his dragon (more on that to follow). Location varies.

<<chair squeak>>

Dr. Masterson: In addition to his secondary form, D174 presents with strong fae magic, which he utilizes in the form of spelled tattoos done for profit. From what I gather, this is rare, and he may be one of only a dozen capable of such work. Note—research this further.

<<typing>>

Dr. Masterson: D174 is despondent. Withdrawn. Fully in denial about his potential and his dragon's importance. I've never encountered a dragon shifter with fire as powerful as his. But the notes provided upon intake confirm my suspicions. D174's flames burn so hot the sandy earth beneath the ruined village turned to glass.

<<fingers drumming on desk>>

Dr. Masterson: *sigh* In order to fully realize his skills and strengths, extensive work will need to be done with D174 to break down the barriers he has raised not only emotionally, but quite literally. The previously mentioned sentient tattoo is not mere artwork, but is, in fact, an avatar of his secondary form. The spell woven into the tattoo is acting as a sort of prison to keep him from taking control of his host. This is problematic, and I fear if his dragon isn't acknowledged and accepted, a catastrophic splintering will occur, and both will be lost.

<<chair squeak>>

Dr. Masterson: *musing hum* My suggested treatment plan as of now is to force the reunion of D174 and his dragon. I can only assume heightened mental aptitude, so I will need to be careful in my approach. If he realizes what I am after, he will actively seek to thwart my attempts. If only he had a mate I could recruit to my purpose. It would make things so simple. No male can resist the lure of his mate for long, and her presence would most certainly force the issue of D174 and his dragon rejoining.

<<fingers drumming on desk>>

Dr. Masterson: *sigh* Best not to dwell on that, as the likelihood of finding her is less probable than the metaphorical needle in a haystack. *chuckles* The needle would be easier to find, no doubt. So, short of her falling into my lap, I will have to find another way. He's too important to lose. For now, I will assign him a tower in addition to his quarters. Every dragon needs a hoard, after all. Best to do what we can to foster those baser instincts and see if that doesn't help to offset, or at the very least mitigate, the damage caused by his forced separation.

<<static>>

End of transcript.

CHAPTER
ONE

DAHLIA

I'd never been this cold before. It was a bone-deep chill that ached in a way I couldn't describe. My limbs felt like they'd been cast in lead. I couldn't lift anything, not even a finger. The frigid December wind whipped around me, but even that felt warm compared to the chill that had settled all the way in my marrow. Even with Tor's body heat as he held me against him, I wasn't able to combat the cold.

Distantly, I knew it was due to the blood loss and that I was dangerously close to bleeding out. All of that seemed secondary to the giant fucking dragon arcing through the star-speckled sky.

"Eyes on me, beauty. Don't you dare close them," Tor said, his voice tight and frantic. "Caspian, get something to stop the bleeding."

"What do you suggest I use? I don't exactly have a medical kit in my frock coat."

"Your shirt has more fucking ruffles than a pair of pantaloons," Hades grumbled. "Useless idiot."

I heard rustling before the scent of my shadow daddy

enveloped me. He'd draped his suit jacket over my chest, and the warmth of his body lingered in the fibers of the fabric. I inhaled deeply, closing my eyes and drawing his scent into my lungs. It didn't do much for the chill, but it was comforting in the way of chicken soup or a stuffed animal.

A strange ripping sound came from behind me before a shirtless Caspian appeared in my periphery, strips of his ruffly pirate shirt held in his hands. He made a valiant effort to make tourniquets, but I knew these wounds were too long and deep. Nothing would stop the bleeding except for stitches or maybe one of those magic healers. Alas, I didn't think anyone was carrying one around in their pocket.

A husky chuckle escaped at the absurdity of my thoughts. It hurt to laugh, though, and the sound immediately became a wince.

"Quiet now, baby doll. You need to save your strength." God, even Hades sounded worried. It really was serious.

"You're not the boss of me," I forced out.

His face came into view, brows drawn, mouth a tight line, eyes burning blue and intense. "Yes I fucking am. Now be a good girl and stop wasting your breaths. I won't lose you again."

"Asshole would never speak to me that way," I grumbled, feeling equal parts bullied and loved. If I wasn't about to pass out from the blood loss, I probably would have swooned like one of those fancy Victorian ladies in a Kerrigan Byrne novel. I wondered if the guys would think it was sexy if I flashed them some ankle. Technically, I was flashing them everything up to mid-thigh, so probably not.

"Dahlia, I swear to—"

I clumsily lifted my arm—which was fucking hard—

and slapped my fingers down on his kissable mouth. "Shadows can't talk. Didn't you—"

Annnd his lips weren't under my fingers anymore. They were on mine. I wished I could feel them better. In fact, I wished I was fully in Tor's arms and not still on this disgusting altar.

"Save the sass for when I can properly deal with you, baby," he murmured against my lips. Then he straightened to his full height and looked off into the distance.

My gaze followed his. The dragon made a shadow in the light of the moon, cutting a breathtaking picture. As we watched, a column of flames rushed from Kai, lighting up the night and promising death to his target.

"Fucking hell, that's marvelous," Cas said under his breath, awestruck. "Guess that's the Ripper managed, then."

"Cas, go as fast as you can and get the healer. She will have something to put our girl back together. Meet us in Dahlia's room," Tor commanded, sliding an arm beneath my legs as he scooped me up.

"Wait," I protested weakly. "We can't leave Kai."

"The dragon will manage just fine," Tor said, already moving toward the castle. I think he'd have run if he wasn't worried about jostling me.

"It's what he'd want, baby doll," Hades said, keeping pace with my Viking. "Let us take care of you."

My eyes grew heavier with every step Tor took, the swaying too soothing to fight off the urge to slip into unconsciousness's comforting embrace.

"Eyes open," Hades snapped.

It took every bit of energy I had to obey. I knew they were worried. Hell, so was I. But my body and my will were not equal partners right now.

9

"We're losing her," Tor said, his voice sounding like it was coming from the other end of a tunnel.

"Dahlia? Dahlia, stay with us."

Hades's frantic pleas weren't enough to keep me conscious this time. Even with my eyes open, my vision faded until darkness overtook me.

When I blinked my eyes open again, I found Tor's stubbled jaw tense with worry above me.

"Hey," I breathed.

"She's back," he announced, his pace quickening as he took the stairs two at a time.

"Don't do that to us, baby doll. My rapidly unraveling control can only take so much."

"Your control," Tor muttered.

I'd have laughed if I could.

Hades trailed his fingers over my arm, or maybe his shadows did. I couldn't tell because, unfortunately, I was about to go under again.

"She's lost too much blood," I heard Tor say as my vision went dark again. "She won't last long."

"She fucking better." Hades's voice whispered through my mind even as I drifted away. "Listen to me, Persephone. I will be furious with you if you make me chase you back to the underworld. I will dredge the River Styx until I find your soul, and I won't rest until you're back by my side. You. Are. Mine. Do you understand me? Not even Death can have you."

I would have sworn his words were accompanied by a peal of female laughter, but there was no way to know for sure.

The next time I opened my eyes, we were standing in the hallway outside my room.

"Goddess, she's so pale. She looks like a ghost," Cas said

from my side. I wanted so badly to turn and tell him I'd be okay, but it was too hard.

"Where's the healer?" Tor bit out.

"I'm the best kind of healer there is, Mr. Nordson. Now put her on the bed so I can help your mate." Oh my God, was that the hot Irish priest? What was he doing here?

Somehow we made it into my room. My eyes couldn't track anything anymore. I had to close them because the movement made me dizzy. Tor laid me on my bed, his barely contained growls somehow comforting.

"Oh, my sheets," I protested faintly.

"Fuck the sheets," Hades barked. "Fix her."

"I don't take orders from you," hot Irish priest said, cool as you please. If I survived the night, I definitely had to give Sunday a high five. That man's voice was sinful.

"You're certain you're okay with this, a stor? A mated vampire sharing blood with another is . . ."

"Caleb, you can save her. You were right to offer. Do it." That Sunday, she was a fucking star. I'd have to put her at the top of my acknowledgments in my next book.

Everything felt as though it was happening to someone else. Sort of like I was experiencing it secondhand or watching it play out on the TV. I was there, but my brain was so fuzzy I didn't feel like I was all that present. Was this what an out-of-body experience was?

I opened my eyes and saw the most beautiful pair of sapphire-blue irises looking back at me. Oh, I definitely understood the appeal of Father Gallagher.

"He's spoken for, darling. Settle down," Cas warned.

"And so are you," Tor added.

Oops. I guess I said that out loud.

I tried to wave a hand but ended up hitting myself in the face instead. "Just shopping for windows."

"Was that supposed to make sense?" Cas asked.

Sunday snickered. "She meant to say window shopping. And feel free to look all you want, sweetie. He's a work of art, definitely worth appreciating."

Before I knew it, Caleb put his wrist to his lips and was bringing the bleeding wound toward my mouth. My stomach rolled, and fear brought clarity to my addled brain. I turned away, but Hades stopped me with a gentle but firm hand.

"No . . . don't want to be a vampire."

Caleb's gaze was warm and kind. "You won't, lamb. It takes a great deal more than what I'm giving you to turn a supernatural creature into one of my kind."

"I'm a human," I slurred.

"No, baby doll. You're not." Hades held my head in place so Caleb could fit his wrist to my mouth. "Now drink. Take what he's offering, please, darlin'. For me."

"For all of us," Tor said.

My nose crinkled in disgust, or I thought it did. It was hard to know what the rest of my body was doing at the moment. But instead of repulsive, the first drop of the warm liquid against my tongue was surprisingly nice. Not chocolate brownie sundae nice, but not too far off from a semi-sweet red wine. That knowledge helped me relax enough to take what he was offering. It also didn't hurt that I immediately felt relief. Say what you will about vampires, but their blood was the best kind of morphine. I could see why people became addicted.

Caleb pulled his arm back, and I instinctively leaned forward, searching for more of the delicious, life-giving blood he'd offered me. "That's enough, Miss Moore. You'll drain me dry if I let you keep at it. Then my Sunday won't be so understanding."

"Been there, done that," Sunday muttered. "Zero out of ten, do not recommend."

Hades repositioned me against his chest, and I let my gaze drift over my bloodied arms. The wounds were knitting together as I watched, nothing left to indicate I'd been harmed save the dried blood coating my skin. Fuck, I felt better than I had in a long time.

"I'm not going to sparkle, right?"

"No more than you already do." Cas winked and gave me a roguish smirk for good measure.

Caleb sat back, sweat beading across his forehead, skin paler than when I'd first seen him. "Did Kingston tell you to say that? That fecking arsehole of a wolf is asking for it."

I didn't know what that meant, but I giggled anyway. Honestly, I felt so rejuvenated I thought I could do anything right now.

"No wonder you guys stay hidden," I mused.

"What's that?" Caleb asked.

"If humans found out what your blood can do, they'd capture you all and build a pharmaceutical empire out of the stuff."

"Stupider mortals have tried."

A little shiver raced down my spine, and I was instantly thankful that Caleb was on our side. He was a little scary when he wasn't saving my life and Irishing all over the place.

Sunday settled a palm on his shoulder and smiled at me. "Let's get back to our room, Father Gallagher. I need to replenish your supply."

Caleb cut her a hard glare, but there was a hint of a smile playing about his mouth as he did. "How many times do I have to tell you all I'm not a priest any longer?"

"At least one more, *Father*."

There was something about the way she looked at him that told me when she said 'Father' what she really meant was 'Daddy.' Amen, sister.

Sunday took his hand and tugged until he stood, his tall frame now towering over her. "Now let's go and leave our new friends to recuperate in privacy."

"Thank you, truly. I won't forget what you've done for my mate," Tor said, holding out a hand for the hot former priest to shake. Caleb nodded and returned the gesture.

"You'd do the same for mine, lad. In fact, I'm certain you have already."

"She's family," Tor said, as if it was that simple. I guess for him, it was.

With that, the two left, and I finally let the gravity of the night's events sink in. "Where's Kai?"

Cas glided across the room, his movements as graceful as any dancer I'd ever seen. When he reached the window, he used two fingers to pull the heavy drape away from the glass and peer out into the night. "Sky's clear. He must have landed."

"We have to find him. We have to make sure he—"

Before I could finish my sentence, the door burst open and revealed Kai. Naked, sweaty, and streaked with dirt and scrapes.

He heaved for breath, his eyes wild and still glowing with power.

"His dragon tattoo is gone," Cas breathed.

I didn't have time to process that, though, because my dragon mate stumbled forward, one word on his lips as his eyes rolled back in his head and he collapsed.

"Dahlia."

CHAPTER
TWO
KAI

"He's asleep in your bed on Christmas morning? Did he stuff your stocking?" Kiki's hushed voice pulled me out of the deep slumber I'd been lost to as Dahlia's scent overtook everything else around me.

"Oh my God, be quiet. He's been through a lot. He's been sleeping for days," Dahlia whispered.

Relief flooded me at the sound of her voice. She was safe. I'd killed the bastard. But then her words hit me. She said days. How long had I been out?

Kiki mentioned Christmas. I did some swift mental math. Three days.

"A dragon! The—shit, sorry, I'll be quieter. A dragon?" she finally lowered her voice to a hissed whisper, but I could hear everything. "I thought you said he couldn't release it. Fuck, that's really hot, Dee."

"It was pretty incredible," Dahlia admitted, but she sounded distracted.

My dragon chuffed, answering another question before I could give voice to it. The last time he'd had free rein, it hadn't taken such a toll on me. But if he was able to eaves-drop and preen at our mate's compliment, he was fine. The deep sleep was likely caused by my sudden and excessive use of our power. My body hadn't been prepared for the drain and needed time to recover. Next time would be easier.

"You should see him. He's magnificent. His wings . . ."

A low hum of pleasure rumbled from deep in my chest before I could stop it, and Dahlia let out a soft gasp.

"He's waking up. I'll call you back, Keeks."

"But I need to kno—"

"Merry Christmas!" Dahlia interrupted, slamming her laptop closed as I opened my eyes.

I had to blink a couple of times before I could make out the sight of Dahlia scrambling across the room to get to me. The bed dipped as she climbed in, and I laughed as she peppered my face with kisses.

"We were so worried! Are you okay? How do you feel?"

"Better now that you're here," I said, exaggerating for my own benefit. I just needed her next to me, touching me. We'd nearly lost her to that psychopath, and just the thought made fire burn in my lungs.

"Your tattoo is gone," she murmured, trailing her fingers over my bare chest.

My brows pulled together as I frowned and glanced down at myself. "Is it really?"

"I looked everywhere."

If I wasn't so confused, I'd have made a dirty joke, but that tattoo was never supposed to fade. I'd ensured it.

"Dinnae be thick. Ye know as well as I that magic can only last until the spell is broken. Ye released me from my chains. I'm as much a part of ye as ye are of me."

Right. That tracked. I'd have known straight away that

was the reason, but it would seem I wasn't firing on all cylinders just yet.

"That's because he's not locked away anymore, gem. We're one and the same now."

"As we always should've been."

Yes, well. You promise to never again murder a village of innocents, and it'll stay that way.

My dragon grumbled, but had nothing to say to that.

"I'm sorry I wasn't there to care for you," I said, forcing myself to look into her eyes even though I was afraid I'd see disappointment.

She surprised me by laughing. "What are you talking about? You killed him for me, Kai."

"Aye, I did." I swallowed hard, sitting up so I could pull her close. "I'd do anything for you, gem."

"Even if it means accepting your inner monster? I mean, that's what brought you to Blackwood in the first place. Just a couple weeks ago, you weren't super keen on the idea of making nice and singing Kumbaya with him."

Inhaling her scent, I let go of the anxious energy that had settled beneath my ribs. "This wasn't like the last time. I chose it. I welcomed my dragon. And I'd do it again in a heartbeat, lass. Like I said, I'd do anything for you. I'd burn the entire fucking world to the ground to protect you. One man or a hundred, it doesn't matter. No one harms you and lives."

"Oh, that line hits just as hard in real life as the books." She melted into me, one of her hands resting against my cheek. "Phew. Okay, now that I'm pretty sure I've ovulated at least three times, you're sure you're okay? Physically, I mean."

We'd circle back to the ovulation talk later. As much as it turned me on to picture her on her knees, letting me breed her, I needed to assure my wee mate I was up for the job. "I'm fine, lass. Dinnae fash yerself."

"But is it normal to pass out after you shift?"

"No, but it's not uncommon either. I did too much too fast. My dragon had been locked away for years, and then . . . Well, consider it the same as sprinting when I should have just been learning how to walk."

"Aw, so you're like a cute little baby dragon."

The dragon in question growled.

"Full grown and ready to prove it, more like," I said, but the tone of my voice was all my beast.

Her eyes flared with interest, but I could see the hesitance there as well.

Of course. I felt like such a bleeding idiot. She damn near been sacrificed not even a handful of nights ago. She was probably still recovering.

"Are *you* well, gem?"

"Fine."

I snagged her wrist and shoved up the sleeve of her festive jumper that said *Jingle My Balls* to expose the skin the Ripper had marked. Smooth, undamaged flesh was all that greeted me.

"Who healed you? None of them can do that." Was this a dream? Some kind of hallucination? Not even the healers could have left her without a reminder of that monster's savagery.

"Father Caleb. He gave me his blood."

A grumpy, possessive sound escaped without my permission. I dinnae like that she'd needed to rely on another to care for her. By the same token, I was so fucking glad she was safe and whole. It was a confusing place to be.

"Kai, I would've died without it."

The tremor in her voice made me check myself. She

shouldn't feel guilty for accepting his help. Cupping her face in both my hands, I pulled her toward me until our lips brushed. "I'll be forever in his debt, then."

She rested her forehead against mine, her eyes fluttering closed while a soft smile played about her lips. "I didn't realize how worried I really was until I heard your voice. It feels like an entire house just fell off my shoulders."

I chuckled. "Isn't it usually the other way around?"

"You calling me a witch, dragon?" she teased, one eye popping open with mock accusation.

"I wouldn't dream of it, gem." I ran my fingers across the sides of her throat until I reached the collar of her jumper.

She wasn't afraid of me, not disgusted by the creature I changed into, not horrified to know I'd killed for her and wouldn't hesitate to do so again. She was mine. Plain and simple.

It was time to remind her of that fact.

Gripping her hips with both hands, I kissed her hard while I simultaneously rolled us until she was underneath me. I felt her smile spread even as I kissed her, and it took the will of a god not to rock my hard length against her.

"Now back to that ovulation stuff," I crooned against her lips.

Her giggle made my cock twitch. "Oh, you liked that, huh?"

"I'm a dragon, gem. There's no greater treasure than creating a life with my mate. And yes, the thought of putting my baby inside you and caring for you while you carry my young gets me fucking hard."

"I can feel that," she teased, writhing beneath me.

"If you want it, love, I can help you feel me from the inside."

21

"Kai," she said with a laugh, "I never took you for a Nine Inch Nails fan."

"Nine inches of what?"

"Hopefully your dick."

I grinned. "Oh, it's bigger than nine inches."

"You're right." She parted her thighs wider, her pajama bottoms wet with clear evidence of her arousal.

I reached between us, sliding my hand under the waistband until I found her slick folds. She groaned and rocked into me. Fuck, all I wanted was to shove her pants down and fill her here and now.

"If you let me, I'll give you as many babies as you want," I whispered as I rubbed her clit in gentle circles. "All you have to do is say yes."

Her breath left her in shallow pants as she rolled her hips in time to my movements. "I'm going to be pretty insulted if you already forgot about our special tattoo session, dragon boy."

"Oh, I dinnae forget."

"Then you already know you can't get me pregnant."

"Easily remedied, gem. Just one little flick of my claw riiight here," I smirked when she wriggled violently beneath me as I traced the faint glow of her tattoo. To the naked eye, it would be invisible, but this magic was mine. Just as she was. I'd always be able to spot it.

She squirmed as my finger shifted into a sharp claw, her gaze locked on mine with a mixture of apprehension and excitement. Did she want me to do it? Fuck me, did my sweet treasure want me to fuck her and fill her with my child?

"Y-you can't want this right now," she breathed.

"Who says I can't?" I continued tracing the ink with my sharp claw. "The Ripper is gone. Threat neutralized. What better way to celebrate than for us to start building a family? All I want is you, Dahlia."

"B-but," she sputtered, her eyes fluttering closed as I continued my slow torment. "We're still stuck here. A-and, th-the, oh—"

"What was that?"

"The ghosts," she blurted.

"I don't see any ghosts. Besides, I have it on good authority ghosts like babies."

I flicked her swollen bundle of nerves, and my mate whimpered in response. "You're t-toying with me, aren't you?"

"I do love to play. But, gem, the thought of seeing your belly round with my child, your tits full of milk, your cunt dripping because pregnancy makes you so horny for your mates . . ." I growled low in my throat before I could continue. "I'm not playing. Not at all. Tell me I can breed you. Right. Fucking. Now."

She gushed around my fingers, and my smile stretched. "You love the idea. You're fucking soaked."

Her cheeks burned crimson as she blinked up at me. "Well, yeah . . . But not anytime soon. Definitely not this second."

"It'll take at least a month for your body to go back to normal. We have time."

She swatted at my chest, but there was no real force behind it. "Kai, you are nuts. A month is basically a sneeze away from today. That's too soon."

"Your slick cunt says otherwise."

Biting her lower lip, she flicked her gaze away from me and then took a shuddering breath. "God, Kai."

"What was that look, gem? Why won't you meet my gaze?"

She kept her eyes averted until I gripped her chin and forced her to look at me.

"What is it?" I pressed.

"It's just . . . I do want it. All of it. I never thought I could have it, honestly. I mean, my dad was a cult leader weirdo in the extreme who probably fathered at least a dozen little weirdos just like me, and he either abandoned us or abused us until we were so fucked up we ended up in an asylum with dragons, ghosts, vampires, and whatever the hell Joffrey is. I never thought anyone would want me the way you do, and to know you want to have babies with me is a lot to process, and my body might not even be capable and . . ."

My heart felt too big in my chest. I loved this woman more than anything. I wanted to give her everything she wanted. Everything she thought she'd never have.

"And what?"

"And I don't want to lay an egg, Kai."

It was such an unexpected response I couldn't contain my laughter. It came out in loud guffaws, so strong tears sprung to my eyes.

"I'm sorry, what? Why do you think you're going to lay an egg?"

"Well, you're a dragon, and dragons are reptiles, and . . . Do I really need for an explanation this to you?"

"Gem," I said through uncontrollable chuckles. "I'm fae. I'm not a shifter. My dragon is part of a curse, but my body, my blood, is fae."

"So . . . fae babies?"

I grinned. "Aye, lass. Fae babies."

"No eggs?"

"No eggs."

"Well. That changes things."

24

I returned my fingertip to the tattoo and locked eyes with her again, watching hers widen as my finger shifted into a claw once more. "Does it?"

She rolled her lower lip between her teeth and goddess, her nipples were so hard I could see them under the fabric of her jumper. Taking a deep breath, she readied herself to answer me, eyes sparkling with need.

"And here we find the rutting beast." Caspian's voice killed the moment as he strode into the bedroom. "Of course, as is befitting a dragon, he's woken up and gone straight for the prettiest present under the bloody tree."

Dahlia and I glanced over my shoulder in time to see Tor and Hades right on his heels.

"It smells like sex in here. Glad to know you're feeling better," Hades said.

"Fuck off," I growled, already mourning the loss of our privacy. Not to mention the potential baby making.

"Is he always this grumpy after a three-day nap?" Tor asked, not that anyone answered.

"Give me five more minutes, will you?"

"Only five?" Dahlia whispered while Hook scoffed.

"Not bloody likely. We've got prezzies, and a tree," he crowed, fists on his hips. "All we're missing is our girl."

"It's okay, dragon boy," Dahlia said before leaning close enough to put her lips to my ear and whisper, "You can knock me up another time."

Well, fuck. Now I wasn't going to be able to walk straight without showing the entirety of Blackwood exactly how she affected me. I stood, the tent in my pants painfully obvious.

"Did you need an ornament for that? Perhaps some tinsel?" Tor asked, a teasing glint in his eyes.

25

"I'll remember this moment the next time you have her to yourself," I muttered.

Tor clapped me on the shoulder. "Eh, cheer up. It's Christmas."

"Bah humbug."

CHAPTER

THREE

HOOK

If that dragon thought he was going to railroad me out of my very first Christmas morning, he was wrong. Christmas in the human world was something I'd never had the pleasure of experiencing, and now that my darling was with me and those dastardly whispers weren't plaguing me any longer, I was intent on having the best Christmas ever.

It was touch and go there for a minute, honestly. If Dahlia hadn't been so keen to do Christmas with us, Kai just might've gotten his way and ruined everything. The Grinch. But luck was on my side, and she got him to follow us all to the magical holiday display we'd created while the dragon slept.

"Step right up, folks. The Christmas Extravaganza awaits," I called, shoving the door to Tor's newly redecorated room open and swinging my arm wide to reveal the decorations within.

The lads, minus said grinchy dragon, had already seen it, but Dahlia's expression as she took in our handiwork was priceless.

"What in the Hallmark fairy godmother did you do?" she squealed, eyes bouncing all over as she tried to take it all in at once. "I don't know what to look at first! Stockings? Garland? Lights? Are those fucking chestnuts roasting on the fucking fire? Is the ghost of Nat King Cole going to pop out from behind the tree?" She squinted a little at one of the branches. "Is that a squirrel? Oh! It's a pixie!"

The little blur of gold light rushed out of where he'd been hiding in the branches. "Ye menaces! Can't a man collect bark for his newborn babies in peace? All I wanted was to make them rocking horses for Christmas, and then I end up kidnapped and in a Viking's torture chamber. It's bad enough you destroyed our home. You should be ashamed—"

I snatched the pixie up by the furiously flapping wings, stopping him mid-sentence as I held him up in front of my face. "Sod off, you overgrown firefly. You're killing the vibe."

He leaned forward, mouth snapping at my nose.

"Oi!" I barked, giving him a little shake and watching the glittering dust float off him. "Behave, or I'll properly hold you captive."

"You could try, you walking codpiece!"

"What was that? You don't want to return to your shimmers?" I threatened.

His mouth snapped shut in mulish displeasure.

"That's what I thought." Moving to the window, I threw it open and dropped him on the ledge. "Away with you before I change my mind. You're lucky I'm in such a festive spirit."

"Yeah, you're really Father fucking Christmas," the pixie shouted, his voice little more than a high-pitched buzz as he flitted away.

"God, all that's missing is snow!" Dahlia marveled as she focused on one thing after another.

Tor, that thunder-stealing showboat, snapped his fingers, and cold flakes of snow began floating gently from the ceiling.

"Oh, that's rich." I rolled my eyes. "He has snow, folks. If I didn't know better, I'd say you were a Kringle, not a Nordson. If I poke you in the belly, will it shake?"

His low growl told me I was treading on thin ice—pun intended.

Music began playing on the record player Hades had insisted we include. He said it sounded better. I really didn't bloody care.

Dahlia's brow lifted as she looked at Hades. "That record player has you written all over it."

"Guilty."

"And the song?"

"It's a classic."

"It's rapey."

"Still a classic."

"True," she said with a little sigh.

The grumpy dragon was still hovering by the door. We couldn't have that. His frowny face would ruin everything. "What do you think, Kai? Did we do right by our girl with our holiday surprise?"

Kai let out a soft grunt. "I suppose the look on her face makes it worth it. Still rather be buried balls deep inside her."

"Wouldn't we all," Hades murmured, picking up a cup of what was probably whiskey but could have been eggnog or hot chocolate for all I knew.

"Is that your Christmas wish?" she teased, crossing the

room and settling on Hades's lap. "Seeing as I didn't know we were doing presents, I guess that's what I'm giving you all."

Hades unbuttoned the second button of his black shirt before pinning her with a smoldering stare. "Not yet, baby doll. We've got a few things to give you."

She shook her head, her smile stretching from ear to ear. "I can't believe you managed all this."

Hades raised a brow. "Why's that?"

"It's just so *not* you," she said with a laugh.

"How do you figure?" Tor asked, moving to the tree to select the little wrapped package he'd stowed beneath it earlier that morning.

"I beg your fucking pardon, this was *my* idea. Don't you three try to take credit for it. I had the vision. You just helped make it happen." I couldn't stand by and let them swan in with their furrowed brows and dark dispositions and steal my shine.

Dahlia shot to her feet and rushed over to me. "It was a universal 'you,' Cas. I didn't mean to leave you out. Never in my wildest dreams would I have expected this as my Christmas surprise. A mind-blowing orgasm or seven, sure. But not a Christmas card come to life. I'm honestly stunned you were able to find the time. I guess all those shift rotations you three did over the last few days make more sense. This is where you were running off to, wasn't it?"

I nodded, still a titchyroo annoyed.

"I wanted it to be perfect for you. It's our first Christmas together. It should be special."

Oh my goddess, I sounded like such a wanker. But it was true. In fact . . . "If I'm being totally transparent, it's my first Christmas ever. We don't do holidays in Ravenndel. No

Hanukkah, no Christmas, not even New Year. Time stands still there. Every day is exactly the same. Beautiful. Warm. A light breeze perfect for sailing. Nothing like this."

She blinked at me, dumbfounded. "Your first . . . You're joking, right?"

I shook my head.

"We don't usually celebrate mortal holidays in the fae realm," Kai chimed in. "We have our own traditions."

"Well, now I feel even worse for not getting you a present," Dahlia pouted. "If I'd have known, I would have . . ." She trailed off again, eyes darting to the side as she thought. "Well, ordered you something online, I guess. Not too many shopping options here. But I could have written you a short story! Or a poem!"

"Stop working yourself up, beauty. This is about giving, not receiving. Allow us to give you your gifts, please?" Tor held out a small box he'd wrapped in sparkling silver paper, complete with a white ribbon and a sprig of . . . fucking holly? Wow. Big man really takes his gift wrap seriously.

Dahlia's eyes were wide, and her lower lip wobbled as she took the present. Preemptively, I pulled a handkerchief from my pocket so I could gallantly offer it to her once the inevitable waterworks began.

She gave the package a tentative shake. "It's not teeth, is it?" she asked, brow low with worry.

Tor laughed. "Not this time."

At his reassurance, she unwrapped her present with a considerable amount of enthusiasm. "Oh, Tor," she breathed, letting all the wrapping fall to the floor as she pulled out a simple silver band. She moved over to the fireplace to get a better look at the details. "Are these runes?"

"Yes. It says, Kærasta, just there." He joined her and

pointed out the word, then whispered, "And my name is inscribed on the inside. Wear it on your left hand, so I'm always near your heart. As you are to mine," he said, holding up his own hand.

Matching rings. Gag. Why hadn't I thought of that?

She inspected his ring and pressed a kiss to it before asking, "When did you have time to get these?"

"I made them in the Novasgardian tradition, as passed down to me by my father and his father before him. They were forged from the blade of your enemy in the fires of Hades."

Her gaze flicked to the man himself. "You helped him?"

"'Course I did. There wasn't a fire hot enough since our dragon was down for the count."

Returning her attention to the rings, she ran her fingers over hers, then Tor's, pausing and looking up at the big beast. "Why is yours different? It looks almost the same as mine."

The Viking's cheeks went pink and I nearly let out a loud snort. He was embarrassed. "It says Kærasto."

"Kærasto? But you said that wasn't a thing."

"It's not, technically. But you said it and it makes me smile every time I think about it," he added with a shrug, looking as uncomfortable as I'd ever seen him. "I guess you could say it's our thing now."

The way she was looking at him had me feeling all sorts of jealous. I needed to move this show along, or she'd shag him here and now, and we'd never get to my present.

"Hades, you're next," I blurted, interrupting their tender moment.

It was his turn to look a little bashful. "Right, uh. It's not much, but . . ." He picked up a leatherbound book and held it out to her.

34

"A book? A little on the nose, don't you think?" I scoffed. "And you didn't even wrap it. Bad form. Did no one ever teach you how to Christmas?"

Hades rolled his eyes. "The gift is what's on the inside. Don't make me get the shadows out."

"Ohhh, I'm sooo scared," I mocked.

He raised an eyebrow, silently reminding me of just how much damage he could do to me with the mere touch of a hand. Right. Point taken.

"Save those for later, Daddy," Dahlia whispered as she plucked the book out of his hand.

She took a seat on Tor's bed and cracked it open, her fingers gently running over the ink-covered pages. "Hades . . . it's your journal."

"I know you don't remember your previous life with me, baby doll, but there's so much we shared. I was hoping this would give you insight into exactly what we had and why you and I are inextricably linked through lifetimes. You're not Persephone, I realize that. But your soul and mine have been bound for all time."

Once again, my Dahlia was blinking back tears and looking lovingly up at someone else. This would not do. This would not do at all.

"Kai," I snapped, knowing the dragon would be my salvation. He'd been unconscious for the better part of three days. No way he'd be able to show me up. "Your turn."

The giant Scotsman rubbed a hand along his jaw. Honestly, he had no right to be so enormous. Neither he nor Tor. There came a point where it was simply too much. Not that Dahlia seemed to think so, what with the way they could hold her up betwixt them.

"I, erm . . . I'm sorry, lass. I don't have anything ready for you."

Bingo.

"It's okay, Kai. You were unconscious."

"But . . . I do have something I've wanted to offer. Now seems like the perfect time, as long as you three are amenable."

I pressed a palm to my chest. "Us? What do you want with us?"

"A spell to bind us to her. Forever."

"One of your special tattoos," Tor murmured, catching on before the rest of us, which made sense since he'd experienced Kai's work firsthand.

Kai nodded. "Precisely."

"What does it entail?" Hades asked, arms bent at the elbows as he leaned back against the desk.

"What does a tattoo entail?" I snorted. "You can't possibly be that sheltered in the underworld."

He picked up a pine cone off the desk and chucked it at my face. "The spell, numbnuts."

"Oh, I see."

Kai shook his head, exasperation in his eyes. "It would join our souls to hers, much like a shifter or vampire mate bond. We'll be branded as her protectors and mates, our bonds cemented through the magic of my dragon fire. More importantly than that, it will allow us to share some of our power and be able to locate Dahlia no matter how far she is. We'll be able to avoid any situations like the one we were in the other night when we lost precious time getting to her."

"Do it," Tor demanded, stepping forward.

I burst in before the epic arsehole lord of the underworld could. "Me also, as well. I'm in." Tearing open my shirt and baring my unmarked chest, I said, "Mark me with my true love's bond."

"Wait just a damn second," Hades said, ever the spoil-sport. "Share our power how, exactly?"

"Nothing you'd miss, but with a bond like this, it's impossible to avoid taking on some of the traits of those connected. From what I've read, it's usually an echo of one's strongest ability."

"What's the matter, Hades, afraid to have a little pirate in you?" I teased.

Dahlia howled with laughter while Hades, you guessed it, glared.

"Do you already have a design worked out?" Hades asked, not bothering to answer me.

"Why are you asking so many questions?" I demanded. "This is an obvious choice. Anything that helps us protect Dahlia is a no-brainer. Are you afraid of needles or something?"

"No, I am not afraid of needles, you insufferable pissant. The only thing I'm afraid of is losing that beautiful creature right over there. What I don't want to do is sign up to be stuck with you three for all eternity, you sucking back my power like it's candy. I've been bound to Dahlia for centuries. I'm not worried about that. Not in the least. But you? I can barely tolerate you on a good day."

"Aw, you say such sweet things. You know you love me." I smirked at him. "I see the way you look at me."

"I love you about as much as anyone can love a festering boil on their ass."

"Enough, you two," Tor interrupted. "Kai, go get your equipment. Or do you need more time to prepare?"

"To answer your question, Hades, I do have a design in mind, but there are a couple of things I'll need to procure for the enchantment. A spell of this magnitude is a little more intricate than my usual work."

"How long do you need?" Hades asked.

"A couple of days, maybe more. Not too long."

"Brilliant! It's decided then. The gang's getting matching tattoos," I said with a grin, more than ready for my big moment. "Now, on to my—"

"Do I get one too?" Dahlia interrupted.

All the wind left my sails, but I held it together like a fucking gentleman as Kai's lips twisted in a slow grin.

"Absolutely. You'll go last."

"Usually the lady comes first," she teased, a siren song in her words.

"Do you remember the last time I tattooed you? Pretty sure the matter of you coming won't be an issue, gem."

Seeing no end in sight to my misery, I snagged Hades's unoccupied chair and plopped down unceremoniously. All I wanted to do was give Dahlia my present. I'd searched high and low for the most *perfect* gift. An item just as meaningful as those other fuckheads and not something easily replicated. Something that couldn't be construed as anything other than the undiluted truth. A window into my soul, if you like.

But noooooo, this absolute dicknose—as Dahlia would say—was ruining my first Christmas. So were the others, but dicknose number one was my target right now. I'd deal with dicknoses two and three later.

"Cas, what's wrong?"

I couldn't help it; I was having a proper sulk now. "Oh, now you remember I'm here? Are you sure you don't want to fawn all over the others a while longer while I am cast to the outskirts of your loving gaze?"

"Does anyone have their miniature violin handy? The pirate is telling his sob story."

I might have to suffocate Tor while he slept for that one.

"Leave him alone. He's right. He's been trying to give me space to enjoy what you've all done, but he's just as excited as I am." My sweet girl came over and sat on my thigh, her delectable scent making me hard already. "I'm sorry, Cas. I didn't mean to ignore you. This is just so wonderful and perfect. I love it so much, and I've never had a big celebration like this either. Just me and Keeks and my little Charlie Brown tree."

I propped my chin on my fist, turning my head just a little to look at her. "This isn't your present, darling."

"It isn't?"

"I guess it's part of it, but it's from all of us. I have something else just from me."

"Well," she said expectantly. "Where is it?"

"In my pocket," I said with a roguish grin.

"Jesus fuckin' Christ," Hades groaned.

"Go find it, love," I whispered.

"It better not be his dick," Tor grunted.

"Twenty quid says it is," Kai answered.

I ignored the hecklers, my attention locked on my girl. It didn't take Dahlia long to find the rectangular parcel, wrapped in brown paper and tied with a string. You know, because of that one song?

She carefully unwrapped the gift I'd so thoughtfully stolen for her. "A tape recorder?"

"More importantly, a tape. A very special one."

"Did you steal this from Dr. Masterson?"

"Technically it's my tape. I can't steal from myself, can I?"

Though to be fair, I definitely stole it. No two ways about it. But I didn't want her to diminish its value for that reason. A little white lie never hurt anyone.

"Do you want me to listen to it now?"

I glanced around at the men who were watching us. I could've asked for privacy, but I wasn't ashamed of what she was going to learn. In fact, I was fucking proud of it.

"Go on, love. Press play."

TRANSCRIPT: HOOK'S TAPE

Hook: I doubt hypnosis is going to work on me, love. But I could use a nice nap. It's your time you're wasting.

<<couch cushions rustling>>

Dr. Masterson: All right, now I want you to close your eyes and take a series of deep breaths. With every exhale, I want you to remind yourself that you are safe. Let your body sink down into the comfort of your surroundings. Feel each of your muscles relax, starting with your toes, now your feet, ankles, calves.

<<clothes rustling>>

Dr. Masterson: How do you feel, Caspian?

Hook: Relaxed. A little bored, if I'm being honest.

Dr. Masterson: Hold on to that as we move into this next part. If at any time you feel threatened, I want you to take a deep breath and remind yourself that you are safe. That I'm right here and I will not let anything happen to you.

Hook: *sigh* Okay.

Hook: *snores*

Dr. Masterson: Caspian, I know you're not asleep.

Hook: You're no fun. All right, I'll get serious.

<<clothes rustling>>

Hook: Mesmerize me, Doc.

Dr. Masterson: *huff* Imagine you are standing at the top of a staircase. Can you picture it?

Hook: Yes. I have quite the active imagination, as you well know.

Dr. Masterson: Lovely. Now, you're going to take a step down, and as you do, I want you to remember your arrival in this realm.

Hook: Glorious day, that. My arrivals always are.

Dr. Masterson: Caspian, be serious.

Hook: As a heart attack, love.

<<ticking metronome>>

Dr. Masterson: All right, Caspian. I want you to focus on the ticking. Do you hear it?

Hook: How can I not, Doc? It's bloody distracting. Ticktock. Ticktock. Like that bleeding crocodile.

Dr. Masterson: Anytime your thoughts begin to run away with you, I want you to refocus on the metronome.

Hook: Fine, fine. *mutters under breath* Tick . . . tick . . . tick . . .

Dr. Masterson: Tell me about the crocodile, Caspian.

Hook: Don't want to. He's been after me since I woke up as Hook. He's a menace.

Dr. Masterson: I didn't realize Ravenndel had crocodiles.

Hook: Just this one.

Dr. Masterson: Why do you think that is? Why is it fixated on you?

Hook: How should I know? It follows me everywhere. That ticking.

Dr. Masterson: Caspian, can we talk about the ticking? It's an interesting feature for a crocodile to have. As far as I know, they don't tick.

Hook: *grumbles* This one did. It ticked down the seconds, haunting my nightmares. I thought I'd be rid of it when I got to Ravenndel, but once I woke on that bloody ship, it was back.

Dr. Masterson: Wait, so you heard it before you became Hook?

<<clothes rustling>>

<<ticking metronome>>

Dr. Masterson: Caspian? Are you remembering something?

Hook: Maybe . . .

Dr. Masterson: Let's return to the staircase. I want you to picture a door at the bottom. Can you see the door, Caspian?

Hook: Aye.

Dr. Masterson: Your life before you became Hook is on the other side of it. We're going to move down the staircase, and when you open that door, your prior life will be available to you, all right?

Hook: If you say so.

Dr. Masterson: Are you at the door, Caspian?

Hook: Aye.

Dr. Masterson: Open it.

<<clothes rustling>>

Hook: I didn't want to marry her. That was why I broke the clock.

Dr. Masterson: A clock? I thought we were looking for the crocodile.

Hook: The crocodile was the clock. Rather, it was turned into one. It was a gift from my betrothed's family.

Dr. Masterson: Tell me why you didn't want to marry her.

Hook: *scoffs* Would you want to marry someone you didn't love? If I am going to be tied down forever, it will only happen for true love. My fated.

<<pen tapping paper>>

Dr. Masterson: And what makes you think you have a fated? Those are incredibly rare, even amongst the fae.

Hook: The Court Seer told me I did. She read my cards and promised me my fated would come to me.

Dr. Masterson: And you believe her?

Hook: *snorts* She's never been wrong. Sure, some of the details tend to be wonky, but the big things were always true.

Dr. Masterson: And what details were wrong for you?

Hook: She told me my fated would ride into my life on a pale horse with the dead trailing in her wake. That was a little far-fetched even for me. But she was clear about one thing: I wasn't meant for Drusilla or anyone my parents forced upon me. My mate would find me when I least expected her.

Dr. Masterson: You don't believe that could still be true?

Hook: How can it be? I was a different person then. A prince. *bitten off laugh* She called me a hero.

Dr. Masterson: Capsian . . . are you . . . crying?

Hook: I was supposed to be the heart of my people. Now I'm heartless. ***angry shuddering breath*** I'm nothing but a heartless villain.

Dr. Masterson: Perhaps you'll find her here.

Hook: Even if I did, Doctor, people like me don't deserve love. Happily ever afters are only guaranteed to the do-gooders, and my soul is blacker than ink. There's no chance I'll ever find what I was promised. If she's still out there, she's no longer meant for me. I've lost her. My one true love. My fated. The only love I'll ever know is the sea.

Dr. Masterson: And what if you find her despite all odds? What if destiny is on your side even though you're a villain, as you say?

Hook: Then I would stand at her side and be hers to command. Her villain. Her mate. Everything that I am would belong to the woman fate sent to me, even the black-ened remains of my heart.

End of transcript.

CHAPTER

FOUR

TOR

Dahlia clicked off the recorder and looked up with tears brimming in her eyes. Oh, the pirate was good, I'd give him that. He knew exactly how to tug on her heartstrings. But from the vulnerable look on his face, I could tell it cost him something to let us all listen in on that deeply personal session. Truth be told, it made me hate him a little less. Rutting bastard. At this rate, I'd actively start liking him by New Year's. Fuck.

"Caspian, do you really think that? That you don't deserve love?" Dahlia asked softly as she cupped his scruff-covered jaw.

He swallowed thickly before pressing his forehead to hers. "Just because I don't deserve it, that doesn't mean I don't want it . . . or feel it."

"Cas . . ."

"That wasn't the important part of the tape, though, sweet girl," he blurted, interrupting her. "The part I wanted you to hear was the last bit. About if I ever found the one fate intended for me, what it would mean. How all that I am would be hers. I meant every word, Dahlia. Even before

49

I knew who you were, it was true, and it's as true today as it was then." He laughed, but it was heavy with the weight of his emotion. "Probably more true, truth be told. I'd give you anything you asked of me, darling. My life, if that's what you required. All that I am is yours to command."

"Well, hell. That was even better than what I told her," Hades grumbled. "Slippery fucker came in swinging."

Dahlia grinned as she wiped a stray tear off her cheek. "Yeah, he did. Don't worry, boys. I have a high capacity for swoon. And unless I'm mistaken, now it's time for me to give you your presents."

She leaned into Hook, nuzzling her nose against his. "Thank you for my gift, Cas. I love it." Then she stood and held out a hand for him to go with her. Dammit, I should've gone last.

The remaining three of us watched as she shoved him onto the bed and dropped to her knees between his spread legs.

"Merry Christmas, indeed," he murmured as she worked open his pants.

"Are we all getting the same thing, or . . ." Kai trailed off as he adjusted his erection.

Dahlia peeked at him over her shoulder. "Are you asking me if you should all line up?"

"It's not the worst idea I've ever heard," Hades offered.

I didn't disagree. If you'd have asked me a month ago if I would have been okay with my mate getting on her knees and servicing four men at once, I would have ripped your fucking throat out. Now, though . . . There was definite appeal. Especially knowing how wet it would make her. I was sure if I shoved my hand down her knickers, I'd find her slick and ready to take my cock. The pleasure we could all provide her with as a unit was addictive.

"Is that what you want?" she asked as she palmed Caspian's cock and gave it a cursory stroke. Cas grunted as she squeezed around the base.

"Don't distract her. She's busy."

I ignored Caspian and focused on Dahlia. "What do *you* want, Kærasta? You're the one giving the gift. It's up to you what that looks like."

Her lips curled. "How come when you say it like that, it sounds like I'm the one getting the present?"

"Because you know you're gonna come either way," Hades answered. "One or all of us will ensure it. Fingers, lips, tongue, teeth, cock. Whatever you want, it'll happen, baby doll."

"Shadows?"

He let out a dark chuckle. "If you wish."

"Oh, for fuck's sake, can you lot shut up? I'm trying to get a hand job over here, and you're ruining it."

Dahlia let out the sweetest giggle before she returned her attention to Hook. "Well, I was going to suck your dick until you came down my throat, but if you'd rather I use my ha—"

"No! Mouth, please. I would like that very much."

I almost laughed at Hook's frantic interruption, but she leaned forward and licked his length, making him writhe under her ministrations. My own cock hardened as I pictured her doing the very same to me.

Kai was the first to move closer. He stalked across the room toward the bed, kneeling beside Dahlia so he could touch her while she worked her way up and down Caspian's length. Not wanting to miss out on my chance to do the same, I took the other side before Hades could.

"I need to touch your skin, gem. Are you overly attached

to this jumper?" Kai asked, his fingers shifting into sharp talons.

She released Caspian's cock and whispered, "Shred it, Kai."

Fuck, I loved this side of her. Wild and free, trusting us completely.

With one precise drag of his claw down the back of her jumper, all she had to do was shrug out of the ruined fabric. Her perfect full tits greeted us all, and I had to palm my length to relieve some of the ache the sight caused. I didn't think I'd ever grow immune to her sinful curves. A soft grunt left me as my mind was filled with images of painting them in ropes of my cum, then using my fingers to rub my spend into her skin so she'd smell like me all fucking day.

"Fucking perfect," Hades groaned from where he stood near the tree. His pants were open, hand down the front as he adjusted himself. He wasn't trying to hide what she did to him either.

"Goddess, if you keep doing that thing with your tongue, I'm going to fucking come, darling," Hook warned, his thighs trembling, hands fisting the sheets.

His admission didn't dissuade her. She only sucked him harder, one of her hands sliding back between his legs so she could tease him further.

"Oh, fuck yes, darling girl," he moaned, completely under her spell, and I couldn't blame him. If I was on the receiving end of her hot, wet mouth and teasing fingers, I'd be the same.

Kai kissed a path along her neck and shoulder as he reached down with one hand to shove his joggers past his thighs. His other hand was busy tweaking one of Dahlia's nipples.

"Fuck, sweet girl. I'm close," Cas barked.

Whatever she did with the hand that was between his legs made him jerk and cry out in pure pleasure. His body tensed as he groaned out his release. From my vantage point, I could make out the muscles of her throat working as she swallowed him down. It had my own balls aching in anticipation. Part of me needed it to be my turn next, but another wanted desperately to be the last man to fill her mouth.

I stepped up behind her, then fisted her hair in a tight grip and tugged until she was forced to look up at me. With my free hand, I trailed my fingers down the exposed curve of her throat as the back of her head came to rest on my thighs. A pearly drop of Caspian's release had escaped her mouth, so I used my thumb to wipe her chin clean, then slipped the digit between her lips.

"Suck," I ordered.

"Mmm."

Fuck, I loved the way she hummed in pleasure at that.

My cock twitched happily as she obeyed, the warm heat of her mouth a perfect echo of her sweet cunt.

Cas was still draped like a starfish on the bed, his climax taking him out of commission for the time being. That was fine by me.

"Go on without me," he panted. "I just need . . . a minute. Fuck."

"Which one of us is next, gem? You have us at your disposal." Kai nipped her shoulder, and she gave a soft whimper at the contact. "From the look of things, we're all ready for you."

"If you're going to make me choose, then I choose all three of you," she said with a cat-that-ate-the-canary grin.

"How do you think you're going to do that, baby?"

Hades asked, his eyes blazing blue as he stepped closer to us.

"Take out your cocks and I'll show you."

I released her hair and followed her order, my length already weeping with need for my mate.

Adjusting her position, she slipped out of the pajama bottoms she was wearing and tossed them aside. Her back was to the bed now, chin lifted to look up at my large frame as she waited for me to close the distance between us.

"Tor, I want you in my mouth first."

Hades and Kai stood at her sides, both of them ready with their dicks in their hands.

"Look at you, baby doll. You have us at your mercy even when you're on your knees. Do you understand the power you have over us?"

"I do, but only because it's the same power each of you has over me."

My dick twitched in anticipation as I reached down and grabbed her by the jaw, needing her attention in the worst way. "I'm dying without you, Kærasta. I need you to touch me."

She offered me a wicked smile before leaning forward and licking the precum off my tip. My hand slid from her jaw to her throat so I could lightly collar her while she teased me. Two could play this game. I knew exactly what the feel of my powerful hands around her vulnerable throat did to her.

A soft whimper escaped her, and at first I thought it was because of me, but then I noticed the inky tendrils disappearing between her thighs.

Fucker just couldn't wait his turn.

Growling low in my throat, I said, "Eyes on me, beauty.

Don't pay attention to what he's doing to you. Not when my cock is going to be in your mouth."

Hades chuckled, but it was cut off by a groan as she wrapped her palm around his length, then did the same to Kai with her other hand.

"Our girl is a multi-tasker. Of course she is," Hook said from the bed. "It's dead sexy watching her like this."

He was propped up on his elbows now so he could watch the show. Based on the thickening of his cock against his belly, he was enjoying it.

Dahlia slipped her velvety mouth around my eager shaft, taking me all the way to the back of her throat in one move. Thank the gods above my mate didn't have a gag reflex. She was made for us in every way.

My fingers threaded in her hair again, if only so I could hold on to something to ground me in the moment. I knew if I gave myself over to the sensation of her, the vibrations caused by the pleased hums she released, and fuck, the way her throat convulsed around me when she took me to the root, I'd be spilling down her throat too soon.

Without warning, she let me go with a wet pop and twisted her head to the side, swallowing Kai down. I nearly protested, but my words were cut off when she used her hand to replace her mouth on my cock.

"Fuck," Hades grunted, his eyes locked on her. "You are so damn beautiful, baby doll."

"Of course she fucking is. She's ours," Kai forced out.

"You should feel her cunt, Tor. Sucking you off made her flutter around my shadows like she was nearly going to come. Ah, fuck, baby. I need you to slow down," Hades said, his hand shooting out to brace himself on one of the four posts on the bed frame as she swapped so he was now the one in her mouth.

She must have tried to say something, causing those same delicious vibrations I'd been feeling to ripple around him.

"Sonofabitch," he barked, eyes rolling back in his head and knuckles going white against the wood. "Watch out, baby doll. You keep at it, I'll make it so you can't. I'm not ready to finish."

"Why would you go and do something stupid like that?" Caspian asked. "Her mouth is a gift. If you don't want it, shove over and I'll take your place."

"You had your turn, pirate," he grumbled as Dahlia once again rotated so her lips were wrapped around me once more.

"Fuck, beauty. This is . . . gods, this is the hottest thing I've ever done. Your perfect fucking mouth," I groaned, fingers twisting in her hair to hold her in place before she could leave me again.

Hades may not want to come, but I sure fucking did. And I knew exactly where my spend was going to go.

"Enough," I bellowed, pulling out of her mouth. I stroked my length as I stared down at her, a frantic plea in my eyes for her to give me what I silently asked for.

She tilted her head back, baring her throat and those gorgeous tits a mere second before my orgasm raced through me.

A nearly incoherent string of sounds left me as jet after jet of my cum striped her flushed skin. Exactly as I'd imagined. The perfect decoration for her to wear.

"I cannae even be jealous you did it first. She wears your cum so well."

"Why don't you add yours to the mix?" Dahlia breathed as she furiously stroked both Hades and Kai.

Kai sucked in a sharp breath, his body trembling, eyes

flashing vibrant amethyst as his pupils turned to slits and his voice deepened. "Nae, my wee mate. The only place I'm coming is inside you."

"Not if I get you off first."

She turned to him and opened her mouth, but he backed away. "Lass," he warned. "Please."

Giving him a stroke instead, she looked to Hades, licking his tip and sucking on him like his cock was a lollipop. She released him and rolled her eyes up to stare into his before releasing the head of him with a wet pop. "My lord Hades will let me drink him down. Won't you?"

A frustrated growl escaped him as he fisted her hair and let her choke on his dick. But I saw it the moment he realized he was approaching the point of no return. There was a flash of panic, a primal gleam in his eyes, and I had to fight a chuckle when he tore his cock from her mouth.

"Stop, baby doll."

Dahlia leaned forward again, desperate for it, but he rocked his hips backward. "No. You aren't getting my cum down your throat."

"I want it."

"You'll get it, but just like Kai, there's only one place my seed belongs. That's inside your cunt."

She stiffened and reached for him, but he stopped her with a hard stare. "Don't make me restrain you, goddess. I will. The gods help me, I will."

"No restraints," Caspian said, no hint of teasing in his voice. For once, he was dead serious. "It's a hard limit for her."

Dahlia shifted on her knees, glancing at each of us in turn. "Well, maybe if—"

"No. There's no *if* when your limits are part of the equation. No restraints." Hades reached out and wiped a tear from her cheek, one I proudly recalled causing while I was shoved down her throat.

"It's different when it's you," she whispered. "When it's any of you."

"Why's it different, gem?" Kai asked, wanting the words likely as much as the rest of us.

"Because I know no matter what, I'll always be safe with you. You'd never hurt me."

"I'd die first," Caspian vowed.

A low growl escaped me as I glared at him. That was my line.

"As would I," I added, frustrated it lacked some of the same power as a mere echo of the pirate's promise.

"Aye, gem. Me as well."

Dahlia glanced at Hades. "And what about you, my lord Hades?"

"I rule the realm of the dead, baby doll. Pretty sure I can't technically die. But if I could, it would be for you."

"See? Safe. Pretty sure there isn't a safer place in any realm than with one or all four of you."

He looked at her long and hard, seeming to come to a decision. "Well, in that case, stand up, baby doll."

CHAPTER
FIVE
HADES

I bit back a groan as Dahlia obeyed my command, her lush, full curves on display for us all. More than her body, it was her expression that had me enraptured. Her cheeks were flushed with drying tear streaks, and her eyes were jewel-bright with excitement. She wanted this. Us. And I was so fucking ready to give it to her.

"Fuck me, she looks good enough to eat," Kai murmured, his voice rough with desire.

"Excellent idea, dragon. Get on your knees in front of her. Tor, something tells me our woman would do better with you acting as her restraints than my shadows. Give her what she wants."

Tor shifted until he was standing behind her, trailing the blunt tips of his finger from her shoulders down to her wrists. Placing his lips at her ear, he whispered, "If it gets to be too much, just say the word. Since we're testing a limit, no special safewords are needed today. Stop means stop. No means no. Got that, beauty?"

"Yes," she panted, her chest rising and falling with each breath as he shackled her wrists with his hands.

"And the rest of you? Are we in agreement?" Tor looked from Kai to me, but my attention wasn't on the Viking. It was on my love.

My goddess was the picture of wanton beauty as she locked gazes with me, wrists pinned behind her back, tits jutting forward as if they were an offering. I didn't break eye contact as I uttered one word, a solemn promise for her and her alone. "Yes."

Kai knelt in front of her, whispering kisses up the inside of her thigh as he murmured his agreement.

And then there was Caspian. Even though he wasn't technically participating at the moment, he wouldn't allow any of us to forget he was there, try though we might.

"Aye," he agreed. "I'll make sure they all stay honest, darling. Don't you worry."

"I'm not worried. God, this is weirdly the most intense thing I've experienced."

"It's about to get even better." I was wound tighter than a drum, watching Tor's lips descend to her nape and Kai's palms skate up her inner thighs, following the trail of his mouth.

I wanted to touch her, to be the reason she was already mewling in pleasure, but anticipation was delicious for a reason. I loved holding out as much as she hated waiting.

"Stop teasing me," she whined when Kai sat back on his heels.

He grinned up at her. "You'll like what I have in mind. Promise, gem." Then he glanced over her shoulder at Tor. "Let go of her just for a second so I can get her in position, yeah?"

When he released her, Dahlia gave a whimper of protest. Tor quieted her with a whispered, "I'll be right back to restrain you to your heart's content."

"I'll hold you to that, big guy." Her gaze returned to Kai as he adjusted his stance, widening his knees before he slid his palms under her round ass.

It was then I realized exactly what he was going to do. The dragon was going to turn his face into a seat for our beautiful mate. Lucky bastard.

In a move too practiced to be the first time he'd done it, Kai picked her up and lifted her until one of her knees rested on each of his shoulders and that perfect fucking cunt was hovering just above his lips.

"Kai!" Dahlia squealed, her shock at going airborne momentarily overriding her desire. But then he licked her seam, and her protest turned to moans of pleasure.

"Tor, she's ready for you."

"I don't need to be told how to care for my mate, Hades. I'll thank you to remember that." Tor's words were a ragged growl as he banded his arm around her biceps, holding her in place against his chest and forcing her back to arch.

"Oh God. I . . ." she started, trailing off into a pleasure-filled groan as Kai buried his face deeper between her thighs.

Every inch of her was on display. Dahlia's body was everything I craved. Her nipples were ripe berries begging for my mouth, thick thighs and full hips promising sensual nights wrapped in the sheets, soft round curves desperate for me to hold on to. I balled my hands into fists at my sides, suddenly regretting my decision to let the others get her ready for me.

Ah, well. Just because I couldn't physically touch her didn't mean I couldn't participate.

Drawing on a few wisps of shadow, I sent them to her, allowing them to tease her as they flowed up her spread legs. Kai was busy lavishing her clit with attention, but that wasn't the only place that made her squirm. And for what I had in mind, she was going to need a little preparation.

I sent my shadows moving along her skin until I traced her pussy lips ever so gently.

"Oh, fuck, Hades. Is that you?" she whimpered.

"Yeah, baby doll. It's me. You know I can't resist making you feel good."

She whimpered again as I worked through her wetness and teased both of her entrances, not quite giving her what she really wanted.

"How do you like being at our mercy, doll? Knowing that you're bound and helpless to do anything but take what we give you."

As far as restraints went, this was pretty tame, but it seemed like the perfect stepping stone to test the waters. With her arms pulled back the way they were, it gave the illusion of being restrained, as did the way she was precariously poised on Kai. Once again, she was sort of balanced between Tor and Kai, one pulling her back while the other held her up. It meant she couldn't squirm, couldn't fight against what they were doing. Instead she had to give her trust over to them completely.

I was envious for about one second before she answered my question, then all other thoughts left my head.

"I fucking love it. God, I fucking love *you*."

And there it was, those powerful little words that could still bring me to my knees when my soulmate said them. I faltered for just a moment as my heart stuttered, just like it did whenever she told me. I was a fool for her. Every. Damn. Time.

"Not as much as I love you."

She was going to fight me on that one, but then Kai did something with his tongue, and she mewled instead.

"Fuck, I'm so close."

"Then come, baby. Come all over Kai's face. I want to see you dripping down his chin."

"Jesus, your mouth."

I was unclear if she was talking about his or mine, but with the way the color built in her cheeks and bloomed across the rest of her body, I realized it didn't matter. Wanting to help her across the finish line, I pressed two of my shadows into each of her openings, filling her up until she had no choice except to come.

"Give it to me, baby doll. I want to hear it."

"Fuck, Hades." She rocked her hips forward, grinding her pussy against Kai's mouth as Tor bit down on the soft flesh where her neck and shoulder met. "Kai, I'm coming." She moaned and called out Tor's name next.

Not to be left out, Caspian got out of bed and strolled over to the group as he stroked his dick. "Don't you look pretty like this, darling? Trussed up like a siren at the mast of a ship. Fuck, you're beautiful."

"Cas . . ."

"You're missing one thing, though. Don't worry, I'll take care of it for you."

And with that, he gave his cock a few strokes and came all over her, his cum joining Tor's across her chest and belly.

He sighed and ran a finger through his release, chuckling softly as he murmured, "I know it's not technically the right position, but all I could think about while watching you was, that's the London Bridge experience I want to have."

Her laugh was a husky rasp as Kai gently set her back on her feet. Tor continued to hold on to her, likely to ensure she had her footing.

"Easy," he cautioned, earning himself a kiss.

Once she was steady, her eyes dropped to Kai's face, and she giggled. "Oh shit, I really am dripping down your chin."

Kai grinned at her and licked his lips. "It's because you're such a good fucking girl."

"Guess that means I'm ready for you," she teased, her eyes slipping over to find mine.

"Are you ready for both of us, goddess? Because I'm aching for you." I couldn't wait any longer. I needed inside her.

She nodded, eyes fever bright. "Can I ride you, Kai? It's been too long since I had my dragon."

The burly Scot got to his feet and nodded, threading their fingers as he tugged her toward the bed. My cock gave a throb at the sight of her arousal glistening on her inner thighs.

Kai laid on his back and Dahlia climbed on top of him, glancing over her shoulder and back at me. "Are you coming, my lord Hades?"

"Not yet, but he's about to," Caspian chirped.

I would have punched him, but he wasn't wrong. "Settle yourself on your dragon, baby. Get nice and comfortable for me. Then I'll fill you, and if you're a good girl, I'll make you come so hard your soul leaves your body."

"As long as you put it back," Tor warned.

"Her soul has been mine since the beginning of time, Viking. I'll never be careless with it."

"According to Kai, I've already proven I'm a good girl."

I strolled over to the side of the bed and gave her ass a resounding smack. "But I'm the one who matters right now, baby doll. And all I'm seeing is a smart fucking mouth. If you want to be a brat, that's fine, but only good girls get rewarded."

"I'm listening, Daddy. Tell me what you want me to do."

"I already told you. Now I guess I'll have to show you." I grabbed her by the nape and used one of my shadows to position Kai's cock where she'd need it to be. Kai's eyes rolled back in his head, but he didn't protest. Then, with deliberate slowness, I pushed her down until she was fully seated, filled with him.

"Fuuuuck," he groaned, his fingertips digging into her hips. "You squeeze me so good, mate."

"Goddess, I'm hard again," Caspian announced. Not that I paid him any attention.

Instead, I ducked my head and pressed my lips to Dahlia's ear as I whispered, "Lean over him as far as you can. Show me your tight little asshole before I fuck it."

A shudder of pleasure rippled over her, and she let out a ragged moan. But my little flower didn't listen. Instead she turned her head and kissed me, hard and hungrily.

I sucked her lower lip and bit down just enough to make her whimper before breaking the kiss. "I said, lean over him and show me what I want." Gripping her nape again, I forced her into the position I needed. Then I crawled up on the bed behind her, a smile tugging on my lips when I noticed Tor standing off to the side, mutely holding out a bottle of lube.

"Are you ready, baby?" I asked, uncapping the lube and pouring a liberal amount down her crack before filling my palm with the liquid as well. While not the massive girth of Kai or Tor, I wasn't a small man, and my goal wasn't to hurt her, only to make her feel pleasure.

"Yes," she panted, her hips rolling as she gently rode Kai.

Lining myself up, I slowly began pressing myself into that tight ring of muscles, little bolts of electricity racing across my skin at the sensation. Pair that with the sounds she was making, and I was going to embarrass myself if I didn't get a handle on things.

My jaw was tight as I fought against the urge to slam into her. It didn't help that she reached back, her nails digging into my thigh as she tried to pull me deeper.

"Don't, Dahlia. I can't. It feels too good." I had to bite the words out because resisting her was futile. I sank as far as I could go, and she let out a desperate cry of my name.

"Oh, fuck," Kai grunted, his face twisted up in pleasure.

For a moment, the three of us held that position, each trying to adjust to the intense sensation. But then Dahlia rocked her hips, and my fingers clenched at her waist. She was hot and tight, her walls clamping down on me enough to make me come.

"Can't take it, can you, Daddy? I thought you were the one in charge."

Oh, I fucking loved her feisty attitude.

"Tor, get over here and put something in her mouth to shut her up. She's trying to get me to spank her."

"I've got something to put in her mouth," Caspian offered.

I was about to snap at him, but Tor beat me to it.

"Stand down. You already got to come twice."

"And I should be penalized for that because? It's not my fault you all sat around with your thumbs up your arses instead of having a wank."

I glared at him. "If you want to participate, make her come all over our cocks, pirate."

Dahlia's body clenched, making Kai and I both groan.

"She likes that idea," Kai said as his hands went to her hips, just under where I held her. "Don't you, gem?"

"Yes. God, Cas, touch me. Tor, let me suck your dick. I need you all."

"Well, when you ask so prettily, love," Cas drawled, shifting until he was close enough to do exactly that.

It was hard to keep track of what was going on, my body primed for the climax that I was only just managing to stave off.

Cas's fingers crept in between her body and Kai's, and I knew it the moment he brushed her clit because she clamped down on me again. She couldn't say anything, though, not with her sexy mouth full of Tor's cock.

I couldn't hang on much longer, and I'd never been more thankful for that pirate than right at that moment because the way he was working her had her fluttering and moaning. She was close. Just a little more . . .

Fuuuck.

She came with a frantic—albeit muffled—cry, and so did the rest of us. Tor grunted and tensed, Kai bellowed his release, and I nearly burst into flames as my orgasm rocked me with the force of a hurricane. Even Caspian managed to join us. I'd have said his stamina was impressive, but that meant I'd have to give him a compliment, and that was going too far.

Before any of us could move, there was an electric tingle in the air preceding a happy bark.

"Well, I can see you were lost without me," Asshole grumbled. Without waiting for me to respond, he jumped up onto the bed, giving my leg a little lick.

"Who invited the fluff ball?" Caspian asked.

"Since when does he teleport?" Tor added.

Dahlia made an embarrassed sound, one arm banding about her tits as if that would somehow preserve her modesty. "Asshole? You're back!"

An ominous creak filled the room, preventing us from saying anything further. With one shift of my knee, a loud crack shot through the air before the bed came crashing to the floor, making the three of us still connected cry out in shock and sensation.

Caspian looked from me to Dahlia, then smirked. "Oopsie daisy."

"Motherfucker stole my line."

I glared at the pup. "You just can't help but get the last word, can you?"

He panted at me, and I swear on all that is good and holy, there was a twinkle in his beady little eyes. *"You want a last line? Here's one for you. Merry Christmas, you filthy animals."*

CHAPTER
SIX
DAHLIA

"Fucking *finally*! Twenty-four hours, Dahlia. You made me wait a whole day for the callback. Not cool. What if you'd died?"

I rolled my eyes. "I was with my mates. They wouldn't kill me."

"They might choke you too hard with their dicks."

I made a considering sound and nodded. "That is a valid fear. You've seen the size of them."

"Seen? Pfft. Not when it actually counts." She held up her banana and raised her brows. "Bigger than this?"

"Yes."

"Hang on!" Kiki darted away from the screen and then returned with a flounce back into position. "What about girth? Bigger than this?" The woman held up a can of Coke, eyes wide, expression expectant.

"You accidentally saw two of them naked that one time."

"Oh, I know, and it is a gift I'll never forget, but I'm not talking about when they're behaving." She waved the can in front of the camera. "Eh?"

"I'm not answering that, Kiki."

She whistled and muttered under her breath, "Definitely bigger than a Coke can." Then she winced. "Your poor vag. They're basically fisting you, aren't they? I'm just imagining the four of them with forearms dangling between their legs. It's surprisingly sexy. Forearm porn has a whole new meaning."

"Ew, Kiki. Stop it."

"It's your fault. You abandoned me."

"I—" I protested, but then I stopped. I'd done exactly that. "Yeah, I'm sorry. Kai was so out of it after shifting, and I just really wanted to make sure he was okay. I mean, it was a lot for all of us to go through."

"No, I get it. You had to Florence Nightingale for him. He'd have done the same for you. That's what fated life partners do. Still, besties have complaining privileges. I get to give you shit for at leeeasst . . ." She drew the word out and trailed off, pretending to check an imaginary watch. "Twenty more minutes."

"Would it shorten my time if I told you he saved me from a psycho killer former member of my dad's cult who wanted me to help him summon the goddess Death?"

Her eyes went comically wide. "I'm sorry, you didn't think to lead with that?"

"Lead with the ritual sacrifice? Seems a bit heavy-handed. I wanted to warm you up first. Ease into it."

"It's not anal, Dahlia. I don't need to be prepped first. Give me the deets. All of them. I'll know if you're holding out on me, woman."

I snorted. Fucking Kiki.

"Well, the Ripper is dead. Kai burned him to ashes, and good riddance. He'd been posing as Dr. Temperance."

"Hot doc was a serial killer?" she screeched. "God, why is it always the pretty ones?"

"Yeah, fake name, fake accent, probably a fake medical degree. He was trying to *finish my father's work*," I said, using air quotes on the last.

"Bastard," she breathed. If she'd had a bowl of popcorn, she totally would have been shoving it into her mouth.

"He did this thing with the lights and snuck up on me. Chloroformed me or something, so I woke up on an altar in the—I'm not shitting you—cemetery. There was a special dagger. He sliced me open, collected my blood, had a whole villain monologue prepared. The dude had clearly been planning for his big moment for the last decade. Oh, oh, and I'm pretty sure I hallucinated because that woman I saw the time my dad tried to do the same showed up again and was whispering in my ear. She got me to use my power to raise some zombies. I swear it was like Stephen King got the manuscript of my life and started tossing spooky obstacles in the way. Oh, and I heard your voice too . . ."

Kiki was staring at me, her mouth hanging open like a broken ventriloquist dummy. She blinked, and I mentally added the cartoon sound effects.

"I'm sorry, back the fuck up. Zombies?"

"Did I not tell you I'm a necromancer?"

"A necro-whater?"

"I can raise the dead and talk to them. Oh, and I lost so much blood a hot vampire priest had to feed me to keep me alive."

"Now you're just fucking with me. There's a hot priest? Hotter than hot doc?"

"Way hotter. He's Irish."

"Single?"

"Not remotely."

"Balls."

"Keeks, he's a vampire, and you faint at the sight of blood."

"Not anymore. Besides, I can work on it. I'm willing to do all the inner work I need if there's a confessional booth and an Irish accent in my future."

"Kiki," I chastised.

"Okay, okay, tell me more about this thwarted ritual sacrifice. Kai turned into a dragon?"

I shuddered in pleasure, remembering the sight of it. Fuck, it was so hot to watch him give in to his dragon. "Yes. He's fearsome and fucking enormous. His fire was so hot it actually melted the dagger." I swooned a little. "Did I mention he can manifest his wings in his human form?"

"Get out. You have a real-life Rhysand. No, better than Rhysand, because he's a mothertrucking dragon." Kiki's expression grew thoughtful. "How on earth are you going to explain them when you bring them all home? Hi neighbors, these are my new roommates, four hulking hot guys with dicks the size of Coke cans, and by the way, one of them is a real hothead, and yes, those are wings."

"Technically I don't really have neighbors. That was the beauty of my place, remember? And well, actually, we aren't going to be coming back."

"I beg your actual pardon," Kiki said, affronted.

"We can't."

"What do you mean you can't?"

I guess that answered my unspoken fear that Kiki had known about Blackwood's little secret before sending me here. Not that I actually suspected her, but literally every other person I'd trusted in my past had betrayed me, so it wouldn't exactly be out of the norm for me if she had gone and done it too.

"I'm not sure how to break it to you, Keeks."

"Spit it out. Like cum."

"We don't spit, Kiki. We're good girls. We show it to them first, then swallow."

She didn't even crack a smile.

I sighed. "Blackwood isn't a wellness center. It's a prison. We're all trapped here."

Her face drained of all color. "What do you mean?"

"Exactly what I said. The Belladonna witch just strengthened the wards. We're never leaving. No one does."

"But . . . what . . . how?" she sputtered.

I shrugged, because I didn't really have any more answers than she did. "Apparently it's a whole big conspiracy. The High Council's way of keeping us out of sight and mind. The supernatural world's dirty little secrets."

"The high what now?"

"Council. It's made up of the leaders of the various species."

"So like the United Nations."

"Sure."

She was quiet for a second, her focus drifting as she stared at something off-screen. Then she huffed and straightened, her posture rigid and her expression filled with her usual take-no-prisoners intensity. Kiki had come to a decision, and heads were about to roll.

"Well, they don't have any fucking jurisdiction over me. I'm not going to let them dictate what my client-slash-bestie does."

I didn't have the heart to tell her she was up the creek without a paddle.

"Are you really just going to sit there and accept this, Dahlia? I'm so disappointed in you."

Scoffing with pure indignation, I said, "You're disappointed in me? What did I do?"

"Nothing, that's the point."

"I didn't know I'd be trapped here when I walked through the doors."

"Neither did I, but you're just over there taking it lying down. Literally. I get that you're being fucked to within an inch of your life, and that's great, but you've got obligations out in the real world. You're not supposed to go on a permanent vacay and never come back. I need you. Romancelandia needs you."

"Kiki, that was a low fucking blow. I don't know what I can do. I'm not a witch. I'm barely a necromancer. But I'd rather make the best of a bad situation because the alternative leads to some really dark places I don't want to go." My voice wobbled as anger made tears spring to my eyes.

"Dee, I get that your hands are tied, but you're just over there taking this BS at face value. Maybe you can't physically do anything, but did you really not think to flash the bat signal and call in reinforcements?"

"Who am I supposed to call, Keeks? Ghostbusters?"

"Me! You're supposed to call me. I'm your person. When have I ever let you down?"

"Keeks . . ."

"No, seriously. When have I ever not come through? Is it because I'm human? Do you think I'm not smart enough to figure out something? I know people."

I huffed, frustration getting the better of me. "You didn't even know paranormal creatures existed in the first place, Kiki. What on earth could you have done?"

"Have you forgotten how good I am at leaking news to the press? Give me access to one of your creatures' names and connections. I'll find them, and before long, it'll spread like wildfire. You said that Sorcha chick is like royalty or something, right? I bet her family won't be happy to know they're never getting her back. Besides, you said it yourself. The SUN or whoever has gotten away with this for so long because no one knows about it. So we make sure everyone fucking knows. Who is better than me at getting the word out? No one."

My heart felt three sizes too big. Even when she was mad at me, Kiki still wanted to come to my rescue. I didn't deserve her.

"The sun?" I asked, because it felt like the safest option with as emotional as I was in the moment.

"Supernatural UN."

"Of course." I was getting slow in my confinement. "I've never even heard of the Blackthornes. How are you going to find them?"

"I have my ways. Give me two hours, a red-string theory board, a glue stick, and a couple energy drinks. I'll find them."

"Don't forget the snacks. You get cranky without a steady supply of salt."

She pointed a pink-tipped fingernail at me. "Good call."

We stared at each other for a second, some of the tension leaving us both. When she smiled at me again, it was filled with a bit of sadness but also resolve. "I'm still pissed you didn't think to mention this."

"I know. I'm sorry."

She bit on her bottom lip. "Did you think I did it on purpose?"

Her eyes were filled with so much vulnerability it broke my heart.

"No. Fuck no, Keeks. I didn't know what to think about

any of it, to be honest. Things have been happening so fast I'm just sort of doing what I can not to drown."

"I wouldn't do something like this. I'd never have agreed to send you there if I'd known."

"I know that. It was *him*, Dr. Temperance. He pulled the strings, and we went along because we didn't know better. It's not your fault."

"If I could trade places with you, I would. You're more than just my bestie. You're like my platonic soulmate. I'd die for you. That's what ride or die means."

"Let's hope it doesn't come to that," I said with a laugh, my heart aching. "Besides, if one of us has to go down, it's gonna be me for you."

"No way, you have those four hotties to bang. Who's sitting around waiting on me?"

"I am."

Kiki stared at me, all traces of humor gone, as she put on her big black-framed glasses and pulled a pencil out of her bun. "Okay, Blackthorne. Is that with an e?"

"Pretty sure."

She nodded, jotting down some notes. After a second, she looked up at me and smirked. "Are any of them single?"

We wrapped up our conversation and hung up less than a minute later. I felt a bit like laundry that had gone through one of those old-school wringers. Kiki was right. I'd fucked up when I didn't bring her in on everything going on at Blackwood, but it wasn't intentional. The real world felt so separate from life here. Besides, I'd had a lot on my plate recently, not the least of which was the return of Brother Sam, aka the Ripper, aka Temperance, aka dicknose. It was hard enough for me to stay up to speed with things, and it was my fucking life.

But I had to admit, knowing that she was on my side,

hard at work trying to come up with a plan to get me and the boys out, filled me with much-needed relief. Finally, that happy ending everyone always wrote about—myself included—didn't seem so unattainable.

Less than an hour later, my phone vibrated in my pocket and I pulled it out, grinning at the message from Kiki.

KIKI:

> Found them. Meeting up next week to break the news.

My heart lurched when a second message came through. Not because I didn't want it to be true but because of the sense of foreboding that curled in my gut as I read her words.

KIKI:

> Pack your bags. I'll be there to get you soon.

CHAPTER
SEVEN

KAI

"I can't believe they're gone."

Ursa, the Russian bear shifter I was currently tattooing, took a large swallow from the bottle of homebrewed moonshine he clutched like a lifeline.

"I hadn't realized how hard certain areas were hit by the death rattle. I thought it spread slowly and wasn't always fatal."

Ursa snorted before taking another gulp. "That's what they always say. It decimated Aurora Springs. It wiped out half the town. My pack didn't stand a chance."

I hummed in acknowledgment, but was too focused on the line I was inking into his skin to comment further. This was not one of my magical tattoos, but for Ursa, it was every bit as special. He'd asked for the North Star MC patch to be tattooed across his back. A memorial tattoo as much as it was a lifetime commitment to his brothers.

"I never wanted to be Prez. Never thought this would be the only way the North Stars go on." He took another swallow, the movement forcing me to lift my gun off his skin while he downed a third of the bottle in one go. "I'm the last remaining North Star. Ivan!" He shouted into the void, his voice echoing off the walls of the study I'd commandeered for this session. "I will avenge you! I will rebuild and carry on our legacy. I will . . ." The man broke down sobbing and hung his head.

"How can you avenge a plague victim?" I muttered under my breath. Soap? Vaccines? Short of eradicating the germs themselves, it seemed a pretty futile promise. But that was Ursa's problem.

"They were good men, you know? Brave. Fierce. Loyal. Too good for this earth." He hoisted the moonshine up high, making me bite off a curse as he shifted away from my needle once more. "May your ride through the stars be eternal!"

"Sit still, Ursa. I'm nearly finished. Then you can rattle the windows with your mourning all you want."

He took another long swallow before setting the bottle on the floor near his booted foot. "Continue," he grumbled.

Twenty minutes later, I was finished, and Ursa was wasted. I envied him the oblivion. I hadn't seen Dahlia but for a few stolen moments between food deliveries and proof-of-life check-ins in three damn days. I understood she needed to work. The muse was talking to her, and she'd hit her stride on her manuscript. She was determined to finish it before the end of the year. That meant the four of us were giving her the space she needed to work her magic. Even if it made us all edgy.

There may no longer be a murderous madman on the loose, but the need to protect and watch over her was instinctual. It would never truly subside, even if we were technically in a time of peace. The next threat could be lurking around the corner, and if we stayed vigilant, we wouldn't be caught with our trousers down.

I finished up the last of the shading before turning off the tattoo gun and sitting back to inspect my work. Goddess, I was good. I wiped down the excess blood and ink, smiling to myself as the slight hint of magic within the ink shimmered in the light. For works like this one, I only allowed the tiniest glimmer of my power to ensure the art never faded.

"All right, my friend. You're done. You honored your fallen comrades today. You should be proud."

Ursa got to his feet and glanced over his shoulder at his broad back in the mirror.

Clapping me on the shoulder, he trained his focus on me with watery eyes. "I'll never forget this, dragon. If you ever need aid, call on the North Stars." Then he snagged his bottle of moonshine and thrust it at me. "Drink!"

"Oh, I'm fine. More of a Scotch guy myself."

"Drink!" he insisted.

There was the slightest hint of a grizzly's growl in the command, and while I had no doubt that my dragon trumped his bear, I wasn't really in the mood to go a round or two with a drunk Russian anything.

Accepting the bottle from him, I took a swig, wincing at the burn down my throat. Potent didn't begin to cover it. The fumes alone were enough to singe the hair in my nostrils, and being a fire-breathing monster, that was saying something.

"Do svidaniya, Kai," he slurred before he stumbled into the doorframe and apologized to it.

I had a bottle of liquid fire in my hand and an uncomfortable urge to go find my mate when I knew she needed me to give her space. So that meant I'd take myself outside for some fresh air and perhaps drink myself into a state of relaxation.

85

With that goal in mind, I made my way outside, my long strides making easy work of the journey. It wasn't long at all before I found myself on the edge of the forest beside what had once been a kitchen garden. Now it was little more than unkempt weeds, but it did still create a striking picture in the spring when it was in bloom.

I took a pull from the bottle but stopped when I saw a bright flash of light out of the corner of my eye. Then another. And another.

"You can do it, Blossom! Flap your wings faster!" Jax's voice caught on the wind and had me turning toward the sound.

"Don't rush her. She'll come to it in her own time." This was Liam. He stood on the post of a rotting wooden gate with a squirming shimmer in his arms.

"My turn, Da! Fancy go next!" The tiny baby pixie cried.

I'd forgotten how fast these little Scottish pixies grew. It seemed the smaller the fae, the faster they matured. I'd known human-sized ones who aged at the same rate I did. Magic was a wondrous thing indeed.

Knowing this was likely a once in a lifetime occurrence, I remained quiet and still so I could watch the wee little ones learn how to fly. It was really quite something.

"There you go, Nova! Just like that," Owen crowed.

"Me next! Me next!" another shimmer insisted, this one a male with a shock of black hair.

Rhys wore a smile that only a proud papa could manage. It was a combination of exhaustion, exasperation, and adoration. "Do you promise not to tackle your sister again?"

"Aye!" the little one swore, already squirming out of his father's arms.

"All right then, Clarence. Careful now. That's a good lad."

Grinning to myself, I took a deep swig of the moonshine. Familiarity did not seem to breed any sort of immunity, because I immediately started coughing, drawing the attention of four very fierce daddies.

Each of them drew a sword from sheaths at their sides, though the tiny wee blades would do nothing to me aside from perhaps cause the equivalent of a few paper cuts.

"Easy," I said, holding up my hands to show I meant no harm.

Owen's hand trembled slightly, betraying his fear. "What's a great oaf like you doing spying on us?"

"Yeah, come to finish what you started, have you? Well, you're not going to harm our shimmers. I'll poke out your eyes before you can blink," Jax threatened, handing his shimmer to Rhys and fluttering near my face.

"Calm down, ye wee beastie," I grumbled, swatting him away. "I'm only enjoying the air. I'm not here to cause any trouble."

"Then perhaps it's best you get tae walking," Liam said with a pointed lift of his tiny brow.

"We saw you flying through the night, laying waste to the grounds beyond that hill. Don't come near our shimmers." Rhys frowned, his stance protective, wings fluttering with agitation.

"I have no intention of harming your bairns. Or you, for that matter."

"Maybe we'd be more inclined to believe you, dragon, if you dinnae try to burn down our home." That was from Owen, who seemed to have recovered from his initial fear.

"Erm, I suppose I do owe you a bit of an apology for

that," I muttered, rubbing a hand along the back of my head.

"You think?" Jax was spilling pixie dust in a column of gold glitter, and I had to take a step back to ensure he didn't accidentally dose me.

"If you'll allow me, I'll help you rebuild your home."

"And how do you plan to do that? Are you a woodcarver in your spare time?"

I'd dabbled a fair bit, but actually had something else in mind. "You'll see. But you will have to trust me."

Liam laughed. "It'll be a cold day in the deadlands before I trust a dragon without proof he won't roast us. Prove yourself trustworthy, and we'll revisit that topic."

"Da! More flutters!" Blossom screeched, whacking her father in the face.

Another of the shimmers began to cry and squirm, and I realized this was my opportunity to get away from this conversation.

"Looks like you're being summoned, lads. Good luck with the flying lessons."

They didn't respond, nor did I expect them to. I was hardly their favorite person, and the children had already commanded their attention. The interaction had left me feeling a bit out of sorts. Or maybe that was the moonshine.

It had to be the strongest alcohol I'd ever ingested. Despite only having a few sips, the tips of my nose and fingers were tingling, and the ground went a bit spongy every time I took a step.

As I crested the hill, my gaze raked the decimated valley below. Scorch marks and burned husks that were once trees littered the scene, but my attention was drawn to the inky black stain on the bare patch of earth where I'd sent the Ripper to meet his maker.

Dark satisfaction sizzled through my veins. There was no guilt or remorse over what I'd done. I'd do it all over again if I could. The bastard had deserved to die for his crimes, but he'd deserved to *suffer* for what he'd done to my mate. I'd never regret avenging her. If I could've, I would've taken him to my tower and tortured him slowly, given Tor, Hades, and Hook the opportunity to participate. But I couldn't allow him the chance to escape.

As if the thought summoned the man, Tor stalked through the trees, blood and gore smeared across his body. The second his eyes landed on me, his posture relaxed.

"I thought I heard something," he said by way of greeting.

"I'm assuming your hunt was a success?"

"It always is," he said with a feral grin.

"Well done."

He crossed his arms over his chest and jutted his chin toward the place where the Ripper had died. "All of us would've done the same. He put his hands on her."

"I know."

"Then why are you out here with a bottle of booze? You can't possibly be feeling remorse."

"Nae, not remorse. I didn't realize this was where I was headed when I started walking, but I guess I needed to see it for myself one more time."

Tor lifted a brow, silently encouraging me to finish my thought.

"He's gone, but it still feels . . . unsettled here."

At that, he dipped his chin in a slow nod. "Aye. I feel it too."

"Cas would say it was the spirits of the forest."

"Cas barely knows his arse from his elbow on a good day. I'm far more interested in what you think and feel."

I took a pull from the moonshine and grimaced, wondering if smoke was curling from my nostrils. "I feel like something is off. Like I'm waiting for the other shoe to drop."

Tor nodded again, his eyes scanning the trees around us as if sussing out a hidden enemy. "I always feel that way. Glad to know it's not just me for once."

"Do you think it's this place, or is there something else looming on the horizon?"

Tor shrugged, and there was something about the motion, covered in blood as he was, that made the act sinister. "Why can't it be both? Blackwood is a dark place with a darker past. Seems likely it will bear witness to more foul deeds in its lifetime."

"You might be right."

I handed him the bottle and stared off into the trees as he took a swig, delighting in the cough that came from him because it made me feel like less of a lightweight.

"What is this swill?" he said through a cough.

"Moonshi—" I began, but my words died on my tongue as a man identical to the Tor I'd known before his curse had taken him manifested a few feet from us.

Tor gasped in shock, his posture stiffening beside me as the blond man approached, expression a mixture of betrayal and relief.

"Alek?"

He stopped directly in front of Tor and simply said, "Hello, brother."

POST-SESSION
TRANSCRIPT: TOR

Dr. Masterson: This is Dr. Elizabeth Masterson. Today marked my first session with new resident Tor Nordson. These are my observations.

<<footsteps pacing>>

Dr. Masterson: Subject name, Tor Nordson—hereinafter referred to as N001. Species, demigod. Sub-species, Berserker. Nationality, Novasgardian. Age, approximately twenty-six years. Height, six foot five, though he does swell in size during fits of rage. Weight fluctuates in the same manner as his height. Notable markings, scar on his left cheek, rose tattoo in the center of his chest. Also appears that his hair is changing color. I wonder if this correlates with how often he takes his beastly form. Something to keep track of in the future.

<<chains rattling and dragging along the floor>>

<<chains dropping on desk>>

Dr. Masterson: Subject N001 required restraints for our entire session, as well as magical binding held in place by Bruno, one of Blackwood's strongest staff members. I have assigned Bruno exclusively to N001's care for the safety of all residents and staff.

<<chair squeak>>

Dr. Masterson: Until N001 has grasped greater control of his beast, I must insist he remain locked in No Man's Land. It is possible he came to us too late, which will be a massive disappointment as I doubt I will be able to find a suitable substitute for his power. Not only is he the first Novasgardian Blackwood has ever seen, he is also the first Berserker —a species that has long since been believed to be extinct —that has stepped foot on these grounds. What we stand to learn from his presence here is too important. I only hope that some time alone will help him calm enough that Bruno and I might work together to reach him.

<<fingers drumming on desk>>

Dr. Masterson: Having never worked with one of his ilk, it's impossible to know which method of treatment will be most effective. However, a close colleague of mine has had extensive experience with another very similar to him. Perhaps a chat regarding best practices is in order. If all else fails, I don't suppose it would be entirely out of line to attempt old-school behavioral modification techniques. And if memory serves, Blackwood is still in possession of the requisite equipment. Note—ask Joffrey to search the storage rooms for an ECT machine. And maybe a wooden spoon.

\<\<knock on door>>

Dr. Masterson: *sigh* Yes, come in.

\<\<door squeaks open>>

Joffrey: My apologies, Doctor. Bruno has run into some . . . trouble in Tor's cell. We require your assistance in handling him. I think perhaps heavy sedation will be required, but we need you to sign off.

Dr. Masterson: *grumble* Fine. I'll be there shortly. Don't give him anything until I can assess him.

Joffrey: Very well, ma'am.

\<\<door closes>>

Dr. Masterson: N001 may very well be my greatest challenge thus far. I am confident, however, that I will get what I need from him before he is useless to my cause.

\<\<static>>

End of transcript.

EIGHT

Shock held me hostage. This wasn't how I wanted to see Alek for the first time since I'd run. Of course Sunday had told him I was here, and if it hadn't been her, Kingston wouldn't have been able to keep his mouth shut. The second my twin's mate had set foot on Blackwood's grounds, this confrontation had been inevitable. Still, part of me hoped to avoid it.

"Alek . . ."

"Hello, brother." His smirk was devoid of all sincerity. "I'd ask if you'd missed me, but since you went to such lengths to avoid me, I'm guessing not."

"You can't be here," I snarled, desperate to keep the truth from him. If he knew I'd taken on this curse to protect him, he'd never forgive himself.

"The hell I can't. You abandoned us all! You're lucky I didn't contact Father and tell him you were missing when you left. He would've rained fire across the land to find you."

I rolled my eyes, knowing that was the least my father

would have done. Still, I played dumb. "Missing? That's a bit dramatic."

"Is it? What else do you call taking off in the middle of the night and cutting off all contact?"

"Vacation?" I drawled, aiming for bored, although I was sure my racing pulse was going to give me away. A Berserker on edge was a Berserker two seconds from losing control.

"A vacation? You call *this* a vacation? What has happened to you? Sunday said you were changed, but I certainly didn't expect to see you looking like this. You're barely recognizable. A beast."

"Your mate should've kept her mouth shut. This doesn't concern her."

A growl tore from my twin's throat as his muscles swelled.

Kai stepped forward, but I stopped him with a hand on his chest. "Leave it, dragon. My brother won't harm me."

He gave Alek a dubious once-over. "Are ye sure?"

I nodded. "You can go. I don't need a babysitter."

"Perhaps not, but I think I'll stay all the same."

"This is a family matter, dragon," Alek snarled, his eyes flickering like bolts of lightning.

"And Tor is my family."

Alek laughed, low and angry. "Is this why you ran off, then? You replaced me?"

"I don't need to justify my reasons with you, brother. You live your life the way you want. I'll live mine."

"We've always done so together." Alek sounded hurt, but still simmering with fury.

"Have we? I remember a time not so long ago when you stole my destiny from me. You abandoned me in Novasgard so you could fuck your little mate and forget about the rest of us."

When Kai winced, I knew my blow might have been aimed a little too low. But if that was what was needed to get my twin away from here and preserve his ignorance, then it had to be done. I'd already committed myself to this path when I accepted the curse in his place. I would see it through to the bitter, bloody end.

I had to convince Alek to leave this place without me because unless Moira figured out a way to free us from the spell trapping us here, he wouldn't get me back. Ever. And the second he found that out, there wasn't a force on Earth that would prevent the war Novasgard would bring to this realm. I couldn't bear the weight of the deaths that would follow.

"Get out of here, Alek. I didn't invite you. I don't want you here."

"No," he said mulishly. The stubborn arse. I should have known better. My Loki-blessed brother never did what was asked of him.

Reaching for the nearest object, I tore a young fir from the ground and hurled it at him. "I said go!"

He caught it and tossed it aside, his eyes flashing and body growing as his Berserker took shape.

"You think I'm afraid of you?" I laughed with a sneer, allowing my rage to swell and my body to transform. "You aren't the only one touched by bloodlust, brother."

Alek's eyes widened as my fingers turned to claws and the scales rippled their way across my body. For the first time, maybe ever, staring at my twin was no longer like gazing into a mirror. We could not look more different. The knowledge hurt more than I thought it would, considering I once wished for some space from him. Now it felt as though there was an entire galaxy, and it was nearly unbearable.

"How did this happen?" Alek snarled in disgust.

My chest ached, but I wasn't going to share the details with him. All that would do was make him more resolved to fix me. I wasn't broken, Dahlia saw to that, and I didn't want to go back to the prince I'd once been.

"Destiny, brother."

Alek shook his head. "No. This was never your destiny."

"And yet here I am."

"Just come home with me, brother. Together we'll find a way to fix you."

"I am not broken!" I bellowed, the beast within taking full control and lashing out. "This is the destiny *you* put in my path when you stole my time at Ravenscroft. There is no going back. Now leave before I send you back with a scar to remember me by. I'm sure Sunday will still love you, even if your pretty face is mangled by my claws."

"Even scarred, I would still be the prettier twin."

I knew he hadn't intended for it to be a dig at my new devilish form. He'd made comments like that for as long as I could remember. That didn't mean it didn't cut deep due to my own newly discovered insecurities.

"Care to test the theory?" I asked, voice low and dripping with violence.

"Tor," Kai warned.

He could have been a fly for all the attention I paid him as I stalked toward my brother.

"It's why I found my mate, and you've chosen to be . . . this," Alek taunted.

My lip curled in a sneer. He must not have known about Dahlia, but there was something in me that wanted to keep her to myself.

98

"You're right, brother. It would take a special kind of mate to want either of us looking like this. Sunday certainly wouldn't."

That did it. Alek raged, shoving me hard as he growled, "Say that again to my face."

Words were impossible to form as the red haze of my fury engulfed me. My brother and I had fought before. It was basically a birthright, given our upbringing. We had boyish tussles, warriors' sparring sessions, and even a few hot-headed fistfights. This wasn't the same. Never before had we come up against each other while controlled by the white-hot rage of our Berserker blood.

I lunged at him, slashing my claws in the air less than an inch away from his chest, a warning he was lucky to get. But Alek had less practice than I when it came to managing his rage. I'd bet he could count on both hands the number of times he'd let the rage consume him. Which meant he was less controlled, less cognizant of what he was doing. He was all fuming instinct while I was able to draw on years of training and strategy.

He didn't stand a chance.

Kai shouted our names, but it was easy to dismiss him as Alek barreled into me, taking us both to the ground. We grappled, rolling around in the dirt and broken twigs and leaves. It was a constant battle for dominance, the same violent dance we'd been engaged in since we were old enough to care about such things. Only this time, we weren't play-fighting.

My claws dug into his shoulders as he pummeled my abdomen, and we rolled until the two of us slammed into a giant tree trunk, shaking the thing so fiercely branches fell to the ground.

"Take it back!" Alek snarled.

"No!" I shouted, headbutting him to knock him off me. It was a move I'd long ago perfected, and the addition of my horns only made it deadlier. Sadly, not even the sight of my twin's blood dripping into his eyes was enough to cool my wrath.

"Never speak of my Kærasta."

Sucking in deep lungfuls of air as I got to my feet, I went in for the kill, leaving behind all of my reservations about telling him the truth. "She'd run from you if you weren't so pretty, brother. You and I both know it. Now go home. To your happy life with your beautiful child, and remember what I did for you."

"What you did for me?" he asked, breathing hard as he stood and spat out a mouthful of blood.

"Tor . . ." Kai tried again.

"You want answers, brother? What if you can't handle the truth?"

"There's nothing you can say to me that I can't accept."

I laughed, a deep booming sound that sent the remaining birds fleeing. "You have always been a short-sighted fool. It's your trickster nature."

Alek scoffed, using the back of his arm to wipe the blood from his brow. "Say your piece so we can finish this."

"I will never return home, Alek. Not to your life, not to Novasgard."

"Do you really hate me that much?" he asked, pain lancing his features.

My truth was a roar as it all finally came pouring out of me. "No, you damned idiot. I did what I had to because I love you. I'd protect you from every evil to see you happy. Even knowing the cost, I'd do it all over again."

"Do what?"

"Take on the curse meant for you."

He faltered, his eyes returning to their normal shade as he stared at me and let my words sink in. "What curse are you speaking of?"

"The one the Shadow Court demanded for the slaughter of their warriors."

"The Shadow Court . . ." he trailed off, his skin leaching of color. "The night you left, when there was that freak storm."

"That was no storm. He thought I was you, and I allowed it. You had already done so much, fought through impossible odds, had Eden and your forever in your grasp. I couldn't let them take it from you."

Alek mutely shook his head, horror and pain flickering in his eyes. "No. No, Tor. That wasn't your choice to make."

"It is done."

Alek shoved me again, though this time, it was the move of a desperate man rather than an angry one. "No. We'll fix it. We'll go to the Shadow Court and explain. Have them reverse it. If it's payment they demand, then it's mine to pay. Not yours."

"It's not that easy," Kai said, his whisper doing what his shouting had not.

"What?" Alek snapped.

Familiar enough with my rage, Kai didn't so much as flinch at Alek's. "We've already spoken to them. They know, and there is no cure," he explained, pity in every word.

"Then you haven't been persuasive enough," Alek snarled, his eyes darkening again. "I'll speak to Father. No one will dare say no to the Jarl of Novasgard."

"Alek," I said, shaking my head. "It's too late. What's done is done. This is my path. I made my choice, and now I must live with it."

"It wasn't your choice to make!"

"It doesn't matter. It is done."

"Tor," he whispered, voice cracking.

"You should go," I forced out, my twin's pain hurting me far more than any physical blow. "Leave me."

"I won't. You're my twin. I won't ever leave you. We came into this life together and we shall leave the same way."

I let my bitterness and anger fuel my next words as the rage built inside me again. "There's nothing for you here. You have your wife, your daughter, waiting for you at home. Go. Go back to the life you fought so hard for and live every moment like it's your last."

Alek's jaw clenched and he shook his head. I could already see the protest building in his throat. Realization struck me like one of my father's lightning bolts. Alek would never leave. Not willingly. Not unless I played upon the guilt eating him up inside. I knew it as surely as I knew my name. Because that is the only way he'd get me to walk away were our roles reversed.

"Don't you get it? I don't want you here."

"You don't mean that."

"Yes, brother. I do. You are a constant reminder of everything I have lost. Everything you've taken from me since the moment you were born. You are living the life that was meant for me, wearing my face, making our family proud. The battles you fought, the glory you found, your mate . . . All of it should have been mine. You stole that from me the day you took my place at Ravenscroft."

A tear trickled from the corner of my twin's eye, and that was when I delivered my killing blow.

"I never want to see you again. Be gone when I get back, or I'll remove you myself."

My gaze met Kai's as I spun around. He knew my words

for the lie they were. My love and contentment with Dahlia were proof enough of that. I would never trade a second of my time with her for anything. Not even the life I once chased with the single-minded devotion of a fanatic.

"Go," he mouthed, knowing that I would not last another second without caving.

I took off running, trusting Kai to pick up the pieces of Alek's broken heart.

A torrent of emotions swirled in me, too much to bear at the same time. I gave myself over to my beast, letting the urge to forget everything else win out as I headed deeper into the woods toward the town beyond. I couldn't allow guilt to consume me because if I did, I'd return to Alek. He had to leave. And for him to do that, he had to think I hated him.

He had to let me go. We might be twins, but his life no longer belonged to me. It belonged to his mate and that sweet little girl. They needed him. And maybe I did too, but I could learn to live without him.

I had to.

Alek had paid the price for his happily ever after.

It was time for me to pay mine.

CHAPTER
NINE

HADES

"A walk? Since when do you take me for a fuckin' walk? You'd better not try and put me on a godsdamned leash. Especially not without my favorite treats. Yes, plural."

Asshole sat at my feet, head cocked to one side, beady eyes looking from my hands to my feet as though he expected me to drop a treat for him.

"Do you see a leash?" I asked, already over this plan. I don't know what the fuck I'd been thinking when I suggested it.

"You could be planning to use your shadows. How am I supposed to know? Now that you're embracing your inner shadow daddy, anything goes."

I closed my eyes and squeezed the bridge of my nose, forcing myself to take a deep breath before I gave in to the urge to punt the ball of fur at my feet across the river.

"You wouldn't dare," Cerberus growled, reminding me that he could hear my every thought.

"Keep it up and I just might. You really want to test me?"

"You want I should piss on your leg? Cause I will, moth-erfucker."

"Remember that football player who came to stay in the underworld for a while? Real good punter. He taught me a few things before I finally assigned him a punishment. I got pretty skilled, and you are about the size of a football."

"You keep threatening me with that. Funny thing is, there's not even a river nearby. And this puppy can doggy paddle like nobody's business."

"So then there's no harm in me testing out my kicking leg, is there?"

Asshole bared his teeth and growled at me.

"Oh, calm down," I grumbled, striding toward the wrought iron gates that would lead us off Blackwood grounds and down the path to town. "Are you coming or not?"

He yipped, bouncing excitedly as his tail wagged. See? He wanted to go; he just had to be, well, an asshole about it first. Can't imagine where he picked up that stubborn streak.

Somewhere in the multiverse, the Fates were laughing at me.

"I can't control it. Little dog energy might be more powerful than big dog energy, boss."

I popped the collar on my coat as a soft snowfall began. I was warm by nature, but the last thing I needed was a human townsperson catching sight of me wandering outside in nothing but a button-down shirt and trousers. They'd peg me as a Blackwood resident, and then I'd get the dirty looks and fear associated with my status. I didn't want to deal with all that nonsense today. I was already in a foul mood because Dahlia had work to do, which left me nothing but scraps of her attention.

Scraps I had to share with three other men.

No wonder I was filled with so much restless energy.

"And her favorite puppy." Asshole's voice was filled with longing. *"It's okay, boss. Don't be embarrassed. Persephone's been holding you by your balls since the moment you saw her. Makes sense Dahlia would have a vise grip on them too."*

I opened the gate and Asshole slipped through first, his little bark letting me know the guard wasn't at his post, just as I'd expected. The man was off somewhere in the woods, taking his usual smoke break.

"Let's go," I said, my steps quick and sure as we put Blackwood in our rearview.

Though his legs were far shorter, Asshole easily kept pace with me, sometimes bounding ahead to sniff at something or lift his leg to mark a tree before trotting back to my side.

"Enjoying yourself?" I asked, barely suppressing my smile.

I'd die before admitting it, but it was nice seeing him like this. I think I might've even been having fun.

The snow began falling more heavily, and the puppy at my feet barked and chased the flakes as they made their way to the ground.

"Gods, has anyone told you how adorable this form is? Are you planning to stay like this?"

"I'm having a blast. You should try it sometime. You don't always have to be the king of the fuckin' grumps, my lord Hades," he said, hitting the last with sarcasm so strong there was no way I could've missed it.

"Real reverent," I deadpanned.

"You know me. Always your most faithful and loyal servant."

"Ha!" I laughed. "You, loyal?"

Asshole stopped dead and glared up at me. *"Name one other denizen of the underworld more loyal than me. I'll wait."*

One second bled into two.

He and I both knew there wasn't a name I could give, even if I'd wanted to.

"Exactly. I left the underworld twice to be with you in your time of need. Do you know what those bitches made me do to get back here?"

"Sit? Stay? Roll over?"

"Ha ha, very funny. They made me fuckin' beg. You know I never beg."

I had to bite my cheek to stop from smiling. "Did they at least give you a bone and tell you you were a good boy?"

"No!"

There was so much righteous indignation in the single word that there was no stopping the chuckle that burst out of me. "Fuck, I missed you."

"I knew it! I knew you'd be lost without me. Take that, Apollo. Hades is my bitch!"

My palms lit with blue fire. "Watch it, dog. I'm no one's bitch."

"Not even Dahlia's?"

The mention of my mate was enough to put out my flames. "No. I'm her daddy."

"Gross, man. I don't want to think of you fuckin' while I'm out enjoying myself. It's bad enough I have to watch it near daily. Your ass is whiter than this snow. Would it kill you to use some self-tanner? Tor's is all golden and beautiful. Even the damn pirate looks like he gets out and bathes his balls in the sun."

I balked. "Do you readily investigate their under-carriage?"

"From my vantage point, it's hard not to notice."

"Do the respectable thing and avert your damn gaze, then."

"Would you turn down free porn? I thought not. Don't come for me, Hades. Not unless you've got receipts."

We were nearing the town at this point, and even if a lot of the townspeople knew about supernatural creatures, I didn't want to be talking to my dog like he was a fucking person when I strolled past them. "Stop talking unless it's an emergency."

"It's always an emergency. I'm little, but I've got a lot to say."

"Don't I fucking know it."

"You're the one who just admitted you missed me. No taking it back now."

"I'm not trying to."

We walked almost half a block in silence.

"So, you really missed me, huh? Is that what this walk's really about? You wanted some quality time with your best boy?"

"You got me."

A woman bundled up in a heavy coat and scarf frowned at me as she walked past, so I held a hand to my ear and muttered, "I've gotta go. Talk soon," and pretended to hang up a phone call. Asshole could talk to me all he wanted, but I'd need to ignore him until we didn't have an audience.

The puppy's laughter floated through my mind. He loved making me look like an ass.

I hadn't been to Briarglen before, but Caspian had given me the rundown when I'd asked him about the best route to take. He'd warned me to stay on the main drag so I wouldn't find myself alone and outnumbered by the less friendly locals. Ever since the Ripper started killing off folks left and right, they didn't take too kindly to strangers. Understandably so.

Hopefully that would change, though, now that we'd rid the town of their serial killer. Not that anyone knew about it yet. Wasn't exactly like Kai was flying around announcing to all and sundry that he'd flambéed the fucker. Fuck, they'd be screaming and running for the hills if they saw a dragon flying overhead. Dragons were rare, and Kai wasn't even a true dragon shifter. His beast was predicated by his father's curse, not a drop of shifter blood in his veins.

"No, Charlie, I saw it. The beast was running through the woods, snarling and snapping, blood dripping from its maw. I'm telling you, it was the Ripper come back to collect."

"That doesn't sound good," Asshole intoned as we came upon a man chatting animatedly on his phone.

I couldn't help but agree. What the hell had they seen? Cause it sure as fuck hadn't been the Ripper.

"I heard Stacy McGinty got a better look than I did. Saw it outside The Hag's Tooth, she did. Yes, when she was taking the rubbish to the bin last night. She said it had great big horns sprouting from its head like the devil himself. And she kept going on about its black eyes, soulless and vicious. Barely escaped with her life."

Just that fast, it all clicked into place. There was only one person they could be talking about. Tor.

Fuck.

Someone must have seen him while he'd been on one of his hunts. And in the way of all superstitious small towns, they'd turned him into a devil.

"Kai said he was in a bad way after the dustup with his brother. Do we know if he came home last night?" Asshole pawed at my leg when I didn't answer.

I shook my head.

"He should be careful. Place like this, all these scared people, it's a powder keg."

"Mmm," I murmured.

Continuing on our stroll, we passed by The Hag's Tooth, the warm light spilling from the windows making the place inviting. As a patron exited, I heard the sound of the crowd singing a sea shanty accompanied by what sounded like a fiddle and . . . an accordion?

Before I could investigate further, the sound of someone clearing their voice pulled my attention.

"I wouldn't go in there if I were you, Hades," the slightly bored, sonorous voice said from behind me.

Turning, I found a blond man dressed in motorcycle leathers standing behind me, one arm resting on the statue in the center of the roundabout.

"Gabriel," I snarled. "What the fuck are you doing here?"

The Messenger of God looked me up and down before turning his attention to the statue. "Dolores Polk," he read off the inscription. "Founder of Briarglen, the original Hag." He shrugged. "Seems a bit on the nose if you ask me."

"Let's not waste time, angel. You and I both know you're not here to take in a bit of the local flavor."

Gabriel sauntered over to me, looking every inch the cocksure pissant I knew him to be. He and I never played on the same team, and it was safe to say we didn't have a history of seeing eye to eye. If memory serves, the last time I came across the righteous fuck, I fed him my fist. Well, I tried to. Fucker was surprisingly fast and wily.

The angel heaved a long-suffering sigh before reaching down to pet Asshole. My pup growled at him and snapped.

"Good dog," I praised.

"I'm trying to help you, Hades. Not everyone is out to get you."

"That's not how it's felt anytime you and I have interacted . . . what did Lilith start calling you after War's failed apocalypse? Leather feathers?"

Gabriel bared his teeth in a mockery of a smile. He never did know how to take a joke. And he absolutely despised being the butt of one, which was why I always made it a point to do so.

Clearly there was no love lost between the two of us.

"All water under the bridge," he said, adopting his bored mien once more. "Listen, Hades, I'm a very busy messenger. I wouldn't be here if it wasn't a matter of life and death."

"How appropriate for me."

"Yes, well, I suppose that is your domain. Maybe you should pay a bit more attention to what I have to say."

"Why should I listen to you? Everything you've ever told me has done nothing but cause me pain."

"You have to give her up, Hades."

I scoffed, my blood running cold even as I bolstered my facade of indifference. "No."

"I know we've had our differences, but I need you to listen to me. You cannot have her. She's the beginning of the end. We thought hiding her would protect the world. Sadly, it has done the opposite."

My temper flared. "You hid her from me?"

Gabriel's brows lifted. "You may find this hard to believe, but not everything is about *you*. We hid her from the world. We kept her soul bound until the Siren Coven sent Lucifer back to hell and his apocalypse was stopped. I gave my wings to fight him, and it was all for naught." Shaking his head, he took a deep breath. "We thought

Death's daughter was no longer needed. We were wrong." If I was of any mind to feel compassion, I'd have said he looked worn down.

But I was the farthest thing possible from compassionate. I was fucking livid.

"I came to you. I fucking begged you to tell me where Persephone was. All this time you knew?"

"It wasn't time for you to know," he said simply, as if that forgave the very grievous error in judgment he had made.

I grabbed a fistful of his shirt and tugged him forward until his nose was less than an inch from mine.

"Your creator is not the only god around, son. If you want to survive past this moment, I suggest you show me some fucking respect."

Gabriel rolled his eyes. "Don't make me smite you, Hades."

"She was my soulmate!" I thundered. "You've never understood the power of deep and eternal love or what that loss can do to a man, you sexless angel."

The man I held in my grip vanished, then rematerialized, his movement causing my ears to pop as his power shifted the air. Now he was sitting on the edge of the statue's base, expression shattered.

"You think I don't know what it means to lose your soulmate? I've given this world everything I had in order to save ungrateful heathens like you. I found her and left her because if I hadn't, the world would've burned. And you can't even do something as simple as stay away from Dahlia."

My pulse roared in my ears. I couldn't remember a time I'd ever been this angry. Sparks flew from my fingers as I took slow, measured steps to where Gabriel perched. "I

MEG ANNE & K. LORAINE

don't believe you. Because if you did actually know what it was like to have the other half of your soul torn away, there is nothing that would ever stop you from searching for it and putting an end to that kind of pain. That kind of wound isn't one that can simply be ignored. You don't just decide to get over it and move on with your life. There is no life for me without her."

"And that's just one of the many ways the two of us differ, Hades. I left her so she could live, because a world without her light wasn't worth being in. I'd have watched her exist from a distance, loved her from afar, to ensure she had a future. You're selfish enough to steal her away and let the world die because of it."

I snorted. "You're right. While you suffer on your moral high ground, I have everything I've ever wanted. There's nothing a villain wouldn't do to keep the woman he loves at his side. And you . . . you *heroes* will languish in heartbreak and die with nothing but tragedy as your legacies."

Gabriel's cheeks turned a soft shade of pink, the only visible sign of his anger. "I should have known better than to come to you. You will never see past your pride long enough to consider the greater good."

"I serve no master but myself, Gabriel. If my Dahlia is the daughter of Death, who better to be her mate than the god who rules over it?"

"You are condemning this world and all the innocent souls within to suffering without end. Does that mean nothing to you?"

"There's only one soul I've ever cared about, angel. And now that she's returned to me, I couldn't care less about the rest. Regardless of any choice I make, those souls you speak of were always destined to come to me in the underworld.

114

She will sit at my side and we will greet them together. As we were always meant to."

Disappointment washed over him. "Lilith warned me that you were no hero, Hades. I should've believed her."

"I told you as much myself. I've never tried to hide what I am, I have no qualms about being the bad guy. But if you have a problem with my being a villain, Gabriel, maybe you should take it up with the person who made me one."

The angel didn't respond. Instead, he stood and walked past me, straight into The Hag's Tooth without looking back.

CHAPTER
TEN
HOOK

"Okay, now, everybody!" I crowed as I stood atop the bar with a flagon of ale in one hand while I slapped my knee to the beat with the other.

"Put him in the long boat 'til he's sober
Put him in the long boat 'til he's sober,
Put him in the long boat 'til he's sober,
Early in the mornin'"

The crowd erupted into a series of cheers as I executed my version of a courtly bow. God, I loved a bit of attention, didn't I? But honestly, I deserved some time in the spotlight since I've been so cruelly denied its glow in the form of Dahlia's gaze.

"Mischief and malice."

"Drink it down."

"Burn it all away."

The band continued on with the next verse of Drunken Sailor as I wobbled on my feet, the whispers disorienting. Gathering my wits, I hopped down and then leaned against the bar top with a lazy grin twisting my lips.

"Another, love. And one for my friend here," I crooned, clapping my palm on the shoulder of the blond man who stood stoically next to me. "He looks like he needs to loosen up a titch."

"Coming right up," the bartender said with a flirtatious smile, pulling two pints and setting them in front of us. "Can I get you lads anything else?" she asked, the invitation in her words utterly transparent.

"Not right now, love."

I had no interest in taking her up on her offer. I was a mated man, after all, but it wouldn't do to upset my barkeep when I had every use of indulging in her services for the better part of the evening.

If I couldn't spend the night buried between my Dahlia's thick thighs, then I was damn sure going to do something useful, like test out the strength of the bloody spell keeping us prisoner. What better way to do that than drink myself into oblivion? So far it'd been going on four hours of nonsense here at this pub. I was hoping to make it past five.

I didn't recall ever keeping track of the length of my exploits before, but since I was the one with the most experience setting foot outside Blackwood's walls, I would be the only one who knew whether that Belladonna woman's hijinks had worked.

That was the theory, anyway.

As I said, I'd started drinking as soon as I'd gotten here, and my vision had taken on a hazy glow at the edges.

"Fire in the sky."

"All the dead things."

"The end is near."

I grunted in dissent, waving my hand about my ear as if

I could send the whispers scattering. "Leave me be, you pests."

"Talking to yourself, Caspian. That's not a good sign," the biker said from beside me.

Grabbing my fresh ale, I knocked it back, giving him the side eye the whole time I swallowed it down. When it was gone, I let out an almighty belch and wiped the foam off my upper lip before slamming the flagon down on the bar.

"Your turn," I slurred.

"No thank you. I don't drink."

The prissy fucker. Thought he was better than me. At least I had better fashion sense and knew that a splash of color could do wonders for a man's swagger.

I eyed him distrustfully. "Not sure I want to rub elbows with a man who doesn't allow himself to indulge." Then again, more for me. "Ah well, bottoms up."

I snatched his drink and drained it.

"Are you quite finished making an arse out of yourself?" he huffed.

Glancing around, I smirked and said, "No."

Then I slapped him on the shoulder and made my way into the crowd, swinging from partner to partner as I danced a merry jig. Or at least I did until I found myself staring into the biker's surly face once more.

"Oh, come on. Just because you have a pole lodged up your arse doesn't mean everyone else has got to," I groaned, trying to shove him away and find myself a new partner.

"I've important business to discuss with you, Caspian."

I rolled my eyes. "That's what they all say. Listen, you're a very handsome biker, but I'm taken. I know, I know, it's tragic for the rest of you, but I am off the market. Mated. My heart has been claimed by another." Poking him in the chest, I drove the point home. "You. Can't. Have. Me."

"And where is Dahlia?" he asked.

My blood ran cold, and my mind boomed from the return of my harrowing countdown.

Tick

Tick

Tick

The man stared at me, his brow pulled together so fiercely I almost laughed at the unibrow he created. Until the ticking got so loud I wanted to cover my ears. Then he took my face between his hands and pressed our foreheads together.

"Oi . . ." I protested, but stopped as the ticking faded to nothing. Apparently the man was no mere biker after all. He's robbed me of the ticking and of my buzz. But it was the words he spoke that truly sobered me.

"I'll ask again. Where is Dahlia?"

"What's it to you?" I demanded, menace simmering in my voice. "Who are you?"

"This is a conversation better saved for privacy."

"I already told you, mate. I'm off the market, as it were."

"I don't want to fuck you. I'm here because I need you to save the world."

I stared at him for a second before laughing. Giving him a pat on the chest, I started to move away. "That's a good one. You really had me going there for a second."

He stopped me. "Caspian, this is no joke. If you return to her, you will end the world."

The gravity of his tone had my blood buzzing. Adopting an unaffected mien, I shot him a lazy grin. "Well, which is it, mate? Am I to save the world or end it? You seem to have gotten your lines crossed."

"The two are not mutually exclusive. It all comes down to free will and the choices you make."

I glared at this man, annoyed that he'd not only ruined my jolly good time but that he was speaking about Dahlia when he had no right to utter her name and, worse still, that he was trying to scare me away from her. As if that would ever be a possibility.

"Listen, mate. I don't know who the fuck you think you are—"

Heaving a sigh, he placed a hand on my shoulder, and fuck me, my ears popped like I'd just shot up to the top of the fifty-seventh floor of a skyscraper. When I opened my eyes after the pain abated, we were standing outside The Hag's Tooth with a light dusting of snow on the ground and softly falling flakes floating around us.

"What'd you do that for? I was enjoying myself."

He stared up into the heavens as he let loose a groan of pure frustration. "I was really hoping to avoid the whole introduction thing this time. It does get ever so tedious constantly having to repeat oneself. But if you insist."

Bright light burst from him, a sort of pulsing power emanating from his person.

"I am Gabriel. The Messenger of God. Sent unto you to deliver a message that shall not be ignored lest the world as you know it may cease to exist."

I squinted at him, raising one arm to block out some of the light. "All that fanfare just to tell me you're an angel? Is that supposed to impress me or something? Does it actually work for you?"

He scowled, his heavenly glow dimming. "Usually, yes."

"Huh. Maybe the creatures of this realm are easily impressed. I'm from Faerie, mate. We all have magic, and we can do a far bit more than create a bit of sunlight. Do some research next time. Learn your audience. It'll help you make a bigger splash."

"I don't need to make a bi—"

"Looks to me like you do, Gabe. You don't even have wings or anything. Truth be told, you look more like a handsome devil than an angel. Anyone ever tell you the biker look gives bad boy? That's the whole schtick. Kinda the same as a pirate. No one ever saw all this"—I gestured to my leather pants, knee-high boots, and billowing shirt— "and thought 'good guy'. Well . . . good in bed, maybe. Perfect for the cover of a spicy romance novel." I made a mental note to offer my services to Dahlia. Her books would fly off the shelves with yours truly on the cover.

"Actually, most of the time they don't wear shirts at all. Marketing is important, you know," Gabriel said, bringing me up short.

"I beg your pardon. What did you just say?"

"Statistically speaking, readers want to know what they're getting. They like to be able to judge the heat level of a book. You know, one chili pepper or five. If the man on the front has no shirt on, chances are good they're getting on-page love scenes and a happily ever after to go with them."

I stood there, mouth agape as the messenger of fucking God schooled me on the inner workings of romance novel marketing.

After I collected myself, I cleared my throat and said, "I think you mean a happy ending."

"That's what I said."

"No, you said happily ever after. I think you'll find that a happy ending means something just a tad different."

Once it clicked, he scowled and rolled his eyes. "Get your mind out of the gutter for five minutes and listen to me."

"You're the one who brought up romance novels and on-page love scenes. Where'd you expect my mind to go? You can't mention a smut scene without me thinking about how they end."

Usually with my cum dripping down Dahlia's sweet thighs, but that was probably best kept to myself.

Gabriel reached into his jacket and adjusted something hidden in an inner pocket before muttering, "It's not smut if they're in love. How many times do I have to say it?"

"It's the first time you've said it to me, and to be fair, it can absolutely be smut if they're in love. The filth factor has nothing to do with the depth of one's feelings. If anything, the more connected to your partner, the further the bonds of intimacy stretch."

"I am not debating this with you."

"Clearly you are. I can tell you, I smut the fuck out of Dahlia all night long, and our love is boundless."

"Is it? Even if your love might bring about the apocalypse?"

"So long as I'm buried inside her, what do I care about the end of the world? This isn't the only realm in existence. Let it burn. My love and I will simply return to Ravenndel."

His eyes glowed as he jumped on the word.

"What would you say if I could return you there right now? Put an end to your madness and suffering?"

My heart stuttered. "What are you on about? I can't return, not until I have my compass."

"Are you so certain? I'm an angel. My powers are phenomenal. One snap of my fingers, and you and your crew can be back on your ship in the turquoise waters of Ravenndel, fighting the Lost Boys and Peter Pan like you have been doing for centuries."

I was struck with a wave of homesickness like I'd never experienced before. My mind bloomed with images of my home, of the people and places I'd left behind.

"With her?" I asked, throat tight. Just like the others, I'd jump at the chance to steal her away and keep her forever.

"No. Nothing good comes without sacrifice. Give her up and save the world by returning home. Stay, and Ravenndel becomes nothing but a faint memory as the end times begin."

The death of hope tasted like ash on my tongue.

"I spent my entire life searching for my mate without even realizing it. Why would I ever give her up?"

"To save her. To save the world she calls home."

"This world was never good to her. All she knew before coming here was cruelty and fear. She belongs with me."

With us, I mentally corrected. I might have told myself I'd take her to Ravenndel with me, but I could no more take her away from her other mates than I could willingly leave her behind. The choice was obvious, even if it wasn't necessarily easy.

"I will not leave my mate. Not for anything. If the world ends, it'll end with her in my arms."

The angel's handsome face twisted in outrage. "Why did I ever think there'd be reasoning with you? Selfish, arrogant fools. All of you."

"If I'm a fool for choosing love, then so be it. Better a fool than the soulless void I'd be without her."

"So be it. Perhaps Death was right to choose her pieces the way she did. Villains only know how to serve themselves. Who better to thrust in her daughter's path?"

Before I could ask him what that was supposed to mean, he vanished, leaving me alone with the falling snow and the eerie specter of Adonis D. Edman watching in the distance. Oh well, at least my head was blissfully sile—

Tick

Tick

Tick

CHAPTER
ELEVEN
DAHLIA

"The end . . . motherfuckers." Oh, sweet relief. I fucking finished.

I slammed the laptop shut after making sure that I saved the file and the email to Keeks went through. Then I stood and stretched, my bones cracking and my muscles protesting from being stuck in the same position for hours on end.

I wasn't sure if I wanted to cry or cheer. I'd finished enough books to know that there was a definite ebb and flow to the creative process, but there was always a punch of anxiety that *this* would be the one that did me in. The one where writer's block and that blank page with its taunting black cursor would win. But no. I took that story and I made it my bitch. Now the publisher could get off my back, and maybe I'd be able to write my new passion project in peace.

No shade to Rebel and her boys. I'll always love them and I wrote a hell of a sequel, but that hadn't ever been the plan. Theirs was a stand-alone story until the publisher insisted I give them more. Nothing was worse than creatively thinking a project was finished, only to find out you had to go back and mine the empty, well, mine, for more gold.

Forgive my less-than-stellar metaphors; my brain was absolute sludge. I needed a drink—or ten. Probably a shower. Definitely a meal involving a vegetable, or at least one that didn't come out of a cardboard box. But first . . . fresh air.

I'd been cooped up in my room for days. I needed to remind myself what the sky looked like. Maybe touch some grass. What was that thing the guy in Die Hard said? Make little fists with my toes in it. Or did that only work on carpet after traveling? Whatever, it sounded good. It was supposed to help with something, and frankly, I could use all the help I could get.

I was always more zombie than human after finishing a project. I needed a day or two to return to myself and the world of the living. Lucky for me, I didn't see any of my men lurking in the hall or near Blackwood's front door. Not that I didn't want to see them, but after days of obeying my wishes and giving me space, they deserved me at my best, not barely able to function. A walk would set me back to rights. There was an undeniable pang of guilt, though. I knew they'd want to see me as soon as possible. Which meant I should make the most of this walkabout. Clear the cobwebs from the social function portion of my brain and make sure I could give them all of me when the time came.

If I was being honest, I wouldn't reject any of them if I saw them. A neck rub from Tor with those enormous hands would probably send me into some kind of pleasure-induced seizure. The problem was, I wouldn't be in a place where I could reciprocate, and turnabout was fair play, in all things.

The cold winter air bit at my skin as I strode aimlessly through the grounds, not making eye contact with any of the residents if at all possible. I needed somewhere quieter, less populated. You'd think the fucking snow would keep them indoors. You'd be wrong. Supernaturals ran hot by nature. A little snow was the equivalent of a balmy breeze to most of them.

I huffed, kicking at the bare branches of a bush that had grown enough to encroach on the path.

"Hey!" a tiny voice squeaked, reminding me once again that more than just the residents of Blackwood called this land their home.

"Oops, sorry!" I called, cheeks burning with embarrassment as I walked a little faster.

By the time I reached the crest of yet another fucking hill, I was huffing and puffing because of the speed I'd used to escape my shame. But everything came to a standstill, shame forgotten, as my blood ran cold at the sight of the kirkyard only a few feet from me.

I hadn't meant to come here.

The scene of the crime. Or rather, the scene of my attempted murder.

My eyes were drawn immediately to the slab of stone that Sam had used as his altar. It was still stained with pools of my dried blood. Though it had snowed on and off the last few days, the wind had blown most of it to the ground, so the dark blotches stood out in sharp relief against the gray and white of the snow and stone.

It was clear no one visited this place, not even a groundskeeper. And why would they? If you died at Blackwood, you were already one of the forgotten. A shiver worked its way down my spine. That had very nearly been me.

A low hum built inside me, reminding me of something I'd been neglecting since my attack. My work with the lost souls of Blackwood. Even if the Ripper was gone, they still had something keeping them here, didn't they? Maybe it was up to me to help them cross over. Or something. I was still super hazy on the details of what I was supposed to be doing with my power.

From what little I've pieced together, necromancers weren't exactly heroes. Granted, the only thing I really had to go off was my father and his culty minions. And then there was my mom. Was she a telepath? Was that where I got my set of pipes? When a necromancer and a mind-melter love each other very much . . . for all I knew, my dad killed her right after I was born. Sacrificed her to the goddess Death.

Yeah, I definitely couldn't use my father as the exemplar of my kind. That seemed like a one-way ticket to, well, here, I guess.

Maybe I did belong locked away at Blackwood. My kind didn't seem like they were born to be do-gooders. Could a necromancer be a good person?

Why did it suddenly feel like I was debating major philosophical points with myself? This was not the relaxing stroll I'd planned on, but I guess I'd been avoiding dealing with all these unanswered questions about myself. And you could only live in denial for so long. So . . . what the heck was I? And did I get a say in what that looked like?

Ugh, as far as I knew, I was the only one of my kind at Blackwood, unless you counted Hades, and he wasn't a necromancer so much as a whole-ass god. So that was more like comparing apples to pomegranates. Heh. See what I did there?

Dr. Masterson really had her work cut out for her if she

thought she was going to help me be any kind of productive member of Blackwood's community. So far all I'd been able to do was get haunted, kidnapped, and toss souls into inanimate objects. I couldn't even solve crimes.

Crimes that were kinda sorta your fault.

Fuck off, inner me. No one asked for a guilt trip today. Sam might have only ended up here because he had me in his sights, but that didn't make me responsible for all his other victims.

Still, maybe I should try to help them. Just to even out the karmic scale. If there was such a thing as a karmic scale. Not all necromancers, am I right?

Taking a deep breath, I shored up my strength and walked into the cemetery, my blood buzzing from the energy within the gates. When I found a grave without a soul attached to it, I perched on the headstone and closed my eyes.

"Okay, everyone. The Dahlia Moore spiritual helpline is now open for business. Step right up."

It didn't take long for the energy surrounding me to change. The air all but sizzled with the arrival of not one, not two, but thirteen mother-effin' ghosts.

For a split second, I really regretted my cattle-call approach. But then I realized none of these souls carried any of the tells associated with the malevolent spirit. The only reason I was overwhelmed was because of the sheer volume of them surrounding me. I wondered if there was such a thing as a spirit circuit breaker. A way for me to control how many of them came through at one time so as not to short myself out.

"One at a time, guys," I said, holding up my hands as they advanced.

The group of them stopped with my gesture, which

reminded me once more that I could do a lot more with them than simply talk. If I needed to, I could send them packing.

Feeling a whole heck of a lot better, I sat up a little straighter. "You," I said, pointing to a man who looked a little bit like a pilgrim in his black-on-black-on-black garb and heeled shoes. If the sixteen hundreds had a Vogue, this guy would have been the centerfold.

The rest of the gathered ghosts looked around as if wondering who the *you* I referenced was. The man in question pointed at himself.

"Yes, you," I confirmed with a nod. "The John Smith looking motherfucker."

"My name is Edward."

"Of course it is."

"Edward is a family name. It's one of the most honorable things a man can do for his child, pass on his father's name."

I rolled my eyes. "Okay. Whatever you say, Ed. What are you hanging around this cemetery for?"

His face contorted into an ugly sneer as he floated a little closer. "I need a witch to finish my great work."

"What great work was that? Because it probably took some pretty bad shit for you to end up in Blackwood."

"A curse set upon the family Reeves."

"Why do you want to curse them?"

"They besmirched my good name."

"Besmirched, huh? How so?"

"They told all and sundry I raped their daughter."

"And did you?"

"Well, yes."

"NEXT!"

"But you didn—"

"NEXT!" I grabbed him by the energy ball that was his soul and tossed that asshole straight back into his grave. "Straight to the trash," I grumbled. Four of the remaining ghosts vanished, and I rolled my eyes. "Oh good, I love when the trash takes itself out."

Another ghost, this one a woman with some serious Farrah Fawcett hair, floated closer.

I raised a brow at her. "What sort of help are you looking for?"

She closed the distance between us, her cold energy making me shiver, but now that I'd met one or two in the flesh, I recognized her as a succubus. "I need you to tell me what time that sexy Thor look-a-like takes his showers. I keep missing them, and I have so few pleasures left. I used to date a Viking once upon a time. I'm desperate for a peek at a Scandinavian foot-lo—"

Straight to the trash once again. "NEXT!"

No one seemed eager to step forward this time, so I pointed at my next victim. "You, Willy Wonka with the hat."

A man in a purple leisure suit and matching top hat floated into my 'office.'

"This better be good, mister. I'm not here to help rapists or perverts."

"I need you to find the bundle I hid under the floorboards of my room. Find it and destroy it. That's the only evidence they'll ever have—"

I held up my hand, sensing where this was going. "Evidence for what?"

"To prove I killed that shifter pack in Sydney."

"That was you?" one of the other ghosts asked, sounding far too fucking reverent for my liking.

He grinned and dusted off his nearly translucent lapel.

"Never even saw it coming. Only one who's ever come close to being as seamless as me was her," he said, jutting his chin toward me. "A whole cult with just a scream. I'm in awe."

Anger built swift and furious within me. "I was already going to give you the brush off for being a murderer, but you really sealed your fate with that one." This time, instead of shouting next, I let out a frustrated scream, tossing my arm away from me as if sending a shower curtain flying open. The ghosts scattered, gone as if they'd never been there at all.

Hopping off the gravestone, I crossed my arms over my chest and began pacing through the rows, grumbling to myself. "These clearly aren't the ghosts I am supposed to be helping."

"Well, young lady, what do ye expect? They're villains, all of them."

I turned around to find a nearly corporeal man standing at the entrance to the Mackenzie poltergeist's tomb.

"Let me guess, you're Mackenzie?"

He chuckled, his raven-winged top hat catching my eye as he removed it with a bow. "Adonis D. Edman, at your service. Mackenzie's likely out pinching the bottoms of every lass he can find right about now. He loves to leave a mark, he does."

There was something about this spirit that was different from the others I'd encountered thus far. He was almost solid, for starters. And I couldn't seem to get a read on his energy the way I could the others. It was closer to static than anything.

"Were you a resident here?"

He shook his head. "I lived in the village. Just a normal man made magic by the hand of death. My purpose here on this side of the afterlife is to share the lore of Briarglen and warn people of the perils of venturing into Blackwood territory."

"So you're like the town crier?" I joked, thinking he certainly looked the part.

"More like a messenger, if ye will."

Something about that title sent chills skittering down my spine. I couldn't shake the sense that a skeleton had risen from the bowels of its grave to score my back with the tips of its bony fingers.

Death was here in a way that was becoming all too familiar.

"And do you have a message for me, Mr. Edman?" I asked, knowing in my gut that's exactly why he was here.

He grinned wickedly, his weirdly mirrored irises flashing. "The Ripper wasn't the main event. He was the appetizer. An amuse-bouche, if you will."

"What?" I asked as the words sank in. "My bouche is not amused."

His smile remained fixed in place. "No, lass. Nor should it be. He was a sign of ill tidings indeed."

"For a messenger, you sure speak in riddles," I muttered, hating everything about where this was going.

"She's already here, slinking in the shadows, waiting for the right moment. If you're not careful, you'll walk straight into her web. Mothers are like that, you know."

My blood turned to ice, and I froze in place. For a second, not even my heart seemed to beat. "Wh-what was that?"

Adonis doffed his cap once more. "Heed my warning, lass, and watch yer back. It won't be long now. Not at all."

With that, he started back the way he came, whistling a

jaunty little tune as if he hadn't just turned my shit upside down.

A soft touch brushed the back of my neck, and I screamed bloody murder as I whirled around, ready to cut a bitch. But instead of a psychotic killer, I found my psychotic lord of the underworld.

Hades smirked. "What's the matter, baby doll? You look like you've seen a ghost."

TWELVE

HADES

"What are you up to, my mischievous little flower?" I muttered to myself as I followed the pull of energy that pulsed from the kirkyard.

I knew it was her. I recognized her scent on the breeze. That and she was the only other person here capable of summoning spirits. I felt it the moment they materialized in this realm. It was like a buzzing beneath my skin. Not in an uncomfortable way, more like unrealized potential. The more spirits nearby, the stronger I became. Add Dahlia to the mix, and you had the recipe for an unmatched level of power between the two of us. No, not unmatched. Limitless.

As I crested the hill, my whole body tensed upon catching sight of my wife. She sat perched on a headstone, all bundled up with her hair in a messy bun, as she spoke to a spirit, a crowd of them surrounding her. The one she was talking to must've pissed her off because she grabbed him by the soul and threw him into a nearby grave.

"That's my good girl," I murmured, pride washing

through me at the sight of her coming into her own. Pride and—I wasn't ashamed to admit—arousal.

Fuck, I was in awe of her. She was coming into herself, becoming the queen I always knew she would. We could rule the underworld without interference from any other deity. She would be my partner in all things, my equal. Hell, the two of us never had to return to my realm if we didn't want to. We might as well take over this land right here.

"Well, well, look who's finally got his ego back. Stow it, boss. You don't want to get too cocky before you've even started. Remember last time? Tempt the Fates and see where it gets you."

"Take a hike, Asshole."

"But—"

"It's not too late for us to test out my punting theory."

"Fuck you, man," the puppy muttered, but he heeded my warning and trotted off back the way we came.

I adjusted myself before continuing on toward Dahlia. Seeing her in her element like this had me feeling some kind of way, and I was not about to allow that interfering menace to get between us. She'd left her room and was alone for the first time in days. I was seizing the shit out of this opportunity.

I stayed quiet, letting her conduct whatever business she had with these restless spirits before they all seemed to scatter at once. Then, before I could get to her, she began strolling through the graveyard, stopping to chat with the strongest spirit I'd seen since being sent here. I remained a respectful distance away, allowing Dahlia her privacy. Not that I wasn't ready to come to her aid the second I sensed she might need backup. I didn't like the way he looked at her or the smirk on his lips as he doffed his cap before walking away whistling. She had more than enough suitors to keep her busy. She didn't need a playful old ghost.

Unable to stay away any longer, I closed the distance between my mate and me, reaching out to run my fingers over her exposed nape as I did.

She screamed and turned to face me, eyes wide,

"What's the matter, baby doll? You look like you've seen a ghost." My lips curled with the words.

She punched me in the arm. "You jerk. Give a girl some warning before you scare her shitless. At least step on a twig or something, you skulking skulker who skulks."

"Maybe you need to be more aware of your surroundings. I wasn't keeping quiet on purpose. You were lost in your thoughts."

She bit down on her bottom lip, eyes shifting in the direction the spirit had wandered. "Maybe."

"You all good, doll?" I asked, brushing my thumb down her cheek and pulling her attention back to me.

She flicked her gaze away from mine again and I had to bite back the frustration building inside me at the gesture. Gripping her chin with my thumb and forefinger, I forced her to look at me once more. "Don't do that. Never hide your eyes from me. What happened to rattle you? Was it something he said?" I had half a mind to chase the fucker down and make him pay for his sins.

Overkill? Probably.

Did I fuckin' care?

Do you know who I am? Overkill may as well be my middle name.

"It's nothing. Really."

"Don't fucking lie to me, wife. I can read you like a book. What did that dusty old specter say?"

She forced out a breath and shook her head. "It's not about what he said. Not really. It's everything." She gestured to the gravestones around us. "It's what happened here the other night with the raising of the dead and the ritual sacrifice. It's trying to break the cycle and be a force of good instead of evil and then being surrounded only by evil. How do you help people who don't deserve to be helped? Answer, you don't. So then, what does that mean for my trying to rise above?"

I opened my mouth to answer, but she bulldozed right over me.

"And then there's the rest of it. The Ripper just being the beginning, and something worse is on the horizon. Does that mean the evil spirit that keeps popping up every-where I look? Or is it yet another boogeyman? Is there something even badder than the baddie we already killed? Where does it end, Hades? Why is it *always* something new and terrifying? There's never time to come to terms with one thing before there's something even bigger and scarier."

I took her by the shoulders and locked eyes with her, finding myself nearly lost in her intoxicating gray irises. "Take a breath, baby. You're going to hyperventilate."

"This is too much, Hades. I have so many questions and not enough answers."

"Well, let's see if I can help with that. Let's start at the beginning and work our way through your list."

She slumped in relief, as though I'd given her permis-sion to finally voice all her concerns. "Okay, what the fuck am I supposed to do if I can't help these damn ghosts cross over or whatever?"

"Well, firstly you have to choose the right kind of ghost."

"There are right and wrong kinds?"

"Yes. The spirits you were working with weren't here because they had unfinished business before they could cross into the Elysian Fields. These were the lost. Trapped in purgatory. They weren't even the damned, destined for the Rivers Acheron or Cocytus."

"Rivers? You mean there's more than one?"

"Dozens. All with various purposes and punishments."

"Sort of like Dante's circles of hell?"

I nodded. It was a close enough comparison.

"How do you decide who goes where?"

I gave her a sad smile. "They decide by their actions. I simply place them there. The good and kind are given peace, the wicked . . . well, they suffer the consequences of their choices. Some in a never-ending river of fire, others one of misery and woe, and some . . ." My heart twisted uncomfortably at the thought of the River Lethe.

"And some?" she prompted.

Throat tight, I answered, "And some are made to forget before they return to the realm of the living to try again."

Her eyes widened with understanding. "That's what happened to me, isn't it? My soul, I mean."

"I . . . It shouldn't have happened the way it did, Dahlia. They made you drink from the river and hid you from me. And now they're trying to take you away again. I won't let them."

She flinched. "Take me away? What are you talking about?"

Realizing my misstep, I shook my head. "We're supposed to be finding answers to your questions, not adding to your list."

"You can't just throw that out there and then try to walk it back."

I held her stare, refusing to say another word on the matter. It didn't bear discussion because there was no way it would ever fucking happen. I'd lost her once. It would never happen again.

"And you can't just ignore the questions you have. We haven't even talked about the fact that you raised an army of zombies to save yourself from the Ripper."

"It wasn't an army."

"A small army is still an army."

"I didn't even know it would work. I just called them from the grave after summoning my scary ghost didn't work. It was that or die. Would you have preferred I go the other way?"

"Obviously not, but since it would place you safely back in my realm, it's not the worst option."

She glared at me, hands on her hips. "There's something really fucked up about being mated to the god of the underworld when not even dying is considered a bad thing."

"Oh, it's bad. But as long as you're mine, I'll take you however I can get you."

"You're a hard man to have an argument with, Hades."

"It's one of the reasons you love me."

"Maybe you're right. But . . . are you saying you'd still love me even if I was a ghost you couldn't touch?"

Fuck, she didn't understand. I'd love her until the River Styx ran dry and the sky turned to ashes. "If they hadn't made you drink from the River Lethe, I'd never have let you leave me, my heart. And just because you were a ghost wouldn't mean I couldn't touch you."

She raised a brow.

"Perk of the job," I explained. "I can touch a spirit as easily as you touch me. It's sort of the counterpart of how I can touch you with my shadows."

I could tell by her expression she didn't quite understand, but that was okay. She didn't need to understand the physics of it all to appreciate the truth of it.

"Can I touch a spirit?"

I shrugged. "I don't know. Have you ever tried?"

"No. Just holding on to their souls like you and Masterson taught me."

"I don't know of anyone other than me who could, but if there was anyone else with the ability, it wouldn't surprise me to find it was you."

She frowned, beginning a slow stroll through the rows of graves, her fingers trailing over headstones as she went. "That brings me back to the threat against me. Adonis mentioned something about my mother and a bigger badder, erm, bad guy. And *you* said 'they' were trying to take me from you. Who are they, and what did that mean? Do you think your 'they' is Adonis's Mr. Bigger Badder?"

Something about the way she phrased the question shook something loose in my mind. Without warning, I was flung into a decades-old memory.

LONDON

THIRTY-FIVE YEARS EARLIER

"AND THAT'S ME OUT," Chaos grumbled, slapping his cards face down on the table.

"Fucking pansy. You folded before I even got a chance to bluff." I sat back in my chair, frowning at the horseman as he raised a challenging brow.

"Some of us like to hold on to our assets, Hades. Then there's the rest of you."

I bared my teeth in a silent snarl. The bastard always went straight for the jugular. What else could you expect from War, though? He was an expert at sussing out his enemy's weakness. Even if that enemy was mostly a friend.

"Come on, now, Chaos. Don't poke at him too hard. It's been hundreds of years since the guy's been topside. It stands to reason he's got energy to burn." Grim snapped his fingers and a cute little brunette scampered over, the bottle of whiskey already open and ready to refill his glass.

Sin and I shared a look at the pompous display. Only Malice was more of a snob, which was amusing, considering he had a history of slumming it. How else were plagues started, I guess?

The girl filled all our tumblers, taking extra care to push her tits out as she leaned over me. I didn't spare them a glance. There was only one woman who had my heart, and she was lost to me forever. I'd never be tempted again.

"Brimstone whiskey this time?" Mal asked, holding up the glass and taking a long look at the amber liquid before sniffing deeply. "Aged a thousand years by the smell of it. Who are you trying to impress, Grim? Certainly not Hades."

Grimsby didn't bother with a reply.

Death and I were old friends, or as close to friends as a god and a horseman of the apocalypse could get. He was sort of an accidental foot soldier of mine, not that he would ever agree to any position that made him a subordinate. But what else would I consider him? I was the one who ruled the realm; he just ushered in my subjects.

As we finished out the hand, I knocked back my drink and forced myself not to look at Chaos's smug face when Grim took the pot. Again.

"All right, you tossers, final round. Let's make it interesting this time, shall we? None of this playing for cars and property, yeah?" Grim said, scooping up the deck of cards and shuffling it with practiced ease. "I want a proper wager."

The other horsemen were instantly on alert, all three sitting up straighter and leaning in.

"What do you have in mind?" Sin asked.

"What better than to bet our most valuable assets? Unless you're too scared, Chaos."

Chaos huffed. "Tell me what you're talking about, and we'll see."

"Power. More specifically, the power passed down by blood. We each put up our firstborn in order to win the right to the next apocalypse."

"Sounds fun, except we promised the girls they could go next, remember?" Sin said, his voice filled with annoyance.

"I'll give them a few tries. They'll fail. They always do. Then I'll make my move." Grim was so confident he was going to win this round.

"Unless I win, and then I'll jump in before any of them can. No sense letting them get their hopes up." Chaos knocked back his drink, and I could tell he was already making his plan.

I scratched the back of my neck, wondering how in the hell they expected me to match their terms. "Uh, fellas. I can't exactly compete here." Not only did I not have a firstborn, but the apocalypse was not my game.

Grim waved a hand. "Not the point. If you win, you'll have the power of the four horsemen at your fingertips. That has to be worth something to you."

A spark of hope lit in my chest. If I had that amount of power in addition to my own, perhaps I could call my

Persephone back from wherever she was being held. I wanted nothing more than to bring her back to me.

"Fine. But I don't have, nor will I ever create, a child. I'll have to wager something else."

Mal looked around the table, a sneer twisting his lips. "Are we really not going to address the elephant in the room? I'm the only one with a kid."

"Pandemic is a full-grown demon and has been for some time," Grim pointed out.

"That doesn't matter. I'm the only one playing for actual stakes if I lose. The rest of you fuckers could very well never procreate."

"Why do you care?" Sin asked. "Have you even seen him in the last century?"

"That's a low blow, and you know it," Mal snapped.

I took a healthy sip of my whiskey. I wasn't going to pretend to understand the intricacies of their romantic entanglements, nor did I want to try.

"Yes, yes, we all know the story. She got you drunk. You didn't understand how very fertile a horsewoman would be when paired with her counterpart. Pestilence is mean and never let you be part of your progeny's life. She used you for your sperm. Blah, blah, blah. You were the only one of us stupid enough to sleep with a horsewoman, and none of us pity you, Mal." Chaos was nothing if not direct. Definitely a stab-you-in-the-chest kind of guy. I had to hand it to him. Then he turned his attention to Grim. "But I'm not sure this is a fair wager. What if the three of us never father a child? I mean, you can't even touch a human without stealing their soul from their body. How are you supposed to impregnate a woman?"

"If humans can figure out how to perfect artificial insemination, I'm sure I'll find a way. But to address your other concern, part of the wager is that we all agree to try and reproduce."

"Leave it to Grim to make the art of fucking sound cold and clinical," Sin said with a shudder. "I, on the other hand, am going to have so much fun with this."

"You probably already have an entire football team of your brats running around sucking the lives out of everyone they encounter," Mal muttered.

"What about him?" Chaos said, jerking his head in my direction. "He already said he won't have a kid. He's got to wager something of value, or it's not fair to the rest of us."

Like I said, fucker stabbed straight in the chest.

"I don't have anything of value left," I muttered, thinking of my lost soulmate. Persephone was the only thing in my life I'd ever truly cared about.

Grim's mouth twisted into a wicked smile. "Your heart, then. The only thing keeping you going."

"You've forgotten who I am if you think I can die."

"No, you misunderstand me, Hades. I don't want you to die, but I will claim your power and loyalty when I win."

"Fine," I agreed.

What did it matter to me? The Fates had already ripped it out of my chest when they stole my goddess.

Grim's lips twisted up in a cruel smile. "Perfect, we're all agreed. Let's play."

"Earth to Hades, come in, Hades . . ."

Snapping back to the present, I slowly shook my head.

"You all right? If you forgive the expression, you look like you've seen a ghost."

I wish that's all it had been. What I'd just uncovered was so much worse than a rogue spirit.

"Your mother," I whispered. "Gabriel can't be right about that. He can't know for sure she was Death's pawn. You're mine, not his minion." But I knew the truth. Grim had won that wager fair and square. He'd won and was using Dahlia to collect.

She was my heart. The only thing in my life of any value. The only thing I'd sacrifice everything for to protect.

And I'd unwittingly promised to give her up. It was supposed to be a safe bet. I never expected to find my Persephone again.

"I'm sorry, what now? Death? As in black cowl, scythe, skull face?" Dahlia grimaced. "Oh God, please tell me my dad did not get down with Skeletor."

"No, baby doll. Your father, the man who raised you, wasn't your biological parent. It makes sense now. I didn't want to pay the angel any heed. I was too angry with him for keeping his knowledge of your whereabouts to himself. Death chose your parents carefully and left you there with them until you served his purpose." Then, a bit softer and more to myself, I added, "Guess that fucker found a way to procreate after all."

"Wh-what? I'm not following you. What kind of purpose?"

"The only one a horseman of the apocalypse has. To bring about the end times."

"Time out," Dahlia said, using the hand signal for that same thing. "Nope. I'm noping myself out of this one. Remember when I said things just continue to get more and more fucked up, and you can never even wrap your head around the level of fuckedupness of one situation before getting slapped in the face by another? Well, you just proved my point, buddy. And I am here to say nay, nay. Not today, Satan. Or is that Uncle Satan? Jesus Roosevelt Christ. I cannot with this shitshow."

She waved her hands around as her spiral took hold. "And another thing, I didn't sign up to be the harbinger of the apocalypse."

My lips twitched at her mispronunciation, her emphasis on bing instead of binge, and before I could stop myself, I blurted, "Harbinger."

The glare she shot me would've given Medusa a run for her money. "Don't tell me how to say words, Hades. I don't need an editor right now."

I raised both hands in a placating gesture and waited for her to continue.

"It was bad enough to believe I was the crotch goblin of a cult leader and mass murderer. But no, you had to go and make that seem like a dream situation compared to reality. Death? Death! Come on. Who's my mother, Medusa? No, she was just a misunderstood acolyte. It's probably something way worse. Like a spider goddess or something gross. Ugh, maybe you should leave me while you can. I'm clearly doomed. Maybe I need to do what's best for all of you and leave you. I can't be the reason any of you die, and harbinger seems like a title that equals dying. If I'd never come here, you would all be safe and sound, not at risk of an apocalypse."

Oh, fuck no. This woman wasn't going to leave me. Not ever.

I snagged her by the arms and gave her a slight shake as my gaze burned into hers. "You listen to me, you silly, beautiful thing. I will not hear talk of you leaving me. Do you understand?"

Angry tears beaded on her lashes as she thrashed in my

hold. "You're not the boss of me."

"Yes I fucking am."

"Let go of me, Hades."

"No. I'll never let go. You're mine. What part of that don't you get? Where you go, I follow. I'm your shadow for eternity. Stop trying to fucking leave me."

"If I don't, the world will literally end."

Godsdammit, did she not see how unimportant that was? "I don't care. If the world is going to end, you'll be in my arms while we watch it crumble."

That one seemed to penetrate. This time she simply blinked up at me. But as I watched, her expression morphed from shocked and loving to a cold mask of acceptance. Not in the way I wanted. She wasn't accepting our fate together. She was accepting our future apart.

Tugging out of my grasp, she turned away from me and began walking down the gravel path.

"Where the hell do you think you're going?" I shouted after her, the sight of her walking away from me flaying me wide open.

"Finding a way out of this hellhole."

"Not without me," I growled, sending my shadows straight at her and binding her in place.

"Hades! Hades, let me go!"

"No. Haven't you listened to a fucking word I've said? I will *never* let you go."

She writhed in her bindings, her eyes darkening like storm clouds. "If you keep me, I'll hate you for it."

"Hate me if you have to, baby doll, but I'm not living a life without you in it. I've done it for far too long already." I moved her until she was backed up against a rotting mausoleum door. My lips close to her ear, I whispered, "I've fucked you while you loved me and been inside you when you said you hated me. I wonder what it's like to do it while you're feeling both emotions at the same time."

She could lie to herself all she wanted, but there was no missing the way her pupils dilated at my words. She was more than interested in finding out the answer herself.

"What you seem to be forgetting, Dahlia, is that I know you better than you know yourself. I've spent lifetimes loving you and recounting every single second we spent together. And you may think you could walk away and that there's some universe where I'd let you go, but here's something you've failed to consider. *You* would come crawling back to *me*. You know why?"

"I'm sure you're going to tell me," she gritted out.

"Because you are as consumed by me as I am by you."

My fingers trailed across the waistband of her pants, but I didn't move slowly once I slid them inside. I needed to touch her and feel how our fiery foreplay affected her. Sucking in a sharp breath when I found her slick and hot, I let out a dark chuckle.

"Look at that. Soaked." I nipped her earlobe. "Good girl."

"Hades," she protested, but it was more moan than anything.

"We belong to each other, goddess. No matter what name you use or form you wear. I chased you across lifetimes, and I will do it again because you. Are. Mine."

With a pulse of my power, I broke through the doors and lifted her in my arms. I needed to be inside her, fucking her until she remembered why she couldn't leave me. Why she'd never fucking leave me.

She brought her lips to mine in a bruising, hungry kiss even as I sent blue flames arcing toward the ancient torches set about the space. The two of us were a tangle of passionate kisses, harsh moans, and needy cries as we tore at each other's clothing. We only stopped when I pressed her against the marble wall that housed countless remains of the people buried here.

"Are you really going to fuck me in a crypt?" she whispered, her eyes bright with lust.

"Wouldn't be the first time, baby doll."

"It is for me."

"Then I'd better make it memorable."

Not that there was any doubt about that. Sex between us was always memorable. Grasping her by the thighs, I picked her up and spun her around, setting her atop the one raised tomb running along the center of the space.

She let out a breathless chuckle.

"Did I surprise you?"

"I'm used to Tor and Kai tossing me around, but I don't expect it from you."

I nipped her lower lip. "You should. In case you forgot, I'm a god, baby. There's nothing I can't do."

With an impatient grip, I parted her thighs, knowing I'd find her dripping and ready to take me. Panic rose in my chest as the thought of never having her like this again invaded my mind, but I pushed it back as I sank inside her to the hilt.

"Fuck, Hades," she cried, arching her back even as she dug her fingernails into my shoulders.

I held her hips, hammering into her hard and fast, proving a point more than anything. "You're. Never. Leaving. Me. Again." Each word was punctuated by a brutal thrust, drawing ragged gasps from her.

I didn't stop there. I had to drive my point home. "You're. Mine."

"Yes," she panted.

"Say it."

"Yes, Hades."

I could see my fire reflected in her eyes as I took her, the weight of my climax pressing down on me, but I needed to hear the words. I needed her to say it.

Bringing my fingers to my lips, I sucked on them before sliding them over her swollen clit. She whimpered and rolled her hips in response as I brought her close to the edge.

"Tell me, Dahlia. Tell me you're mine."

"I'm yours."

"Promise me you'll never leave me," I growled against her lips. Vows made during sex were hardly enforceable, but I didn't play by anyone's rules but my own, and this was one vow I would have before I gave her what she craved.

"I promise."

"Swear it, Dahlia. You and me. Forever."

"Yes," she cried. "Forever, my lord Hades."

That was it. I felt her walls clench around me as she fell, and I was done for, pumping inside her and filling my soulmate with everything I had to give her.

As we came down together, she began playing with the hair at the nape of my neck, her gentle touch sending tingles through me.

"I'll never leave you, Hades. I couldn't even if I tried."

"I know."

She gaped at me for a second before laughing and shaking her head. "Then why'd you get so riled up?"

"Because I needed you to know it too. You and me, we're a package deal, baby doll."

"And the apocalypse?"

I smirked. "Bring it on."

THIRTEEN

I stared hard at the hands of the clock, wondering if Dahlia would forgive me if I checked in a little early this afternoon. She was on the final day of her self-imposed deadline, and I certainly didn't want to earn her wrath by interrupting at a crucial moment, but the truth was, I missed her. Splitting these daily check-ins with her other mates meant I had a scant fifteen to twenty minutes to spend with her a day, and it simply wasn't enough.

Perhaps she'd welcome the intrusion today if I were to offer some *inspiration* in the form of an orgasm for her. My wee mate insisted she could do this with minimal breaks and that it wasn't going to negatively affect her health, but every time I saw her during a check in she appeared more and more frazzled. Her shoulders were tight and tense, eyes bloodshot, and we weren't going to mention the dark circles she wore like bruises. Dahlia needed me to care for her, whether she wanted to admit it or not. And at my core, I was a caretaker. Loving her was written in my bones, and I had to be able to do it or I'd go mad.

While she couldn't give me the hours I wanted, all I

really required was thirty minutes so I could bring her off properly with my fingers and tongue. Relax her. Give her that boost of oxytocin she'd get from her release. She'd be a new woman when I was finished with her. And perhaps I would cease feeling like a useless lump of flesh. It was worth a shot.

Emboldened by my plan, I sprang to my feet and nearly sprinted to the door. If Hook or Hades were to see me right now, they'd poke fun at me for sure. Not that they were faring much better. We all seemed a bit lost without our mate to love. There was only so much we could do from a distance, and if they were anything like me, our souls were hardwired to care for and protect her. No one would expect it from the likes of us. We didn't exactly get placed here for being the lovestruck heroes.

Truth was, no one knew about pining and endless devotion like a man with few scruples around murder.

Chuckling to myself, I bounded down the hall, not caring who spotted me or what they thought. When I arrived at Dahlia's door, I forced myself to slow and knock.

"Are ye up for a break, gem? I know you said you were nearly fin—" As I pushed the door open, my words died on my tongue because she wasn't there. The chair at her desk was empty, laptop closed, a bright pink sticky note attached to the top.

I walked to her desk with a frown, wondering if she'd left the note for me or if it was one of her endless lists. She wrote and left them everywhere. The woman had lists for her lists. It was adorable, honestly. If not a little neurotic, just like her. Yet another thing I loved about her.

Yanking the paper off the computer, I held it up and grinned like an idiot because it was absolutely for me.

Finished! Huzzah!
Taking a walk to stretch my legs.
If I'm not back by the time you get here, come find
me, dragon boy.

Smoochies! Love,
Your Dahlia

I smiled and pocketed the note—the first she'd written for me. She even dotted the Is and exclamation points with little hearts. I couldn't bear for it to be destroyed. If anything, it should be commemorated. And I knew just the spot to display the pink scrap of paper in my hoard. Actually, I think it deserved a frame. Or perhaps I could tattoo her words over my heart in her handwriting.

The absence of my mate didn't seem so unbearable now that I'd been issued a challenge. She wanted me to find her. I was very good at finding things. And she said it in her note: she was *my* Dahlia. Mine.

No one else got a note.

I'd have laughed at how smug I was feeling were it anyone else. Never did I think I'd get this twitterpated over a bit of paper, but here we were. I told you I'd been missing her.

If she wanted me to find her, I wasn't about to waste a second. Tugging off my shirt, I called on my wings. Might as well go to her in style. Dahlia loved my dragon and now that she was done with her book, she was going to get me every way she wanted me.

I tore open her window and leapt out, my leathery wings spreading and catching the wind as soon as I fell. I'd only just started practicing with them this past week while not in full dragon form, but flying came to me as naturally as walking. Dahlia had once told me how much romance readers loved a man with a big wingspan, and the sparkle in her eyes wasn't something I missed. I knew exactly what I was doing by hunting her down shirtless, flying, ready to make her mine.

Perhaps she'd wrap herself around me, and we could test out some other firsts. I didn't know if it was physically possible to fuck and fly at the same time, but it sure would be fun to try. We could start our very own mile-high club.

I caught sight of my girl walking away from the kirk-yard with Hades hot on her heels. Something wasn't right. Not with the pensive expression on her face and the set of her shoulders. What had that arsehole done to upset her? It might be nearly impossible to take on a god, but I'd damn well give it a go if he hurt her.

Logically, part of me knew he was no more likely to do so than I was. But dragons were rarely logical when their mates were involved. I was acting on pure instinct, as I usually was when my Dahlia was concerned.

"Gem," I called, landing a little ahead and to the left of them.

Her head snapped in my direction, and for a moment, her face lit up with joy. "You found me," she said with a smile. It didn't quite reach her eyes, though, which told me something was truly weighing on her.

"Aye, I'll always find ye," I promised, opening my arms wide for her to walk into. Once she was pressed against me, I shot Hades a 'what the fuck happened' look as I pulled my wings around her. The last thing I saw before she was fully ensconced was the slow shake of his head. A conversation for later, then.

Dahlia took a deep inhale as she buried her face against

my bare chest, sighing happily like she'd just caught her favorite scent. "Mmm, I love the way you smell. I've missed you."

I was fucking right, and it took everything I had not to preen then and there. "I've missed you too, lass."

"I just had to clear my head. I wasn't planning on being gone this long." She tipped her face up, and I dropped mine so I could kiss her gently.

"It's all right. Gave me a chance to stretch my wings." I kissed her again, then murmured against her lips, "Congratulations on finishing. I'm so proud of you."

She melted into me. "You know . . . I'm not sure anyone other than Kiki has ever told me they were proud of me before."

"Is that so? I'll have to make a habit of it, then, to make up for the lack."

She giggled, but it was quick to fade.

"What's wrong, gem? Are you nae happy with the book?"

"It's not that," she said, moving to step away from me. As much as I didn't want to, I unwrapped my wings and sent them back where they hid when not in use. "I'd rather not get into it right now. In fact, I'd pay a king's ransom to be able to do anything other than think about it."

"Fair enough. How would you feel about a little distraction as we ring in the new year together?"

"Yes, please!" she chirped.

I chuckled, using my chin to gesture to the residence. "Go put on something warm and meet me up at my tower when you're ready."

"Is that offer open to the rest of us?" Hades asked.

Selfishly, I wanted to say no, but since this was about cheering up my mate, I nodded.

"I'll let the others know," he said, earning a grateful smile from Dahlia. "You get yourself all cleaned up, baby doll. We might want to get dirty again later."

Her cheeks went pink, and instead of arousal or envy, I felt unease in response. If they'd already been together, why was she still tense? Something wasn't right.

She left us, casting a few looks over her shoulder at Hades and me as she went. As soon as she was out of earshot, I rounded on him.

"What happened? Why isn't she sated and boneless with bliss right now? You clearly fucked her. I could smell you all over her."

Hades shrugged. "There's a lot going on."

"Such as?" I pressed when he didn't elaborate.

"I can't tell you. It's her story to share."

"That's ludicrous. How can we protect her if we don't know what's happening?"

"Sometimes we have to be patient, dragon. Let her come to us. She'll share when the time is right. The only reason I know is because I saw it go down. Trust her."

I gritted my teeth and grumbled. "I don't like it. I need to fix it for her. Crush any enemy. Defend her."

He chuckled darkly. "You'll get your chance. We all will."

"What the hell is that supposed to mean?"

He shook his head. "Not my story, remember?"

Irritation shot through me, along with a bit of my dragon's heat. A curl of smoke escaped my nostril, clueing Hades in to my state of mind.

He clapped me on the shoulder. "No need to get pissy, dragon. Our girl doesn't keep secrets. She just wants to breathe for a minute before having to face it again. To that end, you promised her a distraction. Best you get on with it."

As I waited for my wee mate to arrive, I did one more cursory look about my tower. It was nearly perfect—music on the record player, food, and a cozy place to sit all set for her. I was just missing one small detail. Lifting the nearest candle from its stand, I blew a small stream of flame at it until the wick ignited, then I went from candle to candle until the entire room was aglow with flickering light. That done, I checked on the provisions I'd procured, pleased with the look of the decanted wine and spread of fruits, meats, and cheeses. I'd made a point to select all of Dahlia's favorite snacks, hoping to tempt her into eating a little something—or better yet, letting me hand feed her.

Just the thought of finally being able to care for her had my dragon perking up and reminding me that while he and I were more connected than ever, it was still his choice to stay quiet.

"I missed her too."

As if our thoughts summoned her, the sound of Dahlia's laughter floated up the spiral staircase, along with a stampede of footsteps. It sounded like a small army rushing up the steps, but I knew better. Dahlia and the other three were nearly here.

Out of nowhere, a wave of doubt crashed into me. Suddenly the spread and flickering candles seemed like too much. Had I gone overboard? Was this like that time Ren wrote a cheesy love song for Rebel and everyone else laughed at him?

Turning on my heel, I blew out a few candles and

flicked the needle off the record to stop the romantic music just as they entered my tower.

I tried to adopt my most casual pose, but knew I was found out the second Hook's crooked smirk bloomed. Shockingly, he didn't say a word.

"I would have sworn I heard Hozier," Dahlia muttered, casting her eyes around the room. "Don't tell me this is a new form of haunting."

"That Irish fuck has a real hard-on for Greek mythology. But he sure can write a song," Hades murmured.

"Mmm, Forest Daddy."

Hades spanked her soundly. "Watch it."

"What? Everyone gets a hall pass, right? He's mine."

"That's your choice? A skinny Irish poet?" Tor asked, clearly offended.

She batted her eyelashes at him. "Have you seen how tall he is? Taller than all of you. I'm just saying. With that poet's soul, there's no telling what kind of damage he could do in the be—"

Tor growled and grabbed her by the nape before crushing his lips to hers and kissing her so hard she swayed on her feet. When he released her, she was a little dazed.

"What were you saying, beauty?"

"W-was I saying something?"

"Do you want me to turn the music back on?" I offered, trying to contain my amusement.

"No," the others said at once, drawing a laugh from Dahlia.

Hook slunk up to her side, taking her by the chin and turning her face toward his. "Your three hall passes are in this room, love. You think any of us will allow you to so much as fantasize about another, you've got a very tiring lesson ahead of you."

"Tiring?"

His answering smile was absolutely wicked. "Positively exhausting. For you, that is. The four of us will be taking turns, allowing for much-needed rest."

"He's gotten a little too good at this taking charge thing," Hades grumbled.

"Agreed," I said, stepping forward and stealing her away from the pirate. "Happy New Year, lass. I hope this is satisfactory. I know it's not a big party with all your—"

She stopped me with a hand in the air. "What about me makes you think a big crowd and lots of noise is my idea of a good time? My only friend is Kiki, and most of our New Years were spent on a video call with her toasting me from NYC while I tried to discreetly wipe away the drool and pretend I hadn't been asleep watching Dick Clark." She cupped my face. "And I don't know if you realize it, but my family is here now. All four of you. There's nothing that could make this better except Kiki being with us, but the things I want to do with all of you can't include her, anyway."

"Now that's my idea of a party," Hook cheered, angling for the wine and pouring each of us a healthy glass.

"You trying to liquor me up, pirate? Cause I should tell you, I'm a sure thing."

"Apparently not," he grunted, frowning at the already empty decanter. "Blimey, dragon, you really don't know how to throw a party. There should be at least a bottle a piece if we're going to loosen her up with wine." He set the decanter down and shook his head, muttering under his breath, "Amateurs, the lot of them."

"The idea was for all of us to relax, not get pissing drunk. If you think you can do it better, then why don't you leave us be and go get the supplies you think we need?

Can't guarantee the door will be unlocked for you, though."

He tossed me a mulish glare over his shoulder before downing his glass.

Hades tried to cover his smile with his hand but couldn't resist goading him further. "Might have been wise to ration it out a bit, don't you think?"

"Fuck off, all of you."

"I mean . . ." Dahlia teased, cheeks pink and eyes twinkling with suppressed laughter.

Tor stalked farther into the room and glanced around, his brows pulling together as he clearly found something amiss.

"What, Viking? What could possibly be wrong?" I asked, frustration in every word.

"There isn't a proper-sized bed. How are we going to make our mate comfortable without that?"

"Well, if you insist on ruining the surprise, I'd planned for us to end the night upstairs under the stars."

Tor raised a brow. "Don't you think she'll get cold?"

"Not when she's pressed between us."

"Fair point," he mused, our gazes returning to where she was standing, as they so often did. She was the magnet leading us all on a merry chase back to her.

"Come, gem, let's make you a plate. If we don't, Hook's going to eat it all before we get a chance."

Caspian looked at us from where he'd filled his plate and had a cracker shoved in his mouth. "What? Are we not supposed to be eating? No one told me that." He loaded another cracker with cheese and prosciutto before cramming it into his mouth. "A little more communication would be appreciated."

"Or a little less," Hades deadpanned as crumbs sprayed everywhere.

"Didn't anyone ever tell you it's not polite to speak with your mouth full?" I asked.

Hook smirked. "Dahlia loves to moan with her mouth full."

Dahlia turned bright red while Hades sighed. "Not remotely the same thing."

The pirate lifted one shoulder in a shrug. "Not what Dahlia says. She also loves it when I eat and talk at the same time. Don't you, sweetheart?"

I could scent her arousal as she squirmed.

"Don't put me in the middle of this," she whispered, cheeks blazing.

"Darling, you're always in the middle. That's how this works."

"So . . . are we moving to phase two, then?" Tor asked, already stripping out of his shirt.

Dahlia's stomach growled, reminding all of us she hadn't eaten. Taking matters into my own hands, I stomped over and stole Hook's plate, handing it to Dahlia. He was about to protest, but as soon as he realized I was offering it to her, he wisely shut the fuck up.

Smart move. If he hadn't, he would have found himself flying off my tower without the aid of wings or a single damn happy thought to keep him afloat.

"That was exactly what I needed. Thank you, Kai," Dahlia said after we'd all eaten and finished our wine. "This is so—" A boom cracked in the air and the sky lit up outside, stopping her mid-sentence. "What was that?"

I gritted my teeth. "Something that wasn't supposed to start for another few hours."

But apparently people couldn't follow the simplest of

directions. Start the fireworks at the stroke of midnight. Make sure they're within view of the tower, over the lake, so Dahlia sees the reflection. Don't forget the one we agreed upon shaped like the flower that is her namesake.

"Come on, gem. We don't want to miss the show," I grumbled, taking her by the wrist and pulling her up the short flight of stairs that opened up to what was essentially my rooftop garden. It was less garden and more nest at the moment, filled with furs and pillows as it was.

"Kai," Dahlia breathed. "You thought of everything."

At least someone appreciates an eye for detail around here.

The sky lit up again as booms echoed over and over. I sat with her in my arms, a heavy fur covering her as the other three joined us. She leaned into me, letting out soft noises of pleasure with each burst of light that appeared.

As the finale came to a close, Cas leaned over. "Well done, Kai. I have to say I'm impressed. But what do you think about the five of us making some fireworks of our own, eh?"

"I'm not opposed to the idea," I replied, shifting a little to look at Dahlia's face. "What do you say, gem?"

Before I finished speaking, we had our answer.

Hades chuckled, reaching over to wipe away a bit of drool off our sleeping beauty. "Looks like she's not gonna make it to midnight this New Year either."

"Shall we tuck her in downstairs?" Tor asked, reaching as if to take her from my arms.

"Perhaps it's best if we just let her sleep where she is," I countered, not ready to let her go just yet.

"Happy New Year, fellas," Hook said. "Let's hope it's not the last."

CHAPTER

FOURTEEN

TOR

S weat dripped down my bare torso as I tried yet another new path through the woods. Ever since the townsfolk had caught my post-Alek rampage, groups of them had been sniffing around my woods, trying their best to smoke me out. Over the last two days, things had escalated. They weren't just sending search parties; now they were leaving traps. It meant my hunting sessions were more challenging, shorter, and, in the case of the villagers, far more dangerous.

I loped through the clearing, covered in blood and dirt from the deer I'd felled, but at least I hadn't been spotted this time. The sun had barely crested on the horizon, the sky painted in striking hues of peach and violet as the new year began. I'd left my Kærasta safely wrapped in the arms of her other mates after our surprisingly enjoyable party in Kai's tower. As much as I hadn't wanted to, these hunts were vital to me maintaining control over my beast. The interference from the townsfolk was starting to wear on me and my beast. Without an appropriate outlet for my rage, I was liable to slip. And I could not afford to slip because that only ended in one way.

Death.

With a frustrated growl, I jogged up the path to Blackwood and snuck back into the residence. Well, as much as anyone could sneak around in the old castle. Joffrey seemed to pop up like a bleeding ghost around every corner.

My room was silent as a tomb, the air stale because it'd been too long since I'd returned, but all I needed was a shower and change of clothes. Then I was back to claim my woman. I needed her next to me—under me, on top of me, the positioning didn't matter so long as I could touch her—in the worst way. Fuck, now I was picturing her luscious body bared for me, and all that did was make me crave her more. I knew from what Alek told me that this would never abate. She was made for me, and my soul cried out for her.

As I got under the hot spray of the shower, my thoughts didn't divert to the deliciously dirty things I wanted to do to Dahlia as I'd expected. Instead, they made an unwelcome left turn and landed on my twin. That instantly ended my arousal and soured my mood. A flash of Alek's expression when I told him what happened had my chest twisting. I fucking hated myself for causing him such pain, but dammit, that was the only way I knew to send him back to his family in one piece.

I scrubbed until my skin was pink and clean, forcing myself to focus on the task at hand and not the guilt over hurting my brother. Dahlia would be expecting me to spend the day with her now that she'd finished her book. And I wasn't going to let her down.

Getting out of the shower, I wrapped a towel around my waist and padded into the bedroom in search of fresh clothes. Something she liked, such as one of my Henleys and perhaps those gray joggers she always said were indecent.

Just as I was pulling open my drawer, a shrill and unexpectedly loud song began to play. I startled, spinning around and staring hard in the direction of my nightstand. My phone was the culprit. I'd forgotten I'd turned it back on. But I'd done so for a very good reason.

There was only one person it could be. She'd selected that damn song herself.

"Moira," I growled by way of answer.

"Well, hello to you too, grumpy Hemsworth. You know, I really prefer the golden retriever version of you I got when you were at Ravenscroft with us. Such a happy puppy. Now you're like Cujo. I never know when you're going to bite my head off and give me rabies. You have had your shots, haven't you?"

"Do you have a solution for me?" I ignored her digs at my attitude because I knew they didn't bear any true weight. She couldn't go more than five words without some well-placed barb escaping her mouth. It was . . . what did she call it? Her love language.

She sighed. "Yes and no."

"What does that mean?"

"We can unravel the spell, but it's complicated and is going to take longer than I thought. I've contacted the Siren Coven for help as well. Helena, Izzy, and Gwen are incredibly powerful witches, even without their fourth, and have volunteered their skills."

"Where's the fourth? Do you need her?"

"No one knows. But we should be able to use what they can give us. It's just a matter of persistence."

I sat on the bed, frustration causing me to drag a hand

through my hair. "So I'm just meant to wait here for you to tell me you succeeded?"

"No. You're meant to continue on with your life. You'll know when the spell is broken."

"How?"

"I used your blood in the ritual instead of mine. You're linked to it now, even more deeply than you were before. You'll feel the spell break in a way no one else who's affected will. For them, it might be like a shiver running down their spines. For you? Like you were shot through the heart."

"That's . . . lovely," I deadpanned.

"Beggars can't be choosers, Thor."

"Don't call me that."

"Don't be so Thor-like, and I won't."

I heaved another sigh.

"You sure are mopey for someone who just got the news they were waiting for."

"But I didn't, did I? You essentially told me to sit around with my thumb up my arse."

"If that's what your takeaway from this call is, buddy, I'm sure glad I'm not your lady friend."

A low growl slipped free, but before I said a word, she gasped.

"Did you just *growl* at me? Look, I'm going to tell myself you're just suffering from low blood sugar or something because there's no way my Tor, my karaoke partner, my hair salon buddy, would ever *growl* at me."

"I'm sorry, Moira. I've been . . . It's difficult to contain my rage these days."

Just another reason my abbreviated treks through the woods were problematic.

"Aw, it's okay, bud. You're just a burnt cinnamon roll

now instead of a perfectly cooked one. Still delicious on the inside, but a little tough on the outside."

I shook my head, not sure how I felt about the comparison. "Uh, thanks?"

"You're welcome. Now go wank one out and get yourself in a good mood, because I need you to do *me* a favor. And before you try and weasel your way out of it, you owe me. Big time."

I raised a brow, knowing I wasn't going to like whatever came next. "I'm listening."

"Please, for the love of Odin and all his ravens or whatever the heck your people believe in, please text your brother back."

She hung up before I could protest, and my stomach churned with guilt.

Hand shaking, I swiped my thumb across the screen until I opened the thread of hundreds of messages from Alek. I scrolled through them all, reading at random.

ALEK:

Where have you gone?

ALEK:

Eden misses her uncle.

ALEK:

Tor, have I done something to upset you?

ALEK:

You're worrying me. Please don't make me get Mother involved. You know how she fusses. You'll have the entire Novasgardian force breaking through the portal within the hour, and then where will we be?

ALEK:

Happy birthday.

ALEK:

You know, you're lucky we're identical, or Eden would have forgotten what you look like by now. Please contact me. We all want to see you.

ALEK:

Tor.

ALEK:

This is ridiculous. Why are you ignoring me?

ALEK:

It's been months, brother. Tell me what's happened.

ALEK:

What did I do to deserve this?

ALEK:

That's it. Either you respond with proof of life, or I'm getting our father involved.

ALEK:

All right, you called my bluff. I know better than to push that button. I won't select the nuclear option until I absolutely must. You're lucky that I know you're not lying dead in a ditch somewhere. You can thank Moira for that, you know. She mentioned that Lilith said you were at Iniquity recently. Is that true? What were you doing there?

ALEK:

Fine, I can take a hint. But just know, I swear on the blood of the Allfather, no matter how hard you try to push me away, I will never stop searching for you, brother. Never.

The uncomfortable ache in my chest returned with the force of a sledgehammer to my heart. I'd behaved so badly.

In my defense, I'd truly believed my actions to be the best for all of us, but in my misguided attempt to protect him, I'd done serious damage. Alek deserved better. Perhaps Moira was right. I needed to contact him, if only to begin the process of healing what I'd broken.

I began typing a message, my thumb hovering over the send button for several drawn-out seconds as I read and re-read the words on the screen.

ME:

I'm so sorry.

Before I made up my mind whether to hit send, an incoming call flashed on the screen. Kai. Why would he be calling me? In fact, how the fuck did he get this number?

I couldn't help but suspect Hook had been snooping around my room again. That sneaky pirate was always up to no good. It would be just like him to mention the re-emergence of my phone to the others.

"What?" I barked into the phone.

"You've been gone so bloody long we nearly sent out a search party. Get your arse back here so we can begin."

"Begin what?"

Unbidden, images of Dahlia and her other mates naked and writhing together in one big sexy jumble filled my mind. Kai sent the thoughts scattering with his exasperated reply.

"The tattoos."

"Oh. Is that today?"

"We were waiting for Dahlia to finish her book. She's done. It's time."

Running a hand through my still drying hair, I forced out a breath. "All right. I'll be right there."

CHAPTER
FIFTEEN
DAHLIA

The only tattooing I'd ever seen in live action was that one time Kai inked up my lady garden. Wait, no, that's not true. There was also that time I caught him tattooing his arm. Anyway, I digress. The point is, he looked so fucking hot while setting up his kit. If he wasn't so serious about getting this ink done, I'd jump on his dragon dick and ride him right here and now. I wasn't lying when I said I had a competency kink.

I'd sort of forgotten about Kai's present. In the rush to complete my manuscript, his promise to give us a group tattoo had completely fallen out of my mind, but now that the day was upon us, I was beyond excited. Not for the needle part—that I'd skip if I could—but knowing my men would be wearing a mark to represent me? It was sexy AF. Better than a ring, if I was being honest. Every thirsty bitch around would know they were taken.

Damn. Apparently I'm possessive when I'm in love.

"You're staring, gem." Kai's voice was a low rumble that made a shiver break out across my body.

"You're hot."

He chuckled. "So are you. Now, make yourself comfortable. This is going to take a while."

"Not like I have anywhere else to be."

We shared a humorless smile about our captivity. It was the last remaining problem, and one we didn't seem to have a solution for. It was hard to summon strong feelings about it, though. Not because it wasn't shitty, it absolutely fucking was, but if I was going to be locked up anywhere, the sprawling grounds of Blackwood with my four soulmates was a pretty good choice.

"All right," Kai said. "Which one of you three wants to go first?"

Tor stepped up, his expression serious. "I will. Brand me with my Kærasta's mark. I want to be as connected to her as possible."

"Try hard," Caspian muttered.

Tor shot him a snarl and stood in front of Kai. "Where do you want it?"

Kai cocked a brow and gestured for him to take a seat. "Shirt off. We're going to put it here." He pulled the sleeve of his tee up until he exposed a beautiful shoulder cap design of dahlias done in grayscale.

It took Tor all of two seconds to bare his chest for the ink. He really had the grab it by the back of the neck and pull it over his head thing down pat. I leaned against the desk and fanned my face. Whew. Was it hot in here, or was it just them?

Kidding. We all know it was definitely them.

Hades was staring at me with a knowing smirk playing about his handsome lips. He enjoyed watching me squirm, and if the past five minutes were any indication, I was about to receive a serious lesson in edging, because this entire experience was hotter than any porn I'd ever seen. Or written, for that matter. Huh. I wonder if Kai broke something in my brain the last time he tattooed me because I had a total tattooing-equals-sex association going on in my head. There was no way this was a normal reaction.

Tor reached out and traced the lines of Kai's fresh tattoo, stopping next to a blank spot toward the bottom. "Is this intentionally unfinished?"

"Aye. I'll close it and seal the magic inside once all of you are done. To that end, before we begin, I need something from each of you." Tor raised a brow in question, and Kai continued. "Magic like this requires a sacrifice. It's blood magic. I'll need a drop from each of us added to the ink. Willingly given."

Tor's fingers shifted into razor-sharp claws. Before anyone could say anything, he raked his index finger down his forearm.

"Whoa, I said a drop!" Kai said, jumping up to grab a towel. "Your finger would have done just fine."

Cas snickered. "And I repeat. Try hard. You're overcompensating, mate. She already knows you have a big dick, no need to prove it."

Hades huffed. "We all know."

Asshole gave a little bark like he agreed before jumping into my lap, turning in a circle, and settling down for me to pet him.

One by one, we all gave a drop of blood to Kai for him to infuse into the ink. I'd seen this before, but only from him, and when he added his donation, just like the last time, the inkpot glowed with power.

"That's wicked," Caspian murmured. "I've missed fae magic."

Kai hummed his acknowledgment, his attention wholly focused on his task. When he whipped out his razor to prep the skin, I had to look away, much to his amusement. His dark chuckle wrapped itself around me, and I swear I could feel it pulsing against my clit.

He really had ruined me.

I was a horny disaster.

"Does this turn you on, baby doll?" Hades whispered in my ear. When did he get behind me? Had I really been so distracted I hadn't noticed him closing in?

"Why do people ask the questions they already know the answers to?" Cas said, amusement in his voice.

"She didn't tell you what I did to her while inking up her pussy?" Kai asked as he wiped down Tor's skin. "You should ask her about it."

Three sets of eyes landed on me, and I couldn't meet a single one. "It was uh . . . really something special."

Kai snorted.

"I've never noticed a tattoo," Cas pouted.

"It's invisible," I said through a tight throat, remembering the glide of Kai's fingers over my clit while the tattoo machine's vibrations rolled through me. Funny, I couldn't seem to recall any of the pain. Would Kai pleasure me again this time?

"I'll have to do a better job hunting for it, then. I'm good at finding hidden things." His expression twisted unexpectedly, and his mood soured. "Well, except the only thing that matters."

"What was that?" Hades asked. I don't think he was actually interested, but the sudden shift in Cas's mood was so marked that I think it struck all of us.

"Nothing," he said dismissively, waving a hand like some sort of king on a throne.

The buzzing of Kai's tattoo gun filled the room, and we all turned our attention to Tor. As expected, he took it like a champ. There wasn't so much as a grimace or a grunt as the needle moved over his skin. If anything, there was a sparkle in his eye. If I didn't know better . . .

My eyes dropped to his lap, and yup, that was a raging hard-on in his sweats. My beast was just as aroused as I was. Guess I wasn't the only one who got horny when it came to tattoos. Though his being a Berserker fueled by bloodlust, maybe it made a bit more sense in his case.

Tor chuckled, the sound drawing my eyes back up his body as he spread his legs a little wider. "You can do something about it if you want, beauty. I won't stop you."

"I will. Don't even think about it, gem. This is too important. We'll get to the fun part later." Kai's voice was stern and sexy as hell.

"Oh look, she's pouting. Come here, sweet girl. I'm not getting tattooed. You can play with me."

Hades locked his arm around my waist and tugged me against him. "No she won't. She'll be a good girl and wait."

"She will?" I asked, wondering why I shouldn't take Cas up on his offer and work off some of this tension.

Hades brushed his lips against my ear. "Yes, she will. Because anticipation makes everything so much better, my sweet little flower. Once this is done, the four of us are going to lay you back and make you bloom for us. But only if you wait."

"I have been told it's best to celebrate the start of the year the way you intend to spend the rest of it," I murmured.

"On your back?" Caspian teased.

"Coming. Repeatedly," Hades corrected.

"Mmm. Yup. That's the one," I said, feeling more than a little lightheaded.

We watched as the design on Tor's shoulder took shape,

first an outline of the petals and leaves, then the detailed veins and shading. The faint glow in the ink made it seem iridescent and ethereal.

"Nearly finished," Kai murmured as he focused on the last bit of the art.

The air was charged as he finished the last line. I could tell we all felt it because each of us reacted—some more than others. Cas, of course, was the loudest.

"What the bloody hell was that?"

"The spell taking hold," Kai explained with the over-taxed patience of a school teacher. "It's only going to get more intense with each tattoo I finish. Prepare yourselves."

Tor stood, pride practically seeping from his pores. "Do you like it, Kærasta?"

I fucking loved it. "Yes," I choked out, not expecting to be so emotional over a tattoo. To be fair, I think it was more about what said tattoo represented.

Kai readied his station for the next of us as I stood and went to my beast of a mate. My fingers traced the already healed skin—thank you, magic ink—and I swear to God, Tor purred under my attention.

"It's so beautiful," I whispered.

"It's you, Dahlia. Of course it's beautiful," Kai offered.

Cas was next to take his place in Kai's seat. Instead of pulling his shirt over his head, he ripped it down the middle. Like a stripper. I was at my very own Magic Mike show, but with less music and hip rolls. At least for now.

"Why are you giggling to yourself, baby doll?" Hades asked, lips at my ear again.

"She's thinking happy thoughts," Cas answered. "Good thing I haven't given her any pixie dust, or you'd have to hold her down."

"I can still do that if she wants me to."

Sweet mother of God, these men were going to need to buy me a whole new supply of panties before the day was over.

"Go on, dragon. I'm ready to wear my love on my body for the rest of my existence."

There was no hiding my smile as I bit my lip and shook my head. He was overdoing the swoon, but I was eating it up.

Tor moved so that he was standing on one side of me while Hades stood on the other. We silently watched Kai work, Tor resting his chin on my shoulder while Hades's shadows twined their way around my leg. I think it might have been his version of holding hands. Asshole snored softly on the pile of blankets he'd taken ownership of.

"Oh, that spot at the armpit tickles a bit," Cas said, a smirk on his lips.

"Don't move."

"I'm not. I'm just making an observation."

"Fine," Kai muttered.

Just like with Tor, as soon as Kai finished Cas's tattoo, a pulse of energy hit the room. As he'd warned, it was stronger than the last one. Charged was the only way to describe the atmosphere. While the reaction when Tor's was completed felt more like the release of static electricity after shuffling across carpet, this made the hairs on the back of my neck lift and goosebumps break out across my arms.

Cas stood with a cocky grin, sauntering over and taking my chin between his thumb and forefinger so he could lay one on me. There was something about the possession in his kiss that felt different this time. Like now that he'd marked himself for the world to see, he felt more settled and safe. Like he had a home.

"It looks so good on you," I whispered against his lips.

"I can't wait to see it on you."

Hades didn't wait for Kai to summon him. He claimed the seat with the same infuriating sense of calm and control as he did everything else. Before he sat down, he met and held my stare, taking his time as he rolled down his sleeves and undid the buttons of his shirt.

I think I might have been panting by the time he finished.

Bastard knew it too.

His skin was unmarked, with a scattering of golden chest hair. A thrill shot through me knowing the first and probably only piece of art he'd ever have etched onto him was to represent me and our bond.

"Don't worry, baby doll. I'll let you see it whenever you want."

"I wasn't worried."

He winked at me. *Winked*. Then Kai began. As the hum of the tattoo gun droned on, I watched the flowers take shape until a soft tickling sensation trailed over my ankle. I was pretty familiar with the slide of Hades's shadows over my body by this point, so I knew exactly what that mischievous asshole was up to.

"What happened to anticipation?" I asked.

"I have no idea what you're talking about."

I quirked a brow, silently calling him on his bullshit.

He quirked a brow right back. "I'm just helping build it."

"Lean back against me, darling. I'll hold you up while he toys with you."

Tor was uncharacteristically quiet through all of this. I turned to peek at him, wondering if maybe he'd fallen asleep, but no, he was leaning against the wall, bulging biceps crossed over his chest, eyes locked on me. He was a predator lying in wait.

And I was the prey.

Why did that make me so hot?

Thoughts of him chasing me through the forest filled my mind, and I pressed my thighs together, trying in vain to alleviate some of the ache.

Hades played with me the whole time he was being inked but never touched the spot I wanted more than anything. I didn't think I'd be able to sit still when it was my turn. But I had to be a good girl for them. I was pretty sure I promised, didn't I?

When his tattoo was complete, the air sizzled with electricity. Or maybe it was just magic. Either way, it felt like the charge in the sky right before a lightning strike. Once again my body was covered in goosebumps, but this time the tingle of the shock lasted longer and was beneath my skin, almost a vibration.

By the time Kai was ready for me to take my place in his chair, I was a mess. And I wasn't the only one. Each and every one of my mates were tenting their pants. At least my shame was hidden by my black leggings.

Kai proved me a liar when he took a deep inhale, his pupils elongating into slits when they lifted to mine.

"Something on your mind, gem?"

"Nope. Not a thing."

"Pretty little liar," Caspian teased.

"You'll need to remove that jumper, lass. I cannae do this with your clothing in the way."

I slipped out of my sweatshirt, this one emblazoned with the words *I like tacos, books, and maybe five people.* I held it out to him like an offering, the fabric hanging by the crook of my finger.

"Do that again later when ye remove your bra," he whispered, taking it from me and carefully folding it.

"What makes you think I'm removing it myself?" I flicked my gaze toward the other guys. "Tor's really good at ripping my clothes off."

"You'll do it if we ask ye to."

Where's the lie, folks? I would do pretty much anything they ask at this point.

He prepped my skin carefully, his warm hands making me forget I was about to feel pain for a two-hour session, then dropped a kiss on my lips.

"Are you ready?" he murmured.

"Yes."

Kai started the gun, and his face changed from playful to deeply focused at the first touch of the needle to my skin. I wasn't as much of a badass as the rest of them and did flinch, but I wasn't trying to hide my reaction to the pain either. There was nothing wrong with showing emotion. It didn't make me tougher for pretending I couldn't feel the sting of the needle. If anything, showing that it hurt and I was taking it anyway was probably the more badass approach. So take that.

"Look at our girl, taking it even though it hurts," Caspian said in the same low tone we'd all used while each session was going on.

"She's fucking gorgeous." That was my Hades, his eyes burning a bright blue as he watched me. Asshole was curled up at his feet, happily snoring and ignoring everything going on around him.

Tor remained in his spot, leaning against the wall, gaze never leaving me. "Of course she is," he mused, "she's the mate of a Berserker. She knows that a little pain reminds you that you're still alive."

"I would have said a little pain makes the pleasure sweeter, but sure, we'll go with your version," Cas said, winking at me.

Surprisingly, my arm kind of went numb after a while, the buzz of the needle making my eyes heavy as sleep threatened to take me under. Was I a weirdo? My first tattoo had been in such a delicate place; there was no way I'd be soothed enough to relax like this, but something about Kai's skill and my other three mates being there calmed me.

"Is something wrong with me?" I blurted, trying to stay awake.

"Nae. You're doing so well, gem. Why would you ask that?"

"Because I can barely feel it anymore. I'm actually drowsy."

He chuckled as he continued working. "Some people find getting ink soothing. Sort of like meditation."

"It's probably the blood loss."

"Perhaps," he agreed with a smile. "Almost done, love. Just a little longer."

I locked gazes with Tor as the final drags of the needle against my skin were completed and my eyes widened as an even more intense pulse of electric magic rushed through us all. Kai wiped my shoulder clean, and I moved to stand, but he stopped me with a large palm.

"No. You sit right there. I need you to finish mine for me."

Panic hit me hard. "What? I'm not a tattoo artist. What if I fuck it up?"

He laughed. "It's one wee line. You won't. It's important that you do this."

I gave him my best squinty-eyed glare. "I'm pretty sure you're bullshitting me, dragon."

"You'll never know, will you?"

I huffed but paid close attention as he talked me through the basics of the machine. He took care of prepping his skin and loading the ink. All I had to do was hold my hand steady as I connected the final petal.

Kai took the gun from me the instant the ink closed the petal, and a bright glow emanated from the tattoo—from all our tattoos.

The electric pulse was so much bigger this time. It felt like pure liquid energy crashing through my body. The buzz was deep in my skin, in my core. There was no way I could contain my reaction, a wanton moan ripping from my throat as my body physically responded to the sensation.

But that wasn't all. Something else snapped into place with the completion of Kai's tattoo. I could feel them all within me. Sense them. My God, they were so powerful.

"You're just as powerful, baby doll," Hades whispered, his hands covered in blue flames.

I didn't say that out loud. Wait, did he just read my mind?

"I can hear you thinking."

"No you can't."

"Yeah, I fucking can."

I closed my eyes and thought about exactly what I wanted his shadows to do to me, and he groaned. So did the others.

"Can all of you read my thoughts?"

"It looks that way," Cas said. "Show me what you want me to do to you, love. I can't wait."

Well, this was a surprising turn of events.

"You didn't say anything about being able to eavesdrop in my mind, dragon."

"I dinnae know it was going to happen. Only that portions of our power would be shared with one another."

I huffed. "Convenient excuse. This was supposed to be about protection."

"What better way to protect you than to be able to communicate without being overheard," he offered.

"Or knowing how you're really feeling," Tor added.

Of course they saw the upside. As far as I could tell, this was a one-way problem. None of them had to worry about sharing their deepest, darkest thoughts and feelings.

Then again, I wanted them in the worst way. Maybe we'd use this to my advantage for now and figure out a way to handle it later.

CHAPTER
SIXTEEN
DAHLIA

I glanced from hot man to hot man as we all came back to Earth after the wild ride that was our bond tattoos. It was . . . a lot, being in this fairly small space, and while I should still be concerned about them being able to read my thoughts, I was more focused on the pulsing between my legs and the way my skin was on fire for them.

"What the fuck is wrong with me?" I whispered, more to myself than anyone else.

My thighs rubbed together as I searched for some measure of relief. With each tattoo, this had been building, but fuck, I hadn't realized that the *this* was arousal.

I'd been horny before, but my libido was out of control. I could not stop thinking about sex. Scenes from some of my filthiest novels danced through my mind, each one more seductive than the next.

"Two in one? Ding dong, let's go, Shadow Daddy, we're up."

"Excuse me?" Tor snarled.

Cas rolled his eyes as he started to remove his belt and kick off his boots. "Well, it can't possibly be you or the dragon. You'll tear her in two. Our girl wants to be stretched, not hospitalized."

"Ohmigod," I breathed. The thought of both men inside my vagina at once, with Tor and Kai watching, was almost enough to make my knees buckle. "Is it my birthday?" I asked, channeling my inner Kiki. Unfortunately, no one there appreciated the reference. My men were still concerned about who got the privilege of fucking me first.

Cas turned his back on Tor and stared at Hades. "You're still wearing pants. Did you not understand what's happening here? Two hotdogs, one bun. We're up, mate. If you're not up for the challenge, speak now, but I'm not playing the fluffer."

"Fuck, I'm up for it. I was just trying to process the fact that your dick is going to have to rub up against mine."

Cas shimmied out of his tight pants, tossing Hades a wink. "Bet it won't be the last time. But if it makes you feel better, I know what I'm doing, and I've got a slew of references. You're in good hands, mate."

"Why do you make it sound like you're fucking me?"

"Just trying to reassure you. That's the kind thing to do, right? I figure as the only one with experience, that sort of makes me the top."

"You wish. You're a power bottom at best."

"Better than a blouse."

"A blouse?" Kai asked.

"A feminine top," he explained with a smirk.

"What's wrong with a blouse?" I asked, torn between a laugh and a moan.

"Not a damn thing, darling. It just gave me an excuse to use the expression."

Hades shook his head, his blue eyes finding mine. "Is this really what you want, baby doll?"

I was too turned on to speak, so I just nodded. I'm not sure whose fantasy I just walked in on, but I was here. For. It.

Kai came up behind me and began helping me out of my bra, his big fingers trailing over my shoulders and back as he slowly unhooked the fabric. His lips traveled along the back of my neck, then over my bared shoulder as the bra fell to the floor.

"Fuck, she's fit," Cas said, his hungry gaze meeting mine. He was already fully nude at this point, his dick hard and straining.

"Thanks for that, Captain states the obvious," Hades muttered.

"She's resplendent." This came from my beast as he crossed the room and stalked toward me, taking me up in his arms and crushing his lips to mine.

"Resplendent, huh?" I murmured against his lips. "Are you trying to word porn me?"

"Is it working?"

"Y-yes."

Tor's hand slid down my belly until he slipped under my waistband. His big fingers found my folds, slick and ready. "She's wet."

"Oh, come on, you're not gonna call *him* Captain states the obvious?" Cas complained. "Of course she's fucking wet. She's been gagging for us since the moment she woke up this morning. You'd know that if you'd been here when the sun rose. But nooooo, you have to go do your weird little beast runs."

Tor broke away from me with a growl, bodily shoving Cas up against the wall and holding him in place with a forearm to the throat. "Don't test me, little pirate. I eat things twice as big as you for breakfast."

"Kinky," Caspian rasped. "You like the full English? I've got some sausage prepared."

Tor let him go with an infuriated huff. "You're a menace."

"He loves me." Cas winked at me. "Don't let him fool you."

I briefly pictured Cas on his knees at Tor's mercy while I told them what to do, and while my Viking was clearly not interested, Cas didn't even bat an eye.

"So, boss man," I teased, "how do we do this?"

"I prefer maestro."

Kai chuckled as he dropped to his knees behind me and dragged my leggings down until I could step out of them. When he bit my ass, I squealed in delight. They were all teasing me, making me wait while giving me just a taste of what I wanted.

"As soon as you're free of your dragon, I'll let you know exactly how we're going to make this work." Cas was openly stroking his dick as he watched me with Kai. "Viking, I'm gonna need you to magic up some lube for us. She might be wet, but she's not wet enough for this."

Hades cleared his throat. "And maybe a sturdier bed."

Tor complied with a nod, adding his own special twist to things by including a plush new blanket to the bed as well.

Kai's hands on me felt so good, I was seconds away from turning into a puddle. The need I felt for my men was so intense I was pretty sure a well-placed whisper would get the job done. Although the thought of coming around anything other than one or all of their dicks was disappointing. I wanted them or nothing at all.

And then there was my shadow daddy. He stood in the background, participating but not, and all I wanted was for his dick to be the first one inside me. I hoped so much that was what Cas would instruct us to do. Hades had never gotten to be the first, and I was sure it was because of some weird control thing he had. He needed to leave a *lasting* impression or some nonsense.

"Don't worry, sweet girl, you'll get your wish," Cas said, his devilish whisper nearly floating to my ear.

"Whatever my baby doll wants, she'll get." Hades didn't wait for Cas to tell him the next steps. Instead he went to the bed Tor had manifested and laid in the center. His cock stood proud and thick, the tip glistening with the evidence of his need for me. I wanted to lick it clean, but he chuckled and shook his head. "Not yet, Dahlia. Your cunt is the only thing swallowing me down right now."

"Okay, Daddy," I whispered with far too much glee.

His dick gave a happy twitch as the words left my lips. There was no containing my smug satisfaction as I made my way over to him, adding a little extra roll to my hips for the others to enjoy.

"Mmm, my very own personal goddess."

"Only the best for my lord Hades." Honestly, I felt like a fucking goddess. The way they all watched me, practically panting with their desire, made me feel so empowered. I glanced over my shoulder and saw both Tor and Kai stroking themselves while Cas looked on. "What do I do, Captain?"

"Mount him, beautiful. And then bend over for me. Hades, all you have to do is stay hard."

"Not a problem."

I giggled, though it quickly turned into a groan of pure bliss as I threw my leg over his hips and slid down on top of his rigid length. "Oh, fuck." It felt so good, the way he filled me and hit just the right spot.

"Baby, you're so wet," Hades moaned. "Hot and fucking gushing."

"Ride him for a bit, darling. Open up and get yourself ready to take me too." Cas ran his palm up my spine, then all the way down to my ass before dipping his fingers between my legs so he could slip one inside as I moved.

"Fuck, is that your finger?" Hades asked, a little panic in his voice.

I locked eyes with him as he processed the experience.

Cas laughed. "Well, it's certainly not my cock."

Hades smirked. "Really? I couldn't tell the difference."

"That's just because you're new to this. Don't worry, you won't have any trouble in just a second. You'll never forget the experience, I promise."

I giggled and mouthed, "Ignore him," to Hades as I lifted up and sank back down on him. "God, Hades, you feel good."

"It's about to feel even better, love." Cas pressed his palm between my shoulder blades until I was on all fours, torso hovering over Hades, ass presented to my pirate like a prize.

Hades let out a groan that was part hungry growl as he took one of my puckered nipples into his mouth and sucked hard.

"Put your legs together," Cas said, the sound of a smack catching me off guard because I didn't feel it. Did he just slap the lord of the underworld? Ballsy move.

Hades didn't fight it. He was too busy sucking my tit like it was his saving grace, and I felt his thighs close under me.

"There we go," Cas murmured, crawling up behind me. I felt his heat first, and then the press of his legs behind mine. I was pretty sure he was straddling Hades, same as I was. The idea alone had a surge of lust spiking through me.

"Mmm, our little writer likes that we're touching, *my lord Hades*," Cas teased. "I'll file that away for things future us should discuss."

"Not a chance," Hades gritted out.

Cas ignored him and slid a slick finger inside me. Then two, then three. The burn of the stretch had me gasping but reminded me of Kai's dragon shifting while inside me. It wasn't altogether unfamiliar, and fuck was it welcome.

Then the fingers were gone, replaced by the press of his swollen cock at my already-filled entrance. He held on to my hip with one hand, his fingertips pressing in hard enough to bruise. "Stay still for a second. Let me do all the work, love."

"It's too much," I protested.

"No, it's not. Lass, you've taken my cock in my dragon form. You can do this," Kai said as he approached the bed.

"Breathe, darling. If it hurts, I'll stop." Cas waited, poised at my entrance.

I nodded, eyes screwed shut, but Hades's shadows were already working their way down my body and to my clit, teasing and stroking.

"Eyes on me, baby doll. Look at how good you make me feel."

For some reason, that helped. I don't know why the idea of Cas sliding into me was enough to make me tense up like this, but it must have been the fear of potential pain. As soon as the pleasure took over, I relaxed enough for Cas to begin a slow press inward.

Hades's groan was louder than mine, and that fact had me gushing.

"Fuck that's hot. I didn't think it would feel this good."

Knowing that he was getting pleasure from this as well as I was everything to me.

"Don't stop, Cas," I begged, arching my back to try and make more room for him. The adjustment had both men grunting.

"Goddess, Dahlia, I'm almost as far as I can go." Cas gripped the fleshy part of my hips and thrust as deep as possible, making Hades and I both cry out.

"I need friction," I whimpered.

Hades grasped my thighs and looked over my shoulder. "We take over?"

"Exactly my plan."

Before I had a moment to process what the two of them were plotting, they began moving me on their cocks. It felt so fucking good, their thick lengths brushing every single nerve ending with the shadows paying special attention to my clit as an added bonus. I felt hot and cold all over as waves of sensation crashed into me. One right on the heels of another until I could barely tell them apart.

"I'm going to come," I warned. "I can't keep it at bay. It feels too good."

From the expression on his face, Hades was barely holding on. "No one is telling you to wait, baby doll. Come whenever you're ready, and we'll be right behind you."

Just the mental image of the two of them pulsing in time, pumping me full of their cum, had me detonating like a bomb.

"Oh fuck," I cried, unsure whose name to call out.

"Yes, Dahlia, fucking milk my cock like it's the only thing you need," Caspian groaned as he pulsed inside me.

"Fuuuuck," Hades called out, his eyes blazing as his orgasm overtook him.

From the other grunts and cries in the room, we weren't the only ones who found release.

"Look at our mate, Tor. Isn't she the most beautiful you've ever seen her? I love watching her in the throes of her pleasure."

"It'll be even better when we're the ones responsible for it."

"Aye. We're of the same mind. Are you ready for us, gem?"

I was a panting, dripping mess, but there was only one answer to that question.

"Fuck. Yes."

CHAPTER
SEVENTEEN

KAI

S hould I have given her some time to recover? Probably. But my wee mate wasn't complaining as she stood on wobbly legs, both Hook's and Hades's cum running down her thighs. In fact, the look on her face said she was ready to beg for us both. If I couldn't clearly see the evidence for myself, or had I not witnessed the act, I never would have guessed she'd just been so thoroughly fucked.

"How do you want me?" she asked, her voice breathy, eyes wide with an innocence that didn't match what I'd just seen her doing.

"Can you hold yourself up on hands and knees so Tor and I can both take you?"

Goddess, I wanted her to say yes.

Her answer was immediate, though it didn't form on her lips. I heard it instead in my mind. Not as loud or clear as one of my own thoughts, but almost as if it was coming from behind a closed door.

"Oh God, yes."

My gaze flicked to Tor, who'd clearly also heard her because he was already striding toward the bed and scooping her into his arms as he went.

Tor stared hard at Hades and Hook, his tone leaving no room for argument. "Move."

Caspian, the spry little monkey, was quick to scramble off the bed. Hades was less nimble. He had the look of a man who'd just had his soul sucked out of him by way of his dick. I was familiar with the sensation. Sex with my mate was like that. Satisfying on a level nothing else could match.

He rolled to his side with a soft moan, making Dahlia laugh.

"You gonna be okay over there?" she asked.

He waved a hand at her. "Worry about yourself, baby doll. I'll be right as rain in a bit."

The pirate cupped a hand to his mouth as if sharing a secret, though he did nothing to lower his voice. "I said it once, and I'll say it again: amateur."

Hades formed a fist with his shadows and punched Hook right in the jaw.

"Ow! What the bloody hell was that for?"

"For pissing me off. Now sit down and shut up. You're ruining the mood."

Hook muttered something under his breath, but he did as he was told. Dahlia squealed in delight as Tor deposited her in position on the bed, her perfect arse in the air, the swollen lips of her pussy visible between her legs.

"Mouth or pussy?" Tor asked me, surprising me that he'd even give me a choice. Normally the beast just took up his position, and we didn't have a discussion about it.

"He's too big for my mouth," Dahlia answered for me,

giving her hips a wiggle. "It's the ridges. I can do it, but then he can't . . . get bigger if he needs to."

"Our mate knows us so well," my dragon crooned.

"Aye," I said aloud, confirming both statements at once.

Tor reached down and tugged on Dahlia's bottom lip. "Good thing I love this fucking mouth then, eh, Kærasta?"

She nipped at the tip of his finger. "Guess so, big guy."

"Does this mean you two are finally going to take our girl to Paris?" Hook called from his perch on my desk. The thought of his naked arse on my belongings had my eye twitching, but I did my best to shelve the need to shove him off and wipe it clean. At least for the moment.

Tor shot me a confused look.

"The Eiffel Tower," I explained, recalling the pirate's explanation from before.

"Is that the high-five thing?"

I nodded.

The Viking grumbled and let out a beleaguered sigh, his gaze searching Dahlia's face. "Is that really something you want?"

She lifted one shoulder in a shrug, her grin pure mischief. "I don't hate the idea."

"How is us touching palms while inside you enticing?"

A little shiver ran over her body as she processed his words. I don't think he realized that he painted a very different picture in her mind. It took her a second to clear her throat so she could reply. "It's funny. Something I want to collect for my mental scrapbook."

I had to bite back my laughter because this woman had somehow managed to take this moment and make it amusing while still turning me on like no other had ever been able to do.

"Perhaps. We'll see what happens." Tor knelt on the bed

in front of Dahlia, cock in hand as he threaded his fingers through her hair and balled the strands into his fist with the other. Tugging her head back, he stared down at her. "First, she has to suck my cock until tears stream down her cheeks."

Moving into position, I palmed her arse with both hands and spread her cheeks apart. I shouldn't be so turned on by the sight of other men's cum dripping out of her, but fuck it, I was. Her pussy was swollen and sloppy, and I couldn't wait to make an even bigger mess of it. Knowing that she'd already come but needed more—needed me—it was every fucking thing.

"Please, Kai," she begged as Tor brought his length to her mouth. Just before he shoved inside, she asked again. "Fill me?"

"Well, when you ask so pretty for me," I murmured.

Sliding the tip of my cock through her folds, I got my length nice and lubed for her. Then notched myself at her entrance before pushing just the tip inside her and making her moan.

Tor and I made eye contact, both clearly thinking the same thing. We pulled out of her and nodded just before sliding back inside her in tandem.

"Fuck me, that's never not going to be hot," Hook observed.

"I know," Dahlia agreed, her mental voice once again permeating my mind.

Hades let out a soft chuckle. "You have such a greedy cunt, baby doll."

"Yes I fucking do. And you love it."

Tor's hand was still fisted in Dahlia's hair, keeping her steady as he rolled his hips, and she sucked him down like her life depended on it.

"Look at our girl multitasking like a queen. Taking two cocks and carrying on an entire conversation. I'm proud of you, darling," Hook praised. "And impressed. I can barely string two words together when I'm inside you. Come to think of it, perhaps they aren't doing a very good job."

"But you certainly can string an innumerable number of words together at any other godsforsaken moment, can't you?" Hades complained.

"It's a gift."

"It's fuckin' something."

All I knew was that talking was the last thing on my mind as her walls fluttered around me. I didn't care what else was going on; I was lost to the pleasure of being inside the woman I loved.

"My turn," my dragon demanded. He didn't wait for permission before taking control of my body. The tips of my nails grew pointed, and I knew if I looked in a mirror, I'd find my pupils slitted and glowing. I also didn't need Dahlia's thoughts to know how much she enjoyed my dragon's cock. Her wanton moan took care of that for me, as did the vise-like grip of her pussy.

"You break her skin, and we're gonna have words, dragon," Hades warned.

"The only pain she'll feel at my hand is from an abundance of pleasure," I promised, though it was my dragon's voice speaking through me.

"I'm fine, Hades. God, it feels so good," Dahlia assured him using her mind, and I really fucking loved this addition to our solidified bond. I could feel the added power boost. My awareness of her other mates was different now, a sixth sense, if you will. I knew this was only the tip of the iceberg, but any other benefits would have to be discovered later.

Giving her arse a light spank, I softly chided. "Focus,

gem. Tor and I are the ones loving you right now. Hades had his turn. Your attention should be on us."

She moaned around Tor's cock, which made him suck in a sharp breath before growling, "Do it again, beauty."

She did, and his eyes rolled back in pleasure. I timed my thrusts to his, matching his pace and driving Dahlia wild with need.

Her cries of pleasure echoed through my mind, spurring me on as I drove home as deep as possible.

"Breed her. She wants it. She's your mate. You know what to do to make it catch." My dragon was pushing his primal needs on me, but I wouldn't do that to her without her explicit consent.

Thank the goddess Dahlia and the others didn't have access to my thoughts. Or his.

But fuck if the thought alone didn't do something to me. A soft roar escaped as I picked up speed.

"Yes, yes, yes," Dahlia chanted, wordlessly begging for more.

Tor and I didn't need any urging. We were happy to give her everything she wanted. Especially when everything included us.

"Any other time, I'd decorate your face with my spend, Kærasta, but this time, I need you to swallow me down so I'm inside you too," Tor said through panting breaths. "Are you ready for it?"

She hummed around his dick, and the wicked thoughts she projected had my balls drawing up tight. I wasn't going to last. Especially not when Tor barked out her name and began pulsing down her throat.

She came around me, her orgasm washing over us all as it became obvious she had gained her footing with this new ability of hers.

"Oh fuck," Hades groaned. I'd become familiar enough with the noises he made to recognize that he was coming too.

Hook let out a surprised shout at the same time, but I was too busy filling her with my seed to focus on the rest of them. It seemed never-ending—the waves of release, the squeeze of her cunt around me, the way her body moved as she milked every drop from me.

"Now's your chance, lads. Up top for our girl," Hook prompted.

I huffed out a laugh and lifted one arm, noting the slight trembling in my limb with amusement. "Don't leave me hanging, Viking."

Tor, cock still in her mouth, sighed. "Oh, for fuck's sake." But he raised his palm and slapped it on mine, making Dahlia squirm and moan.

At that exact moment, a soft *click* sounded from the other side of the room. Tor and I both snapped our heads toward Hook, who was grinning and holding up my phone. "There. Now she doesn't need to rely on her mental scrapbook at all."

Tor stiffened as Dahlia released his length, then narrowed his eyes at Hook. "I hate you."

"No you don't. No one really does."

Dahlia giggled, whimpering a little as I slipped out of her. I couldn't help myself—I watched as the mixture of all of us dripped from her cunt. Taking two fingers, I coated them in the fluid before holding them up to her lips.

"Taste us. Go on, gem."

She sucked in a gasp before closing her eyes and letting me slide both inside her mouth as she cleaned them off.

Click

I was going to break that pirate's fucking fingers if he

209

kept taking photos without permission. A growl built in my chest, but Dahlia's eyes fluttered open and she turned her attention to our erstwhile photographer.

"Cas, do me a favor?"

He smirked. "Anything, love."

"Send me those pictures."

He adjusted the angle of the phone and took a quick snapshot of his semi, drawing another giggle from Dahlia. Then he tapped the screen and looked back up. "Sent."

"You better get that picture of your dick off my phone," I growled.

Shrugging, he said, "I thought I'd program my number in and set it as my contact photo."

"I hate you," I huffed.

"See," Tor added, "it's spreading. He's worse than an epidemic."

A soft snore pulled all of our attention to the beautiful woman who'd curled up on the bed as we'd been arguing over the pictures. We'd fucked her to sleep.

Hades prowled over to her and gently brushed some strands of hair off her forehead. "Come on, let's get her cleaned up. She worked hard today. She deserves some sweet dreams before she has to face what's coming."

Tor and I both tensed, our attention lasering in on him. "What do you know that we don't?" Tor asked.

Recalling how I found them yesterday, I couldn't help but suspect it had something to do with whatever had put her in a sour mood.

"Hades," I pressed.

He shrugged, his expression an impassive mask. "It's always something around here."

It was hardly an answer, but it also wasn't a lie. The reminder made me even more grateful we'd taken the time to tie ourselves to her via the tattoos. If something was coming, she wouldn't face it alone. She'd spent too much of her life alone. We were going to ensure she'd never experience that again. And good fucking luck to whoever was stupid enough to try and take her from us.

CHAPTER
EIGHTEEN
TOR

"Bad form!" Hook shouted, jabbing his index finger down onto the board next to Dahlia's tiles. "That's not even a word."

"Quixotry is absolutely a word."

"Oh yeah? Use it in a sentence, smarty pants."

Playing with the ends of Dahlia's hair, I murmured, "The pirate was too stupid to understand the meaning of the word quixotry."

"Well played. But that is not what I meant, and you know it."

I didn't even look at him. He wasn't any concern of mine. Dahlia was truly all that mattered, and she didn't need my help beating Hook at this game. He was witty, but she was brilliant.

Her thoughts brushed my mind, making my body warm. *"I never thought I'd look at Hades and melt, but do you see him? He's such a dog dad. It's adorable."*

"It's a wonder Cerberus tolerates it," I replied, keeping my voice low so as not to be overheard.

I loved that she'd figured out how to focus her inner

voice, a way for her to talk to each of us individually or as a group without anyone else being privy to the conversation. My gaze drifted across the room, taking in the other residents nearby. Three mermaids watching Hook longingly but keeping their distance. Two shifters working together on yet another puzzle. What was it about them and that station? Kai sat in his usual spot at the window seat, sketching with his eyes flicking to Dahlia every few moments. No doubt he'd be drawing her. She was his muse, and I didn't blame him.

She giggled, and Hades flashed through her mind.

My attention drifted to where he sat in the corner, brushing his little dog's fur carefully, making sure he was fluffy in all the right places. His face was tight with concentration while Asshole quietly panted. Without warning, the puppy twisted around and bit Hades's hand.

"Ouch. Fuck, I'm sorry. No, I don't like it either. I'll try to be more careful." Hades sighed, clearly listening to whatever rant was taking place in his mind.

"I don't think he's a dog dad. I think he's the dog's bitch," I whispered against Dahlia's hair.

"Pretty sure that's true of all pet owners. They're the ones doing all the heavy lifting with the feeding and *excrement* pick up." As she said the word, she set the corresponding tiles down, building yet another high-scoring word.

Hook flung himself back in his chair, arms flailing in frustration. "This is bloody rigged. You can't possibly . . . that's so many letters. And a triple word score besides. There's no way I can catch up now."

"You're just upset because you can't come up with any words that are more than four letters. I'm not cheating, Cas, and you know it."

He huffed, crossing his arms and having himself a proper sulk. "I don't like losing."

"Shouldn't you be used to it?" I asked idly. "You're shit at every game you play."

"I am not," he protested.

I glanced at him with a raised brow. "When was the last time you actually won a card game?"

He opened and closed his mouth, looking a bit like a goldfish attempting to feed. "I . . . I . . . You know what, I've had enough. You win, darling. I need to go to the library and brush up on my five-dollar words if I'm going to stand a chance against you."

Hook stood and straightened his cuffs. As he did, I whispered, "At least he knows how to read. I didn't expect that."

Before he left the room, his shoulders stiffened, and he turned his head to look at our mate. She craned her neck and smiled at him before the cheeky pirate smirked and offered her a rakish wink.

"You're getting quite good at that," I said.

"Good at . . . oh shoot, did you hear me?" she asked, immediately assuming the wrong thing.

"No, actually."

"Then how did you—"

"You're not one to let any of us storm off without knowing where your heart lies. And I don't think there's much in this world that would stop that pirate in his tracks, save you."

Her cheeks turned pink as she glanced down at her lap, where I'd placed a hand. I needed to be touching her as often as possible, so honestly, I didn't even think twice about the contact.

"I just want you all to know I love you, no matter what."

I pressed a kiss to her forehead. "I know, Kærasta. And that is one of the many things I adore about you."

"Well, isn't this shmoopy." Sorcha's bored drawl was an unwelcome interruption. "Soak it up while you can, I suppose."

"What's that supposed to mean?" Dahlia asked.

"The villagers are preparing for an uprising."

"An uprising?" she echoed, her voice raising an octave.

"Eh, doesn't that happen every century or so?" Oz asked, stealing Hook's recently vacated seat as he glanced at Dahlia and added, "Silly wabbits. They don't stand a chance against us."

"Not like this," Sorcha countered. "They really mean it this time."

"Dusting off their pitchforks, are they?" Oz asked.

"Exactly. And Blackwood has become their target. Kit heard from the guard he was trying to make a bargain with that the townspeople are amassing an army to come in here and get rid of us once and for all. They're blaming everything on Blackwood."

Unease built in my gut. As cavalier as she seemed, Sorcha's words had an undertone of real fear. She knew as well as I did if there were enough of them against us, we'd be at war.

"What reason would they have to come for us?" Dahlia asked, her fingers tightening around mine.

"All the dead bodies, of course."

"Wait, they're pissed at us about the Ripper's victims? But they were our people."

"Not just ours," Sorcha corrected. "He's targeted a lot of their numbers. Not to mention the growing pile of animal carcasses they've found in the woods. Animals that are part of their food supply."

Dahlia was very careful not to look at me. *"They're talking about your animals, aren't they?"*

I gave a very slow, very subtle dip of my chin. This wasn't good. I needed the runs and hunts if I was going to give my beast the freedom it required. Without the ability to expel that energy, I was certain I'd reach a boiling point, and then we'd have a mess on our hands. One I might not be able to come back from.

As grounding as Dahlia was, I spent my days constantly teetering near the edge, knowing any threat to her would send me over. I wasn't like Kai, who would always come back to himself. It was only my connection to Dahlia that spared me the first time, and even then, I still had to find a way to maintain the balance. It took everything I had to hold on to the man I had been before I was cursed.

Sorcha clicked her tongue. "I have it on good authority that there will be no secret jaunts to the village for anyone, no matter how persuasive they may be. Security is being amped up. Clearly the Ripper hasn't sated his bloodlust. He's just biding his time."

"Maybe he's moved on," Dahlia said.

Sorcha laughed. "Moved on? What a silly thing to say. Why would he willingly leave when we're all stuck here like a bunch of sitting ducks for him to pick off?"

"What if it was Temperance? He just vanished into the night. Maybe he was the Ripper."

Oz shook his head, laughing. "No. He wasn't. There's no way. He was too . . . something. I can't put my finger on it. Up Masterson's ass, maybe? Besides, he left because he didn't need to be here anymore. Dr. Masterson is back, and there's only room for one boss."

That certainly was a convenient explanation. Too bad it was riddled with falsehoods. The others and I had spoken at length about whether to come forward about Temperance's death but ultimately decided to buy ourselves time with his disappearance instead. None of us were keen on the idea of getting locked up in No Man's Land for murder, even if it was the murder of a serial killer. Blackwood was funny that way. They didn't seem to care why you broke the rules, only that you did. We couldn't risk being sent away from Dahlia, and there was no way in hell we'd let her take the fall for what happened.

"Have you heard anything from your family, Sorcha?" Dahlia asked.

The vampire looked at her like she was speaking in tongues. "Why would I?"

"B-because they seemed pretty shocked to see you here. I figured Noah and Rosie would share the news that they'd found you."

A flash of something in Sorcha's eyes betrayed a little glimmer of hope. "No. They won't come for me. They wrote me off for the good of all of us."

"Oh," Dahlia murmured.

There was something she hadn't told me. I could feel it weighing on her. Unfortunately our mental connection was one-sided, so there was no way I could ask her in front of the others. Something to follow up on later, then.

"Don't worry about me, little writer. I'll be just fi—" Sorcha stopped mid-sentence, her focus on the pretty redhead who'd just walked in with Drax at her side. "Since when has she been allowed back in this room? After what she pulled, I'd think her privileges would be permanently revoked."

"Didn't you hear?" Oz asked. "They figured out the problem. The poor girl had been starving herself by accident. That's why she was so out of control. Her body was trying to self-correct."

"Starving? What are you talking about? I saw her at breakfast every day." Dahlia's brows pulled together as she spoke.

"Sex, sweetie. He means sex. She's a succubus. She needs a steady supply of sexual energy to keep herself in tip-top shape."

Dahlia's cheeks turned pink. "And when she first came here, she was celibate. But now that she's full, you mean to say—"

"She's fucking," Oz interjected with a laugh. "Actually, no. Not any of the residents, anyway. I heard she's a cam girl." He waggled his brows. "They gave her computer back so she could resume her work. There hasn't been an incident since."

Now that he mentioned it, I wasn't affected by her like I had been in the past. Everyone seemed more at ease, in fact.

"How can you possibly know that?" Sorcha said with a roll of her eyes. "You are such a horrible gossip, Oswald."

"This isn't news." Oz waved a hand. "You love my gossip."

"Yes, I do. It's better than watching those horrible housewives on the telly." Sorcha continued to track Merri's journey around the room, her lips pinching in a frown. "Still, I think it best not to tempt fate. I don't trust her not to make a fool of me again, and the last thing I want is to find myself spreadeagle on a card table with Scrabble tiles stuck to my arse. If you'll excuse me," she said, not waiting for any of us to bother to reply before she swanned out of the room.

Oz snorted. "Dramatic much?" But he was quick to

stand and follow, offering Dahlia a hasty "Toodles, dollface."

After they left the room, Dahlia turned to me, concern etched on her face. "Tor, what does this mean for you? The people think you're—"

Chest tight, I took a slow, steadying breath. "I can't go without my hunts. It means nothing. I've done nothing wrong, and if they come for me, I'll prove it."

"How?" I didn't need our connection to interpret the emotion bleeding through the lone word. She was worried.

So was I.

But not because I was scared of a fight, I'd trained as a warrior since I was old enough to hold a sword. Battle would never frighten me. No, the thing keeping me awake at night was wondering who else would get caught in the crossfire.

Threading my fingers through Dahlia's hair, I pulled her closer, pressing her cheek against my chest so I could rest mine on the top of her head. Breathing in the scent of her, I willed my inner beast back. She was here. Safe and in my arms. It was enough.

For now.

Continuing to run my fingers through her hair, I took a deep breath and finally answered her question.

"I have no idea, Kærasta. But I will find a way."

POST-SESSION TRANSCRIPT: HOOK

Dr. Masterson: This is Dr. Elizabeth Masterson. Today marked my first session with new resident, Caspian Hook. These are my observations.

<<chair squeak>>

Dr. Masterson: Subject name, Caspian "Captain" Hook—hereinafter referred to as F523. Species, high-born fae with ties to the Sea Court. Age unknown, but appears to be in his late twenties to early thirties, as with all fully matured fae. Height, six feet, though he claims to be six foot two. Weight, undocumented. Notable markings, hoop earrings, multiple tattoos, most notably a Jolly Roger on his right forearm. Presents as a pirate rather than the high-born fae his blood suggests. Claims to be Captain Hook from Raven-ndel. This remains to be seen. *heavy exhale*

<<chair squeak>>

<<typing>>

Dr. Masterson: F523 is going to be a challenge. He believes —wrongly—that he arrived by nefarious means, specifically that he orchestrated his admission to Blackwood unbeknownst to us. As a high-born, full-blooded fae, his glamour is extremely potent. In fact, despite our numerous fae residents, I've never seen anyone that matches him in this area. Even our strongest potion designed to neutralize glamour has proven ineffective so far. We might have to double or even triple the dose. Note—reach out to Belladonna coven. Perhaps they know of something that might be of assistance in this regard.

<<rifling of paper>>

Dr. Masterson: In addition to the removal of several unauthorized weapons upon his intake, we confiscated multiple bags of pixie dust. Due to that revelation, I recommend F523 undergo a detox program prior to beginning any further treatment. It is also my recommendation that F523 be kept under close surveillance. Until his glamour is successfully managed, he is a risk both to staff and the other residents. Also, it is important that we uncover his motivations for quote 'sneaking into' end quote Blackwood. He does not appear to recognize that he was already on our admissions list, but the fact that he wanted to willingly be placed here suggests ulterior motives that might threaten our own mission.

<<fingers drumming on desk>>

Dr. Masterson: *musing hum* Yes. Yes, I think that will do nicely. *clears throat* I will assign additional security to covertly watch him. He's crafty, and cannot know he's being watched, so as he identifies as a pirate, I will ask some of Blackwood's mages to take the forms of a gossip of mermaids and keep tabs on him. Nautica, our only current mermaid resident, will benefit from having some perceived fellow merfolk around as well.

<<phone receiver being lifted>>

<<dial tone and dialing>>

Dr. Masterson: Joffrey, please collect the mages and send them to my office.

<<static>>

End of transcript.

NINETEEN

HOOK

The spade pierced the damp earth, the sound of it sliding along rocks and mud almost like a song under the night sky. "Nighttime is the best time. It's the right time for trouble. That's what the lads said when we'd go on our secret missions, wasn't it?"

I gave an emphatic nod, answering my own question.

"Darkness to hide all manner of sins. No witnesses but the stars, or the lady on the moon, and she's not exactly talking, is she?" I chuckled, my endless stream of chatter much more preferable than the haunting whispers crowding my head.

"You'll never find it."

"You're wasting your time."

"You'll die here."

And then a new voice joined the chorus, one I recognized from my encounter the other night at The Hag's Tooth.

"You may as well crawl in there and lie down. This hole will be your grave at this rate."

Raising my voice, I spoke louder to drown out the

225

mental intruders. "But you stars. You're tricky little bastards, aren't you? You tell all the secrets because you just can't help it. Shh! Shh! Don't tell on me. I'll fill in all the holes. I promise."

After a few more tosses of dirt, I leaned against the wooden handle of my tool, sighing in defeat. "It isn't here either. Bloody hell, if I get my hands on that sniveling poltergeist, he's done for. Leading me on a merry chase. He better not have been lying."

Reaching into my pocket, I pulled out my makeshift map and the pen I'd been using to track my progress. Hands full, I used my teeth to pull off the cap, then spit the bit of plastic in the dirt. I'd find it later.

"Not here. Not there. Not anywhere. What a mystery."

I marked an X across the quadrant I'd created on my brilliant map before narrowing my eyes and looking from the illustration to the actual patch of the grounds I'd been searching. Holes littered the garden from every unsuccessful digging session.

"Usually X is supposed to mark the *right* spot," I muttered with a frown. "Drat. Have I been doing it wrong again?"

Tick

Tick

Tick

Panic flashed through me, a white-hot warning of approaching danger.

"Faster. Faster. Dig deeper, Caspian."

"The better to bury you in."

"Ah! No. You're not welcome here. Leave me!" I shouted, swatting at the air by my ear as if I could force the voice to leave.

I stepped backward, trying to put some distance

between myself and the nonexistent creature hissing in my ear. My foot landed in a hole some inconsiderate prick had dug, and I toppled arse over tea kettle onto the ground, landing with a thud.

"Just give up."

"Stay here forever."

"Death is the inevitable end."

"Yes, that is what I've been trying to tell you. Creator above, why does no one ever listen?"

Huffing, I got to my feet and brushed the mud off my backside before glancing frantically around.

Tick

Tick

Tick

The crocodile was getting louder. He was closing in on me. I couldn't let him catch me.

Deciding the holes were some other sod's problem, I turned back toward the castle and made a run for it. There wasn't time to follow the clearly paved path. The quickest way to get from one point to another was a straight line, hedges be damned. I leaped over the manicured row of shrubbery and bounded through the rose garden, thorns catching on my clothing.

"No, not that way!" the interloper groaned. *"You're going the wrong way, pirate. You're supposed to be fleeing* from *Blackwood, not running headlong toward it."*

The certainty in the words made me falter.

"Leave Dahlia. Leave Blackwood. It's the only way."

Just the thought made my heart ache with agony.

"She's your mate."

"The only true path."

"Dahlia is the cure."

For once, the whispers' commentary was welcome.

Whether they spoke true or not, well, it was the only truth I wanted. Without my compass, Dahlia was my north star, always leading me back to myself. Leading me home.

Dahlia was my home.

I'd already given up one. I would not willingly give up another. No matter the cost.

Tick

Tick

Tick

Letting out a startled cry, I took off again, singing to myself beneath my breath to offset the persistent cacophony in my head. If I didn't listen to their words, were they even really talking?

I burst through the door and tore up the staircase, not bothering with so much as a hello to the vampire and demon necking in the alcove. That terrible ticking was still hot on my heels, but perhaps the crocodile would go for Sorcha instead of me. I wondered vaguely if she'd be willing to dispatch him for me?

Maybe if fang and claw weren't enough, she'd disagree with his belly. Poison him from the inside out. So what did I care the manner of the fiend's demise, so long as he left me alone?

Blissful silence. That's all I wanted.

No one appreciated silence until they were robbed of their sanity.

I'd read once of a town somewhere in the UK where the residents heard a persistent humming. One by one, the townsfolk went insane because after they heard it, the sound couldn't be ignored.

Was this the same?

No. Dahlia could make it go away. She would. I'd crawl

into her bed, and she would mute the noise until all I heard was her sweet voice.

Better still, her moans.

Dahlia was the cure; wasn't that what the whisper had said?

Time for Hook to take his medicine.

Reaching her door, I threw it open and then slammed it closed behind me, not caring who I woke. For one suspended moment, I pressed my ear to the door, listening hard to see if I was still being followed.

Tha-thump

Tha-thump

Bless the gods above and below, it was only my heart-beat chasing me. Rolling my body so that my back was pressed to the door, I stood there and sucked in lungfuls of air, closing my eyes and working hard to calm my racing heart.

A blissful silence washed over me as my pulse evened out and Dahlia's sweet scent filled my nose. Everything was better when she was near me, and it was abundantly clear my madness had become a danger. I didn't think that was ever really a question, but before, at least it was manage-able. The madness came in fits and bursts, but now it was constant. As soon as I slipped away from my mate, the whispers would return as if they never stopped.

A conversation told in pieces.

Part of me had hoped that the tattoo would be some sort of bandage. But no. Whatever other power I'd obtained, that was not among them. Perhaps I was suffering from a much stronger curse. It certainly felt like my madness was a curse.

Or a death sentence.

Was this what Tor had felt like moldering away in his cell?

Dahlia had set him free. Helped him find a path back. Why, too, could she not do the same for me? Surely that blasted compass couldn't be the only remedy.

Her soft moan filled the room, pulling me out of my reverie and into the moment. The curtains were open, allowing moonlight to spill across the bed. Goddess, she was startlingly beautiful. She sighed and rolled onto her back, her hand resting between her breasts, wrist displaying my bracelet as though she knew I was there.

If solace was what I sought, then what better way to find it than buried between her thighs? Heart racing for a different reason now, I stalked across the room, tugging off my soiled clothing.

My sweet darling was wearing nothing more than a camisole that covered her full breasts but still offered me a perfect view of her hard nipples beneath the fabric. I hoped when I pulled down the sheets, I'd find her in a thin pair of knickers I could easily remove without waking her. Or perhaps nothing at all. Would I be so lucky?

Quiet as a church mouse, I grasped the corner of the blanket she was snuggled beneath between my thumb and forefinger, carefully lifting it and pulling it off her slumbering form. Dahlia let out a sleepy little groan, but otherwise didn't move.

"White cotton? Well, well, look at my Wendy-bird, all innocent and sweet. Just waiting for her captain to come ruin her." My voice was nothing more than a rough whisper as I ran my fingertip over the gusset just over her pussy. I wanted this fabric translucent from how wet I could make her even while she slept.

But I couldn't risk waking her with foreplay, not when

230

her darkest desire was to be taken fully while she slept. When she opened her eyes, it would be to the realization that my dick was deep inside her.

Still, I didn't want to hurt her. Reaching for the drawer beside her bed, I took out the bottle of lube she kept there and liberally coated my cock. I couldn't help but take a second to appreciate how it glistened in the moonlight.

That handled, I climbed up onto the bed beside her, my movements slow and measured as I carefully took her by the ankle and pulled her leg to the side. I kept waiting for her to wake up, to catch me before I could complete my mission, but the gods must have been on my side because she didn't so much as twitch an eyelash as I got myself into place.

My whole body hummed in anticipation as I pulled her knickers to the side and bared that plump, perfect cunt. If I had more time, if I knew she wouldn't wake, I'd dive in face first and make her come in her sleep before sliding inside her. But the way her eyelids fluttered and the little furrow between her brows deepened indicated she wasn't far from consciousness even now.

I was desperate to give this to her. She'd done so much for me, more than she even knew. Dahlia wasn't just the balm to my madness. She was the answer to decades-old prayers. It was only fair I repay her in some small way. To my knowledge, I was still the only one of her mates who knew about this specific fantasy. It was time to make it a reality.

Pressing my tip to her entrance, I bit back a groan as I pushed forward and her tight walls gripped me. As slowly as I possibly could, I inched deeper, holding my breath, limbs trembling from the effort not to slam home. Goddess, she felt so good.

It was a tight fit, far tighter than usual, as unprepared as she was, but she didn't stay that way for long. As I slid back out, just as slowly and carefully as I went in, I bent over so that my face hovered just above hers. I wanted to watch the play of her expressions. I didn't want to miss a second of her realizing what was happening.

This time my thrust was smoother as her cunt became slick and welcoming. A soft mewl of pleasure escaped her now parted lips, and even though her eyes were closed, I could see the flush creeping up her face. She was waking up for me. Any moment now, my darling would open her eyes. I was sure of it. Fuck, I was running out of time. I wanted her to wake up with my cum inside her, but even more, I wanted her to come around my dick in her sleep if I could get away with it.

I rocked my hips, sinking deeper into her warm, slick pussy as I chased my release, eyes never leaving her face. When she opened for me, I needed the first thing she registered to be me.

"Fuck, darling. How are you still sleeping?" I bit out, reaching between us and toying with her clit as I continued moving carefully inside her.

By normal standards, I wasn't fucking her particularly hard or fast, but you'd think any motion of the ocean would be enough to wake her up. Not to mention that most excellent curve I was blessed with. Usually she was a moaning mess with each thrust because I knew exactly how to hit the spot.

Another rush of wetness flooded her pussy as her walls fluttered around me, and her breaths became rapid pants. A sweet whimper escaped her, and she squirmed before it happened, the rhythmic pulse of her release.

"Ah, fuck, Dahlia," I grunted, spilling inside her as her warm inner walls milked me dry.

Her eyes were open now, her lips parted in a sleepy smile. "Mmm, that was even better than I imagined."

"Were you awake that whole time?"

"No," she murmured, leaning up to press a kiss against my lips. "Not until the very end. I've gotta say, orgasms are the best alarm clocks."

"How did you stay asleep? I thought for sure you would've woken the moment I touched you."

She flicked her gaze to the bedside table, an empty mug the only thing there.

"Tea?"

"I got a sleeping draught from one of the healers."

Confusion collided with horror. "Oh shit, Dahlia. I'm sorry. You were wearing your bracelet . . . If I'd known, I wouldn't have—"

She lifted her finger and pressed it to my lips. "I took it so I could stay asleep once you realized I had the bracelet on, Cas. You didn't do anything wrong."

"But drugging is a hard limit for you. You were very clear about wanting to be fully coherent."

"Yes, Cas. Being drugged is a hard limit. Not me willingly taking something that would help me sleep so we could do this."

I frowned. "So . . . I can't spike your wine, but you can take whatever you want?"

"Exactly."

"Somehow that's even hotter."

Her smile took a sinful cast. "I know." Her gaze moved over my face, her smile dimming as she took in my dirt-smeared countenance. "Rough night?"

"I'd rather not talk about it," I said, bumping her nose

with mine. I'd only just managed to reclaim my equilibrium. I didn't want to invite a return of the madness.

"Sleep, then?"

I pulled out of her, making us both groan before flopping down at her side. "Sleep. And perhaps a round two in the morning."

"Or before then, if I'm lucky."

Chuckling, I wrapped her in my arms and pulled her against my body, needing her near in a way I wasn't sure she'd ever fully comprehend. Before long I was drifting off to sleep, the ticking long since banished, and the whispers a faint but terrifying memory.

No one was going to take my Dahlia from me.

Not even a motherfucking angel.

TWENTY

"Who's the most handsome boy in the whole world? It's you. That's right, don't let anyone tell you different. You got that big dog energy."

I watched Hades, the king of the underworld, baby talk his bichon. The tiny, teacup-sized puppy was on his back in the middle of my bed as my tall, dark, and dangerous mate massaged a moisturizing balm into the pup's toe beans.

There was no stopping my giggle before it escaped.

Hades pinned me with glowing blue eyes. "You laughing at me, baby doll?"

"Nope," I said with a shit-eating grin before I averted my gaze and returned my focus to Kiki's notes.

I definitely was.

"The winter air is hard on his pads. I gotta make sure he's looked after."

"Uh-huh."

"I'd do the same for you if you needed it."

One brow raised as I glanced at him again, this time finding the man using a—I shit you not—steam brush on

Asshole's face. I didn't even know what that was supposed to do, but the little pup was eating up every second of his pampering sesh. Hell, I would, too, if Hades was the one giving it to me.

Heh. I loved when Hades gave it to me.

"Are you offering? I could use a massage," I said, reaching my arms into the air and stretching my sore muscles. I knew what I was doing, the movement arching my back and pushing my tits out so he'd have a better view.

But my lord Hades didn't answer me because he'd already turned back to the dog. Now he was using tiny cotton swabs to clean out the puppy's ears. Wow. Cock blocked by an Asshole. Who would've thought?

I couldn't find it in myself to be jealous. Hades just looked too damn cute catering to his familiar's needs. For as grumpy and rough around the edges as he could be, he had a soft spot for that dog. And there was something undeniably sexy about a man who took care of the ones he loved.

"Tell him if he needs a wee bow tie, he'll find one in the top drawer of Joffrey's dresser." I jumped at the sound of Myrtle's voice from behind me. I'd gotten so accustomed to the soft hum of her energy I hadn't even noticed she'd materialized.

"Jesus Jones and the Apostles! Myrtle, don't sneak up on me like that."

"Sorry, I thought you sensed me. Your handsome man there clocked me as soon as I came in."

Hades didn't spare her a glance; he was now rubbing ointment on Asshole's little black nose.

"Perhaps the beastie would look better with little pink bows for the ears."

Asshole opened one eye and growled.

"Don't help me, spirit. He's just fine as he is." Hades put the cap on the salve and snatched a small bottle of what looked like dog cologne.

Asshole barked once in what I could only assume was agreement. Not for the first time, I wished I had a doggy translator. I was dying—no pun intended—to know what that pup had to say.

"Fine. I was just trying to help." She began to fade away, but I stopped her with a cry of her name. I'd been stumped over my ghost-helping issue for days, but maybe she was just the ghost I'd been looking for.

As soon as she heard me, she popped back into her mostly corporeal form. "If you're going to holler at me, you might try using my real name."

Uh . . . fair point.

"What is your name, Myrt . . . I mean . . ."

The sassy ghost rolled her eyes. "Nellie. Nellie Brown," she said, bobbing a curtsy. "Now, what is it you're after?"

"You're not a former resident here, right? I mean, you didn't do anything to get stuck here, did you?"

"Besides live and die here, you mean?"

I knew the moment I had Hades's full attention because there was added warmth on the side of my face. "What are you up to, baby doll?"

"You told me I was trying to help the wrong sort of ghost, but what if Myr—Nellie, here, is the *right* kind of ghost? If she wasn't a resident, that means she should have some redeeming qualities, right?"

"Gee, what a ringing endorsement. I'll be sure to add that to my tombstone if I ever get one. Nellie Brown, she had some redeeming qualities."

I waved a hand. "You know what I meant. You're not stuck here because you did bad, bad things like the other ghosts in the cemetery. Why were you at Blackwood, Nellie?"

Hades pulled Asshole onto his lap and settled in to listen, his shadows shooting out and wrapping around my waist before yanking me to sit next to him. Apparently my desk chair was just too far away for his liking.

I didn't think it was my imagination that Nellie's form glowed a little brighter as she clasped her hands in front of her and began recanting her life's story. "Long ago, I worked for the Duke of Canterbury and his family. I was a simple scullery maid, just a human working for nobility, as was my lot in life. I didn't know they were vampires until I fell in love with the handsome duke. I was a bloody fool, letting him feed from me whenever he wanted. I'd naively thought I'd become his duchess one day. We talked of him turning me so we could be together forever. It's the oldest story in the book. Naive girl, older man, he promises her the world to get beneath her skirts. I knew better, truly I did. What could a nobleman want with a no-name girl like me? But I was blinded by love, see?"

"Who among us," I whispered, my chest tight with empathy for her. "So then what happened?"

"What always happens in these sorts of situations, I'd expect. He was intended for another. We were going to run away together. We had a plan, and I was all packed. I was waiting for him in the spot we'd picked, but he wasn't the one who was waiting for me."

The gasp I gusped. This was up there with my favorite romantic thrillers. I was practically salivating for the big reveal.

"Oh my God, who was it?" I breathed.

If there'd have been popcorn, I'd have been choking on it.

"The dowager duchess. She was so fast I almost didn't see her coming. She snapped my neck and tossed me down the well, along with all my worldly possessions. They sealed it the next day, and I've spent the past many centuries waiting for someone to find me."

"Unfinished business," Hades murmured.

"What's that?" I asked, tearing my eyes away from poor Nellie to look at him. I felt like a bag of dicks for taking her presence here for granted. All this time, she'd just been stuck and I could have done something about it. No AITA post needed. The answer was clear. Yes. I was the asshole.

"Her unfinished business. We need to find her body. Bury the bones. It's what she needs to be ready to cross over."

I glanced at Nellie. "Have you really gone this long without people being able to see you? Surely someone else has."

"They've seen me in fits and bursts. I'm not usually strong enough to manifest. But you, miss. You can see me even at my weakest."

"And why are you tied to this room?" Hades asked.

"It was mine. I can only visit the well and my room. I'm not powerful enough to roam the halls."

God, that was depressing. I couldn't imagine being trapped in one room for the rest of my immortal days. Okay, a room *or* my murder scene. Somehow that was even worse.

"Well, Nellie," I said, slapping my hands on my thighs after releasing a deep breath. "Today's your lucky day. I'm sorry it took me so long to get my head out of my ass to think of helping you, but we're making up for it now, okay?"

"Don't be so hard on yourself, you're only just figuring all of this out," Hades said.

Nellie nodded her agreement. "I've already waited centuries, miss. What's a couple more months? And I'd be lying if I said watching you hasn't been the most fun I've had in ages."

Hades grumbled something unintelligible under his breath, and I ignored the last part of her statement out of sheer self-preservation.

"Well, let's get you out of here, then, Nellie. I don't know about you, baby doll, but the only audience I want is one we consent to."

"I'll meet you at the well!" she chirped.

"Wait! Where's the well?" I asked, but Nellie was already gone, just winked out of existence.

Asshole barked and leapt off the bed.

I raised a brow, feeling a bit like I was a cast member in an old episode of Lassie. "You know where she's going, boy?" I asked, feeling like it was somehow my line and really leaning into the cheese of it.

Asshole barked again and did a little spin.

"You're gonna take us to the well?"

Hades stood and curled his arm around my neck, reeling me into him so he could place a kiss on my temple. "That's enough of that. Asshole, lead the way."

We followed the fluffball outside and to a secluded, overgrown spot I'd never have realized was a fucking well. That was dangerous. Someone could fall in, and we'd never find them.

Oh.

"I should have grabbed my gardening gloves," I muttered, eyeing the thorny branches with a grimace.

"Don't worry, I've got you covered," Hades said, sparks already dancing along his fingertips.

"Burn, baby, burn," I said, waving my arm for him to go ahead.

"Mmm, I think I like it when you call me baby." Fuck me, the warmth in his voice made tingles dance down my spine.

He sent his fire into the brush, setting the entire thing ablaze in moments. We stood beside each other, Asshole sniffing his way along the path and Nellie's ghost hovering next to the flames.

"A wee bit dramatic, don't you think?" Nellie's voice floated on the wind, a little more detached than it had been before. She was weakening after all her conversation.

"Do you want to be at rest or not?" Hades snapped.

I stepped closer to the well, my heart in my throat as I glanced down into the dark pit. Nothing but a black hole greeted me.

"I didn't think this through, did I? Do we have a ladder or a rope or something?"

"Baby doll, when are you going to stop underestimating me?" Hades asked, his palm warm on my lower back.

Before I could sputter an apology, he released a stream of shadow down into the inky depths. Watching him show off had me feeling a lot less guilty.

I stood back, arms crossed over my chest, as I watched him work his magic. His brows were furrowed and lips pressed into a tight line as he focused, but mere moments later, his shadows returned, laden with what most certainly used to be Nellie. Blackened, waterlogged bones were cradled within the shadow tendrils, a skull clearly visible on top.

I don't know what I really expected to feel watching Nellie come face-to-face, or spirit-to-skull if you will, with her remains. It wasn't a happy moment, but it wasn't sad either. It was more of an inbetween. An acceptance muted by grief.

"The servants have a kirkyard just beyond that copse of trees there. It's hidden so the duke and his family never had to see it."

Of fucking course. "Royalty," I grumbled. "A bunch of pompous assholes."

Asshole barked in protest.

"Sorry, buddy. I meant musty scrotums."

Hades cleared his throat.

I threw up my hands in exasperation. "What's wrong with that one?"

"You do know I'm royalty, right? As are at least two of your other mates."

"Yeah, well . . . something."

"I do love to render you speechless," he said before lowering his lips to my ear. "But my preferred method is to fill your mouth with something other than words."

For once I was certain I had the perfect comeback. "If you render me speechless, I don't have *any* words. So there!"

He chuckled and shook his head. "That one went right over your head, didn't it, pretty girl?"

"I . . . you . . . Stop flirting with me! We have a body to bury, Hades."

"Oh, by all means, please go on. I have so few pleasures left." Nellie's teasing tone made me feel a little less guilty about not heading right for the kirkyard.

Once again, Asshole led the way, using his doggy expertise to find the perfect spot. He took care of most of the digging for us, Hades stepping in with his shadows when the hole got too deep for Asshole to carry on.

"Can I take them from you?" I asked Hades, gesturing to the bones.

"Are you sure you want to?"

"I need to do this. It's important to me that I lay her to rest."

Nellie's death had been filled with cruelty and a blatant disregard for her life. I wanted to give her final moments the honor and dignity she deserved. That every living soul deserved. Well, except for scumbag murderers and the like.

Hades kept them aloft with his shadows while I carefully selected them one at a time before placing them into the fresh grave. A tear slipped down my cheek when I rested her skull just above her bones.

Using his shadows, Hades filled in the grave, and when it was done, we stood in silence, waiting for something to happen.

Maybe I needed to say something? "I'm so sorry this happened to you, Nellie."

She gave me a nod as if to say it was fine, then began glancing around the area, clearly looking for her way out.

"Hades," I hissed. "Why isn't the light lighting?"

"I'm sorry, what?"

"You know, the big glowy light? Or the door that opens so she can cross over? I'm supposed to shed a few tears as the ghost thanks me, and then the music swells and she's, you know, sucked off."

Hades choked on a laugh. "That's not what happens. There's no sucking off, I promise."

Asshole let out a series of enthusiastic yips, and I was certain he was asking for a suggestion box. Especially when Hades shook his head and muttered, "No, we cannot make that a reality."

Hades turned his attention to Nellie. "When you died, did a reaper come for you?"

She nodded. "I was so confused. She tried to get me to go with her, but all I wanted was to find my love. He was waiting for me. I didn't realize I had died, not until it was too late."

"I see."

"Are you telling me there's no way to help her cross over now? She missed her chance, so she's stuck here forever even though I helped her with her unfinished fucking business? If so, you suck."

Hades met and held my infuriated stare. "King. Of. The. Underworld." Each word was bitten off and growled. "Seriously, stop underestimating me. I'm a fuckin' god, baby doll. There are always loopholes."

I blinked a few times, not wanting him to see how damn hot that was. "I'm waiting. Explain these loopholes."

Hades glanced past me at Nellie, his expression going gentle. "I can take you over. Just follow me."

"W-wait!" I shouted, grasping his arm and tugging him back. "Where the hell do you think you're going, mister? You are not just taking off and leaving me behind. I remember what you said about Asshole. How if he left, he might not be able to come back. And you were just going to what, prance off without so much as a by-your-leave? Or even a goodbye kiss? What the actual fuck, dude?"

He opened his mouth as if to protest, but I stopped him. "And another thing! What if you can't get back? You had your whole fucking rant about how I was your destiny and your soulmate and goddamned Persephone. You think you can just leave me here? No way. Not today, Hades."

As with most of my rants, he just watched me with a small, amused smile. "You done?"

"Not remotely."

"Too bad," he murmured, taking my chin between his thumb and forefinger and laying one on me. Once he'd rendered me speechless, this time with his tongue in my mouth instead of his dick—no, his earlier joke had not gone over my head—he whispered, "I already told you, you're stuck with me. If you can't go with me, then I'm coming back to you. The end. There's no other option, baby doll."

Asshole barked as just beyond us, a portal opened, the swirling energy the same flame blue as Hades's eyes.

He laced his fingers through mine, his grip firm and strong. "Come on, then," he said, giving my hand a squeeze. "It's past time you got to see what your home looks like."

I glanced from the portal to the estate in the distance, a little bit of panic racing through me at the thought of leaving my other men. But Hades promised we'd come back, right?

No, actually, he hadn't. He'd just said *he'd* come back if I couldn't go with him. Not exactly the same thing.

As we walked through the portal, Nellie at his side and me trailing behind him with our hands linked, I knew something wasn't right. I could feel the magic of Blackwood rooting me to the grounds. Apparently the underworld was a bit too far away. Hades didn't waver, though; he continued walking confidently toward the portal. Then he was stepping through it, and I . . .

I was standing in the same place. The portal was gone, along with my mate, his dog, and my ghostly roommate.

"Well, shit."

TWENTY-ONE

"F uck."

"I told you not to try and bring her, boss. Now she's gonna be so mad at you. You'll be in the doghouse for weeks."

"Wouldn't be the first time." I tore my eyes away from the empty space where the portal had just been and looked down at Asshole's furry body. "You really gonna stick with that form? You don't want to go back to your slobbering, three-headed glory."

"Nah. I kinda like this one. It's grown on me."

"Really?"

"I think it's adorable," Nellie said. "He's a wee beastie."

"See?" Asshole said, wagging his tail. "She thinks I'm an adorable wee beastie."

"Suit yourself."

Nellie's eyes grew wide as she took in her new surroundings. Her form was solid here, her essence matching that of this realm. It was only her eyes that exposed her for what she was, those silvery blue, mirrored orbs a dead giveaway. Pun intended.

Surprising myself, I took her hand and gave it a squeeze. "Come on, Nellie. Let's get you checked in."

She glanced down at where our hands were joined, then looked up at me, an almost pained expression on her face. "I haven't touched another person in centuries."

"That's all about to change. You're where you belong now. Nearly everyone here is just like you."

Asshole snickered, trotting along at my side as I led Nellie down the path that would take us to the reception area. "I really thought you were about to make a dirty joke."

"I'll leave those to you," I muttered.

As we strolled together through my domain, I took a moment to soak it all in. I'd missed the beauty of the dark sky above, the world bathed in nothing but the light of my very own moon and stars. In the distance, I caught sight of the glow coming from the River Styx. My gut twisted in anticipation. I hadn't realized how much I craved the comfort of my realm. Would Dahlia enjoy being here? Gods, I hoped she would.

Despite popular belief, the underworld was not all brimstone and hellfire. That was the other guy's realm. Mine was more peaceful, at least in the central areas. The one thing everyone got right was the river. Filled with the luminescent souls of the dead, it glowed with their light. Every now and then a row boat with a lantern would float down the water, one of my reapers and the soul they were escorting the sole occupants. There was a lone dock for them to disembark and then the main gates.

The gates were misleading in their simplicity, though the demarcation they represented was very real. Beyond the two wooden posts, a soul would find a multitude of possibilities: punishment, salvation, peace, or perhaps a chance for redemption. The path they'd be sent on was chosen based on the way they'd lived. Oftentimes we'd receive a soul who thought they were doomed to an eternity in the hellfire they'd been taught to fear. But that punishment was saved for the worst of the worst. As with most things, the afterlife was a spectrum. Shades of gray, if you will.

Leading Nellie down the main walkway, I ignored the side paths that would lead to other sections of my realm. She didn't need to worry about those.

"Don't worry, doll face. You're gonna be just fine," Asshole said, giving Nellie a little lick on the ankle. "My guy Hades won't let anything happen to you."

"Are you certain?" Nellie asked.

"You'll get what you've earned. Nothing less."

We joined the line of souls waiting to be given their assignments.

"Next!" Janine, the underworld's resident greeter, sat behind a broad white desk at the head of the line, her curly red pixie cut standing out in stark relief against the plain backdrop behind her.

I smirked at her chosen appearance. This woman had been working for me since before I stole my Persephone. Her visage had gone through more changes than trends on this generation's social media. Today she wore a fluffy black cardigan buttoned at the throat, sparkly cat-eye glasses attached with a bejeweled chain around the back of her neck, and crimson lipstick that matched her hair.

"Name?"

"Bethanny Johannson."

"Death date?"

"Uh . . . today?"

Janine blinked at the poor soul and shook her head. "Do you have your papers?"

"P-papers?"

She chewed her gum loudly as she manifested a keyboard and typed something into a nonexistent computer. "I swear, those reapers are getting lazier every year. Did yours give you anything? A receipt? A document? Even a token?"

Bethanny shook her head, her shoulders tense. "I'm sorry. I just followed him onto the boat."

Rolling her eyes, Janine continued typing, then held out a hand. "Gimme your finger, sweetheart."

"What?"

"Your. Finger. I need a drop of your soul so I can run you through the system since *someone* didn't do his job. I bet it was that handsome prick, Chad."

The girl did as she was bade, a little gasp escaping her as Janine took the drop of essence that she needed.

Nellie leaned in close. "She's not going to do that to me, is she? I dinnae like needles."

"Don't worry, doll face. You're with the man himself. You'll breeze through this." Asshole nipped my ankle. "Right, boss? She's been through enough, hasn't she?"

I nodded. Having heard Nellie's story, I doubted she was destined for any major punishments. Would be easy enough to make sure she landed somewhere pleasant to spend the rest of her days.

"All right, sweetheart. Third door on the left. The. Left. It's on your head if you choose the wrong one."

Ah, sweet Bethanny got to go through to the Elysian Fields. Good for her.

"Next!" Janine shouted as a bedraggled man approached. "Name. Death date. Paperwork," she said in rapid fire.

"Um, Scott Alwyn. Death date was . . . a few days ago, I think." He shoved his paperwork at Janine.

She snatched the papers from his hand and read them over. "Oh, lethal injection, huh? I'm assuming you already know where you're going, then?"

"Please, I've paid for my crime. Can't I try again?"

"You paid with one life. You stole seven."

"But I was only convicted for—"

"Save it for someone who cares, buddy. I've heard it all, and I ain't buying the shit you're peddling." She pointed to the right. "Elevator. There's only one button. You can't miss it."

It carried on like this for another handful of recently deceased. Then it was Nellie's turn. My unflappable receptionist nearly fell off her stool when she looked up and found me.

"Boss! What are you doing, slumming it down here? Did you actually wait in line?" She craned her neck around me as if checking for confirmation.

Not wanting to be left out, Asshole let out a series of joyous barks and shot around the desk.

"Oh my gods! Look at you! Love the new look, shnookums."

"You're looking fit yourself, hot stuff," Asshole said, earning himself a couple extra chin scritches.

I cleared my throat and redirected the conversation. "This isn't a social visit, Janine. I've brought someone through the gates who missed her boat."

Janine gave Nellie a once-over. "Oh, by the looks of your outfit, honey, you're really late to the party. But if Hades himself is escorting you . . ."

"We solved her murder!" Asshole piped up. "Poor broad was thrown down a well. It was fuckin' tragic, Janine. I'm telling you. She was in love and everything."

"Oh, honey. All right, let's get you sorted out. What's your name?"

"Nellie Brown."

"Death date?"

Nellie shrugged.

"Right, right, doesn't matter. I'm guessing you don't have any paperwork, what with the missing your reaper and all."

Nellie shook her head.

"Finger, please."

"Wait," I said, "we don't need to process her."

Janine gaped at me. She couldn't have looked more offended if I'd asked Asshole to shit in her coffee cup. "What do you mean? We have protocols for a reason, boss."

"And as the one who wrote the protocols, it's my right to break them when the occasion calls for it."

Janine held up both her hands, scoffing, "Well, I never."

I turned to Nellie and stared into her mirrored irises, searching for the truth in her soul. She wasn't perfect, but no one really was. The woman hadn't lived long enough to do something heinous enough to earn her any kind of punishment.

"You have two choices, Nellie. I can send you off to the Elysian Fields, where you'll never know pain or sorrow again. Or, you can drink from the River Lethe and forget everything you've ever known and start all over with a blank slate. There's no guarantee your life will be kind to you, but there's also every possibility it will."

Nellie swallowed, clearly struggling with her choice.

Asshole took the bottom of her dress and tugged until she looked down.

"Door number two, doll face. Maybe this time your

prince charming and you will ride off into the sunset together."

"I didn't take you for a romantic," I murmured.

"You fucking kidding me? I am *the* romantic. Why else would I have followed your ass around the mortal realm all these years?"

Nellie bit her lower lip and nodded before looking straight at me and saying, "I want to do it again."

Janine sighed. "Thank the gods. Good choice, sweetheart. Down the hall, second door on the left."

I walked Nellie to the doorway, the rushing river audible as soon as she opened the door. She turned to me and wrapped me in a tight hug, catching me off guard as she said, "Thank you."

"Go on now. Make good choices, and don't let me catch you heading for any of the punishments next time."

Then she was gone, and the door shut behind her. I never really interfered with the sorting of souls, but I had to admit, this was a good experience for me. As I returned to Janine and Asshole, my gaze fell upon the small child who was next in line, a reaper escorting him but struggling to comfort him.

It wasn't very often I came across a kid in my realm. Not for any lack of them, but as a whole, they were innocent, meaning they didn't require my special brand of attention. Almost always they were sent straight for reincarnation, but if he was here waiting to be sorted out, then he must have already gone through the process a few times. Poor soul.

I crouched down so we were at eye level. This kid had to be no older than four.

"What's wrong, buddy?" I asked.

"I want my mummy," he whimpered. "Where is she?"

"What's your name, little man?"

"B-Bradley."

"Bradley what?"

"Thompson."

Reaching out, I took his hand and closed my eyes. His mother was in the Elysian Fields. Waiting for him. "See that door?" I asked after I opened my eyes and adjusted us so he was standing in front of me.

"Uh-huh."

"Your mom is waiting behind it."

"She is?" The awe in his voice nearly broke me. "Are you sure?"

"I am." Standing, I scooped him into my arms, his little body so light as I carried him. Tossing a look back at Janine, she simply nodded, understanding exactly what I needed to do.

The door opened as we approached, sunlight and gentle birdsong filtering out. As I expected, there was a woman with Bradley's exact shade of hair standing in the doorway.

"Hi baby, I've been waiting for you," she said, her smile so big it hurt to look at. This kind of joy, the special brand forged from grief, always hit hard.

"Mummy!" Bradley shouted, squirming in my arms until I let him down. "I missed you so much, mummy!" He bolted through the doorway. I only just managed to see him leap into his mother's arms before the door closed soundlessly behind him.

I had to clear my throat and blink away the pressure in my eyes.

"You all right, boss man?" Asshole asked, sensing as he always did when I was out of sorts.

"I'm fine," I lied. No need to admit I was growing a heart over here. "But I think it's time to head back."

"You're taking me with you, right?" he demanded, not giving me any choice but to catch him as he jumped up into my arms. It was just similar enough to the moment I'd just witnessed that I gave myself permission to rub my cheek over the top of his head and steal a little bit of comfort.

"Of course I am. Now let's go. Dahlia's waiting on us."

CHAPTER
TWENTY-TWO

DAHLIA

I stared at the space where Hades and Asshole had vanished, along with my sweet bathroom ghost. Now that she was gone, I was feeling a lot more nostalgic about her presence in my life—and my room.

"He'll be back. Everything's fine. No need to panic." My muttered mantras weren't doing a whole lot to keep me from a full-fledged spiral, so I had to alter course. If I didn't, I'd stand here waiting for him to come back until it was tomorrow, and nobody wanted that. "Hey! You did it. You finished the business and saved a life. Afterlife? Doesn't matter. Go you!"

With my praise kink activated by my own words, I straightened my shoulders and left Nellie's fresh grave, confident my dark lord would return soon. I was an absolute badass ghost whisperer, and according to Kat the spirit doll, I also had better tits than JLH. So basically, I was absolutely killing it.

"One down, a billion more to go," I said, pep in my step and a little extra sass in my ass. "So who's next on the Dahlia business managing express? Hmm, the Dahlia cross-over cruise? Nope. That's terrible. The Dahlia Moore tour to the underworld. Eh, I'll let Kiki workshop it."

How do you think The Haunts got their name? If it had been up to me, they would have been 'that one band with the British lead singer.' Or, even worse, Untrimmed Bush. Yeah. Naming things was not my specialty. No one was perfect. But in my defense, I pictured Gavin Rossdale from Bush every time I wrote about Ren.

"Talking to yourself again, gem? I hear it's only a problem if the voices talk back."

"Negative, ghost rider. It's only a problem if you're arguing with yourself and you lose."

"How can ye lose if you're arguing with yourself?"

"Exactly."

I looked around, trying to find my sexy dragon boy, but he wasn't behind me or in front of me. Was I hallucinating? Oh shit, was he one of the voices?

"Kai? Where are you?"

He chuckled. "Look up, lass."

I rolled my gaze skyward and found him hovering about fifteen feet above me, shirtless—ungh—and slowly keeping himself afloat with those fuck-hot wings. God, he was so sexy. Did he know what he was doing to me? By the smirk on his face, yes. Yes he did.

"How's the weather up there?"

"It'd be better if I had my mate in my arms."

"Well, get down here and do something about it then."

"I have a better idea. How about you join me up here?"

I stupidly pointed at myself in the chest. "Me?"

"Do I have another mate?"

I shook my head. "This ass isn't airborne, friend."

He landed in a crouch, his wings folding back and head

bowed, and I swear, I orgasmed when he lifted his face and those purple eyes found mine.

New kink unlocked.

"You and your arse seemed willing enough when you asked if you could ride my dragon."

"Well, yeah. Cause he's big and won't drop me."

Kai's expression went stormy, and fuck it all, I shivered. But not with fear. Nope. I was a thirsty bitch, and he was my drink of choice.

"You think I'd drop you?" Affronted might be a really solid word to describe his tone if I wasn't so turned on.

"I mean . . . you're strong, but I'm not exactly petite. Do you even know if those are load-bearing wings? What's the weight limit?"

"You're fucking perfect. We've been over this. You're made for me, and I you. Now wrap your arms around me and don't let go, because we're going for a ride."

My next round of protests died on my lips when he pressed a finger to them.

"Do as I say, mate."

"I think you just graduated from dragon boy to dragon daddy."

He let out a low growl of approval and then brought his lips to my ear. "Not yet. You can make me a daddy any time you want, though."

A ripple of arousal hit my lady parts, and our conversation from Christmas morning returned to me. I hadn't given too much more thought to the idea of letting Kai breed me. Of what it might be like to create a family with my men. How different such a unit would be than the one I'd grown up in.

Just a month ago, the thought would have sent me

running—and you know how I feel about running. But now? Now I didn't hate it at all.

I wrapped my arms around the back of his neck and he pressed a kiss to my temple before whispering, "Hold on tight, gem."

"Oh God," I squealed as he lifted off with one big flap of his wings.

"How many times do I have to tell ye? It's Malakai."

"Do not get me all horny when you're carting me through the air, Malakai. That feels dangerous and against FAA regulations."

"If I could, I'd fuck you while we flew over the Highlands. I'd let you ride my cock until you came all over me while my homeland was nothing but a blur beneath us."

Remember those fanny flutters? They were really coming into their own these days, and Kai was a wizard at bringing them front and center.

"Could you do that?" I asked as the wind whipped loose tendrils of hair in my face.

"I dinnae see why not? Shall we try?"

"Uh, maybe not for our inaugural flight," I finally managed when I was capable of forming words. The thought had rendered me stupid, and I got stuck picturing what it would look like if Kai had his way with me while we were flying across Scotland. My pasty ass for all the world to see. The Daily Mail would have a field day. **Smut Writer Fucked by Dragon Man Over Inverness. Full Story on Page 5.**

"Next time, then." Before I could agree, his hold on me changed. "Do you trust me, gem?"

"Enough to let you take me up here without a parachute."

"Good, then let go."

"I'm sorry. I think I just had a stroke. Did you tell me to *let go* of the only person keeping me from plummeting to my death?"

"Ye ken I willnae let that happen."

"I ken you will *try* not to let that happen."

He chuckled at my rough attempt at Scots. "I'm hard-wired to protect ye, gem. I couldn't put you in harm's way if I tried."

"Uh, yeah, you could. Case in point." I would have gestured to the beautiful sky around us, but that would have required loosening my death grip around his neck.

"Close your eyes and trust me, lass. Let me be your wings."

I bit back my Thumbelina joke because there was no way Kai would understand the obscure reference to a movie from my childhood. We had a grand total of five kids' movies on VHS when I was a child in the cult. I had them all memorized. Robin Hood, All Dogs Go to Heaven, Ferngully, Labyrinth, and Thumbelina. Hmm, that explains a lot about the type of men I was attracted to.

I squeezed my eyes shut and released a tense breath. "Okay. Fine. Just . . . please, I'm too young to go out this way."

Kai chuckled, his lips feathering over my temple again as I forced myself to drop my hold. For all of two seconds, I was in freefall, my heart lodging itself in my throat as he spun me around like some kind of Cirque du Soleil acrobat.

"I've got ye, my love. I won't let you fall. Open your eyes and fly."

God, the way he whispered in my ear had my fears vanishing, and I opened my eyes. The breath left my lungs in a shocked squeak as the world below us came into view. Green hills passed under us as white sheep and brown

Highland cows grazed in fields. I'd never seen anything so beautiful, not even when I'd been on an airplane.

"I'm flying," I whispered, feeling every moment of my Titanic dreams being lived in real life.

"You are."

I giggled and held out my arms. "I'm the queen of the world!"

Kai tightened his hold on me and trailed kisses down the side of my neck. "You're certainly the queen of mine."

This man was born to be a fairy prince. Good lord. Just coming out with the swoony lines and walking around with that voice and that body. Oof. No wonder my ovaries were in overdrive. Honestly, I was pretty sure I had just ovulated.

I fought the urge to squirm because I didn't want to give him a chance to prove he'd keep me from falling to my death. But I needed him in the worst way.

"Kai, as much as I'm loving our impromptu tour of the Highlands, I'd really like to go back to your tower now."

"Oh? Are ye cold, gem?"

"Nope. Quite the opposite."

It only took him a second to catch my meaning.

"You might want to close your eyes for this part, then," he rumbled in my ear just before he nosedived at rapid speed.

I didn't close my eyes. I watched us close the distance between us and the grounds of Blackwood, his tower like a beacon calling us home.

Kai was plastered to my back, so there was no mistaking the insistent jut of his erection. My dragon was excited.

Me too, dragon daddy. Me fucking too.

CHAPTER
TWENTY-THREE

KAI

As soon as my feet touched down on the cold, hard stone of my tower, I spun Dahlia to face me and crushed my lips to hers. I'd never flown with someone in my arms before, and knowing the two of us shared this special first between us only added to the experience. Walking her backward as I held her face in my hands and devoured her mouth with mine, I fought my dragon's insistent urging to let him take hold and drive into her here and now.

"Kai, what's gotten into you?" Dahlia breathed against my lips.

"I cannae believe I have you all to myself. I want to take full advantage of the moment."

She smiled against my mouth. "Sounds like you have plans."

"Aye, my wee little mate. Remember what we were discussing before we got so rudely interrupted the last time?"

The way she rocked her hips into me, her breath hitching a little as she did, told me everything I needed to know. She remembered, and she wanted it. I wasn't just going to fuck my mate. She was going to let me breed her. For real.

"Are ye ready for that, gem? For me to fuck you full of my cum and plant my baby in you?"

She gulped, eyes wide as she nodded. "I'm ready for you to try. I won't be heartbroken if it takes a few tries for the baby part."

A deep primal chuckle escaped me as I nuzzled her neck. "It's the trying that's the fun part."

"Are you sure we're . . . compatible that way?"

"One hundred percent. You're my fated mate. There's no question my seed will take root. Eventually."

Her hot little hand trailed over my bare chest until she stopped at my waistband. Goddess, I wanted her to tear open my fly and reach inside. "And what if you break the spell and you're not the one to fill me with your baby? What if it's Tor?"

"I'm not sure I understand the question."

"Well, will it bother you? That you aren't the biological father?"

I shook my head. "Lass, the child will be part *you*. I cannae help but love it and raise it as my own."

She let out a happy sigh. "Couldn't be more perfect if I wrote you."

I grinned, feeling the weight of that compliment sweep through me. "Are ye saying I swept you off your feet, gem?"

"Maaaybe."

I took the opportunity to quite literally do just that, picking her up in my arms and racing down to my room below. Her squeals of delight were music to my ears, her happiness a gift I would never take for granted. If I could hear that sound once a day for the rest of my life, it would be a life well spent.

"Well, mister dragon man, now that you have me all to yourself, what are you intending to do with me?" Dahlia teased as I gently laid her on the bed.

"I thought I made my intentions quite clear. But just so there's no misunderstanding, first, I intend to strip ye bare."

Dahlia's hitched breath and flushed cheeks told me she very much enjoyed where I was going with my explanation, so as I started to strip out of my clothes, I kept going. Outlining in detail how the next couple of hours were going to go.

"Then?" I fucking loved the huskiness of her voice.

"Then I'll break the contraception spell."

"How?"

I smirked, my fingers working their way to the button of her jeans. I needed to bury my face between her thighs and prepare her for my cock.

"With my claw across your perfectly smooth skin. Just a scratch deep enough to disrupt the magic. I'll lick the wound clean and keep going until I'm lapping at your dripping pussy."

"Mmm, that's one of my favorite parts."

"I'm pretty sure when you're with me, mate, they're all your favorite parts."

"It's true. So keep going. What are you going to do to me after I'm a dripping mess?"

It didn't take me long to slide her jeans over her hips and down her legs, the damp patch on her knickers a dead giveaway that she was already wet for me.

"Once you've come on my tongue and fingers, I'm going to stretch you wide, soften you so you're ready to welcome me and take my knot."

Her eyes shifted to the already swelling knot at the base of my erection. She'd seen and played with it before, but she'd yet to feel it inside her. I could sense the smallest hint of apprehension at the thought of the stretch.

"Dinnae worry, love. By the time I knot you, you'll be begging for it. I'll make it so good for you, you will be lost in nothing but pleasure. And when we finally reach our peak together, I'm going to do everything in my power to fill your belly with my child."

She squirmed under me, parting her thighs and raising her hips as though begging me to take her now. I ran my claw over her knickers, shredding the defenseless cotton with ease. Fuck, she smelled good. She smelled like mine.

I was helpless to resist the temptation to taste her. Swooping down, I licked her from arsehole to clit. I would never tire of her taste. Sweet and slick, exactly what I craved.

She arched her back, her cries of pleasure music to my ears as I slid one finger inside her and sucked on every exposed part of her cunt, avoiding her clit on purpose. I was teasing her, of course, but dragging this out was only going to amp up her arousal. I needed my mate as desperate for me as possible in order to give her my knot.

"God, Kai, why are you torturing me?" she whined.

"I'm not. Doesn't this feel good, my treasure? Don't you like the way I eat your pussy?"

She hummed in a mixture of frustration and desire. "Yes, but I want more. I need you inside me. I feel so empty."

Inside, my dragon growled with approval. He was more than ready to fill her. As it was, after her needy words, I was struggling to maintain the course.

"Soon, gem."

I shifted back so I could look at her warm, welcoming pussy, her arousal glistening on the swollen lips I'd been sucking. Tracing them one at a time, I finally rested two fingers on her opening, waiting to feel her try to suck me inside. I needed her so aroused she couldn't stand it before my dick got anywhere near her. She'd taken me before, but this would be far more intense than that.

"Kai, what are you doing?" Her question was a whimpered plea as she rolled her hips and tried to get me to penetrate her.

"Have ye not been paying attention, gem? I already told you. In detail."

"Kai," she groaned, her complaint making me grin. It was working.

Giving her a fraction of what she was after, I slid my fingers through her slick channel, making her cry out when I curled them in a beckoning motion.

"There it is," I murmured, pressing my fingertips up in rapid taps. "Gushing for me, aren't you? You're already doing so well. You'll take my knot like you were made for it."

"Because . . . I . . . oh God . . . I am."

She came around my fingers, a flood of slick release coating the digits and tempting me to taste, but I held off because I knew if I teased her for too long, she'd end up frustrated with me instead of desiring me.

While she was still riding the high of her climax, I added a third finger, pumping it in and out of her, her inner walls squeezing me tight.

"Again, gem. Give me another one."

She bit her lip and closed her eyes, pleasure streaking across her face as she did as I told her. The room smelled of her, and I never wanted that to change. I still hadn't washed the pillow she'd ridden for me as a gift because I couldn't bear to lose the hint of her scent that still lingered.

As her back arched as a second climax crested, I added a fourth digit. Her garbled groan was still all pleasure as she took what I was giving her. The hardest part was still to come, when she was taking my full fist. And even that circumference wasn't as thick as my knot would be. But we'd be close. Close enough that I wouldn't hurt her.

"Can you take more of me?" I rasped, my mouth watering at the way her cum was leaving a wet spot on the bed.

"There's more?" I didn't miss the edge of panic in her tone.

"Aye."

Locking eyes with me, she nodded. "Get me ready for you, Kai. I want to take your knot."

"Tell me if this hurts. I'll go slow, and I'll stop the second you say something."

"It feels good. God, it feels so good."

She rocked her hips, taking me deeper, and I shifted the position of my fingers so I could slide my entire hand inside her up to the wrist. With the way my fingers were positioned, it was a bit like reaching into a bag of crisps.

"Still with me, Dahlia?"

"Uh-huh," she panted, face dewy with sweat, eyelid fluttered, breaths labored.

"You're doing so well, my love," I praised, shifting my body again so I could suck on her clit while I worked my hand inside of her, alternating between slow thrusts and rotating motions. "Come for me, mate. One more, and then I'll give ye what you're really after."

I rolled my knuckles over her G-spot once, twice, a third time, until she fucking squirted, her shocked moan as she came without warning making my cock weep with desperation to be inside her.

While she was coming down, I slid my hand free, not wasting the opportunity to lick her off my fingers. When she saw what I was doing, she whimpered.

"Fuck, why is that such a turn-on? I can still feel the flutters from my last orgasm, and I already want you again."

I winked at her. "That's because I'm good at what I do."

"You're wearing way too many clothes."

I glanced down my body at the black boxer briefs I'd left on simply to keep myself at bay. If I had been nude and that close to her pussy, I wasn't confident I'd have been able to keep from fucking her by this point. "Easily remedied."

Dragging my claw over the fabric, I let it fall to the bed before grabbing her by the hips and pulling her closer to me. My cock throbbed with the promise of what was to come as I positioned myself at her entrance.

"You're a liar, you know," she murmured, reaching between us and stroking me.

I stiffened, my eyes lifting from her glistening cunt to her flushed face. "Me? A liar?"

"Uh-huh. You told me you were going to break the spell and then get me ready. But you're doing it backward. And you still haven't broken the spell. This oven isn't even turned on."

A low, rumbled laugh was my initial response because she was turned on, all right. She was so turned on her cunt was actively trying to pull me inside her right now.

"I didn't know you'd be such a stickler for following an outline. I thought you were a pantser."

"I like to think of myself as a plot gardener. I like to plant seeds and see where they go."

I couldn't resist myself. "I'll help you plant a seed right now."

She giggled, her joy infectious.

"Are ye ready, then, gem? We're at the point of no return. If you're not ready, it's okay. We can wait until you are."

"Malakai Nash, if you do not put that glorious cock inside me right now—"

She cut herself off when I laughed.

"I meant the spell, love. If ye've changed your mind about breaking the spell."

Blinking wide gray eyes at me, she took my hand and placed it over the spot where her tattoo was hidden. "Breed me, Kai."

My claws elongated as the dragon within me flared to life. He loved this, as did I. With a careful drag of my sharp claw over her skin, I broke the spell and sank inside her at the same time.

The only cries out of Dahlia were ones of pleasure as I filled her to the hilt, my knot pressing against her but not slipping inside.

"God, those ridges are magic."

I leaned down until the front of my body was stretched along hers, and then I rolled both of us onto our sides, facing one another. There was something about the gravity of this moment, the thought that we'd agreed to take a step toward building a family together, that made me want this to be intimate and beautiful.

"I love ye, gem. You know that, don't ye?" I asked, reaching up to tuck some hair behind her ear.

"I do. I love you too, Kai. So much."

Grabbing her by the back of one thigh, I hitched her leg

over my hip so I could rock deeper inside her, my knot nearly pressing in this time.

"I cannae wait to see your belly round with a child. Your tits heavy with milk. You'll be even more beautiful than ye already are. If that's possible."

She was wordless as I pressed my knot inside her sweet heat. Her mouth opened on a gasp as I stretched her to the brink.

"Breathe for me, love."

She did as I said and I worked my way inside her, biting back my urge to climax as her cunt squeezed me.

"Look at you, Dahlia. Such a good girl taking my knot like you were made for it."

"Wasn't I?"

"Fuck yes, you were."

I stared into her eyes as I rocked slowly back and forth, unable to pull out and desperate to come.

"I cannae hold back any longer," I whispered through gritted teeth.

"Please come. Oh God, Kai, I need you to. Fuck, your knot is just constant pressure on my G-spot."

"Do you think you can give me one more, gem?"

She was trembling in my hold, her body so stimulated and the pleasure so intense she was struggling to focus. "One more? Kai, the last one's still happening."

Her nearly slurred confession seemed to be all the permission I'd been waiting for, because I came so hard I nearly blacked out.

The walls shook from the roar I released, dust floating from the rafters and the mortar between the stones.

Dahlia was still moaning as my pleasure ebbed, and even though it would shrink down a little, I knew my knot was going to be hitting just the right spot inside her until it was small enough I could slip out of her.

"I know how this knotting thing works, if my fictional research is telling the truth. You're stuck, right? Like a key in a lock?" she asked, raking her fingers through my sweat-dampened hair.

I nodded, pressing a brief kiss against her lips. "Having never knotted anyone before, I cannae say for certain. But from what I gleaned during a very uncomfortable birds and bees chat with my dad, that's the way of things."

"You mean the dragons and the pixies?"

A laugh escaped me, the action making us both moan as we moved. "Whatever you want to call it. I hope you don't mind being stuck with me for a while."

"Kai, I want to be stuck with you for the rest of my life."

I hummed in approval and nuzzled into her neck. "As do I, gem. Eternity won't be long enough."

CHAPTER

TWENTY-FOUR

KIKI

"Now boarding flight S125 to Edinburgh. This is the final boarding call for flight S125 to Edinburgh."

"Sweet baby Jesus in the manger with the donkey," I muttered as I raced down the terminal with my adorable wheelie bag trailing behind me and my phone to my ear.

Fucking Dahlia wasn't answering, and for whatever reason, my text messages weren't going through to her. I had news. Big fucking news, and she needed every bit of it. The last thing I wanted was for her to get caught with her pants down, potentially literally.

"Come on, come on, pick up."

I was so focused on my chant that I didn't notice the six-foot wall of yum until he was slamming into me.

"Oh!" I gasped as my phone flew out of my hand and clattered onto the floor.

His hiss of surprise had me snapping my head up in time to see him grimace at the brown coffee stain on his white T-shirt.

"Watch it," he groused, but to his credit, he bent down to collect my phone before shoving it at me. "Here."

"Thanks. I'm so sorry."

Beautiful blue eyes met mine, and if this was a romance novel, we would've fallen in love right then and there. "Be more fucking careful."

Ooookay, then. This was going to be an enemies-to-lovers trope. My favorite. Challenge accepted, Broody McBrood Face.

He didn't even give me a chance to apologize before he did that sexy man prowl over to the customer service desk. You know the one I mean. It's all swagger and I be fuckin'. Like his internal monologue was telling everyone they needed to make room for his big swinging dick.

Keeping one eye on him, I tried Dahlia again as I lined up behind the rest of the people boarding the plane. Still no answer. Heaving a world-weary sigh, I gave in and decided to leave a message.

"If you've made it this far, you already know who this is. My number's unlisted, which means you're Kiki, so why haven't you texted me yet? You know I hate talking on the phone. Anyway, leave a message if you must. I probably won't listen to it."

Beep.

As the attendant scanned my boarding pass, I launched into my rant.

"Where the heck have you been?" I began, careful of the language I used because there was a little girl with pigtails right in front of me, and her mom looked like she might cut a bitch. "I've been trying to text you, and I've called you four times with no answer. I'm sorry, but you need to get the donkey di—uh, donkey kongs out of your, erm . . . hands? Oh, you know what I mean. I've got news. Big news, and it involves the . . . shmampire shmouncil and some serious stuff that's about to go down."

The attendant waved me forward, and I followed the other travelers down the jet bridge to the plane.

"I can't believe you've been so busy you would ignore me. Me! You better not have do not disturb on. I know I showed you how to give my number emergency access, and bi—babes, this counts as a nine-one-one emergency." I sighed gustily. "They'd better be worth it, and when one of them inevitably knocks you up, you'd better name them after me. Girl or boy. I don't care. Now listen to me, Dahlia, I'm on my way to mother . . . trucking Scotland on a red-eye for you. A *red-eye.* I don't fly overnight, ever. You know that."

I found my spot at the back of the plane and settled in my seat, looking out at the tarmac beyond.

"The last seat available was a fucking middle seat next to the bathrooms at the ass end of the plane, Dee. It already stinks back here, and this is an international flight."

The dude sitting by the window cleared his throat from where he was waiting in the aisle, and all I did was scrunch up a little so he could climb over me. It only took me one fleeting glance at him to recognize Mister Meet Cute from earlier.

"I'll be there in . . . some ungodly amount of time, but I'll be there. We have to get you out of that place before the" —I eyed the hottie and dropped my voice —"shmampire shmouncil gets there because all hell is going to break loose."

He made a soft grunt beside me and shifted in his seat. It was probably too much to hope he wasn't paying attention to my message.

"Anyway, Dee, I told you I would do the thing, and as

always, your girl came through. You better have those bags packed and—"

"Ma'am, I'm going to need you to hang up the phone and put it in airplane mode."

"I'm almost done." I glanced at my seatmate near the window. "He has his computer plugged into seat power. Why aren't you yelling at him?"

"I'm working, and I'm not plugged into anything, lady. Why don't you hang up like the flight attendant said?"

"Because I'm also working, and my bestie needs me. What are you working on over there, anyway? Something ridiculous like financial projections or . . . oh . . . a puffin sanctuary?"

"There was a crisis," he grumbled in what I dare say was an adorable fashion.

"You don't say. Please, tell me more. I love puffins. Did you know their beaks fall off after mating season?"

"Ma'am, your phone, please? I will have to ask you to get off the flight if you can't follow protocol," the flight attendant urged.

My phone? Oh, fuck me.

"Dee, I'm coming for you. Don't worry. We're going to fix this, and you're getting out of there."

"Lady, if you just get off your fucking phone so we can take off, I'll hack into the system and get you back on a call as soon as we hit cruising altitude." God, puffin boy's voice was H-O-T when he was leaning in and whispering in my ear.

I hung up without another word, smiling at the attendant before turning my attention to the man next to me. I gave him the sweetest smile and batted my eyes. "So, tell me about the puffins."

"My partners and I are opening a sanctuary in Scotland. I'm heading there to check out the progress."

"Oh, like business partners? Are you the CEO?"

"No. Like *partners*." He raised his left hand and wiggled his fingers in my face, crushing my dreams of falling in love with my airport meet cute. Or not so meet cute, as it turned out.

Oh well, better luck next time, Keeks. There's sure to be loads of eligible Scotsmen waiting for you. Maybe you have a bearded hottie in your future. One who doesn't have a weird affinity for puffins.

~

Dahlia

"Dee, I'm coming for you. Don't worry. We're going to fix this, and you're getting out of there."

"Lady, if you just get off your fucking phone so we can take off, I'll hack into the system and get you back on a call as soon as we hit cruising altitude."

I shook my head, chuckling to myself as the message cut off. For Kiki's sake, I hope the guy sitting next to her was single and ready to mingle. He sounded hot. Hopefully that would take some of the sting out of her middle seat on a red-eye. For as long as I've known her, Keeks only traveled first or business class. That she'd given that up to get to me spoke volumes.

"Everything okay?" Merri asked, taking a seat next to me before the group session got started.

"Yeah. My friend Kiki has been trying to get in touch.

She is the queen of rambles. Somehow she takes what should be a one-minute message and turns it into a fifteen-minute memo. Which is funny, actually, since she's an editor."

Merri smiled, but it didn't reach her eyes. "At least you have a way to get in touch. I need to talk to my aunt something fierce, but I don't have so much as a phone number for her. She won't answer my emails."

"How does she not have a phone number? I'm basically the queen of the hermits, and even I have one."

Merri shrugged. "She told me once that it's important for a woman in her line of work to always be a bit unattainable."

"Her line of work?"

"She runs *Iniquity*. You know, the sex club?"

"Uh . . . no?"

"Have you never been there?" she asked, eyes wide. "I thought all supernaturals knew about it. It's a hub for them to gather safely."

"I'm not a supernatural."

"Oh, aren't you, darling?" Cas teased, entering the room and the conversation. "You seem pretty supernatural to me. Ghosts, necromancy, that scream of yours. You might be more supernatural than me."

Huh. He had a point. I guess it was hard to unlearn years of misinformation. "Yeah . . ."

Tor stalked in next. I could just make out Bruno in the hallway behind him, his expression strained. They'd resumed their daily sessions in addition to Tor's morning hunts. Today's must not have gone well since they both seemed to be simmering. In what, I wasn't sure, but neither looked particularly pleased.

Tor dropped into the empty chair next to me as Cas approached the same one.

"Hey, I was going to sit there," he complained.

"Not anymore," Tor growled.

My pirate must have sensed the same tension I did because he surprisingly kept his mouth shut and pointed to the chair across from me. "Guess I'll just take that one instead. It has the best view." He tossed me a little wink, making sure I knew he was talking about me. The man was astonishingly unflappable.

It was a relief to see. The last couple of nights, I'd woken up to him crawling into my bed, mumbling to himself about ticking and whispers. He had near-constant dark circles under his eyes and, more often than not, seemed to zone out of conversations. His only reprieve seemed to be when he was with me. I was worried about what would happen when even I wasn't enough to soothe his restless mind.

Kai and Hades both walked in at nearly the same time, Asshole barking and running up to me, his sweet little face begging me to pick him up.

"At least one of us should get to be close to her," Hades grumbled, clearly talking to the dog.

"Later," I whispered, his smoldering stare making my blood heat. He and I hadn't had a chance to be alone since his return from the underworld. As grateful as I was that he was able to come and go at will, either thanks to the weakening wards or just his own godly power, I'd hated being separated from him. Maybe it was the ghost's warning, or maybe I was just codependent on my men after these months of forced proximity. Either way, I wanted to spend some alone time with him to make up for it.

Another flash of desire rocked me when thoughts of my

alone time with Kai came to the forefront of my memory. My cheeks burned, and I was certain they could all tell exactly what I was thinking. Oh wait, they fucking could, and I'd completely forgotten to shield my mind.

Hades chuckled.

Kai smirked.

Tor growled.

And Cas? He spread his legs wide and offered me an invitation to sit on his lap without even saying a word.

I cut a glance at Merri and wondered if she truly had been able to put the lid on her succubus powers. Were my wandering thoughts due to her influence, or was this just me being thirsty?

The roll of Hades's laughter hit my ears again, and I had my answer.

This was all me. It had always been this way when it came to my men.

Dr. Masterson came into the room after we'd all settled. Wisps of hair had come loose from the no-nonsense bun she always wore, her lips pursed and shoulders tense. Very different from her typically calm visage.

"Everything okay, Doctor?" I asked, unable to ignore the sense that something was wrong.

She blinked at me as if surprised by the question. She attempted a smile that I suspected was supposed to be breezy. Instead, it just looked strained. "It's just been a challenging day. Temperance is missing, and Swift returned home unexpectedly, leaving me to deal with the unrest in the town along with overseeing the residents all on my own."

It took everything in me not to flinch when she mentioned Temperance. She could never know. It would crush her to find out her friend and colleague had been a psychopath. "Is there anything we can do to help? Do you really think the townsfolk will try to hurt us?"

Her stare was hard as stone. "They can try. We won't let them."

"Oh, Dr. Masterson, I didn't know you had it in you to be so fierce. I'm a little scared and a tiny bit aroused, if I'm being honest," Cas teased.

"What else is new?" Hades muttered.

"I think it's my fault," Tor said, drawing everyone's attention. "The unrest, I mean. Some folks saw me after one of my hunts and assumed I was the Ripper. I've already adjusted my hunting grounds and cut back on the time I spend in the forest. That should help settle some of the tension."

Masterson smiled at him. "You don't have to take the blame all on yourself, Tor. The Ripper has created a problem for all of us. You are just an easy scapegoat, but it could have just as easily been any one of us. Blackwood is shrouded in mystery and suspicion, as has always been its lot. We will weather this storm as we have every other."

"Would it help if I stood watch in my tower?" Kai asked. "No one willingly comes up against a dragon. If they see me, perhaps it'll scare them away from any ideas of attack."

"Or encourage them to take up arms," Hades said softly.

"What was that?" Masterson asked.

Hades cleared his throat and exchanged a look with Asshole before clarifying. "In my experience, once the fuse is lit, the bomb always goes off. If you give the people a target, they will take aim. Fear is a powerful motivator, and it has a way of making people bold when they should be scared."

"Wise words, Cain. For now, none of you need to worry about what you should be doing. We have security for a reason. I assure you, we have everything well in hand." She straightened in her seat and put her little recorder on the table next to her chair. "Now, let's get down to business," she said, pressing record, "This is Dr. Elizabeth Masterson..."

POST-SESSION
TRANSCRIPT: CAIN

Dr. Masterson: This is Dr. Elizabeth Masterson. Today marked my first session with new resident Cain Alexander. These are my observations.

<<pacing footsteps>>

Dr. Masterson: Subject name, Cain Alexander—hereinafter referred to as U002. Species unknown, but a canine familiar appeared upon his arrival. I suspect he is some sort of powerful mage. Age unknown, but appears to be in his late thirties. Height, six foot two. Weight, undocumented. No notable markings. Abilities, unknown. U002's intake at the referral of Dr. Temperance was unexpected, but he is clearly going to be an asset to my cause. Even without his memories, power bleeds from him.

<<chair squeak>>

<<typing>>

Dr. Masterson: While U002 appears to be an enigma, his attraction and subsequent aversion to Subject M120 is painfully obvious. The two are drawn together, and I wonder if it's due to a similarity in their power? U002 has a darkness inside him I am eager to unleash. Perhaps M120 is the key. I will come up with a treatment plan that keeps the two in close contact. His resistance to her is a clear indicator of something he's repressed.

<<chair squeak>>

Dr. Masterson: If treatment can unlock his memories and release his power, perhaps he will be one of the final ingredients needed to achieve my goals. The energy during group V's first session was palpable. As hypothesized, all of them coming together visibly changed M120's entire aura. U002 might be the last of her mates.

Dr. Masterson: *musing hum* Not who I was expecting, but if my suspicions as to his identity are correct, exactly who I require. I do not feel comfortable stating my theories at this time, but suffice it to say if he's who I suspect, he will be the first of his kind on our premises. There's no way to know if we are properly equipped to handle him if he has an episode. Note—it may be time to look into strengthening the wards.

<<phone receiver being lifted>>

<<dial tone and dialing>>

Dr. Masterson: Instruct all staff to take any and all opportunities to put Dahlia and Cain together. *pause* Yes, we need them to grow closer. *pause* I understand. Yes, all of them do need to bond. *irritated* Yes, that is why they are in group sessions together, but Cain won't open up if anyone else is around. We need them to connect. *huff* If I wanted your opinion, I would've asked for it. *pause* Just see that it's done.

<<phone receiver being set down>>

Dr. Masterson: *heavy sigh* Lizzie dear, I don't know how you do it.
    <<static>>

End of transcript.

CHAPTER
TWENTY-FIVE
LILITH

The familiar strains of static filled the room before the tape clicked off, leaving me and my companions in uneasy silence. My office wasn't unnecessarily large or garish. But with the three of us contained within the walls, it felt small. Perhaps it was the weight of everything we'd learned bearing down on us. We were nearing the end of this little mission, and we were still missing crucial pieces of the puzzle.

"Do you think she knows?" I asked, my question not aimed at anyone in particular.

"Knows what?" Gabriel asked. The angel was perched on the corner of my desk, his legs stretched out in front of him and crossed at the ankles.

"Are you thick? Did God drop you on the head when you were created?" my Drystan spluttered. "Does she know he's Hades? We can only assume these last few happened prior to the previous box of tapes based on the way she was talking about her *subjects*. So, by now, has she figured it out? Clearly Hades knows who he is. Shifty bastard."

"Thank you, *Crombie*. I wasn't speaking to you," Gabriel sneered, but I ignored him.

"If we're going off the information we've gotten from these recordings, I think she suspects, but doesn't truly know who he is." I stood and began pacing the floor, my spiked heels clicking with every step. "We need to get to the bottom of what Death is doing at Blackwood. She's pulling the strings, that much is obvious, but how?"

"She's much more subdued than the other two were. Almost invisible," Gabriel muttered.

"Of course she is. Death comes quietly to every mortal creature, no matter what. She doesn't have to herald her arrival like her sisters. War is loud and brash, bloody and terrible. Pestilence . . . well, doesn't that stand on its own? She starts with a sneeze and ends with a rapid deterioration and ugly demise." Drystan followed behind me, only stopping when I did, and he caught up to me. "She's hiding at Blackwood, unassuming and probably right under all our noses."

"But to what end?" I muttered in exasperation. At the looks on the men's faces, I rolled my eyes and clarified. "Yes, the apocalypse, obviously. But how? What is her goal here? Why Blackwood? Why Dahlia? What are we missing?"

Gabriel sighed and rolled his eyes. "We know exactly why Dahlia. She's Death's child. Created for this very reason."

"Fine. But what about my other questions?"

"Blackwood is the perfect place to build an army where no one can see. As much as the wards keep them contained, they also keep most of us out. Those who might be able to make a difference, anyway. I have to give it to her. She really did come up with a brilliant plan," Gabriel mused.

I blew out a frustrated breath. He wasn't saying

anything we hadn't already known for months. Ever since he overheard her little meeting with the other horse-women. We'd planned our defense to the best of our ability, sending sweet Merri in as our very own Trojan horse to act as our eyes and ears on the ground. Her cover story was perfect, based in truth as it was. And after her little episode in the rec room—that orgy was no accident; it was a well-executed plan—no one paid her much attention at all, giving her the wide berth required for her to sneak around and pilfer these session recordings. And the gala had provided the perfect opportunity for her to hand them over. It gave Drystan and me a reason to be on the grounds, and when we snuck off, no one had been the wiser. All in all, Merri had played her part perfectly. She was an exceptional spy, though I expected nothing less. Our kind were uniquely equipped to ferret out secrets.

"So far these tapes have given us insight into how Masterson conducts her sessions and how each of Dahlia's and her mates' power has grown, but we're no closer to finding out who Death is masquerading as. My money is on Bruno. No man is that handsome and nice unless he's trying to get something," Drystan grumbled.

"Why has no one mentioned the best friend? Kiki is Dahlia's only connection to the outside world. She is the reason Dahlia ended up at Blackwood, and she's been instrumental in putting Dahlia and her mates together." Gabriel stood and stretched before turning his gaze on me. "They won't leave her, Lilith. I tried. I spoke to Hades and Caspian both, and neither one would heed my warning."

"Did you really expect them to? Who would willingly give up the answer to their every prayer?" Drystan scoffed.

I couldn't help but agree with my fae prince. Though

Gabriel hadn't been willing to listen to reason. He was one of those who had to learn for himself the hard way.

"Is it really that serious, Gabriel? Do you think she's going to win? You never allow yourself to intervene like this. You always wait until the final battle." A chill ran down my spine as I thought of the strict rules he'd adhered to all these years.

"In those instances, we knew they'd ultimately fight on our side. This time we don't know much of anything, save that every player is a wild card. They could just as easily fight for her as for us. She stacked the deck in her favor, and we are woefully unprepared for what's to come. I don't think we've ever been this outmatched."

"This is . . . Bloody hell, angel, are you telling me she might very well win?"

"It's always a possibility, isn't it?"

"Well, yes, but . . ." I started, the defeat in his words bringing me up short.

"This isn't going to be a battle like the others, Lilith. There might be an army, but it likely won't be ours."

"I never thought I'd be the one telling you not to lose hope, Gabriel. The Belladonna coven is already at work on the wards. As soon as they fall, you'll be able to hand off your sword and—"

"Hand it off to whom?" he asked bleakly, his shoulders slumped.

"Ye of little faith," Drystan muttered. "You can't seriously be giving up now. Yes, we're way behind the ball on this round, and yes, we may all die because of it, but you're the fucking Messenger of God. Aren't you fueled by faith and optimism? If we find out who Death is wearing and are able to infiltrate Blackwood, we could still stop this and save our skins. I personally would prefer that option since it keeps me with my Lilypad."

I offered my pet a warm smile. He really had grown by leaps and bounds since he'd shown up bloody and broken on my doorstep. Submission had done him a world of good.

Gabriel dragged a hand through his golden locks and returned to my desk, slender fingers picking up the final tape we had in our possession. "Perhaps you should consider bringing your little emissary back home," he suggested, worry creasing his brow.

I wanted to. In fact, I'd nearly brought her home with me from the gala, but the truth was, we didn't have what we needed, and if we failed, there wouldn't be anywhere for her to return to. "Not until we're certain we have everything. Merri is there for a purpose. She's all we have inside. If we take her out too soon, we will lose any advantage we may have."

A sadness filled Gabriel's eyes, but he nodded. "Very well." Holding up the tape, he cocked one brow and looked to the player. "Shall we?"

"Let's hope this one reveals something we can act on," I said as Gabriel inserted it into the device.

"Only one way to find out," Drystan added, settling back into his chair. "Well, what are you waiting for, angel? Hit play."

POST-SESSION TRANSCRIPT: DAHLIA

Dr. Masterson: This is Dr. Elizabeth Masterson. Today marked my first session with our eagerly anticipated new resident, Dahlia Moore.

<<chair creak>>

Dr. Masterson: Subject M120 will not be referred to by her number. Dahlia is far too important for that. She is truly a beautiful creation. While she is classified as a mage, Dahlia is much more than that. She is a necromancer, but it wouldn't be in my best interest to make her aware of that just yet. Nor would it help me to tell her of her true parentage. She'll figure it out eventually.

Dr. Masterson: *blows out heavy breath* I find that in cases such as hers—where traumatic memories have been repressed—it is best to let her arrive at these discoveries on her own. That way she is both mentally and emotionally prepared for them. So instead of playing the role of doctor, I will play the role of trusted ally and, dare I say, friend. That's what she needs right now. To trust me.

<<paper rustling>>

Dr. Masterson: Her past is dark, as is appropriate for a necromancer, but she's been shielded from most of her abilities from an early age. This was purposefully done, a way to mitigate the madness her power could've caused. But now, it's time to free her of the chains of both her mind and magic—a mission that began the second she arrived. My task is to take her hand and walk with her through all of her repressed memories, bring her out the other side as the incredibly powerful being she is, and only then can I take what I want.

<<drumming fingers on the desk>>

Dr. Masterson: After today's session, it is even more apparent that this is the correct course. And the group session earlier this week was equally illuminating. I was right to place the five of them together. As predicted, they are the keys. One by one, they will help ensure that my name is known in every corner of the globe. With their unwitting cooperation, I can change the world as I was always meant to.

<<chair squeaks>>

<<pacing footsteps>>

Dr. Masterson: *frustrated groan* *drops accent* Ugh, why did I have to pick a Scot? Honestly, this accent is hard to keep up for so long. There's no reason for me to keep it going right now since no one is around. At this stage, it is crucial that they do not suspect my true motives or that every move they make is part of my plan to get my Apocalypse. Even the most seemingly innocent encounter has been curated and overseen by me. Everything is a means to an end. My end. But to ensure the purity of the experiment, they can never be made aware of this. It would ruin everything. If my subjects suspect I'm pulling the strings, they'll fight back. I can't have that. Their willing participation is essential. *musing hum* Perhaps I'll need some assistance to throw them off my scent.

Dr. Masterson: *accent returns* All right, time to get back in character.

<<phone receiver being lifted>>

<<dial tone and dialing>>

Dr. Masterson: Nathaniel, darling. Fancy a trip to Scotland? *pause* You're already here? How fortuitous.

<<static>>

End of transcript.

PART TWO
CHECKMATE

"And I looked, and behold a pale horse: and her name that
sat upon him was Death, and Hell followed with her."

Revelations 6:8

TWENTY-SIX

I wiped my sweaty palms on my jeans as I strode down the hall that led to Masterson's office. Should I have given her all the dirty details of my epic Nellie reloca-tion session? Yes. Had I? Not so much.

To be honest, I hadn't wanted to point the spotlight on myself during the group session. Merri had a lot going on, and I didn't really know her that well. Sometimes, keeping my secrets was the only way I felt secure. But I'd gotten in trouble when Dr. Masterson found out I'd kept other devel-opments from her in the past. I'd learned that lesson. She couldn't help me if she didn't know the truth.

Or at least the version of the truth I felt comfortable sharing. There was no way I was comfortable outright lying to her. Not after everything Masterson had done to help me. But I wasn't going to out Hades either. It had taken me a while to settle on a truth that was, well, truthful but not *too* truthful. Hades helped me, sure, but in this case, I thought it was best to say he was a *person from the underworld* who made certain Nellie could cross over. It wasn't a lie. Hades definitely hailed from the underworld. He just so happened to rule it as well.

Reaching Masterson's office, I gave the door a half-hearted knock. When there wasn't an immediate answer, I tested the door knob. If she was busy, it would be locked, so when it turned without issue, I just let myself in.

"Dr. Masters—"

The office was empty. It still smelled faintly of her perfume, sweet and slightly cloying. Lilies, perhaps?

Well, shoot. There went all my big plans. I'd gotten myself all riled up for nothing. What a letdown. Heaving a sigh, I turned to leave when I felt it.

That electric tingle along my skin and the pressure pushing against my chest.

Ghost.

Specifically Cunty McCuntface.

I hadn't encountered my malevolent spirit since our run-in at the gala. Part of me had been waiting for her to show up again. She was sort of inevitable that way. It was like she hid in the shadows, building up her energy between jump scares. Such a bitch.

"I'm going to turn around on the count of three, and you aren't going to terrify me this time. Got it?" I said, willing my limbs not to tremble.

"One."

No, my breaths weren't shaky.

"Two."

And I definitely didn't have bubble guts.

"Three."

I turned around, eyes wide open, and stared at the shadowy female form that hovered an inch from my face.

I had to swallow my whimper. No amount of prepara-tion would ever be enough. Her skin was a strange ash gray, eyes sunken dark pits, but now there was a faint blue glow in their depths. As with the last few interactions we'd had, she'd taken on even more of a human form. I didn't quite know what to do with that.

It didn't make her any less scary. Or menacing.

She was no Nellie, that's for sure.

The reminder of Nellie, of what I'd accomplished by simply talking to her and learning her story, was the push I needed to swallow my fear. Hadn't Cas asked me if I'd ever tried asking the spirit what she wanted? Or had that been Tor? Shoot, I couldn't remember. The idea had been so laughable at the time I'd immediately dismissed it.

It wasn't so laughable anymore.

The ghost leaned in so close I could feel the cold energy radiating off her. The hairs on the back of my neck stood on end, and as she opened her mouth to no doubt scream in my face, I stopped her.

"Hi, uh, I'm Dahlia. You probably already know that since you're haunting me and everything. What's your name? What do you want? How can I help you?" I tried my best to give her a megawatt customer service smile, but I knew without needing a mirror that it was one hundred percent grimace.

She stopped, tipped her head to the side, and gazed at me. Or at least I assumed that's what she was doing. Hard to tell without pupils, or you know, eyeballs.

"I can do that now. Help. Do you have unfinished business? Maybe I can solve your murder? If we do, maybe you can move on. I know a guy. He can escort you if you need it."

Her energy was frenetic and oppressive as she assessed me. Fuck, I needed to get a handle on this because I really didn't want to touch her soul, but if I had to, I would. I'd toss her into the nearest creepy doll and lock her in a chest. We might end up with a real-life Chucky or Annabelle on our hands, but that could be someone else's problem.

"It must be really dark in your head to be so angry all the time. Did something bad happen to you?"

I was trying to remember what Hades had told me about souls and why they got corrupted. With Nautica, it had been because the vessel her spirit was in was dead, so it was destroying her soul. But this lady wasn't in a body, so what was her excuse? Was she just a big ol' meanie, or did she have a reason for being a ball of vengeful wrath?

Probably.

Maybe she died in the throes of a bitch of a period. I know that makes me pretty damn vengeful.

Her form flickered and disappeared, but the nearly painful hum of her energy didn't dissipate. In fact, it got stronger, causing the lights in the office to flicker. My gaze darted around the room as I tried to get a read on where she might rematerialize. I wasn't going to be caught off guard again. Nope. She wasn't going to make me flinch this time.

Fuck.

She appeared near the door, the sight of her making me jump. Dammit.

This time I couldn't swallow my scream, and I had to stand in place with my hand pressed against my chest while my heart returned to a semi-normal pace.

"Listen, lady. I'm really going to need you to simmer the fuck down. You are a lot to take when you're standing still. Once you start zooming around and jumping out of shadows, all bets are off. If you want my help, just stay where I can see you. And maybe dial down the 'I'm going to steal your soul' vibes. No? Fine, it was just a suggestion."

I was rambling again, but it helped normalize a very not normal situation.

She turned her focus to the white lab coat hanging on the back of Dr. Masterson's door, her hand reaching out as if she was going to touch the fabric but, of course, passing right through. Was she a nurse here once upon a time? A patient? Oh! Maybe she'd also been a doctor a long time ago.

Why did I suddenly feel like I was playing a ghostly version of charades?

While I was trying to parse out the meaning of her actions, she started to shrink.

Wait, no. Not shrink. The bitch was melting into the floorboards.

"Hey! That is not what we agreed on. You're supposed to stay where I can—"

My protest died on my tongue as one of the floorboards rattled, the perfect seal breaking and leaving the board raised just a hair.

"What the actual fuck?" I whispered, approaching it and kneeling down to inspect the damage. With careful fingers, I pried the board up until I found a secret compartment hidden underneath. "You have to be kidding me."

I was fully shaking as I reached inside and pulled out a rolled-up bit of white cloth. I already had a terrible feeling about what it was; I didn't know if I had the stomach to find out whether my suspicions were correct.

The ball of fabric was white—or had been at some point. Now it was dusty from being shoved in the compartment, and . . . stained.

"Oh fuck. Oh God. Please . . ."

I stood as I unballed the fabric, a rust-colored stain clearly visible on the white doctor's coat. The stain spread down the front, but even discolored, I could easily distinguish the blue embroidered name across the breast. Dr. Elizabeth Masterson and the Blackwood Estate logo just underneath.

Before I could react, a crash sounded from behind me, causing me to spin around and nearly lose my balance.

"Now you're just freaking me out on purpose," I grumbled, already moving to collect the fallen object. It must have been important. Why else would she have gone to such lengths to get me to look at it?

"You could try using your words, you know. A please never hurt anyone."

The floor was dented where the heavy award had landed. I glanced up at the bookcase and found the empty space on the very top shelf taunting me because I'd need a stool to put it back.

"This thing is a fucking weapon. I'm going to have a word with Masterson about safety because if that had been my hea—" My words faltered as I inspected the heavy marble trophy with Masterson's name engraved on the front.

Something caught my eye, something that shouldn't be there on the white stone. Blood stained the sharp angle of the bottom corner, and as I turned the statue over, my skin went clammy. The truth in what I'd just been saying hit me hard enough I was speechless.

My gaze went from what was clearly a murder weapon to the ghost now floating next to the desk. Except she didn't look like the terrifying manifestation who'd haunted me for so long. My stomach churned as I took in the bespectacled eyes I knew so well, the cupid's bow lips, and the short stature. But most of all, my attention wouldn't leave the caved-in side of her head, blood running down her face and neck, soaking her white lab coat.

"Dr. Masterson?"

My stomach clenched with a cocktail of nausea and terror.

"Oh no. Not you too." But then I shook my head. "But we killed him. The Ripper is gone, so who . . ."

I trailed off, my heart already realizing something my brain didn't want to acknowledge.

The dried blood on the coat was old, not new. And this ghost had been haunting me since I'd arrived at Blackwood. Which meant . . .

"If you've been dead since I got here, who have I been talking to all this time?"

TWENTY-SEVEN

TOR

Under the cover of darkness, I crept through the Black Forest with the stealth of a jungle cat. There was far too much unrest in the town for me to remain blind to the goings-on simply to avoid being spotted. And after what Masterson had said during our session yesterday, I did not think any of us could afford to bury our heads in the sand.

I was my father's son, and one thing had become increasingly obvious over the last several days.

War was coming, whether we were ready for it or not.

The knowledge didn't scare me. I was the firstborn son of Odin's chosen warrior. The call to battle sang in my veins and a killing field would always feel like home to me.

What did concern me was what could happen to my mate.

I heard the voices in the distance before I saw the glow of their torches through the trees. The townspeople had gathered, and by their angry tones, they weren't having a party.

"What are we waiting for? The beast is out there, killing whoever he comes into contact with."

"If we don't stop him, no one will!"

"Do you have your weapons, lads?"

Weapons? I crept closer, needing to see them with my own eyes, and sure enough, a crowd of what had to be over a hundred people was gathered around the statue of The Hag, literal flaming torches in their hands along with blades, pitchforks, guns, wooden stakes, and who knew what else.

"My Jeremy spent the better part of the last two weeks melting every piece of silver in town to make us bullets."

"They should go right through any shifter we encounter and do a fair bit of damage to the vampires."

"Well done, lad," the first man said, clapping Jeremy on the shoulder. Whoever he was, he seemed like the leader of this little uprising. I took special note of him, knowing it would come in handy when I hunted him down later.

"When do we attack? They're stronger before dawn, aren't they?"

"We should burn the place to the ground. Not even the strongest of them can survive fire. Lock them all inside and torch the estate."

"No! We draw them out and make sure they're truly dead. Cut off their heads, stick them on pikes. A warning to any other creatures threatening our safety."

My fingers turned to claws, the razor-sharp points pricking my palms and drawing my attention back to myself. I'd been growling, my inner monster instinctively reacting to their increasingly bloodthirsty threats.

"They are protecting the Ripper and continue to let him terrorize our town. Who's to say they haven't been sending him out to pick us off one by one so they can take over?"

"I saw him only last week. His eyes were fathomless black pits, like a shark. The only reason he didn't kill me was because I played dead."

I snorted quietly. The only reason I didn't kill him was because I wasn't a cold-blooded killer. Freya's heaving bosom, fear could do a lot of damage to people's psyches.

"Is it really wise to attack Blackwood? These creatures are there because they're out of control."

Finally, a voice of reason. It wasn't hard to spot the woman in the crowd. She clutched a toddler to her, the youngster sucking its thumb as it looked around with wide, terrified eyes.

"If we do nothing, more of us will die."

"If we go against them, many of us will die tonight. Who will raise our children? Who will be left to pick up the pieces? If we leave them alone, there's still a chance—"

The leader cut her off. He made a slashing motion with his arm, making the fire of his torch cut through the crowd.

"If you're not with us, you're against us! So whose side are you on?"

"They've passed the point of no return, lad. Best you and yours get clear of that mob."

I flinched at the raspy voice that hit my ears from behind me. Turning around, I found myself face-to-face with the nearly solid spectral form of Adonis D. Edman.

"And go where? The wards are still up and holding us hostage."

"Are they?" he mused, something about the way he stared at me making me think he knew something I didn't. "I guess it'll be your funeral, then. I'll gather a welcoming party for you."

"We can fight them off. They may have weapons, but we are stronger."

Adonis shook his head. "There are more coming. Hundreds, in fact. They'll arrive shortly, and from the way they've been talking, they plan to raze Blackwood to the ground."

"They can try," I snarled, welcoming the rush of bloodlust.

I have never run from a fight, no matter how badly the odds were stacked against me. Today would not be the day I broke that streak.

Adonis's gaze shifted past me, his expression not changing so much as intensifying. It reminded me of an animal who'd sensed a predator in its midst. "These woods are crowded tonight. Best you make haste if you're intending to deliver a warning."

"Tonight, we kill the beasts who threaten our town!"

"Kill the beasts!"

It was harder than it should have been to force myself to move away from the threat. A fight like this is what I'd been created for, but if I stayed, there was a chance Dahlia might get caught unaware, and putting my mate at risk was quite possibly the only thing that could short-circuit my wiring. I'd fight to the death, but protecting her would always be my priority.

I'd only made it a handful of steps at most before another figure came into view. Suddenly Adonis's parting words made more sense.

"A word, Viking. If you please."

"Aren't you a little overdressed for a romp through the woods?" I asked the blond man. He was dressed head to toe in leather and looked as though he was prepped and ready for a photo shoot on the back of a motorbike.

"Oh, father above, do I really have to do this again? I

thought your brother would have clued you in to who I am by now." The man rolled his eyes up to the heavens and sighed before pinning his now glowing stare on me. "I am Gabriel, Messenger of God. I come to deliver unto you a"—he heaved another sigh—"message."

Alek had told me about Gabriel, actually. He'd made a point to mention what an overbearing arse he was.

"I'm a little busy at the moment. It'll have to wait."

"I'm afraid it can't. It's rather urgent. A matter of life and death, if you will."

"Isn't it always? My mate is in danger. These people are champing at the bit to kill us all. I need to return to her."

"You need to listen to me." He stopped me with a surprisingly strong hand on my shoulder.

I growled in warning, unable to control myself. "Unhand me, angel."

Now was a terrible time to try to hold any sort of rational conversation with me. My beast was at the surface, foaming at the mouth to be unleashed. The only thing keeping him remotely at bay was our joint need to return to Dahlia. But even that thread was fraying fast, my ability to keep him in check nothing compared to what it had been even a week ago.

"I can see this curse is weighing on you, Tor. You're carrying a burden never meant for you."

"And I can see you have a real hard-on for leather, even though you'd look more at home in a toga."

Gabriel didn't take the bait. Instead he continued on, his palm still resting on my shoulder. "You were meant to be a prince. A hero. Not this . . . beast. Your destiny was warped by a cruel twist of fate."

"Your point?"

"I can repair your path. Set you on the right one again. Lift your curse and give you back the version of yourself you've always known. You're destined to be a hero, not a villain, Tor."

"And you'll do all this out of the goodness of your heart."

"It's the way it should be."

"No. I don't believe you. You have an ulterior motive. This is going to cost me something, likely something I don't want to give."

I might be more monster than man, but I was no fool. If an offer sounded too good to be true, it always was.

"If you don't take my offer, you'll lose everything. What does it matter that you'll have to give something up?"

"It matters because there are certain things that I value above all else. Including myself. I will gladly suffer on their behalf."

Gabriel rocked back on his heels as he considered my statement, then took a steadying breath before locking eyes with me once more. "Dahlia will not survive this. You lose her either way, Tor. But if you take my offer and leave her here, at least you will have your family."

My patience was waning, and if he'd thought mentioning Dahlia would soften me to his cause, he clearly didn't understand who and what I was. If anything, it had the opposite effect. Grasping him by the wrist, I flung his hand off me, my growls building in intensity as my body swelled in size.

"I will never leave her. She. Is. Mine."

"Yes, yes. That is what you all say. It doesn't change the facts."

"Which are?"

"The world is ending because of her. Because of your connection. Break it, and you can save everyone."

"Never."

Dahlia was my reason for existing. She was the only one who'd helped me claw my way back to the forefront of my mind after my curse took hold. Without her I was nothing, my life without meaning. What did I care of the world and the others in it? She was my world. My thoughts flashed to my brother and his mate, my father and mother. They would all do the same thing. They'd choose each other. Not the title of hero. Not a metaphorical crown.

"She is my Kærasta, and I'll kill anyone who tries to take her from me. Even you, angel."

The angel in question heaved a resigned sigh. "I was afraid you'd say that. For what it's worth, you're making a mistake."

"Yes, well, it's my mistake to make, isn't it? That's what free will means, right?"

He sighed again. "Unfortunately for me and the rest of the world, yes. That it does."

Before I could respond, he vanished with nothing more than a shift in the air that made my ears pop.

No matter. I had to get back to my mate and see her safe. Surely there was some kind of underground bunker on the property where I could hide her away until the worst was over. She wouldn't like it, but that didn't matter when her safety was in question.

Running full tilt through the brush, I ate up the distance between me and the gates of Blackwood with long strides. The noise of the growing army of villagers had been a faint murmur in my ears while Gabriel tried to sway me to leave, but now that I had reached the tall fence and was farther from them, the only sign of the war party was the glow of their torches in the distance. It wouldn't be long now. They were coming. We had to be ready.

I pushed myself harder, bracing to jump the fence when the snap of a branch had me spinning around, fully prepared to attack.

"Ouch, shit! Stupid trees. Get off me!"

That voice was far too familiar. What in Loki's shrunken ballsack was Kiki doing in the woods outside of Blackwood?

I hadn't had a chance to process her appearance before Kiki's eyes landed on me and she let out an ungodly shriek.

"Ohmigod, don't kill me!" she screamed, throwing her arms up in the air.

"Peace, Kiki. It's me, Tor. The Viking?"

Her entire body seemed to relax. "Well, duh. Of course you are. I was more worried that you didn't recognize me. With the claws and the teeth and the grrrr of it all."

"The grr of it all?" I sighed, fighting the urge to squeeze the bridge of my nose. I did not have time for this woman and her brand of logic.

"Well, you're a world champion growler, aren't you? I bet you don't even realize you're doing it. I dated a guy one time who moaned while he ate. No idea he was making a fucking sound, but there we were, eating at Maggiano's in Philly, and he was moaning like a whore."

"Kiki." I couldn't let her continue rambling. Not when the threat of the townsfolk was looming. "We can continue this conversation once we're on the grounds. Things are . . . uneasy in Briarglen."

"Oh, right! That's exactly why I was skulking through the woods. My Uber driver dropped me off on the outskirts of town, and I had to hoof it through a really ugly group of people. At first I just thought it was some sort of protest gone awry, but then I heard the chant. It seemed like a good idea not to mention where I was going because they are *really* upset with you guys."

"Why are you here?" I asked, taking her bag automatically when she handed it to me.

"To rescue Dahlia, obviously."

"How do you plan to do that?"

"Is that doubt I sense in your tone, mister?"

There was no safe answer to this question. I recognized the verbal trap from a mile away.

"Let's just say I know a guy who knows a guy. And by guy, I mean shmampire. Oh wait, I don't have to speak in code anymore."

That was supposed to be a code?

"Vampire," she corrected. "And by vampire, I mean I'm close personal friends with Cashel Blackthorne now. He's none too happy that Blackwood is keeping his sister against her will. Apparently his brother really didn't know Blackwood was spelled to be a prison. They really thought they were protecting her."

While she was talking, she'd moved to stand in front of the stone wall encircling Blackwood's perimeter. When I didn't immediately do what she wanted, she glanced back at me. "Well?"

From the way her arms were up in the air and she was wiggling her fingers, I gathered that she was demanding I help give her a boost. I hoped she had good upper body strength, because I could only throw her so hard before she ended up hurt.

With my hands around her hips, I tossed her in the air, shouting, "Grab the bars and pull yourself over. I'll catch you on the other side!"

I hurled her bag up and over, ignoring her cry of protest, before I took a few steps back and then ran for the wall, easily scaling the rock and landing gracefully on the other side. Kiki was still clutching the iron railing at the top, her mouth hanging open as she stared at me.

"I always thought you had to shout parkour before you did it."

I smirked. "I'll keep that in mind for next time. Now, jump. I'll catch you."

"Talk about a trust fall," she groused, but I had to hand it to her; she didn't waste any time doing as she was told.

I caught her easily, her little 'oof' as she made impact with my body the only sign that it wasn't as easy for her.

"Fancy meeting you here," she said with a forced smile as I helped her get her weight under her.

I didn't bother coming up with a reply, using the moment instead to pick up her bag and sling it over my shoulder. She didn't seem to mind carrying on a one-sided conversation, because she just kept going.

"Oh great, more trees," she said with a wary huff, her eyes scanning Blackwood's side of the forest.

"Blackwood is hidden for a reas—" My words died on my tongue as a harsh tug on my awareness stole my breath.

No. This wasn't my awareness. This was my bond with Dahlia, the one reinforced by Kai's tattoo. Something was wrong. Fear and urgency pulled at me, calling me to my mate.

The sensation was followed by her voice in my mind. "I need you. Meet me in my room. Hurry."

The urgency I'd felt before was nothing compared to what was clawing at me now.

"Come on," I snarled, hoisting Kiki over my other shoulder and not giving her a chance to protest.

"You know I never wanted to examine your ass this

closely, right? I can walk and appreciate it from a distance, big guy."

I ignored her, racing through the woods and back to the woman I never should have left.

I could only pray I wouldn't be too late.

TWENTY-EIGHT

"If you've been dead since I got here, who have I been talking to all this time?" I asked, my voice paper thin.

Instead of answering me, the ghost simply vanished.

"Well, great. Fuck you too, then. All these months of scaring the ever-living shit out of me, and when I finally solve the mystery of you, you just ghost me. I know you're dead and all, and that sucks, but have you ever heard of common decency? In case you missed that day at school, let me bring you up to speed. Not cool, lady. Not cool." I dropped the lab coat on Masterson's desk before gingerly placing her—shudder—murder weapon next to it. "Guess you can't cross over yet, which means I'm not finished with my job, huh? I have to fucking find your body, don't I? I don't like finding bodies. Bodies scare me more than you do. Bodies are gross and all decomposed and sometimes come back to life and try to eat me."

To say that I wasn't handling my little revelation very well would be the fucking understatement of a lifetime. Would you? I mean, Jesus. The woman I thought I'd been baring my soul to has been dead the entire time. Which means I'd been had. Hoodwinked. Bamboozled. Who the fuck was the impostor I'd been talking to? Did Masterson have an evil twin? Oh, shit . . . Did the evil twin kill her and take her place so she could destroy us all? Was she jealous of her situationship with Temperance and wanted to steal her man? Ohmigod, what if she was Temperance's estranged wife, and he'd been having an affair with Lizzie all this time, so she offed her in order to get what she wanted?

I slapped myself, the sound ringing out in the little office. "Get yourself together, Dahlia. Now is not the time to start plotting romantic thrillers. You need to find your men, fill them the eff in, and get the hell out of Dodge."

There were some holes in that plan, but I didn't care. The only thing that mattered was sharing what I'd learned so it wouldn't be on me alone to figure out what to do with the secret.

Yanking open the office door, I stepped out into the hallway, the urge to get to my men so strong I could feel it pulsing in my veins. Something was wrong in the energy swirling through Blackwood, though. It pulled me off center, made me stop and take in my surroundings before I continued on. Was it another spirit? Or had Masterson returned for a little extra haunting?

With a quick glance from side to side, I noted no visible ghosts, nothing out of the ordinary. Well . . . not nothing.

The usually empty halls were not so empty. I wouldn't say they were crowded, but more than a few people were rushing around. Doors opened and closed as they darted into rooms or knocked urgently on someone else's.

Spotting a familiar head of inky black hair, I made my way over to Sorcha. The usually kempt vampire was decidedly unkempt. That was a real departure, and it sent all my spidey senses tingling.

"Sorcha, is everything okay?" I asked as she took a long swig from a crystal decanter filled with what smelled a lot like whiskey but looked like blood.

"No. They're coming for us, you naive little creature. Haven't you been paying attention?"

I rolled my lips together, the news not so much a surprise as a pile-on. Wasn't one crisis at a time enough? Couldn't people take a number and wait their turn?

"So you're going to get hammered and just wait for them?" I asked, gesturing to the bottle in her hand.

"No. I'm going to get pissed and make my escape. If you know what's good for you, you'll do the same."

"Uh, Sorcha, I think you're forgetting something."

She raised a brow at me.

"What about the wards?"

"Devil take them. I'd rather risk my chances out there in the woods than stay locked in here only to burn alive when they set this place on fire."

Kit came tearing around the corner, his expression bedraggled as he rushed to Sorcha. "Come on. We have to go. They've breached the gates. They'll be here within the next ten minutes at the most."

"No! You have to stay and fight. What about the rest of us?"

Kit shot me a withering look. "I'm a demon, darling girl. I don't care about the rest of you."

I shook my head, realizing I wasn't going to get anywhere with these two, and ultimately, they weren't who I wanted to find anyway. If shit really had hit the fan, I needed to find my mates, pronto.

Unfortunately, their rooms were empty, no trace of any

of them to be found, and I wasn't ashamed to admit panic threatened to take over by the time I got to my bedroom. Where were they? Had something happened to them? I'd know, wouldn't I? We had a bond.

We have a bond, I thought to myself, a little lightbulb going off in my mind.

I'd gotten so used to shielding my thoughts that I'd forgotten I should be able to contact them from anywhere. Or, at the very least, sense them. Hadn't that been the whole point? I vaguely recalled Kai mentioning something about how the tattoos would help them find me or sense when I was in danger.

Closing my eyes, I focused on the part of me that felt like them. It was hard to explain it more specifically than that. I guess if I had to describe it in one of my books, I'd say it was like a cabinet, and when I opened it, they were on the other side, just waiting for me to pick them up and play with them. Nope. Scratch that. Kiki would edit the shit out of that metaphor. They were just part of me now, okay? And when I focused on them, it was like that connection became tangible. Like I could wrap my hand around the invisible tethers between us and tug.

"I need you. Meet me in my room. Hurry."

When I opened my eyes, a little squeak of surprise escaped me at the sight of that pretty blonde woman I'd seen a few times before standing in front of me. Her hair was a tumble of golden ringlets, her eyes big and innocent, cheeks like a cherub's.

Oh God, was I dying? She only ever appeared when I was on the brink of death. Fuck. Shit. Fuck.

"Dahlia, I need you to listen to me," she said, her sweet voice reminding me of a kindergarten teacher.

"Are you a ghost? Am I dying? What is fucking happening this time?"

"Does it look like you're dying?"

"No, but every time I see you, I am. Shit. Am I about to have a stroke?"

"Dahlia..."

"I could be dead on the floor of Masterson's office, and now I'm just a ghost who doesn't know she's a ghost."

"Dahlia..."

"Oh God, I don't have a me to help me cross over."

"Dahlia!"

I slammed my lips shut, my face molten when I realized I'd gone full spiral on this woman. "Sorry."

"You're not dying, but you are in danger. I've been watching over you since the day you were born, sweet girl. It's been my purpose."

I looked at her, confusion swirling within me. "Are you like...a guardian angel or something?"

"You could say that. But even more than that, I'm your mother. I promised I'd always protect you, and to date, I've kept that promise. Don't make me break it now."

I sat down hard on the edge of my bed, my knees giving out on me. "My mother?"

Fuck. She must've died in childbirth. She never abandoned me, not by choice. For all I knew, my asshole father killed her.

She cast her gaze out my window, then looked back at me. "I need you to listen to me, Dahlia. Trust that I'm only here to help you, like I've always helped you. We can talk in depth later, once the danger has passed."

"O-okay."

"There's a terrible army of angry people headed this

way. They're going to kill you all, and they won't stop until they're sure no one survives."

"I know."

"Then you must also know we have to fight them. We can't let them win. If they do, it'll change the relationship between supernaturals and humans forever. It will be the end of the golden era. A return to all-out war. Days filled with nothing but death and dismay."

For someone who looked and sounded like she'd be at home on a cheerleading squad, she sure painted a grim picture.

"Residents are already taking off, heading for the forest. Soon there will be no one left to fight with."

"You have to convince them to defend their territory. Your mate is out there in the middle of it right now. Tor is strong, but they'll overpower him. He will be torn to pieces, and it will be your fault."

My heart lurched. "How? How can I convince these creatures to listen to me? I'm not a leader."

"No. But you have something the rest don't."

"Big tits and a witty mind?"

She ignored my bad joke and shook her head. "A captain with the power of persuasion. If anyone can rally the troops for you, it'll be him."

Cas. I'd almost forgotten about his glamour since it had never really worked on me. The reason for that was a question for another time.

"I can try," I said with a shrug.

Cas was hard to wrangle on his best day, and lately he hadn't had many of those. More and more often, I'd catch him staring off into space, his eye twitching, his fingers spasming in his lap while he mouthed things I couldn't quite hear. The only way to bring him back was to touch him and say his name.

"Try isn't good enough. If you don't succeed, it will all be over, Dahlia."

A crash sounded from the hallway, pulling my attention from her and to the door. When I looked back, she was gone. "Damn. Don't these ghosts understand I need a little more than an ominous warning before they leave? An itemized to-do list would be nice. Or maybe a phone tree."

I didn't have much time to sit in the information she'd just given me because Kai, Cas, and Hades burst through the door, all three of them breathing hard, Asshole wriggling his way between Hades's ankles and running to me with a series of concerned barks.

"Gem, what's wrong?"

"Besides the obvious," Hades added, hitching his thumb over his shoulder and gesturing to the ruckus in the hallway.

"Everyone is running. We have to get them to stay and fight if we're going to survive."

Thinking of Tor out there alone with an angry mob focused on taking him down made my purpose crystal clear. My mother was right; I had the ultimate trump card up my sleeve, and I was going to play it.

I didn't look at my other two mates. My gaze was pinned on Caspian, whose expression made my heart ache. His eyes were red-rimmed and bloodshot, as though he hadn't slept, and dark purple shadows had taken up residence underneath them, the hallmark of someone who wasn't well. But it was more than that. His usually neatly trimmed scruff was now the beginnings of a scraggly beard.

"How can we help?" Hades asked.

"It's not you who can help, actually. It's him."

Cas blinked at me. "What can I do?"

I took his face between my hands, holding on to him until I knew he was fully present and locked in on me. He'd mentioned more than once that using his glamour was becoming harder, that it took a lot out of him. I hoped now that we'd bonded, my power would strengthen him and asking this of him wouldn't cause more harm. Honestly, if Tor wasn't in danger, I wouldn't risk asking at all.

Closing my eyes, I inhaled the scent of my mate. Salt and clean air, the sea on a clear day. Then I lifted my lids and stared deep into his eyes, recognizing just how lucid he was. "I know that your mind is a mess right now, and I don't have any illusions that what I'm going to ask of you will be easy. In fact, I'm pretty sure it might cost more than you can afford to give, but I'm going to ask anyway because it's important."

"Anything, love. I'll do anything for you, you know that."

"I need you to use your glamour, Cas. I need you to rally the troops and defend the ship."

"The ship?" Kai whispered.

"She means Blackwood," Hades explained.

"Defend the ship," Caspian whispered. "Captain goes down with the ship."

"Yes, Cas. Get them to defend us. Keep us from going down."

He gripped me by the nape and crushed his lips to mine in a fierce kiss, then murmured, "It'll be done, darling. You have my word."

He tore away from me and fled from the room, my heart aching as I watched him go, worried it might be the last time. I didn't know why I had the sense that whatever version of Cas returned to me once this was over wouldn't be the flirtatious rogue I'd fallen in love with.

"Does this mean what I think it means?" Kai asked, entering the room fully and taking me by the shoulders.

"What?" Hades questioned, his voice low and suspicious.

"We're going to war."

Taking a deep breath, I turned and faced them fully, accepting the weight of his words and knowing that whatever happened next was on me. "Yes. Tor is out there, and they're after him. They think he's the Ripper, and there's no way he'll escape them all. If the residents of Blackwood stay and fight, he might have a chance. I couldn't risk any other outcome. And I won't apologize for it."

Hades sent a shadow to wrap around my waist. "Nor should you. Each one of us would do the same were our positions reversed. That's what mates do, Dahlia."

"Aye, gem. When it comes to the one we love, we burn the world to the ground. Every time."

CHAPTER
TWENTY-NINE

HOOK

"Save the ship. Captain goes down with the ship," I muttered, repeating the words as I made my way through the corridors.

With every step I took away from Dahlia, the static in my mind increased. I hadn't attempted a mass use of my glamour in . . . well, I couldn't remember the last time I'd attempted to influence more than a handful of people at once. Even at my strongest, my mind wasn't able to send more than a whisper out beyond a small group of people. I may have talked up my skills a tad too much, if I was being honest.

What if I couldn't do this for my darling? If I failed her, she'd die, and it would be my fault. I couldn't let that happen. It wasn't an option. It was time for me to show up as the true captain I was. Her power increased after bonding with us all. So had Kai's, Hades's, and Tor's. It would stand to reason I would be more powerful as well. I had to believe that.

And Kai had also mentioned that we might wean a bit of each other's power or even skills as a side effect. I could only hope it was true. Goddess knew I was going to need every drop of help I could get.

Tick

Tick

Tick

I flinched as the ticking took up space in my head once more, but it was still faint at the moment. I had time before the madness dragged me under. Picking up speed, I raced through the estate, frustrated when I found the place all but empty. Bloody cowards.

"Hello!" I called. "Is anyone still here?"

No answer. I kept searching, making it all the way to the greenhouse before someone finally answered. However, the voice that met my ear in reply was not one I'd expected.

"Over here, pirate! Have ye come to help us?"

I narrowed my eyes, finally zeroing in on Rhys, the pixie man we'd seen at Christmas. "Are you lot running as well?"

"Jax has the shimmers already safely tucked away with Polly. We're going to stay and fight. Blackwood is our home."

I had to swallow back a groan as the ticking grew louder. How were the five of us and a smattering of wee pixies going to stave off an entire village?

Tick

Tick

Tick

This was not the glorious showing I'd hoped for.

Rhys's irritation would've been obvious from his posture alone, but the agitated way he fluttered about caused pixie dust to come off him in a flurry, the glittering motes falling from him and coating the table below.

"Where are your cohorts?" I asked.

"They're here. Hiding in the plants."

"Gather them. I have an idea."

Rhys gave me a suspicious look but ultimately obeyed. Good man. I didn't have time to waste, and frankly, neither did he. The roar of the approaching villagers was loud enough that I could hear them from in here.

Or were those shouts in my mind?

A familiar and unwelcome slithering sound caught my ear, causing me to twist my head in search of the wicked reptile I could never seem to escape.

"Where is it?" I hissed, finding no trace of him.

"Where's what?"

The pixies had returned while I'd been distracted. Good, good. More eyes meant we'd been more likely to track the bastard down.

"The crocodile. Where?" As soon as I asked the question, I knew I'd made a mistake. My madness was already sneaking up on me.

"He's lost his marbles, hasn't he?"

"Aye. We should leave while we still can."

Threading my fingers through my hair, I gave a tug sharp enough to bring tears to my eyes. The pain helped me focus.

"No. No. Stay. I have a job for you."

"We're a little busy, if you haven't noticed. We don't have time for a side quest."

I had to pull myself together. If they weren't on my side, I'd never gather the troops in time to fight. Closing my eyes, I willed the ticking to stop, or at the very least, fade. My power was right there, pulsing within me. I grabbed a tendril and opened my mouth, whispering as I did.

"You'll help me because it's the only thing you can do to stay alive. Go, find every last resident of Blackwood and dust them until they're drawn to you like moths to a flame. Bring them to the courtyard. Wait for me there."

As soon as I finished speaking, the pixies blinked in unison, their eyes sharpening as they refocused. Immediately, they began to strategize as if the plan had been theirs all along.

"All right, lads. We need to find those cowards before they clear the gates."

"Divide and conquer. It's our best bet. Rhys, Owen, you go north and east. Tawny and I will go west and south."

"Where the hell am I supposed to go?"

"Search the castle, ye daft bastard. Have ye lost yer brain along with your wife? Goddess."

They flitted off in a whirlwind of pixie dust, and it was only after they were gone that I allowed myself to sway on my feet.

"You're too slow."

"They're getting away."

"You'll never stop them."

Tick

Tick

Tick

Hitting myself in the head with my palm, I forced myself to focus. I couldn't fall victim to this. Not now.

"Captain goes down with the ship. Captain goes down. Captain . . ." I murmured as I lurched out the greenhouse door and into the night. The angry shouts of the mob were louder out here. I could almost make out what they were saying.

I collided with a cloak-covered lump of a creature, the sound of porcelain and silver scraping together unmistakable.

"Ah, a looter. Fancy meeting you here. I'll have to ask you to release your pilfered goods and change course."

The creature snarled, then stood to its full height, which only brought them to my waist.

"Joffrey?"

The troll-like man threw his hood back and shot me a look that would've killed a weaker person.

"What's it to you? Not like I'm taking anything out of your pocket."

"No, but you're fleeing when I require you to stay and fight. That's an offense worthy of walking the plank, mate."

Joffrey scowled. "I don't take orders from you, *captain*."

The insincerity in his sneered words had me ready to throw him overboard. Collecting a fistful of his shirt in my hand, I lifted him into the air, holding his eyes and gathering my magic as I whispered, "You will stay. And you will fight. To the death if need be. Blackwood cannot be lost."

I staggered at the drain on my power and was caught completely unaware when a saucer-sized palm collided with my ear. He was surprisingly strong.

"Unhand me, you blackguard. I'm trying to defend Blackwood. Can't you see the enemy is already at the gates?"

I dropped Joffrey and watched as he skittered back into the estate, leaving his stolen wares behind.

"Result," I muttered, wincing as my head began to throb right behind my eyes.

Slowly, I made my way to the courtyard, happy to note there was already a small crowd gathered and waiting for me. One thing I had to give the pixies, they might be tiny, but they worked fast and that dust of theirs was potent.

One by one, the residents of Blackwood joined our group, as well as every staff member, with the exception of

Dr. Masterson. It couldn't have taken more than ten minutes for thirty of them to arrive, but the insistent tick, tick, ticking would not leave me be.

"You're going to fail."

"They're coming."

"You're all going to die here."

Thankfully, the restlessness of the crowd brought me back before I could descend too deeply.

"What are we doing here, Hook?" The big Russian bear shifter asked, his hands partially shifted into claws.

"We're fighting."

"We didn't come here to fight. We were sent here to recover. This is ridiculous." Aiden, a mage I'd encountered once or twice, popped the collar on his peacoat and turned to leave. "I have better things to do with my time than die here with you." He linked hands with a burly man who must've been part giant. "Come on, Hans. We can catch the next flight out and be back in Berlin by tomorrow if we hurry."

"You won't make it to the airport. Those wards will pull you right back," Sorcha said, her attention not on the Germans but on her chipped nail polish.

More mutters of dissent started up in the crowd. I was losing them. The pixie dust brought them here, but it wouldn't keep them complacent for long. I needed to get myself together before it really was too late.

"Save the ship," I whispered, another image superimposing itself over the crowd of people in front of me. For a second, I would have sworn we were all on deck of my ship. It was so real I could even feel the spray of the ocean against my face.

"What wards? What is she talking about?" a woman I couldn't spot asked.

"Oh, bleeding hell, they don't know," I muttered as the ticking intensified.

If I was going to get them on my side, I needed to do it now.

"Everyone listen!" I shouted.

They quieted down, but the occasional grumble of disapproval still seeped through.

Closing my eyes as I had with the pixies, I grabbed my power with everything in me, knowing this wasn't even the entirety of the Blackwood residence standing before me. That meant I'd have to reach out farther than I could see, and who knew if I'd succeed.

"Save the ship," I murmured again.

Once I held every ounce of power I possessed, I released it in a trickle, allowing it to infuse my words, my whispered speech impassioned and leaving no room for contradiction.

"This is our domain. We must protect it at all costs. These townsfolk aim to kill us all, and we cannot let that stand. We were sent here because we were too powerful, and they've already taken enough from us by locking us up because they're afraid. You won't let the outside world continue to persecute the residents of Blackwood. You will save our ship, or you will die trying."

"That's right. They have no reason to come here and hurt us," Aiden said. "We have to fight them. We have to win."

"I'll stop them before they get far. No one can come up against a bear and survive," Ursa said before he let out an almighty roar and transformed into the very bear he'd spoken of. He was easily ten feet tall, his claws deadly weapons and his eyes shining bright with fury.

Other voices joined him, each and every one of them committed to the cause.

341

Some I recognized: Sorcha, Kit, Merri. Others were new to me. But all were in agreement. They would stay, and they would fight. Relief slammed into me as my head throbbed so intensely I had to bite back a pained groan. Something warm dripped out of my nose, and when I wiped my hand across my upper lip, it came away crimson.

That couldn't be good.

Tick

The crowd had all rushed to take up arms, leaving me alone in my success. Good. That was good. They couldn't see me weak. It would be bad for morale. They'd worry about their captain.

Tick.

"I did it, darling," I muttered, the world swimming and dipping before me.

Tick

I took a couple of unsteady steps, spotting the door to Kai's tower. If I could reach it, I could take a second to regain my strength. "I saved . . ."

Tick

"The ship . . ."

But I didn't reach it. As soon as I attempted my next step, the ground rose to greet me and the world went dark.

THIRTY

DEATH

"And they said I wouldn't be successful." I locked the bunker door as soon as I got inside, humming happily to myself as the energy in the room changed. "Look who's laughing now. Me. It's me. I'm laughing." I squealed and clapped my hands, running the rest of the way down the stairs.

Pausing at the entrance to the bunker proper, I stopped just long enough to switch on the vintage record player, the strains of my favorite animated movie soundtrack echoing in the chamber. Plucking a discarded coat off the rack, I held it out and began waltzing around the room.

"But it's not a dream anymore. It's real. I'm going to win this, and no one can stop me."

"Oh lovely, she's off her bloody rocker," Grim muttered, his deep, gravelly voice breaking through my celebratory dance.

I blew him a kiss as I twirled around his cell. "You're just bitter and it shows, cutie."

"Helene . . ." Chaos growled.

"Oh, my full government name. You must *really* mean it."

Gliding across the floor with pure happiness in my little black heart, I continued my dance, singing along with my pretend prince/coat. I stopped in front of Sin's cell, giving him a beatific smile as I swayed back and forth. Then, as the song reached its final bars, I made my way to the empty cell reserved for Malice. He'd arrive any moment, and I could begin my most important ritual. The air hummed with power, and as I watched, the fourth horseman of the apocalypse materialized, all six foot three, stacked muscle, and smoldering inch of him.

"Alas, my prince has come." I dropped the coat, then leaned close and pressed my pink lips to the glass separating us. "Welcome to the party, Mal. We've been waiting for you."

Pestilence glowered around the room, spotting his brothers in their various cells. "If you wanted to see me so badly, you could have called. You didn't have to kidnap me."

"Where would the fun in that be? Besides, we all know you're not one to answer your phone. They call you a hermit for a reason, darling. Where is it you've been hiding? Switzerland? No. Sweden? Eh, it doesn't really matter anymore, does it? You're here now."

"Where exactly is here? I really expect more from you, Hel. This is a dank hole in the ground. Are you really that hard up? You know I'm always willing to help in exchange for something. I could've hacked into a bank and transferred some funds your way."

"I don't need your money, Mal. I'm just fine on my own." My eye twitched. He was getting to me. He always could, even more so than Grim, and that man was my ex-lover.

Perhaps it was because Malice and my sister had once been thought to be an unstoppable team—until he knocked her up and abandoned her. Well, she says he abandoned her, but he has maintained another story. I honestly don't care what he has to say. Chicks before dicks. Horse before . . . Meh, it just doesn't quite have the same ring to it.

"So what now?" Sin asked as he leaned against the back of his cell. "You've got us all here. What are you planning to do with us?"

Grim's eyes found mine. He knew. Of course he did. We were two peas in a pod, he and I. Okay, not really. He was a lot grumpier and above it all than I was. He'd lost his joy somewhere along the way, whereas I still reveled in our divine purpose.

"Now, Sinclair darling, I steal all your power and start my apocalypse."

Chaos slammed his fist against the glass, making the magically reinforced barrier quake. If I hadn't already triple-checked that it would contain him, I might have been scared he'd escape before I'd gotten what I needed.

"Just like that?" Sin asked.

"Just like that. Well, minus the raising of my army and a nifty little ritual to kick things off. But those are just formalities, really. It's basically in the bag."

"And what are you going to do with us when you finish this little ritual?" Grim asked.

"Leave you all right where you are. You'll be nothing but husks by the end, but that's just fine. I don't care if you spend eternity trapped in your cells. You deserve it for the way you treated me."

Grim scoffed. "How we treated you?"

Chaos picked up the thread. "We're the ones in cages. How can you possibly claim to be the injured party?"

I pouted. "You never take my sisters and me seriously. You four think you're the only ones who could ever succeed at our task. Well, I showed you, didn't I? And I have a secret for you. I didn't even need a penis to do it."

"All you've done, sweetheart, is piss us off," Sin said, his voice thick with lazy seduction. I didn't think he even realized he'd turned it on. It was like that with him, the incubus that he was.

"The four of us may not much like each other these days, but it doesn't mean we won't work together when the occasion calls for it," Mal added. "I don't think you realize the level of shit you've gotten yourself into."

I didn't want to listen to them anymore. They were boring me with their incessant complaining. And, honestly, their opinions really weren't serving me any longer, and wasn't that part of the new me this year? My resolution? Get rid of things that don't serve me.

I'd start with them.

Skipping over to the record player, I snatched one of my favorite albums and replaced the soundtrack I'd been listening to. I selected an appropriate song for the occasion and turned the volume as loud as it would go before training my gaze on the four men in my clutches.

"I'll be back," I said, then I hit play.

If they said anything in response, I couldn't hear them. Instead I left, like the mastermind I was. I had a few loose ends to tie up. But I'd be back. Soon.

The grand finale was about to begin.

THIRTY-ONE

"Oh my God, Tor, put me down. I'm going to hurl if you keep bouncing me around like this." Kiki's voice was a high-pitched whine, but I didn't want to set her down until I knew she'd be safe. Dahlia would never forgive me if Kiki was harmed.

It had taken longer than I'd hoped to sprint through the woods. By the time the castle came into view, the villagers had already breached the gates, and the sounds of battle met my ears.

Fuck.

So much for meeting Dahlia in her room. I could only hope the others had gotten to her and would keep her safe. I was needed down here.

There was just one problem. I couldn't exactly fight with a one-hundred-and-something-pound spitfire on my shoulder. Before we fully cleared the treeline and gave up our position, I dropped her.

She let out a garbled cry as she righted herself, pushing her hair out of her face as she grumbled, "Not exactly what I meant, but I'll take it."

"There's a tower about a hundred feet in that direction. I want you to run as fast as you can and secure yourself inside. The key is hidden in the third brick from the keyhole. Lock it behind you and don't come out until I give the all-clear. Do you understand me?"

She blinked up at me, her expression a little dazed. "Yes, Viking daddy."

I shuddered, remembering the doll calling me daddy. "Never call me that again."

"I can't promise you that. Words just fall out of my mouth sometimes. Shocking, I know, but your girl has no filter. If I thinks it, I speaks it."

Taking her by the shoulders, I gave her a little shake. "Focus, Kiki. Your life may depend on it. Now run!"

I pushed her as gently as I could manage in the direction I'd indicated, but she stumbled like I'd shoved her.

"Use your inside hands," she grunted, rubbing at her shoulder, before picking up her bag where I'd dropped it. "Hey, Tor?"

"Yeah?"

"Don't die, okay? Dahlia needs you."

"I don't intend to."

"Good," she said, giving me a forced smile before trotting off.

A scream tore through the air from the direction of the fray, and I saw Sorcha Blackthorne striding into a group of three villagers, tearing hearts from chests and heads from bodies even as they slashed at her with silver blades. Her skin opened and she bled freely, but she didn't stop. As soon as she reached the next man, her eyes glowed a blinding amber, and she whispered something that was impossible for me to hear.

The man immediately took the dagger he'd intended for

her and plunged it into his own eye. He was dead before she stood up.

With long, powerful strides, I ate up the distance so I could join my fellow residents. This was my fault, after all, and I never shied away from a conflict. For the first time, I willingly let my beast take over when human lives were at stake. My body swelled as the fury of their attack seeped into my bones. My mate wasn't here. She wasn't in direct danger, but they'd kill her if they found her. I would kill them first.

The second one of the villagers laid eyes on me, his mouth dropped in horror and he turned to flee. "It's him! It's the be—"

He never finished his sentence. My clawed hand slid through skin and muscle like butter as I tore through his back, grasped his spine, and tugged.

He died instantly.

Pity. I wouldn't have minded at least a gurgle from him.

It was much the same with the next human to face off with me. And the one after him. I quickly lost count of the bodies I left in my wake, pausing in my slaughter only long enough to scan the battleground and track what my allies were doing.

Across the grounds, Oz and Bru faced off with enemies of their own. The mind reader grasped a woman by the face, her mouth open on a scream, while Bru used his magic to hurl folks out of his way and bind them to various objects to keep them there.

"Tor!" Sorcha shouted, just in time for me to turn and catch a shovel to the face.

"Got him," the man snarled, but I simply spat out a mouthful of blood and some teeth before turning on him and slashing his belly wide open.

He gasped, his hands going to his gut as though he could hold it all in. It took seconds for him to collapse and bleed out. My favorite part was when his leg twitched and his bladder released.

I reached up and wiped the blood out of my eyes before turning to see a terrifying ginger blur leap into the air with a screech before landing on a man's head and plunging two curved blades into his shoulders. It was Joffrey, his eyes wild, a hat I'd never before seen on him identifying him as a redcap.

"So that's what you are. Go figure."

Just as I was about to dismiss the man and go in search of my next victim, I spied the arrow a heartbeat before it slammed into him. Joffrey dropped to his knees, blood gurgling from his mouth as he tried in vain to tug the arrow free.

"Iron?" he choked out. "They've killed me."

Even as he was dying, he lashed out with his blade, cutting a man down at the knees before falling to the ground lifeless.

Joff was hardly a friend, barely an acquaintance, but he was on our side, and his death sent me into a blinding rage.

I had just finished snapping a man's neck when I finally saw her. My moonlight-haired beauty. She and her other mates had arrived.

Her voice rang through my mind, a scream of my name before pressure in my side indicated my distraction had gotten the better of me. I looked down to see a spear sticking out of me, but luckily it hadn't hit anything vital. With a roar, I snapped the end off and pulled the rest clean through. I would heal. And the person who launched it at me would pay with their life.

Using the handle of the spear, I tossed it at my attacker

like a javelin, sending it through their eye socket with enough force they were thrown to the floor.

"My eye! My eye!"

Stalking over to him, I leaned down, not stopping until he could feel my breath on his face. "It's not your eye you should be worried about."

He opened his mouth to speak, already dying due to the spear in his brain, but I simply raised my foot and slammed it down on his throat, crushing his windpipe and killing him.

Ensuring I was safe for the moment, I finally allowed myself another glance in the direction I knew Dahlia to be. Thanks to the tattoo, I could sense her at the periphery, almost like an orbiting planet. She was busy talking to Hades, who was using his shadows to deal with those foolish enough to come near him. Hook was nowhere to be seen, and Kai . . .

The dragon shifter was looking straight at me, an unspoken message aimed my way. Then, with a slight nod, he released his own inner monster and took to the sky with a mighty roar I couldn't help but echo.

We would win the day.

We had to.

But even as I made the vow, I realized that despite the bodies littering the ground, they kept coming. We were horribly outnumbered.

THIRTY-TWO

KAI

I took to the sky the moment I saw the look on Tor's face. He'd been out here holding them at bay the best he could while we'd done what we could to pack and prepare for the worst. But as time passed and the sounds of the battle below only intensified, we knew it was time to join in.

Hook had never returned, and I could only assume he'd been successful in his mission, given the number of residents who were fending off attackers of their own.

But how many of us were there against how many of them? From the ground, it appeared as though we were winning. I knew better. There could be thousands just waiting for their turn. It all depended on just how much they hated us.

Learning the answer to that question could be the difference between winning or losing the day. That was why instead of focusing on the villagers already on Black-wood's grounds, I flew high, jetting over the gates and beyond. The hope was that the crowd would die off, that the majority of their numbers were already inside.

That was not the reality.

More than double the number of fighters were waiting their turn, weapons in hand.

This was no half-cocked, drunken brawl. This was a strategic battle. One they'd planned and prepared for, likely for months. The Ripper had just been the excuse they'd needed to strike.

"Intruders! Turn them to ash!"

Building my dragon fire in my chest, I dropped within range, dodging their arrows and bullets. I knew this was my chance to do some damage without my compatriots getting caught in the crossfire.

"Aim for his heart!" a man yelled from below. "That's where he's vulnerable."

Before they could even try, I released a column of flame, turning my head from left to right as though I were an enormous flamethrower. They burned, the entire line of ten men. And I didn't regret a single one of their deaths.

One thing that did pique my interest, however, was that my flame was blue. I instantly recognized it as the same blue as Hades's fire. This must be one of the effects of our bond. For some reason, my dragon liked that. He let out an approving roar, appreciating the sense of clan that came with the connection. He'd been alone for so long, kept separate even from me. Belonging to his mate and the rest of her men satisfied something inside him—inside us—we hadn't even realized was missing.

"He's bleeding. You got a hit in," another man said. "Ready the archers!"

Bleeding? I wasn't bleeding. I'd have felt it if they'd hit me.

Swooping low, I snatched the lying prick up, eating him

in one clean bite. The shouts of protest from his comrades did nothing but encourage me to do it again.

So I did.

Dragons had to eat, too, you know. What better meal could there be than that of an enemy?

Landing in the midst of a small grouping, I roared loud enough that they had to cover their ears before swiping a few of them off their feet with my tail. I hit them so hard they flew into the trees, then I reared up on my hind legs and used my powerful wings to create a gust that knocked them all on their arses.

Ursa bellowed and charged them, his bloodied maw proving he'd already taken out at least a few of our foes. A bear as large as him could be brought down, but he'd destroy his attackers in the process.

I heard them gathering for another attack, the warning sounds of a commander rallying his troops. My fire still needed time to build, however, so I took off, flying higher into the sky, needing to put my eyes on Dahlia before my next attack.

She stood within the protective shadows of Hades, the god refusing to let her leave his sight. My heart ached for the fear in her eyes. It burned bright, along with a righteous fury.

"Kai! Watch out!"

Her warning came too late.

I dove to the left, anticipating some sort of missile, but their aim had been perfect. The bolt shot through the membranous part of my torso, where it connected to my right wing. Twisted as I was, I finally noticed the dozens of other arrows lodged into my side and wing.

How had I not felt them?

Tor, I realized. Just as I'd inherited Hades's fire, I'd taken on his Berserker's imperviousness to pain. Ideal in theory, but perhaps not as useful as one might initially think.

Unfortunately, just because I couldn't feel the pain, that didn't mean I was invincible. Another spray of bolts punched through my already battered wing, leaving gaping holes and shredding the thin membrane as easily as a hot knife through butter. Iron and the fae didn't play nicely together. We were all taught that from an early age, and the damage these arrows had done made that clear as day.

And that wasn't the only trick they'd used either.

A heavy weight clouded my mind, the sensation not unlike a net capturing its prey. Despite the adrenaline and fury pouring through my veins, I was inexplicably sleepy. Lethargic.

Tranquilizers.

The fuckers had drugged me. Of course. They knew Blackwood had a dragon.

Attention on Dahlia, I tried my hardest to aim my large body away from her, not that there was much I could do. I was already plummeting, my wings no longer working, thanks to the iron and sedatives in my system. I'd lose consciousness before hitting the ground if the way my vision was blurring was any indication. But I had no doubt when I crashed into the earth, those would be my final moments.

I hoped she survived.

I hoped she was proud of her dragon.

I hoped she could forgive me for leaving her.

THIRTY-THREE

I've written my fair share of fight scenes. I knew that war was bloody and brutal, that it was chaos in all its glory. But this . . . I had not been prepared for this. Dismembered limbs were literally everywhere. Along with corpses, blood, and, well, I wasn't exactly sure what I was looking at, but I think at one time it might have been some-one's stomach.

The butcher knife I'd snagged before leaving the main house seemed like a ridiculous child's toy compared to what the rest of them were using. Claws and teeth, brute strength and guns, arrows and fire. But I needed something to defend myself and my men with, didn't I?

At least, I'd expected to. But Hades wouldn't let me anywhere close to the fight. Every move I made to engage was met with his shadows stopping me.

"I can help, damn you," I growled, my frustration over feeling useless making me exaggerate my skills. I've never so much as trained with a knife. I couldn't even lie and say I had some long underutilized self-defense skills from a course I took after I moved out on my own. I was a writer, not a fighter. And if I tried to go out there on that field and use my kitchen knife, I was as liable to gut myself as I was one of the villagers.

"You can't. You're a distraction, baby doll. None of us want to see you harmed, and you going out there would mean us willingly putting you in harm's way. I know you want to fight, but there's nothing on this earth or any fucking realm that will get me to allow it."

I didn't appreciate his use of the word 'allow' like I was some kind of child who needed permission instead of a grown-ass woman. But since he was the one with the shadow magic currently keeping me in place, there wasn't a whole lot I could do about it either. I also knew I was the reason Hades hadn't really joined in the fight. Our side could certainly use the help of the god of the underworld, but he was fully focused on keeping me alive rather than taking down our foes. I wasn't sure how to feel about that. Maybe he wasn't either, because Hades glanced down at Asshole, who stood at my feet. "Go. Protect your goddess and do your worst, Cerberus."

Asshole yipped, and the shadowy barrier keeping us safe opened for him. He ran for the battle, body morphing to over ten times his size, white fluffy fur replaced with a sleek black coat. But it wasn't that change that brought a gasp to my lips. It was the three heads, mouths filled with razor-sharp teeth, that stopped me. Cerberus attacked with a fury I'd only seen from Tor. But for every enemy he killed, three more came through the gates.

I watched, frustration and horror churning inside me as more and more blood was spilled. Joffrey went down, followed by Logan, his howl of agony when a silver spear punched through his chest reaching my ears and making me cry out.

"You might not be a fighter, but you have other gifts that might help."

I flinched at the unexpected sound of my mother's voice in my mind. I looked around, wondering if she was here somewhere, but I didn't see her.

She had a point, though. I did have a certain set of skills that definitely packed a punch. Problem was, I wielded my scream more like a sledgehammer than a scalpel, and the last time I'd tried to bring the dead to my aid, it was a short-lived affair. In sum, a bitch lacked control. This is the exact reason I'd been trying to train and build up my metaphorical muscles.

Tor's bellow called my attention to where he was literally tearing limbs from bodies. My beautiful demigod was coated in blood, his eyes burning black, Berserker rage pumping through his veins. But he staggered and fell to his knees as I watched, his palm pressing on the wound in his side as blood—his blood—poured freely down his leg.

Before I could even process that, a bellow of pure outrage shook the trees as Kai's dragon took a hit. I didn't think something as small as an arrow would have any impact on such a massive creature, but apparently I was wrong. Horror and fear turned my insides to ice as Kai tried to flap his great wings, but one seemed to be stuck at a weird angle. Almost like he no longer had control of the muscles within it. Then, without warning, his enormous form went slack, and he was no longer flying through the night sky but falling.

Fucking falling.

"Get back! He's coming down. Fuck," Hades growled, arm banding across my chest as he pushed me away in case Kai crashed to the ground near us.

My dragon landed less than a hundred feet from where

we stood, the force of his body hitting the ground akin to an earthquake, causing everyone nearby to lose their footing and fall. Everyone but Hades and I. His shadows kept me in place.

"They're not going to stop, Dahlia. There are too many of them. Your men will die."

No. They couldn't die. I couldn't lose them.

My eyes darted across the battlefield. Where was Hook? Why hadn't he come back to me?

Out of my four mates, only one was still standing, so far as I could tell. They weren't dead, though; I could sense them through our bond. They were hurt, critically so, and I couldn't get to them.

"You know what you need to do. You can end this here and now."

"We need more fighters," Hades muttered. "Is this all we have? I can't use my shadows and keep you alive at the same time."

"You've done it before. One, a hundred, a thousand, it's no different. This is what you were born for, Dahlia."

Hades wasn't going to let me into the conflict. There was no possibility of that happening, but there was a way I could join without ever leaving his protection. My mother was right. I was born to do this.

Crouching down, I planted my palms on the cold, damp earth and tapped into my power. They were there, so many of them. Hidden underneath the grounds, buried like the secrets they were. All the former residents of Blackwood who'd never been allowed to leave. My limbs shook as I siphoned all of my magic into the dirt, picturing it spreading like a drug through veins until each and every remaining body was touched by me. Commanded by me. My very own army of the dead. I didn't need their souls. I didn't need information from them. All I required was their ability to fight, and my power would give them exactly enough life to do that until I released them.

It's what I'd done when I summoned them in the cemetery. Granted, I'd been suffering from massive blood loss and hadn't been able to keep them going for long, but it had done the job. Now, though, I wasn't injured, and I was fueled by incredible purpose. My men were suffering. They were in danger. There was no way I'd let anything happen to them, so these corpses, these zombies, or whatever the technical name for them was, wouldn't stop fighting until every last one of these assholes was eliminated.

"Dahlia, what are you doing? That's too many of them," Hades warned. He'd clearly tapped into my thoughts and worried I couldn't do this, but with the magic binding us all together, I was stronger than I'd ever been.

"Too late. I have to do something."

The ground shook, a vague tremor like an aftershock, but before long my army was clawing their way out of the dirt, some doing so in the middle of the battlefield, others coming from all angles. There were shambling creatures with clumps of dirt in their hair and most of their flesh intact. Others were yellowed skeletons, their clothing or what was left of it in tatters. Others still were barely more than crawling torsos. And then there were the animals. Dogs, cats, horses, all of Blackwood's familiars and pets had also risen.

Sorcha had warned me that many creatures died here. I didn't think she understood how true her statement had been.

"Holy hell," my dark lord whispered. "You don't have their souls in your grasp, do you?"

I shook my head, needing every ounce of control I had to keep them focused before I assigned them their task.

Hades's lips were at my ear, pride in his voice. "Give 'em what they have coming, baby doll."

Power sang through me, lighting me up from the inside. I didn't feel drained at all by using my gift to reanimate the dead. If anything, their existence made me feel stronger. Energized. Like somehow they were empowering me.

With a pulse of energy through the tether between myself and the bodies, I whispered, "Fight for us."

The shambling zombies turned their attention to the villagers, their attack pressing forward without stopping. Sure, they could be destroyed, but they didn't feel pain the way the rest of us did, so they'd keep going until they were nothing but powder, and all because I willed it.

I scanned the melee, heart pounding as I searched for Tor. I needed him to come to me and remove himself from the danger now that my army was at work. Then he, Hades, and I could go search for Cas and rescue Kai. When I caught sight of his towering form, horns glinting with the blood of his enemies, eyes strained with fatigue, I opened my mouth to call his name. But before I could, a large arrow, twin to the ones used on Kai, hit him in the chest. Shock registered on his face as he glanced down his body, and he lifted one arm in an attempt to pull the arrow from his flesh. Only his limb was sluggish, his steps staggering, and as I watched on in horror, my untamable Viking's eyes rolled back in his head and he fell.

It was too much. The straw that broke me. I'd already watched my dragon fall from the sky, my pirate was missing, and now my beast was dead or dying.

No.

This wasn't happening.

It couldn't.

I needed it to stop. I needed everything to stop.

So I did the only thing I could. The one thing that felt instinctual and appropriate for a woman who'd reached the end of her rope.

I screamed.

I screamed, and they died.

They all died.

THIRTY-FOUR

KIKI

"Dahlia," I croaked as I swear I heard an echo of her screaming.

My head throbbed, the wave of nausea accompanying the opening of my eyes causing me to screw them tightly shut again while I got my bearings. Blinking until my vision cleared, I took in my surroundings. Where the fuck was I? Oh yeah, Blackwood. Dahlia's Viking had sent me to the tower so I could be *safe* while he fought off angry villagers. Except I hadn't made it up the stairs, instead slipping and falling on a patch of ice and soundly knocking myself out. I was a real help in a crisis, let me tell you.

Life had gotten a lot more interesting since Dahlia came to Blackwood and learned the truth about herself and the world she belonged to. Some days I still had to pinch myself to make sure I wasn't dreaming. Days like the one where I knocked on a vampire's door and willingly entered their McMansion. Or today when, I shit you not, a whole-ass zombie walked by me.

Panic, followed by disgust, crept up my throat. She was

bloody and partly decomposed, but I was pretty sure I recognized her.

"Is that the fucking doctor?" I said, clapping a hand over my mouth because, rule one of the zombie apocalypse, don't draw attention to yourself lest they eat your brains.

"Down with the ship. Captain goes down with the ship." The voice filtered to my ears, capturing my focus and turning my attention to the unconscious man I'd seen when I first ran over here. Safe to say he wasn't unconscious any longer. He pushed himself upright, and recognition shot through me.

"Pirate? Is that you?" I got to wobbly feet, stumbling to him.

"Are you lost? Do you need a happy thought?" he asked, his eyes unfocused.

"Caspian. It's Kiki. I'm here to get Dahlia."

"Dahlia? My darling Wendy-bird. Where is she?" He stood, head swiveling as he searched for her. He looked worse for wear, drying trails of blood coming from his eyes, nose, and ears.

"Yikes, buddy. What the hell happened to you?"

"Ticktock, ticktock . . ." His attention shifted past me to the zombie still shuffling her way to wherever it was zombies go. In search of brains, I guess.

He stood ramrod straight, his shoulders so stiff he could've doubled as a hanger.

"What is i—"

"Hold that thought," he said, finger pressed to my lips.

Then the man rushed straight up to the zombie, somehow not getting eaten by her. He stopped her with a palm to the shoulder, but she continued to attempt to move forward. The guy was stronger than he seemed.

"My, my, Lizzie. You've looked better. What the devil

happened to you? You look like you've been dead and buried for months."

The zombie didn't have much to say to that, just a low, drawn-out groan that made me think those people in charge of the video games knew more than the average bear.

"It would appear you have something I've been looking for." Without even an ounce of reverence, Hook grabbed a pendant that was hanging around her neck, yanking hard enough to break the chain.

He stepped aside, giving her a courtly bow as she continued her journey past us. "As you were."

"Caspian, what the fuck was that?"

"Hold on, love. I need a moment." He proceeded to press the dirty pendant to his lips, his nose curling in disgust as he spit out some—bleck—grave dirt. "How I've missed you. I'll never let you go again. Next to my heart, that's where you belong."

Despite the somewhat fanciful words, there was something different about the pirate. I couldn't quite put my finger on it. He seemed more focused, maybe. Alert and present in a way he definitely hadn't been when he'd woken up.

"No wonder I couldn't find it. It *was* buried, but obviously in a place no one would think to look. Poor Lizzie. I wonder how long she's been dead. Someone did a good job of bludgeoning her and covering it up. Hmm, perhaps it was the Ripper? But no. He seemed very invested in her."

"Caspian?"

"Hmm?" he asked, glancing over at me as if he'd forgotten I was there.

"What are you talking about?"

"I found my compass," he said, waving the pendant like it was a prize.

"Um . . . congratulations?"

"Yes, thank you. Oh, this is brilliant. The day has been saved, don't you see? I'm myself again. Not a trace of madness to be found."

I cocked one brow. "That's what you say. There's a fuck ton going down just over that hill, man. I don't think the day has been saved in the slightest."

He grinned, his attention shifting yet again as he looked in the direction Zombie Masterson had disappeared. "Come to think of it. It's not every day the dead just up and walk about. I wonder . . ."

He started walking.

"Sure, sure, I'll be right there. No need to wait for me or anything."

Guess I couldn't exactly be surprised that a pirate didn't have manners. I stumbled after him, chasing him up the cobblestone ramp until the main grounds came into view. What I saw wasn't a fight. It was a massacre. Everyone within the gates was dead. The state of their deadness, however, varied. Some were long dead, like the doctor, though instead of shambling toward something, they were standing still and swaying in place. Others had only just been recently killed. Like *very* recently. My stomach churned as my eyes landed on a corpse I recognized. The last time I saw him, he'd been delivering my box of dresses to Dahlia. I think she said his name was Bru. He was so handsome; he almost looked like he was just sleeping. Except for the way his vacant eyes stared at nothing.

"What are they doing?" I whispered as I tore my eyes away from him and back to the zombies doing their best streetlamp impersonations.

"Waiting."

"For what?"

"Dahlia's orders."

Dahlia had done this? She'd brought forth an army of zombies to fight the villagers? But why, when they'd clearly been killed already?

The bodies littering the grass were reminiscent of that one time I went on a date to see a fucking WWII movie. Spoiler alert, I hated it. I hated this too. Especially when I realized that the only living person standing was Dahlia. Hades was there, but he was on his knees, head cradled in his hands, blood leaking out of his ears.

Suddenly the carnage in front of me made sense. I'd seen this before. Lived through it, technically. The footage from the Rebel premiere came back to me. Dahlia's scream, the creepy look in her eyes, and the way her hair floated like she had her own wind machine. The bodies as they dropped all around her. Our bodies. Because, yeah, I'd gone down with the rest of them.

"Oh, my darling girl. What have you done?" Hook murmured.

"Dahlia wouldn't do this on purpose," I said, instantly coming to her defense.

"She would if she thought her mates were at risk."

"What do you mean?"

Hook pointed to the left, a large black lump of something in the way of whatever he was trying to show me. "That's Kai." He pointed somewhere else. "And that's Tor. Plus, I was missing. Draw your own conclusions, love."

"You seem to be drawing them on your own just fine."

He tapped his temple. "I have the added benefit of her thoughts, you see."

My brows lifted. "And you want me to believe this is the

sane version of you I'm talking to? I'm not sure that compass did all you hoped it would, buddy. You're still mad as a hatter to me."

"She's my mate. We're bonded. Believe what you want, but we have to get down there and stop her because she's so consumed by her rage we're going to lose her if we don't. Dahlia may be willing to do anything to save us, but I doubt she'll be able to live with herself once she realizes she killed as many friends as she did enemies."

The urgency in his tone brooked no argument. He was dead serious. Also, Dahlia's hair was doing that scary floaty thing again, and Hades still hadn't managed to get to his feet.

"Right, so she's spiraling. I know how to deal with this. Stand back and let the master work."

Then I was jogging, doing my level best not to think too hard about what I was jumping over and weaving around as I crossed the yard to get to her. These zombies may have seemed calm and unaware of their surroundings, but I'd seen my share of horror flicks, and the last thing I was going to do was let one of them sink their teeth into me.

"Kiki, wait! I don't think you should . . . Oh, bloody hell."

I didn't stop. He could chase me all he wanted. If that pirate thought I was going to let my bestie's doom spiral consume her, he clearly didn't know me.

Friends don't let friends commit mass murder. I'm pretty sure it was in the bylaws, right below mentioning lettuce in the teeth and before no crying alone.

I just hoped I wasn't too late.

THIRTY-FIVE

E choes of her scream still ricocheted through me, the fury-filled wail having taken down every living thing within range. Even I was affected by the power inside her, and while there was no chance she could kill me, it still hurt like a motherfucker.

My brain felt a bit like it was dripping down the inside of my skull, or maybe more like Jell-O that hadn't quite set. I pressed an index finger to my ear, wiggling it around as if it might do something to mitigate the ringing.

"Fuck me, baby doll," I muttered, glancing up at my goddess, hoping she heard me. But when I caught sight of her, I realized she was lost to the rage, and I wouldn't get her back until she relinquished her hold on the zombies in her thrall.

I scanned the battlefield, looking for one particular form, when my breath punched out of my chest. No. Fuck.

Cerberus hadn't been unaffected by Dahlia's scream. My heart lurched at the sight of him, not in his towering three-headed form, but returned to his favored tiny white fluffball visage. He was so still I had to hold my breath as I watched him. Immortal he might be, but that didn't make him any more immune than I had been. I nearly cried out when his little belly lifted on a deep breath. Not dead then, merely unconscious. Thank fuck.

This had gotten out of hand. Dahlia had killed indiscriminately. She'd never recover from the guilt of it once she came back to herself.

"Dahlia, I need you to look at me, baby," I urged, desperate for her to snap out of it.

She didn't even spare me a glance as she held the zombie army at the ready, all of them focused on the quiet mouth of the property.

While she was distracted by them, I allowed myself the opportunity to cast my senses out to see if there were any other survivors. The sheer number of souls roaming the property overwhelmed me. They were confused, waiting for someone to explain what had happened. I couldn't pay them any attention, not yet. Not until I got my answers.

Ignoring them and their need, I searched for those whose deaths would truly destroy my love. When my mind brushed against Tor's and Kai's, finding them both unconscious rather than dead, I released a breath I hadn't realized I'd been holding.

The soft sound of a woman calling out Dahlia's name called my attention away from Dahlia's other mates, and when I saw Kiki rushing toward us, Hook hot on her heels, another rush of relief hit me. Blood ran down her face from a wound at her temple, and Hook looked even worse, with rust-colored stains coming from his nostrils and ears. Given the injuries they'd sustained, it was obvious they both must've been unconscious when Dahlia loosed her scream.

Recalling a detail from Dahlia's story about the night her father attempted to sacrifice her, that was how Brother

Sam had survived as well. She'd kicked him and he'd hit his head, rendering him unconscious before she screamed, which sparked his decades-long reign of terror.

So clearly the mind needed to be engaged and conscious in order for Dahlia to destroy it with that special gift of hers. Or be a god, I supposed. Good thing for silver linings.

"Baby, I need you to look at me," I urged again, but it was no use. Her eyes were clouded over, hair swirling around her even though there wasn't a single gust of wind in the air.

Kiki stumbled up to us, her breaths heaving, worry on her face. "Dahlia, what are you doing?"

"She can't hear you," I said, finally pushing my way to my feet. "She's lost to—"

"Her rage, yeah, yeah. He already told me."

I glanced over her shoulder at Caspian. "Good to see you're alive."

"I very nearly wasn't." When his eyes met mine, there was a clarity there I hadn't seen in a long time, if ever. Whatever had happened while we'd been apart, it seemed that he'd turned some kind of corner.

"Oh, fuck, there's more of them," Kiki whispered, her attention trained on the flood of new enemies coming in through the gates. Armed, dangerous, and nothing to focus on but the zombies and us.

Their presence penetrated the fog Dahlia seemed to be lost in, drawing forth another hissed command. "Attack."

As a unit, the zombies turned toward the villagers and descended upon them. Terrified screams, wails of agony, and useless gunshots filled the once silent night.

"It's a slaughter," Hook said, shock heavy in his tone.

That wave of attackers was dealt with so quickly it was

almost like they hadn't been there at all. And the zombies returned to their state of stasis.

"Dahlia, you have to stop this," Kiki said, grabbing her friend by the shoulders and shaking her.

Dahlia didn't respond. There was not so much as a twitch of her eye to indicate that she'd heard a word Kiki had said. Nothing except the whisper of her voice in my mind.

"I can't stop. Not until the threat is exterminated."

"Keep going," I urged. "She can hear you."

"Come on, Dee. This isn't you. You don't kill people. I know what your scream did, but you've undone it before." She grabbed Dahlia's face and tried to make eye contact. "You brought them back at the premiere, remember? All of us. We don't even remember it happening. You can fix this. It's not too late. You're not the villain of this story, Dee. You're the heroine. Come on. They don't deserve to die like this."

Dahlia blinked, some of the cloudiness leaving her eyes.

"You've almost got her," I whispered. "Don't stop now."

"Oh, shit, Tor's still alive," Hook said, his attention trained on the Novasgardian as he slowly got to his feet.

Tor stumbled a few times, dazed, and to my surprise, Hook ran to meet him and offer a helping hand.

"Come on, Dee. They're innocents. Most of them. A few, I think, might even be your friends, or on their way to it. I mean, no one is coming for my spot at the top, but it's never bad to have a backup in case you want to throw a dinner party or something one day."

I chuckled at the tangent, relief making my limbs heavy as Dahlia's thoughts grew even more aware.

"Why would I ever throw a dinner party?"

"Dahlia Moore, you listen to me right now. Do better

than this. If you leave these people dead, I will be so ashamed of you. You'll be just like your father. Worse, because he only killed a few dozen. This is hundreds. Hundreds, Dee. All their blood will be on your hands. I know you don't want to do this."

"I . . . don't," she whispered, her voice hoarse as her attention locked on to Kiki's face.

"There's my girl. Welcome ba—"

I had a split second to catch the horror in Dahlia's expression before everything went to hell.

THIRTY-SIX
DAHLIA

"All their blood will be on your hands. I know you don't want to do this." Kiki's voice broke through the haze of vengeful energy controlling me, hitting me where it hurt.

She was right. I didn't want to be like him. I wasn't a cold-blooded killer. I'd only wanted to protect Tor and Kai. I was supposed to be one of the good guys, not the baddie.

It was harder than I wanted to admit to let go of the fury storming through me. I wondered if this was what it felt like for Tor when his beast was in control. Was this something I'd taken on from him, or was this all me?

"I . . . don't." My words were just a faint whisper, but I knew she heard them when her lips spread in a smile.

"There's my girl," she said, her voice warm and filled with relief.

I wanted to hug her, but I was still coming out of the trance-like state I'd been in. I blamed that for what happened next.

Out of literally nowhere, Masterson—the alive impostor version, not the once evil ghost—materialized.

385

Her eyes met and held mine while her lips twisted up in a malevolent smirk.

"Welcome ba—" Kiki's words were cut off as blood bloomed across her baby pink T-shirt.

"I think that's enough out of you," Masterson crooned as she ripped the dagger out of Kiki's back and laughed.

"Kiki!" I screamed as my best friend fell into my arms, blood already bubbling out of her mouth as she choked.

Hades was off and running, shadows snaking out ahead of him to latch on to Masterson. But it was too late. She vanished as if she'd never been there at all.

"Keeks," I breathed, sinking to the ground with her limp body against mine. "Hold on, don't leave me. I can fix this."

Once we were on the ground, I pressed my palms to the wound in her chest, trying to stanch the blood loss. Cas and Tor stood over us, and my gaze flicked frantically from one to the other.

"Do something! Help me! Go get a healer, something!"

But there was no healer. I'd killed them all. The healers and everyone else.

Caspian tore off his shirt and handed it to me to help with stopping her bleeding. "Here, use this."

"Gem," Kai breathed, his human form bearing all the injuries he'd taken as a dragon. But he was alive. All my men were. I'd be happy about that later. Once I knew Kiki would be all right.

"It's going to be okay, Keeks. I've got this. We'll get you to a doctor, and you'll be good as new."

Her lips trembled as she tried to form words, more blood—far too bright a red—bubbling out of her mouth.

"It's okay. You don't have to talk. Just think about your cool scar and all the stories you'll be able to tell. Maybe you'll get a hot doc of your own."

"Dee . . ." she gasped. "Stop."

"No. I won't. I can't do this . . . w-without you. You can't . . . Keeks, you have to get through this."

Tears were streaming down my face because I knew the truth. My hands, her clothes, the shirt Cas gave me, were all soaked in her blood.

"Th-this isn't y-your fault, Dahlia," Kiki managed to force out as she shivered so hard her teeth chattered. "Don't b-blame yourself."

I hated that she was wasting her energy trying to comfort me at a time like this. But that's who she'd always been.

"Keeks," I whispered, my heart fucking breaking as her eyelids fluttered. "Please don't leave me. I need you. You're my best friend."

"Al . . . ways . . ."

And then she was still. So still I had to hold my breath so I could try and register hers. Except none came.

"No. No. No. This can't be happening." I stroked her face, staring down at her and willing her to open her eyes. "She's cold. Get her a blanket, a coat. Something. Don't just stand there." I glanced around me at all of my men, who stood like solemn sentinels. "What are you doing? Help us!"

"Kærasta—" Tor wrapped his hands around my biceps and tried to lift me.

"No, stop," I shook out of his hold, not ready to be parted from Kiki. I shot Hades an imploring look. "Bring her back. Please. I'll never ask you for anything else, ever. Just please, give her back to me."

"You know I can't, baby doll."

"Fine," I growled, hating my men in that moment. "I'll do it myself."

I still wasn't one hundred percent sure what I'd done

the night of the premiere, but like Kiki had said, I'd brought everyone back to life before. And I'd done it in the greenhouse with those plants, so clearly this was part of my gift. I just needed to do what I always did. Grab hold of the spirits I wanted and send them where they belonged. It was Kat all over again, but on a mass scale.

Easy peasy.

Closing my eyes, I held tight to my friend and let my power flow as I called back every soul I could. I felt each and every one of them hovering around like they'd been waiting for this very thing. It was surprisingly easy. Almost second nature. Some souls I recognized by feel alone. Sorcha. Oz. Bruno. Kiki was there too, but I couldn't seem to grasp her as easily as the others. They all returned to their bodies, standing and looking around in confusion, readying themselves for another round of fighting. All of them but Kiki.

"No. Dammit. Kiki, come back! Come on."

I must have messed up. Tried to do too many at once.

Closing my eyes, I tried again, calling out her name. Hades's hand was on my shoulder, giving me a little shake. "Stop, baby doll. You don't want to do this."

"What the fuck do you know about what I want?" I snarled, grief making me vicious. He was the god of the fucking underworld. He could help me if he wanted to; I knew it. He'd made all those deals in the stories. This wasn't beyond his power.

In a flash, the lord of the dead was in my face, crouched down at my level, his eyes blazing blue fire. "I know you don't want her to end up like Nautica. I also know you are desperate. Don't do something you can't take back. I'll forgive you anything, but you won't forgive yourself."

I shook my head, rejecting his words for no reason other than I needed him to be wrong.

"The others came back just fine. Look at them," I said, flinging my arm out to indicate all the people milling around. They didn't seem to realize what had happened and sounded as if they were regrouping before the next attack. Others were trying to figure out where the zombies had come from.

"About that . . ." Hades started, his eyes scanning the field before returning to me. "Did you notice that only those you reaped were returned?"

"No?"

How could I notice something like that? I hadn't been aware of who I'd . . . reaped. If that's what it had been.

"Anyone that was slain by someone else's hand is still down. I think you can only return those you purged. Because it wasn't a natural death. Their bodies didn't actually die. Not like Kiki's did."

"That . . . that's stupid. You have to be wrong."

"No, baby doll, I don't. I watched it happen with my own eyes."

"We all saw it," Cas said, Kai and Tor nodding along in confirmation.

Tears swam in my eyes. "She's right there. Can't you see her?"

Hades nodded, stroking the back of his hand down my cheek.

"Kiki!" I shouted. "Keeks, it's me!" But the spirit of my best friend didn't acknowledge me. She just stood there, staring off into the distance with a bit of a wistful expression. "Why isn't she talking to me? Spirits always want to talk to me. Usually they don't shut up."

"She's waiting for you to release her so she can take her place in the underworld."

"No. Please. Not Kiki. Don't take her from me."

"I'm not doing anything, Dahlia. This is the natural order."

"No," I whimpered.

"You have to let her go, sweetheart. If you try to force her to stay, it will be Nautica all over again. Or Nellie. She deserves better than that. She deserves to spend her after-life in the Elysian Fields."

Asshole approached us, nuzzling my knee with his fluffy little snout.

"Cerberus has volunteered to be her escort. He'll take care of her, Dahlia. I promise." Gentle blue eyes met mine. "Please, baby doll. Trust me. This isn't goodbye. You have my word. You'll see Kiki again. I'll make sure of it. One of the bright sides to being mated to the god of the under-world is unlimited access to his realm."

Heavy tears rolled down my cheeks. I wanted to sob. To rage. To demand that he make her come back, but I knew I couldn't. I couldn't risk Kiki's soul, not for my selfish whim.

Kai knelt down and scooped Kiki from my arms, and this time, I didn't fight. "I've got her, gem."

Asshole yipped and approached Kiki's faint spectral form, wagging his tail as she followed him without even looking back. I understood why, though. She wasn't meant to stay on this plane. All her business was finished. A portal just like the one I'd seen with Nellie opened and together, they walked through. My Kiki, my best friend, the woman who'd gotten me through the hardest parts of my life, was gone.

I curled in on myself, sobs breaking free as grief unlike anything I'd ever known slammed into me. Nothing would ever be the same again. Who would I call when I got good news? Who would tease me about donkey dicks?

"Dahlia..."

"Gem..."

I forced myself to suck in a breath as Tor and Kai called for me. This was not the time or place to fall apart, but I couldn't exactly help it. My entire world had just imploded.

"Um . . . are they supposed to do that?" Caspian asked, his worried voice stealing my attention.

I followed his gaze to the fight that had broken out between the zombies—my zombies—and the rest of the living creatures on the battlefield. Unfortunately, they weren't under my control any longer, and it was painfully clear they were attacking without prejudice. Villagers and Blackwood residents alike.

"I can't control them anymore." My voice was tight and frantic as I tried to send my power into the zombies.

"Lovely," Cas said, sarcasm thick in his tone.

"They're coming this way. Fuck," Kai said, carefully placing Kiki's body atop a stone bench and readying himself for a fight.

A horde of at least fifteen of the undead pressed closer, most of them fairly well preserved, all of them covered in ichor from those they'd already consumed. They snapped their teeth and reached for us, faster than I expected.

"Fuck!" Hades shouted, sending his shadows to dispose of a few of them, but grunting in frustration when they simply rose again and kept coming. He shifted to his fire, shooting out jets of blue flame. That seemed to help, but it didn't stop more from taking their place.

Not even Tor seemed to be able to rip heads from bodies fast enough to make a dent.

"We need Dahlia safe!" Tor called as he shoved a zombie away.

"Go, baby doll. Go inside and lock the door." Hades sent a blast of shadow fire into one of the approaching corpses, the body continuing to approach even as it burned.

"I don't want to leave you," I protested, the loss of Kiki still raw and painful, bringing to the forefront the understanding that if I were to also lose any of them, I might not survive it. I felt a bit like one of those people who was convinced that they couldn't fall asleep on a plane because it might drop from the sky. If I was here, if I could keep my eyes on them, then they'd be all right.

I knew it was a stupid fallacy. My being here before hadn't done a damn thing to protect Kai's dragon or stop Tor from being taken out. But my heart was struggling with the idea of willingly leaving without them.

"Gem, go. We'll be fine. We can fight better if we're not fearing for your safety."

Kai's words hit me with the force of a freight train. Hades had said it before; I was a distraction.

"Please, darling. Go inside. We will be all right. I swear it." Cas shoved me toward the door, his eyes filled with anxiety.

I nodded, not able to push out the words I really wanted to say, so I thought it instead.

"I love you. All of you. Don't you dare leave me."

Then I ran inside the enormous estate, hoping with everything in me that I'd be able to help somehow. I slammed the door closed, resting my forehead on the glossy wood as I tried to calm my racing heart.

"You look like you've seen a ghost, Dahlia," a sweet voice I recognized whispered in my ear.

I spun around, my mother's spirit standing inches from me. "I have. Too many of them."

"There is quite a conflict raging outside. It's a shame. Are your mates all right?"

I nodded, my hand pressed against my chest as if it could do something to soothe the insistent ache. "For the moment."

"What if I told you I know a way for us to stop it all?"

Interest sparked at her words. "You do?"

"Yes, my sweet daughter. I do."

"This is not the time to be coy. Tell me what to do."

Her smile stretched, her eyes flashing with something I couldn't name as she held out her hand. "All you have to do is come with me."

I placed my hand in hers out of pure reflex. The warmth of her skin against mine drew me up short. I shouldn't be able to touch her, let alone feel her warmth.

"Wait. You're not dead."

Her hold on me tightened to the point of pain, the tips of her fingers digging into my wrist hard enough to draw blood. "No, darling. I'm Death."

THIRTY-SEVEN
DEATH

"Wakey, wakey," I said, throwing cold water on Dahlia's face. "You don't want to miss what Mama's got planned."

Dahlia blinked, slow to return to consciousness after our little jaunt to the bunker. Interplanar travel wasn't easy, and the first time was always the worst. Which worked out in my favor, honestly, because it made it that much easier to position my daughter in the place of honor.

"W-what are you . . ." she murmured, tugging on her restraints. "Let me go. What is this?"

I sighed. "Oh, sweetheart, it's your very own crucifix. You should be excited. Not every girl gets to experience the same fate as Jesus. That's reserved for the very special."

"Weren't common criminals crucified back in the day?" Sin asked.

"Can it. No one's talking to you, Sinclair."

"Cut me down from here. I have to go help them!"

I laughed at her. "You're so cute. They're already dead, I'm sure of it. Your beautiful army of the undead saw to that."

The way her chin wobbled and her eyes filled with tears made me giggle. "You're not my mother. You can't be. She'd never do something this horrible."

"Pfft. Where do you think you got your gifts from, Dahlia? Certainly not that father of yours. He was a clown. A charlatan. Everything of value in your life you inherited from me. A chip off the old block, if you will. I'm going to need you to reevaluate your rather skewed and narrow-minded view of the world, darling one. Power is neither good nor evil, but it is absolute. And I? I'm about to have all the power in the universe at my fingertips."

"I can't believe this one is actually going to win," Malice muttered. "I really thought it would be one of your sisters. Where are they, by the way?"

I gritted my teeth against the rage threatening to make me slip up and do something stupid like snap Dahlia's neck before I was ready. "They weren't invited. They have a way of messing things up."

"Well, you're not wrong," Grim mused. "But I don't think they'll appreciate being left out."

"They'll live," I snapped, my temper momentarily flaring. "Unlike you," I added with a simpering grin.

"You can't kill us. We're immortal," Chaos protested.

"Oh, can't I? Is anything truly immortal these days? Even Hades himself seems to be weaker than ever. Perhaps it's because so few believe in anything other than the power of their social media following. No one worships any longer. Where is the reverence? The fear? The absolute devotion?"

Dahlia scoffed, drawing my attention back to her.

"Something amusing you, daughter?"

"I just find it ironic that my father had a literal cult in

your honor, and when he tried to show the ultimate act of devotion, you snuffed him out."

"Not me, sweetie. You did that."

"You told me to."

"Of course I did. But that's because I had plans of my own. I couldn't let his misguided faith result in the death of my progeny. How else was I to put the pieces on the board and make my strategic moves so we'd end up here?"

Dahlia shook her head, denial stamped across her face.

"You're just starting to realize how brilliant I am, aren't you? Every choice you thought you made, you're realizing I was behind it. That there's no such thing as coincidence. Not even back then." I nodded sagely. "I know, I know. My plan was flawlessly executed. Though it was a bit touch and go there at the end. You really made me work for that last piece."

Dahlia's complexion drained of color as she trembled. "What last piece?"

"Why, you stepping into your power. You were so close for so long, but then that final battle, the way you called the dead to your aid and used your scream to wipe the earth of your enemies." I made a chef's kiss gesture and beamed at her. "It was beautiful. You called up your power like it was a missing part of you, which, honestly, it was. I just gave you the nudge you needed to break down that last little wall.

"Your foolish little friend very nearly ruined my plan. It's why she had to die. She almost got you to return the horde to their graves."

Her eyes widened. "You?"

This was the best part. The grand reveal. My sisters told me all about it. For the final time, I donned my disguise. Elizabeth Masterson's form shimmering into being, the shift between my true self—or at least my preferred one—and hers instantaneous.

"And how does that make you feel, Dahlia?" I asked in Masterson's voice.

"You killed Kiki. You . . . tricked me. I trusted you." A fat tear slipped down Dahlia's cheek, and I almost felt bad for her. Almost.

Ditching the accent, I offered her a simpering smile.

"Yes. Yes. And yes, you did. For someone as untrusting as you, I'm shocked at how quickly you believed every word I said." I sauntered through the room, making sure everything was set. "I'd say I was sorry about your little friend, but that would be a lie. If it makes you feel better, it wasn't personal. But the second she took you under her wing and declared you her family, her fate was set in stone. I was always meant to be your only family. I couldn't have your loyalties divided, sweetheart. I did you a favor, really. Her death was the catalyst. Your last tie to the mortal world and the final thing I could take from you that would push you to accept your full potential. She died. You blossomed. You're welcome, by the way."

"I thought you were my ally."

"No, daughter. *You* were *mine*. My pawn, really. All I had to do was kill the doctor and take her shape, and you played right into my hands."

"You should stay like that, by the by. You look better as a brunette," Grim said.

"Careful, I can still castrate you," I said, dropping the persona.

"I'd like to see you try. In fact, why don't you come over here and do just that?"

"You just want to trick me into releasing you. You should know better, Grimsby. I'm not that stupid."

He shrugged. "It was worth a shot."

Rolling my eyes, I turned back to Dahlia.

"I can't believe it was you. All those sessions, the secrets . . ." She shook her head. "Why pretend to help me if you just wanted to hurt me?"

"I wasn't pretending. I needed you to accept the truth of who you were. More than that, I needed you to trust me. And no one wants to trust someone more than a girl who was cast off and betrayed by the most important people in her life. You wanted to believe in me so badly, you'd have done anything to earn my approval. Poor girl. It was a double whammy. Mommy *and* daddy issues."

The clock chimed, and I let a wide grin spread over my face. "It's time."

"Time for what?" Dahlia asked.

"For my apocalypse. Places, everyone. Oh, wait." I giggled. "You're already there. I'll just hop into my spot, and we'll finish this in style." I skipped to the middle of the room, equidistant from all five of them. In fact, the five of them were all strategically placed on the points of a star, and I was dead center. "Just a warning. This is going to hurt."

Closing my eyes, I took a deep breath before taking a straight pin from my pocket and pricking my finger. "Mmm, I feel just like Sleeping Beauty." I began humming "Once Upon a Dream" as I squeezed my fingertip until a bead of dark blood welled on the surface. Then I turned my hand over and watched as the drop fell and splashed between my feet.

An earsplitting crack of thunder shook the walls, and the lights flickered once, twice, before we were plunged into total darkness. That was, until the glow began in each of the four cells.

"Welcome, Dahlia. You've got a front-row seat to the end of the world. Pity you won't live long enough to enjoy it."

THIRTY-EIGHT

TOR

"Why won't you die, you zombie scum?" I snarled as I bashed in the head of the approaching corpse with a well-thrown boulder.

Exhaustion was getting the better of me, though. Even if I couldn't feel the pain of my injuries, I was still mortal, and I'd lost too much blood. After Dahlia had lost control of the undead army, the battle, such that it was, had definitely shifted. Villagers were no longer coming after Blackwood's residents. Instead all of the living had allied against the dead. Unfortunately, the dead didn't seem to want to, well, die.

Instinct warned me this was a losing battle. How could one defeat an opponent that couldn't be bested?

My gaze swept the chaos, and I caught sight of Kai, naked, bleeding freely, and not faring much better than I. Hook stumbled into view in front of me, one hand clutching his chest, blood pouring from between his fingers.

"What happened to you, pirate?"

"Nicked by an iron dagger. It's just a flesh wound."

"You're bleeding profusely, Hook. That's no flesh wound," I said with a frown. It was unlike the pirate to downplay any situation. That told me more than anything he could say about his injury.

"So are you." He gestured at my body. "Where's the off button for these nightmare creatures?"

The two of us stood our ground, watching the horde of zombies creep up the slight hill where we'd gained the high ground. I had to admit, if I wasn't stitched up soon, I'd lose consciousness. I'd be a veritable feast for the undead.

I shuddered just as Kai cried out from where he was fighting a zombie. He hadn't been able to return to his other form due to the iron lodged in his body, so he'd been left on the ground with the rest of us. Unfortunately for him, the iron was like a slow poison. Not only did it hurt like hell and cut him off from his dragon—and consequently his dragon's fire—but the longer it remained, the slower his reactions became. Which was likely why he didn't notice the half a corpse crawling up on him until after it had taken a chunk out of his leg.

"Bitten?" Hook whispered. "Poor sod. That's the end of him. Unless you know of anything we can do?"

I stared on, shaking my head. "It's doubtful we have the time. And look at the battlefield. We're not going to win this fight. We're vastly outnumbered."

"Then what are we supposed to do, just lay down and die?"

"No. We fight to the bloody, bitter end. And when we reach Valhalla, all I can hope is that Dahlia eventually joins us there."

"Dahlia," he said, her name filled with unmistakable longing. "I should have known a happy ending wasn't in my future. The captain always goes down with his ship."

Hook and I readied ourselves to fight as three shamblers and a crawler approached. Reaching down, the pirate plucked a blade out of the chest of one of the villagers' bodies and gave it a flashy twirl.

"If we're gonna fight, we might as well make it stylish," he murmured. "I'll see you on the other side, brother."

He looked at me expectantly, and I realized he was waiting for a similar sentiment. I clapped him on the shoulder. "You weren't as useless as I once suspected. It will be my honor to die on this battlefield by your side."

His lip curled, but then he laughed. "If we manage to survive, I'm going to teach you how to give a proper compliment, Viking."

I wanted to toss back a barb, but my vision went gray and my knees weakened, causing me to sway like a tree in a windstorm.

"Easy there," Hook grunted as I stumbled into him.

An apology died before ever leaving my lips, my legs failing to support me as I knocked us both to the ground. I struggled to push myself upright, but I was no longer in control of my body. My mind went dark and hazy, my consciousness seeming to float away. The last thing I recall before going still was a feeling not unlike knuckles brushing over my cheek.

Kærasta.

As soon as the word took shape, there was a terrible pain in my chest, like someone had wrapped their fist around it and tugged. Then all sense of her was gone. Vanished. Our bond severed. There was only one way that could happen. I let the darkness take me, hoping when I woke, I would be in Valhalla with my Kærasta.

$\sim$

Hook

THE LAST THING I thought I'd be doing tonight was spending time underneath a giant Viking. But here we were, him nearly crushing me with his weight, zombies approaching with their disgusting teeth gnashing, and rancid breath strong enough to fell a tree. They were going to eat me. I just knew it. I was a delicious delicacy, you know? Pirates were rare and so well-seasoned. All that sea salt.

I didn't know which was worse, though. Dying of iron poisoning or dying by zombie attack. Both were horrifically embarrassing. I think I might prefer the crocodile, truth be told. Was that still an option?

The crawler had his one remaining eye on me, his fingers digging into the ground as he closed the distance between us. Surprisingly, I was more focused on the agony ripping through my chest as Tor's body went limp atop me. It felt worse than the dagger as that stupid villager ran me through. Something was wrong with my Dahlia. She was gone from my senses, her presence snuffed out as though she never existed at all.

"No," I whispered, struggling with all my might to dislodge the heavy weight across me.

I was no match for his bulk, and I could do nothing but watch in mounting horror as the crawler inched ever closer.

"Not like this. Captain Caspian James Hook cannot go out this way. Where's the dignity? The honor?"

Before I could finish my well-deserved rant, several shadow tendrils snaked around us, wrapping both Tor and me up and plucking us up off the ground as if we weighed nothing at all.

"Hades?"

The god stood at the top of the short bank of stairs

leading to the entry of Blackwood. His eyes blazed with divine fury as shadows worked to bring Kai, Tor, and me all to him. He had a knee-high wall of shadow fire between him and the horde, and he was using a combination of said fire and his shadows to dispatch as many of the creatures as he could.

"Took you long enough," I grumbled.

"Should I have left you there to die? It's not too late, you know. I can toss your ass back through the barrier here and now."

I shook my head, letting out a pained *oof* as he dropped us on the stoop. Kai followed, his labored breathing and already necrotic blackened leg revealing he was worse off than any of us.

"She's gone," he rasped.

"I felt it too," Hades said, anger making his voice brittle.

"Is she dead?" I asked. If anyone would know, surely it was the god of the damn dead.

"I can't see her soul. I'm not sure. There's no way to know until I return to the underworld."

I coughed, the metallic taste of blood filling my mouth. "I'm halfway there. I suppose I'll find her first."

He shot me a withering look, but truly, the three of us were pathetic, mostly dead, lying on the steps of our prison.

"Say, you don't suppose there's anything you can do about that, can you? Being a god and all. Can't you use your fancy powers and patch us back up, good as new?"

He shook his head, looking sincerely apologetic. "My power is tied to death, not life. There's nothing I can do for any of you right now."

I coughed again, my spittle foamy and pink as it hit the stone. "Well, I guess . . . now you will have her all to yourself . . . like you always wanted." I sucked in a ragged breath. "You prick."

"Stop," Kai growled, though it came out more kitten than dragon. He was barely holding on. "You cannae talk like it's over."

Without warning, the ground beneath us shuddered, then began a terrible quaking. "Oh, gods, what now?" I muttered.

"What the blazes is that?" Hades glanced up, his face illuminated by something coming from the estate.

Doing my best impersonation of a crawler, I . . . well, I crawled to where he was standing and rolled to my back so I could see whatever it was he was looking at. A shocked gasp left me. Blackwood's facade cracked right down the middle as I watched, and a column of light burst from the roof.

"Bloody hell."

"You're more on the nose than you think," Hades mumbled.

"Meaning?"

"Last time I saw something like this, the gates of hell had just been opened."

I blinked at him, certain the blood loss was making me stupid. "What are you saying?"

"Pretty sure the world is ending, kid."

"Don't call me kid. I'm a captain."

KAI

"WHAT HAPPENED?" I asked, every word labored. It was getting harder and harder to speak through the crippling pain. Tor's Berserker gift had been no match for the iron, and I was fading fast.

The air pressure changed rapidly, my ears popping just like they did when I ascended to the sky as a dragon.

"Obviously good triumphed over evil, and the gates were closed." The dry tone of the man standing over us didn't match the current dire straits we were in.

"Are you . . ." I started, my eyelids heavy.

Fuck, I was tired.

"Who are you?" I finally managed, trying hard to keep my eyes locked on him. They kept going in and out of focus, and there were currently two blond men in leather pants wiggling around.

"You really didn't tell him?" he asked Hades. Scoffing, he spread his arms out as a golden glow emanated from all around him. "I am Gabriel, messenger of—"

"We got it. Unless you're here to save us, you can sod off, mate."

Gabriel scowled at Hook. "Did you know it's considered terribly rude to interrupt someone?"

"Hello, pirate," Hook sang before devolving into a series of painfully wet coughs.

The angel rolled his eyes. "Did you never think to try and rise above your station?"

"Why would I want to? Pirates have all the fun."

"What are you doing here, Gabriel?" Hades interjected. The suspicion radiating from the god put me on alert. Or on as much alert as it could.

I hadn't heard my dragon's voice in my mind since I fell from the sky, and each blink of my eyes lasted longer and longer. I feared the worst. That he was gone, and I was soon to follow.

"I already warned you about this, Hades. I gave you,

Caspian, and Tor chances to keep this from happening. But you were all too selfish to see past your obsession with Dahlia. You could have cut this off before it became a problem. Thwarted Death's plot. Saved the world. But no, you had to think with your dicks. Father save me from oversexed mated creatures."

"Why didn't you come . . . to me?" I asked, confused that he would have approached the others but not bothered with me. Not that I'd have left her, but still. They'd had an opportunity to prove their love and commitment to her, and I'd have appreciated the same.

"The wards only just dropped, and you never left the grounds," he said matter-of-factly.

That made me feel mildly better.

"Where is she?" Hades asked, his voice harsher than I've ever heard.

"I can take you to her. We have to stop Death from finishing her ritual."

"What . . . good are we to . . . her . . . like this?" Caspian choked out.

The fucking angel illuminated from within and the world went white, burning heat engulfing me for only a moment. When the flash of pain was gone and the light dimmed, I felt . . . strong again.

And not just me. My dragon woke, mentally stretching his wings in my mind.

I never thought I'd say it, but I'm grateful you're alive.

"I'm harder to kill than ye'd imagine."

"Bloody brilliant, you are! You know, I've never been a praying man, but I'll light a candle in your honor, Gabe," Hook crowed, getting to his feet.

"Gabriel," the angel corrected, emphasizing the second half of his name.

"Whatever."

The angel cleared his throat and held out a bundle of clothes for me. "You might want to put that away. Something tells me you don't want to walk into a fight fully nude."

"Handy guy to have around," Cas said with a whistle. "See, Hades? He's more of a god than you."

"Stuff it, pirate," Hades said as I pulled on my clothes. He was the only one of us who seemed nonplussed. The god was still staring at Gabriel, arms crossed over his chest. "Why should any of us believe anything you have to say? By your own admission, you tried to make us leave her. Why should we believe you're just going to willingly take us to Dahlia now?"

"Have you looked at the sky lately, my lord Hades?" Caspian asked. "That looks pretty fucking believable to me."

"Precisely. If you recall, I tried to mitigate the problem. You, in turn, caused it. Now you have to clean up your mess, and we need to put the genie back in the bottle, as it were. Dahlia needs you."

Tor got to his feet, his eyes immediately finding mine, before he said, "Where is she?"

"Finally, someone talking sense. Who would have thought it was the Berserker? Not me, I can assure you."

"Focus, Clarence," Hades drawled. His intolerance of the angel was not hard to pick up on. Whatever history the two of them had, it wasn't a pleasant one.

"You wish you were Jimmy Stewart," Gabriel sneered.

Tor stalked over to him, wasting no time before grasping Gabriel's jacket. "I asked you a question, angel. Stop fucking around and take me to my mate. Right. Fucking. Now!" he roared.

411

Gabriel's eyes flashed with his angelic power, but he reined it in. Likely because Tor was ultimately giving him the opening he'd been after. "Gather together. You'll need to touch each other's shoulders before I take you where you're going."

"What about them?" Hades asked, his focus going to the zombies kept at bay solely by his dwindling blue flame barrier.

"I'll handle them."

Standing in a circle with Gabriel in the center, we did as he said. He reached out and touched my forehead, and the world around us swirled as though we were inside a cyclone. When everything was set right, I found myself staring down a dark staircase, the sound of the song "The Final Countdown" by eighties hair band Europe filtering through the corridor.

"What the actual fuck?"

HADES

THE WORDS LEFT my mouth as the music grated against my ears. The rapid shift from battlefield to stairwell was disorienting, even for me. It was akin to jumping into a pool during a raging party and the water silencing everything aside from the pounding bass.

"What are we waiting for?" Tor asked, his voice a harsh whisper.

"Before we go charging down there, maybe we take a second to get the lay of the land," I said. Despite my phrasing, I made it clear that it was not a suggestion. "The last thing we want is to spook her while she's got a knife to Dahlia's throat or something."

A growl was Tor's only response, but Kai and Hook both nodded.

"How do you suggest we do that without giving ourselves away?" Kai asked, voice barely audible over the music.

"You stay put. I've got this." I sent my shadows creeping down the stairs and through the hall.

As my helpful spies slithered into the room, I took stock of what we were up against. Set deep underground, Dahlia was being held in a cement bunker of sorts. It reminded me of a large bomb or storm shelter. Low ceilings, no natural light—in fact, the main source of light came from the portal of pulsing energy in the ceiling—and mostly bare walls. The only decoration, in addition to the four containment cells made of what looked like glass, were the handful of needlepoints with odd platitudes, each one more snide than the last. *Cell sweet cell. Death is my homegirl. Your mother lied; you aren't special. Life is like a box of chocolates; they both have expiration dates.*

What a fucking piece of work. I'd admire her if she didn't have my Dahlia trussed up like she was an offering. She'd been latched to a crucifix, arms stretched out on either side and held up by bits of rope. She was arched back, her head lifted to the portal though I don't think she was trying to get a look at it, so much as it was an involuntary act.

Concerning as it was, that wasn't what held my attention.

A constant bolt of energy was being pulled straight from her chest and into Death. It melded with the same flow that came from each of the cells. Death was using

413

them all to get what she wanted as she became the conduit that powered the tear in reality above her.

My shadows wanted to remain focused on Dahlia, but I needed to know who else was being sacrificed for Death's power play. One by one, the horsemen of the apocalypse came into view. Each of them arched in pain as their energy was siphoned from them.

"Oh, fuck," I whispered, pulling my tendrils back before Death noticed them. "So much for the horsemen being in on it." Guess my theory about Grim coming to collect on a gambling debt hadn't been quite right. Then again, I'd been wrong about a few things, so I wasn't exactly batting a thousand here.

"What is it?" Kai asked.

"Some kind of ritual. She's draining them."

"Them?" Tor asked. "She's got more than Dahlia down there?"

I nodded. "Four other supernaturals. They're locked up. It looks like she was collecting them."

"What like a zoo?" Hook asked.

"Maybe."

"Did you recognize them?" Tor asked.

I blew out a breath, wishing I could avoid answering, but knowing there was no way around it without flat out lying. "Yeah. It's the four horsemen."

"Do you think they'd help us if we freed them?" he pressed.

"It's possible," I hedged. The horsemen were hardly what I'd consider good guys, but at least I had somewhat of a relationship with them. Better the devil you know. "Right now, they're supercharging her and fueling whatever spell she's doing to open that portal. It might be draining them, but more importantly, it's killing our girl. We need to stop her."

Tor snarled, ready to burst in there and crack skulls. One specific skull, to be clear, but I stopped him with a shadow around his wrist. "You said we have to stop her. I will tear her head from her shoulders and crush her skull with my boot."

"She's a horsewoman of the apocalypse. There's no way your usual methods are going to work here."

"All right, what do you recommend, boss man?" Hook prompted.

I rubbed a hand over my chin, shaking my head. Truth was, I had no fucking clue. But she'd been one hundred percent focused on her ritual, so at least we'd have that going for us. At the very least we'd have the element of surprise on our side.

What I did know was what I'd learned from the other horsemen. If she was anything like her counterpart, she wasn't one who enjoyed getting her hands dirty. Grim preferred using others to do the dirty work for him. His smug superiority meant that he assumed he was above that kind of thing. Unlike Chaos, who loved a good fight, as you might expect from the Horseman of War. But the same couldn't be said for the others. Death came quietly through nefarious means. Meaning she might not be as skilled in an actual fight. So maybe if we could restrain her, we might win.

Maybe? Might? I grimaced at the amount of uncertainty in my plan. Unfortunately, it was the only one I had.

"She's distracted right now, her focus solely on that portal she opened above her. Clearly that's what she needs. She's summoning something, and I think if we can stop her before she's successful, the world will be saved."

415

"You mean Dahlia will be?" Kai asked, his dragon front and center in his question.

"Is there anyone else who is our world?" I asked drily.

"Just making sure."

"One of us must prioritize getting Dahlia down from that fucking cross," I started.

"Me." Tor didn't leave room for argument, and I offered him a curt nod.

"I'll take Death down because one touch from her on any of you and you will be meeting me in the underworld."

"Are we leaving the horsemen in their cells or freeing them?" Kai asked.

"There is a risk if they're freed, but I think it's minimal. They're more likely to side with us since she took them hostage."

"You don't think they'll just finish what she started?" Hook inquired in an unexpected display of forethought.

I shook my head. "No, that would mean they'd have to admit she helped them. If they're going to start an apocalypse, they'll do it themselves when the time comes."

"Guess it's a good thing I held on to this then," the pirate said, plucking a key out of his pocket.

"Is that . . ." Kai started.

Hook nodded. "Masterson's skeleton key. She thought she took it back, but I made sure to recover it."

"Will it open the cells?"

"Only one way to find out, but it stands to reason that it would. It's bespelled to open literally anything."

"What do you want me to do?" Kai asked.

"Death loves to have others fight her battles for her, so keep an eye out for any unexpected guests."

"Got it."

"You guys ready?" I asked.

They nodded, and I could feel the purpose rolling off them.

"Let's go."

I didn't even pay attention to the men at my side as we rushed down the stairs and into Death's bunker. I trusted that they'd do their assigned jobs to the letter. The music blared as Death's face glowed from the power racing through her, her eyes open but sightless as the energy overtook her.

Not wanting to get too close to her, I sent my shadows to wrap around her waist in an attempt to yank her bodily out of position and break the circuit. But my fucking shadow power didn't work on her. The tendrils went straight through her.

Grim's strained voice came from the cell nearest where I was standing. "Use your fire, Hades. Now!"

I wasn't going to look a gift horseman in the mouth. If anyone knew what would take her down, it was her mirror.

Drawing on the full extent of my power, I channeled a massive bolt of the deep purple flame her way. It collided with the golden beam of energy she'd siphoned from the others, cutting off the stream and sending all five of them to the ground, Dahlia sagging in her bindings while Tor got to work undoing them.

I didn't let up, even as the portal closed above her head, even as the spell was clearly interrupted.

I couldn't believe she was able to force out any words with the power I was hitting her with, but as she slowly turned to nothing but charred dust, her voice filled the room. "I . . . still . . . beat . . . them."

"You may have beat them, but I beat you." She might have been Death, but I was Hades God of the damned Dead and that meant she'd always answer to me.

My fire didn't let up until there was nothing left of her. I couldn't stop, not until I was sure she was vanquished.

"She's gone, mate." Hook's hand on my shoulder made me flinch.

"For now," Chaos said. The horseman looked like he'd been ridden hard and put away wet. All of them did. Whatever Death had stolen from them came at one hell of a price. There was no knowing if they'd recover it, or how long it might take before they did.

"Still, we did it," Hook persisted, his attention shifted to where Tor cradled Dahlia. "We saved the world."

Our girl was a little worse off than I'd like, but her eyes were open and she was alert. Face pale and brow dotted with sweat, she appeared like she'd been on the wrong side of a fight with consumption.

"You okay, baby doll?" I asked, rushing to her, just like the other two.

"You stopped her."

"Of course we did. We've all told you we'd burn the world down for you. Do you believe us now?"

"I didn't think you meant literally," she teased with a raspy chuckle.

A tug on the back of my shirt had me unwillingly turning away from my goddess. "What?" I snapped.

Sin held up his hands. "Don't bite my head off. We just wanted to say thank you."

"I didn't do it for you."

"No, but you still freed us. Consider your debt to me repaid," Grim said, his eyes bruised with exhaustion.

"For a minute there, I thought this was all you coming to collect. I'm really glad it wasn't."

"Aw, would you look at that? Hades got his heart back," Malice teased, his voice warm, but his expression haggard.

"What will you four do now? Get the band back together?" I asked.

Sin exchanged a meaningful look with the others. "No. I don't think so."

"We have other business to attend to," Chaos added.

"You gonna fill me in?"

"It doesn't concern you." Grim's pointed stare told me in no uncertain terms that I needed to leave it alone.

"You're right. I don't want to know."

The horsemen left us, not looking back as they made their way down the corridor.

"Should we be worried about that?" Tor asked, pointing in the direction the horsemen had disappeared.

The four of them being who they were, there was no simple answer to that question. Because of that, I just shrugged. "Guess we'll find out."

"Is it really over?" Dahlia asked from her place in Tor's arms.

"It seemed a wee bit too easy, don't you think, lads?" Kai stared down at what used to be Death, except the ashes were already gone.

Caspian shoved him. "Would you bite your tongue? Everyone knows that's the quickest way to invite bad luck." He glanced nervously around the room as if expecting Death to jump out of the shadows.

"She's not permanently gone. Death can't die. But we stopped whatever she was doing and at least delayed her for a while."

"She was my mother, I think. Unless she lied about that too," Dahlia said, her eyes finding mine.

"She didn't. That was what Adonis and Gabriel had been trying to tell us."

She heaved a sigh, her thoughts turning inward for a

second before she seemed to shrug them off, not ready to dwell on what all that meant for her just yet, if I had to guess.

"How did you find me?" Dahlia asked, wriggling until Tor put her down, his beast really not liking that. "I don't even know where we are."

"Special messenger." Hook's quip wasn't lost on me.

"What?"

Hook smirked. "Divine intervention in the form of an angel, love. Dressed in leather, if you'd believe that."

Tor leaned down, nuzzling Dahlia's neck and taking in her scent as she spoke to Hook. "Tor, why are you doing that? I'm fine. You saved me."

"I nearly lost you twice tonight. I need to calm the beast. I was holding you as much for my benefit as yours."

She turned to him, taking him by the face and pulling him in for a kiss. "Let's get out of this place and find somewhere we can go. Then I'll let you hold me all night long."

Tor let out a rumbling purr. "It's a deal, beauty."

"Me too. Don't forget about your captain, darling girl," Hook interjected.

Dahlia smiled. "As if you'd let me. I'll need all of you tonight. Every night."

"It's a good thing the feeling's mutual, then, isn't it?" Kai added, leaning in to press a kiss to the top of her head.

"Come, then, baby doll." I led the way up the stairs, not looking back for her because I knew she'd always be with me. "Let's see what's left above ground."

THIRTY-NINE

My mind was reeling. I hadn't begun to process everything that had happened. I'd made a deal with myself to take everything second by second because otherwise I would cease functioning. I would curl up in a ball right here on the staircase and sob until I died of dehydration. Or a broken heart.

Don't think about it, Dahlia.

One second at a time.

Focus on the feel of Tor's hand against yours. How many steps until you reach the top? Seven more. You can make it seven—six more stairs.

We came out behind the estate near the lake. The grounds were eerily quiet back here. Most of the fighting had taken place on the other side of Blackwood. I wasn't sure what we'd find waiting for us when we got there, but I was pretty sure it was going to look like the aftermath of a Civil War reenactment, aka bodies fucking everywhere.

One body in particular would be waiting.

Breathe, Dahlia. Just breathe.

Feel the air against your cheeks.

As we rounded the estate and approached the battle-ground, I braced myself. I didn't want to see the carnage. I'd lived it once already.

Maybe that was why the sound of voices startled me. These were not throes of battle voices. These were calm, talking about the weather voices. Or at least that's what it sounded like as the main courtyard came into view.

The fighting had officially stopped, and villagers and residents alike were scattered across the field. As with any natural disaster, the mood varied wildly from group to group. Some folks wailed, mourning the loss of friends and loved ones. Others celebrated that they'd survived. Some were still in shock and stared unblinkingly around them. And then there were those who were more akin to first responders, walking around the field to check for the injured and potentially to see if they could find a missing companion.

It was easy to tell the dead from the living now. Every last zombie was nothing more than dust where they'd fallen.

"What . . . How did you guys stop them? I lost control."

"It wasn't us, gem. It was the angel Gabriel."

"How?"

"The power to smite isn't used lightly, but that looks like exactly what he did," Hades mused.

"Ohmigod, Dahlia!" Oz cried, rushing over to me and nearly knocking me over when he wrapped his arms around my neck and squeezed. "You're alive! I was so worried."

I hugged him back, relief making me sag against him when I spotted Bru walking at a more leisurely pace toward us. Tor's handsome handler grinned at me, and I hoped to God or whoever was up there that none of them remembered me killing them all. I wasn't going to say a damn word.

"Sorcha?" I asked.

"That cockroach?" he said with a watery laugh. "It'll take more than a couple grumpy villagers and some zombies to take her out."

"So where is she?"

"Took off as soon as the wards fell. A lot of people did. The Council is going to have their hands full when they realize they have escapees to round up," Bru answered, gently pulling Oz away from me so he could hold him. It was such a Tor move that I couldn't help but swoon a little.

"The wards are really down? We can leave?" I asked, disbelief coating my question. "Kiki will be so . . ." The words died on my tongue.

Kiki would be nothing. Kiki was gone. She was dead, and I was responsible.

"No, gem," Kai whispered, his fingers brushing my arm until he shackled my wrist. "She told you not to blame yourself."

"Where is she?" I asked, glancing around the grounds and not finding a trace of her.

A tall blond man dressed in black leather strode toward our little group from where he'd been standing in the middle of the battlefield. I'd clocked him earlier but assumed he was just a villager.

"I took care of her, Dahlia."

"Who the fuck are you?"

His chest puffed out, and he opened his mouth to speak, but Hades stopped him. "He's Gabriel. The angel."

All the air left the angel in a rush of pure annoyance. "What he said."

"Who told you to do that, Gabriel?" I snapped, panic

425

and grief clawing their way through the Kiki-sized hole in my heart. How was I supposed to say my goodbyes now?

"It was do that or let zombies desecrate her body. I assumed you'd rather she be cared for and laid to rest."

"Where is she?" I insisted.

"Well, I . . ." Gabriel glanced from me to Hades, almost as though he was pleading for help.

I didn't blame him. I was scary.

"It doesn't matter where she is, baby doll. Her physical form may be gone, but you're forgetting one key benefit of being mated to me."

I frowned, locking eyes with him. "Which is?"

"I can take you to see her whenever your heart desires. Every damn day if you so choose. She may be dead, but she's not gone. It's more like a relocation."

I could already hear Kiki's long-distance relationship jokes.

"Can you take me there now?" I think the question came out somewhere above a plea, but just shy of a beg.

"Don't see why not. The wards are down, and there's not really anything keeping us here anymore."

Tor's arm snaked around my waist. "You'll take all of us."

Hades sighed but nodded. "I thought that went without saying."

"You're Hades, nothing goes without saying," Tor countered.

"Fair enough."

"Are you satisfied with that, Dahlia? Although, honestly, after what the five of you caused, I don't technically owe you anything." Gabriel crossed his arms over his chest.

"Why are you still here, then?" I asked.

He cocked one blond eyebrow. "Because there's more work to be done yet."

"We just closed a portal to hell and stopped a rabid army of the dead. What more is there?" Technically, I didn't know where the portal led, but given who my mother was, one could only assume.

"I suppose it's none of your concern now. You've done your part. You survived. Congratulations."

"Anyone else think he's being sarcastic?" Hook asked.

Hades shot Gabriel a considering look. "You were wrong."

"Was I?"

"You said the world would end if we stayed with her. Look around, angel. We're all still standing."

"Hmm..."

I think it was safe to say that the angel Gabriel was not my favorite person. Not only was he underwhelmed by what we accomplished, but he also exuded a strong sense of disappointment. Or maybe that was disapproval. Either way, not a fan. I'd like to see how he'd handle being crucified by his own mother. Probably not too well. He'd probably cry.

"Well, as lovely as it's been shooting the shit with an angel and all, I need to see my bestie. My lord Hades, would you mind?"

"You kidding? I've been waiting for you to ask since I remembered who I was. Let's go home, baby doll. I know there's at least one pup there who will be happy to see you."

"We won't be stuck there, will we?" Kai asked.

Hades shook his head. "No. In fact, there's a bit of a limit on how long the living can stay in my realm. So we'll have to make other plans eventually."

"I think I'd like to return to Faerie at some point. I have

427

some matters to address with the Shadow Court," he said, giving my hand a squeeze.

"And I will need to return to Novasgard. My parents won't forgive me if I keep my mate from meeting them." Tor frowned after he said that, his fingers lifting to touch the horns on his head. "Though I don't know how my mother will handle my new appearance."

I stood up on my tiptoes to kiss his cheek. "She will love you no matter what, because you are her son."

"Do any of you get seasick?" Caspian asked, mischief in his tone.

"I'm not sure. I've never been on a boat," I admitted. "Why?"

"Because now that I've got my compass back, I want to take us all on a cruise to Ravenndel. We'll have to pop to Alaska first and pick up my ship and the crew, but then I'll show you wonders you never thought could exist."

"I don't know about that. I wrote about vampires and ghosts before I knew they existed. I have a pretty spectacular imagination, pirate."

"I know you do, darling girl, which is why I love putting it to use."

Gabriel made a gagging noise. "I thought you were all leaving."

Hades chuckled. "We are. Keep your feathers on."

It seemed so easy; I would've missed his intense focus if I hadn't been watching him, but Hades opened a portal to the underworld right next to where the angel was standing. So close, in fact, Gabriel jumped out of the way. Clearly he did *not* want a ride downstairs.

"You ready, baby doll?" Hades asked, holding out a hand.

I took it, glancing at each of my men in turn. "Embark

on a lifetime of adventure with four handsome men who are devoted to me?" I smirked. "Let's do it. I'm ready to live like one of my heroines."

"Does that mean we get to live happily ever after?" Hook asked.

We'd already stepped through the portal, so I couldn't be sure, but I would have bet my left tit that Gabriel's voice floated after us.

"For now."

EPILOGUE I

DAHLIA

"The underworld really has a waiting room? Wow." My gaze swept the area: sterile white walls, a sort of backlit white reception desk, and then a small woman with the cutest head of curly red hair behind it.

"Can you think of a better form of psychological torture?" Caspian asked.

"But why punish them before they've been assigned heaven or hell?" Kai slipped his hand into mine and squeezed. "Wasn't dying hard enough on them?"

"Contrary to popular belief, not everything about my realm is a punishment." Hades shook his head and tightened his grip around my waist on my other side. "But to answer your question, the ones who aren't pre-screened and immediately filtered to where they belong have to endure the wait. It ensures no errors are made and, in some cases, that souls who belong together are reunited properly."

"Soulmates?" I whispered.

"Exactly."

"Next!" the woman at the desk called. "Name, death date, and paperwork, please." She glanced up from whatever she was looking at, and her eyes went wide behind the adorable dark-rimmed glasses she wore. "Boss! You've gotta stop sneaking into the line. I feel like you're out there checking up on me and making sure I'm doing my job."

Hades let out a low chuckle, and surprisingly, he gave her a warm smile. "Janine, I need passes for these mortals. They're going to be visiting my realm for a while, and I don't want them to experience any negative effects."

"Now he mentions the negative effects?" Cas whispered loudly.

Tor elbowed him, drawing out a dramatic "Oof."

"What was that for?" he wheezed. "It's important to know these things. You wouldn't sign a contract without reading the fine print, right?"

Janine cleared her throat.

"Why does it matter, Caspian? It's not like you would have opted to stay at Blackwood without Dahlia," Kai pointed out.

Before he could answer, Janine started speaking.

"Prolonged exposure for the living to the underworld may lead to the following: hair loss, premature aging, dick shrinkage—"

"Hey now!" Caspian protested.

"-—symptoms of an enlarged prostate, joint pain, age spots, abdominal discomfort, impotence—"

"All right, we understand," Kai interjected.

"— rapid weight gain or conversely rapid weight loss, incontinence, trouble breathing, diminished sex drive—"

"Wait just a damned second," Tor growled.

"Best just to let her finish," Hades said.

"Thank you, boss. I never get to recite this, and you

have no idea how long it took me to memorize it." She cleared her throat and pinned Caspian with a hard stare. "Painful orgasms, blindness, loss of hearing, unexplained vomiting, heart palpitations, chest pain, and finally, death."

"So what were you saying about those passes?" Caspian asked.

I quietly snickered, more than a little amused by the entire exchange. Usually I'd be the one panicking, but I didn't have a doubt in my body that Hades wouldn't have brought us—specifically me—here if he thought there would be a chance of it negatively affecting me.

Janine gripped the arm of her glasses between her thumb and forefinger before taking them off and letting them hang like a necklace. Then she cocked one perfectly arched brow. "Name!" she shouted at Caspian.

"Erm, Hook. Caspian James Hook."

She laughed. "Just kidding, I know. You've been moving up the watch list for the past couple of months. I thought we might nail down your death date not too long ago, but you surprised me. Give me your finger, hun."

Cas shot me a worried glance as he obeyed. She pricked the tip of his finger, then forcibly flipped said finger over to smear the ruby bead on a white placard. The little badge glowed for a heartbeat and then returned to its original unilluminated status. "There you go, sugar. All set. Next!"

"Make sure to keep that on you at all times," Hades warned softly.

Hook wasted no time obeying, and Hades and I shared a silent laugh at his expense.

Once all my men were protected from every horrible side effect known to man, I stepped up to the desk, finger already out.

433

Janine shook her head. "Not necessary, sweetie. You're already cleared for entry."

"What? How?" I asked, automatically turning to Hades for an explanation.

"The underworld is as much your domain as it is mine. Not only are you my mate, but you're Death's daughter. There's nothing here that could ever hurt you."

My whole fucking chest warmed at the knowledge I belonged here. I'd never really had that, not until I found the four of them. "Okay then, my lord Hades. Give us the grand tour."

He made a low growling sound in his throat and leaned over to kiss me. As was always the case with him, the kiss was no half-hearted affair. He bent me back and kissed me like I was breakfast, lunch, dinner, *and* dessert. Once he'd thoroughly ruined my panties, he pulled away and winked at me.

Janine tittered behind us. "It's good to see you happy, boss."

He waved away her words, but there was no missing the way his smile widened at them.

"Come on," he said, leading us through the set of double doors to the right.

My god of the underworld didn't even have to touch the doors. They simply parted for him like he was fucking Moses and they were the Red Sea. Or my thighs. It was hot as fuck.

"How come doors don't open like that for me?" Cas muttered.

"Because you're not a god. Come on, pirate. This tour's for you too."

Hades led us down a winding path that somehow turned from a boring white business suite to a winding path leading to a castle on a hill. I turned my head to look back, but the hallway we'd been wandering through was no longer there. I didn't question the physics of it all. We were in the underworld; I was just going to accept everything as it came.

"So you're taking us to your mojo dojo casa house, are ye?" Kai asked, a teasing note in his voice.

"What the fuck did you just say?" Hades asked.

I laughed, and Cas shot Kai an accusing glare. "When did you watch Barbie? We were supposed to watch it together!"

Kai shrugged. "When you'd gone full nutter and she was writing her book."

"Bad form," Cas complained, shoving Kai aside so he could take his place on my other side. "You have to walk in the back with the Viking."

"I chose to walk in the back," Tor said mildly.

"So you can check out my ass?" I asked over my shoulder, tossing him a saucy wink.

His lips curved up in a grin, and he nodded. "You know it, Kærasta."

I wasn't sure how long we'd been walking. I also had no way of knowing what time it was. Only that it seemed, for all intents and purposes, that we were strolling together during a warm summer's night. Fireflies flickered off and on, the scents of jasmine and pomegranate filled the air, and I couldn't help but smile at how much joy it brought me. How familiar it all seemed.

For the first time, maybe ever, it felt like I was home.

Hades twined his fingers with mine, gripping tight. "You *are* home, baby doll."

"I think this might be my favorite place," I admitted, feeling a little bashful about the confession. "It makes me feel . . . the same way I do when I curl up on a rainy day in front of the fireplace with a book."

"Safe?" Hades offered.

"Happy. Content in a way nothing can match."

"Just wait until I get you on my ship, love. You'll be singing a different tune."

"Nothing compares to Faerie, or the Highlands, for that matter."

My eyes shifted to Tor, already knowing what was coming. "Novasgard was created by the gods for their chosen. There is no comparison in any realm."

Hades simply shook his head and kept walking. He showed us the castle, taking us through every important space and making sure we knew our way around before stopping outside a closed door.

"What's in there?" I asked, excitement and hope lighting up in my chest.

"Your room."

I deflated. "What do you mean? I'm not sleeping with you?" I glanced at all of them in turn. "I don't want to be away from any of you."

"Not that kind of room, sweetheart. There's only one bed you'll be sleeping in, and it's mine. But we'll get to that later. Now open the door."

Little tingles licked up my belly at the thought of Hades's bed and what later might entail. But my curiosity was too strong to ignore, so I did as he suggested and pushed the black lacquered door open and crossed the threshold.

When they didn't follow, I glanced back at them. "You're not coming with me?"

"No," he said with a soft smile. "Come find us when you're finished."

Curiosity prickled in the back of my mind. There were very few things that would get my men to leave me to my own devices. My writing was one of them.

As I stepped deeper into the room, a soft laugh caught my ear and my eyes filled with tears in response.

"Stop drooling on me!"

"Keeks?" I warbled, running toward her voice. "Ohmigod, Keeks?"

"Dee? Took you long enough," she called, jumping up from the bench she'd been sitting on, her and Asshole racing toward me.

I barely spared a glance at the night garden I'd found myself in. I would have sworn it was an actual room not a second ago, but none of that mattered right now. Only the woman who had flung herself into my arms and felt as solid and real as she always had.

"Kiki," I whimpered, clinging to her.

She hugged me fiercely and then pulled back to look me in the eyes. "Girlfriend, why did you never tell me about the ghost dick?"

I laughed. "What? I wrote a whole book about it."

"Okay, listen. I need you to sit down and prepare your most expressive shocked face while I fill you in on everything you've missed since I died."

Tears streamed down my cheeks at the familiarity of it all. Hades may have promised I'd see her, but I hadn't thought we'd have *this*. I could touch her, smell her perfume, hug her whenever I needed to.

"Hello? I'm here too, doll face. Did you forget about me?" A deep masculine voice had me glancing around the garden, searching for an intruder. "Down here. Gods, you leave to take a pretty lady to the underworld, and suddenly it's like you don't even exist anymore. What happened to all those head scritches and cuddles, Dahlia? I was your wittle snuggle buddy."

"Asshole?" I asked, glancing down at the fluffy puppy standing at my feet.

"You better believe it."

I dropped down so I could pepper his furry face with kisses. "You are the goodest boy. Thank you so much for taking care of Kiki for me."

He gave me a couple of happy licks. "You don't even know the half of it. I took such good care of her, I even introduced her to her soulmate."

"What?" I went still, pulling back to look up at Kiki. "Is it true?"

Kiki beamed and nodded.

"Why didn't you say something?"

"Hello, I already mentioned the ghost dick. And that I had a story to tell you."

"But how? When? You've only been dead for like . . . ten minutes."

"Time works differently here," Asshole explained. "It's been weeks for us."

"Well, what's his name? What does he look like? Can I meet him?"

Kiki bit her lower lip and looked away, her entire face radiating pure joy.

I drank in the sight of her, the pain of her passing slowly leaving me. Hades had been right, the jerk. She wasn't gone, just relocated. This is where Kiki belonged. Her happy ever after might look a little different than mine, but after everything she'd sacrificed for me, she was finally getting all the joy and love she deserved.

"His name is . . ."

EPILOGUE 2

GRIM

Teleportation was never a challenge for me, at least not until tonight. That bloody witch I called my ex-lover had drained all of us nearly to the point of collapse. I almost hadn't had enough juice to make the jump from her lair to my penthouse. The months of imprisonment had been rough on their own, not to mention the toll her little ritual had taken.

I braced one hand against the wall, struggling to catch my breath as that subtle shift of energy told me the others would be popping in any second. Pushing myself upright, I wiped my forearm on my brow to remove the dots of cold sweat beading there and forced myself to walk normally over to the fully stocked bar cart. If ever there was time for a drink.

My fucking palm shook as I reached for the decanter of Brimstone whiskey and poured three fingers into a highball glass. They couldn't see me like this. Weakness wasn't an option.

One by one the other three horsemen appeared, all of

them wearing haggard expressions, Sin looking worse than the other two.

His needs were a little different than the rest of ours, given his incubus nature. He didn't just have to nourish his physical body, he had to regularly feed off sexual energy as well. Other emotions would keep him going, but nothing would truly sate him the way that lust would.

"I don't know what just happened, but I'm pretty sure we owe Hades a debt," Chaos grumbled. "I hate owing anyone anything."

"Would you rather we be lying there in those cells, drained and blinking mindlessly up at the ceiling? Maybe a bit of drool running from the corner of your mouth?" This from Malice, who'd already taken a seat and was pretending his body wasn't failing him with every ounce of bravado he had.

I was familiar with the spell Helene had used, but only in a theoretical sense. The aftereffects of what she'd done to us, what she'd harvested, were yet to be seen. My hand spasmed around the glass, some of the amber liquid sloshing and spilling onto the polished wood in front of me. Pressing one fist against the tabletop and bowing my head, I forced myself to take a deep, restorative breath. That bitch had to pay for what she'd done to me. To us. There was no way I could let her treachery stand.

Sin groaned, his body folding in on itself as he slid to the floor from where he'd been propped against the wall.

"Guys, I hate to ask, but I need—"

"No," we all bit out at the same time.

"But I'm in a real bad way and—"

"Not a chance," I muttered.

"Mal? Buddy? Come on."

Malice shook his head. "I don't think I could get it up, even if I was willing to let you feed on me."

"C?"

"Has the answer to that question ever been yes?" Chaos countered.

"Well, no. But this is an extenuating circumstance. I've never gone this long without feeding. I'm in serious need. Come on. Be a pal. Just a quick session. Go put some porn on, rub one out, and let me watch. Is that really too much to ask? You won't even know I'm there. I won't make a sound, swear. I'll close my eyes. I don't even technically have to watch, I just need to be in the room."

"No."

"I'd do it myself, but you know it doesn't work that way. I can't eat myself. It would basically be cannibalism."

"We said no, Sin," Malice said firmly, halting any further protest with a hard stare.

"Fine, but if I die here, you three are going to have to—"

"Sin, you can't die. You'll be fine until we get things sorted here," I offered, my voice tired. I faltered a bit as my head swam, but I managed to catch myself and gingerly lower my body into a chair.

"You okay, Grim?" Chaos asked.

"No, I'm not fucking okay. It's a bloody disaster. She siphoned our power, weakened us all, and managed to set him free while she was at it."

"Do you think they realize she successfully started the apocalypse yet?" Chaos asked, jerking his head toward the floor-to-ceiling windows to indicate the outside world.

"Gabriel has to know. There's no way this escaped his notice. Especially once Lucifer's chains were broken." I pinched the bridge of my nose as a throbbing headache began between my eyes.

A hint of sensual amber curled in my nose, and when I glanced down at the table next to me, I saw a piece of black parchment instead of the empty surface I'd been expecting. When I lifted the paper, a fiery red scrawl appeared.

I'm calling in that favor you owe me, Grim darling.
Iniquity. Midnight.
Don't be late.

L

"What do we do now?" Sin asked, his brows pulled together.

Balling up the note in my fist, I gritted my teeth and took a steadying breath. Training my gaze on Sin, I snarled, "Now we get revenge."

Death may have won, but the games aren't over just yet. The horsemen will return in 2025 for The Mate Games: Apocalypse.

While you wait, keep reading for a bonus epilogue from your favorite villains.

BONUS EPILOGUE
HADES

"No, don't give it to Tor. His arm is too good. I'm a little guy. I don't have the stride to run after the stick if he throws it." Asshole's complaint had Dahlia laughing from where she sat at the base of one of the many fountains that decorated my home.

"Give it to Cas," she urged, which caused the pirate to shoot her an affronted stare.

"Give it to Cas? Are you implying my arm isn't as good as Tor's?"

Tor clapped him on the shoulder. "Don't be offended. She's simply telling the truth."

Dahlia spluttered. "I didn't say that! Kai, tell them I didn't say that."

The dragon grinned, his arms crossed around his chest. "Don't bring me into it. You stepped right into that one, gem."

"But I thought you were supposed to fight my battles for me, dragon daddy."

"This isnae a battle, my wee mate. This is you making a mistake."

Dahlia huffed, and I couldn't help but laugh. The weeks had flown by, and I had never known completion like being here with my soulmate. It was everything I'd ever wanted, every dream I'd ever had come true. Do you know what it is for a god to dream? How big of a wish it has to be for it to be something we can't just will into being?

That's Dahlia. My greatest wish. My eternal happiness.

As though she knew I was looking at her, she turned her face toward me and smiled. Fuck, the way she looked at me made my chest tight. I loved her. Fiercely. And I was sure I'd proven that to her beyond all doubt, but fuck if I'd ever let her think otherwise. Which meant there was something we all needed to talk about before much more time passed.

Dahlia lifted her hand to her eyes, like she was shielding them from sunshine, except there wasn't any. My realm existed in constant twilight. "You gonna come over here and join us, or what?"

Tucking my hands in my pockets, I strolled over to where the rest of the group had gathered, Asshole happily chasing his stick—Cas had given in and tossed it for him—the others scattered around the remains of their makeshift picnic.

Kai stiffened, Tor following soon after, and I fought a sigh. I knew there was no way I'd have been able to hide anything from them. Not after all we'd been through.

"What is it?" Tor asked.

"Danger?" Kai got to his feet and all but put himself in front of Dahlia.

"How do you two know something's happening?" Dahlia asked, moving so she could see me.

"Because he's got his hands in his pockets and that murderous look in his eye," the dragon insisted. "Hades isn't easily worried. That face says worried."

"Really?" Dahlia asked, her gaze tracing over my features like a caress. "He just looks his usual level of broody smolder to me."

"Broody smolder?" I asked.

She winked. "It's a thing, trust me."

Asshole returned with an excited yip, dropping the stick on Cas's boot. His doggy grin vanished when he clocked me. "Ah shit, it's time, isn't it? Fuck. But there's still so much I wanted to show them. You promised we could go down to the river and introduce them to the guardians."

"The guardians?" Dahlia asked, curiosity taking her hostage.

"Next time, baby doll."

"We have to leave?"

"For a while. They'll start feeling the effects of the underworld if we don't skedaddle by tonight."

Caspian's eyes flared with panic, and he scrambled to pull out the badge he'd kept tucked under his shirt. "What about these? You swore to me it would protect me, Hades." He began to unbutton his pants and reached down to check his cock, heaving a sigh of potent relief. "Oh, sweet mercies, no shrinkage."

"You're fine, pirate," I said through a laugh. "No smaller than usual."

"Oi, you. Don't try and sell me short."

"I don't have to. You do it just fine."

Dahlia playfully slapped me on the chest. "Leave him alone. He's paranoid. I get it. He's worked so hard to get himself back, and the thought of losing everything is a lot to deal with."

I nodded, my chest squeezing with affection. "I'm familiar with the feeling." Capturing her by the chin, I tilted her face up so I could kiss her properly.

"Mmm," she moaned, melting into me. "I missed you."

"Missed you too, baby doll."

"Who's fault is that? You're the one with all the meetings."

"Next time, I'll just chain you to my chair so I can stare at you while I work."

"Oh yeah?" she teased, but there was no missing the way her pulse sped up.

Unbidden, her voice filtered through my mind, followed by a very clear visual of her, chained to my chair, spread open, naked, and dripping as my shadows fucked every hole she had and I handled paperwork and phone calls until I couldn't stand it any longer. I spun around, tore open my pants, and fucked her with my mouth while stroking my dick until I could come all over her.

"Is that what you had in mind?"

"Fuck, it is now." Here I'd just been thinking I could sneak a blowjob under the desk. Her filthy writer's brain was so much better than mine sometimes.

"We still have time before we leave, don't we, Shadow Daddy?" she asked, blinking up at me.

"Yes we do, baby. We absolutely do." We didn't, but fuck did I want to take her up on that fantasy.

She smirked. "Don't you have some paperwork you need to take care of?"

Kai wrapped his hand around the back of her neck and tugged. "Now, now, gem. Hades said it was urgent. You'll just have to wait until later."

Dahlia pouted. "Boo. Hiss."

I hated that the dragon was right. If we were going to close up shop here, then they'd need the rest of the afternoon to pack and gather anything we might need for the journey. And I'd have to settle my affairs, which sadly involved meeting with my team in person and assigning an interim ruler. If anyone thought I'd let her out of my sight so I could stay here and deal with souls, they were dead wrong.

Tor moved until he was flanking her other side, his eyes on me. "If we can't stay here, where are we going?"

"Well, that's the million dollar question," I said. "The way I see it, we have nothing but options. I figured you all might want to take those trips to your home realms you'd mentioned. Give our girl a much-needed vacation before we return topside and deal with the Blackwood fallout."

"Ravenndel," Caspian said. "We can stop by Aurora Springs and snag my ship and my crew, then we'll head to the second star to the right! I can't wait to take you swimming in the lagoon and sailing around the island."

"A little sunshine does sound nice after so much nighttime." Dahlia was quick to look at me. "Not that I'm complaining. You know how much I love it here."

I ran a hand over her head. "No offense taken. I know my goddess needs to spend time in the sun. You always have."

"Any objections to Ravenndel?" Dahlia asked the others.

Kai shook his head. "I go where you go, gem. That's all I care about."

"What about when you're called back to Faerie? You said they'll need you eventually. What if you're out of reach?"

He pressed his forehead to hers. "Who knows? It may never happen. I've learned a lot about life since I met you. I'm not going to live for something that might not come to pass. You and our life together aren't something I'm willing to squander on worry. So, I'll say it again. I go where you go."

She grinned and kissed his cheek before turning to Tor. "What say you, Viking?"

"As eager as I am to return home, I could use a little more time before dealing with my parents."

Dahlia's expression softened, but she didn't press him on it. I knew she would comfort him in private later. She was always good about handling our feelings and vulnerabilities with care.

Caspian let out a happy shout and clapped his hands. "If you're lucky, maybe I'll even break out the tights you're so desperate to see," he murmured in her ear, tugging her away from me and stealing her breath with a kiss.

"Will I have time to go see Keeks before we leave?" Dahlia asked after Caspian released her.

"I already sent for her. We'll make sure you're all packed. Go spend time with your friend."

She threw her arms around my neck and kissed me hard. "I love you, my lord Hades."

"Love you too, goddess. With every fucking part of me."

~

HOOK

HOW THE BLAZES was I going to get away with this?

Snuggled in my bed with Dahlia wrapped in my arms, I stared out the porthole as the ship rocked back and forth. I was naked. She was naked. My dick was pressed against her round arse, and all I'd need to do was part her thighs so I could slide between the slick folds of her cunt.

A loud snore had me scowling. The giant behemoth in my bed was the only true obstacle. Tor was a light sleeper, and the second I'd begin my thorough plundering of

Dahlia's delectable body, he'd want to join in. Sometimes I didn't *want* to share.

My fingers crept across her hip and down in front where I could play with her a little, see how open she'd be to my attention. If I could keep her still, maybe Tor wouldn't notice.

Goddess, my cock had only been half-mast until now. Now? I was rock hard and throbbing. Maybe it was worth waking Tor.

Before I could explore the thought, a series of thumps met my ears. I'd been a pirate too long not to recognize the sound for what it was. Feet hitting the deck. My crew was staying on the island tonight, blowing off steam with the locals while me and Dahlia's other men enjoyed a bit of quiet. We'd spent most of it in bed, bringing Dahlia off again and again.

So if it wasn't my crew, who the fuck was boarding my ship without permission?

"Tor?" I hissed.

The Viking sat straight up, his eyes wide and attention trained on the door.

"There's someone on the ship. Arm yourself."

Tor brandished a gleaming blade at my suggestion. "Way ahead of you, Captain."

"Where did you get that?"

"I put it under my pillow like any self-respecting warrior would."

"Fair enough," I murmured, sliding out from beneath the blankets and creeping over to the chair where I'd absentmindedly tossed my clothes earlier. Taking hold of my cutlass, I made way for the door.

"Aren't you going to put on your pants?" Tor asked.

"No time."

453

Flinging open the door, I stopped short at the sight of both Kai and Hades in the hallway, tense and ready for a fight.

"Shhh, don't wake her. We can deal with this on our own." I crept past them, not giving two shits I was bare-arsed and flapping in the breeze. Ravenndel was a temperate clime. I could wander naked as a jaybird and be comfortable.

"Who the fuck is on the ship?" Hades whispered.

The sound of steel leaving scabbards was our only hint before several bodies came out of the shadows. My attention had turned toward Hades, so I hadn't seen whoever it was step behind me and hold their blade to my throat.

"Surprise," a husky voice crooned in my ear. I knew that voice. She was one of the most deadly pirates to ever roam the sea, Captain Calypso No Beard.

Tor snarled, his body growing larger, but the click of a gun cocking stopped him.

"I wouldn't do that if I were you." The soft lilt in the words gave away the man's identity as well. Baby Bronn, No Beard's right hand.

Hades gave them no warning as he sent his shadows out in all directions, knocking the gun away from Tor's head and binding every one of the pirates, with the exception of the woman currently threatening to slit my throat.

"Why don't we all just simmer down and talk about this like rational people, all right?"

No Beard chuckled in my ear. "Made a few friends while you were away, I see. Your new additions are quite powerful, aren't they?"

"You have no idea," I managed, doing my best not to press any harder against the wickedly sharp blade. Just those four words were enough to send a trickle of blood down my throat.

Kai snarled, his eyes glowing, and I swore I saw the threat of dragon fire glow in his throat.

I had to put a stop to this before he burned my ship to nothing more than a few planks. In a move I'd bet none of the others expected from me, I disarmed No Beard and brought her to the floor. My bare foot rested on her chest and she closed her eyes tightly shut, turning her face away from me.

"For the love of Nereus, Caspian. The last thing I want to have to look at is your scrotum. Where are your fucking pants?"

"I left them in my room. Along with my woman. Neither of which makes me particularly happy. So tell me, Caly, what the fuck are you doing on my ship?"

I released her, and she carefully got to her feet.

"It's all right, Hades. You can let them go."

"Are you sure?"

"We're old friends."

"Do all your friends greet you with a dagger to the throat?" Kai asked.

"Only the good ones," Calypso answered with a grin, pushing some of her rose gold locks out of her eyes and revealing her trademark eyepatch. "I am Calypso, but everyone knows me as Captain No Beard." She grinned at me. "Bet you never thought you'd see me again, eh, Hook?"

"Why do they call him Hook? Do you see a hook?" I didn't recognize the masculine voice or the accent.

"I can confidently say I do. Look down, mon amour." The pretty blonde giggled, and her cheeks went pink.

"That's nothing. I wouldn't call that a hook," he grum-

455

bled. "It makes no sense. Why call yourself Hook if you have not earned the moniker?"

"Trust me, I do just fine. My Dahlia has no complaints."

Kai and Tor both snarled at my use of Dahlia's name, likely not wanting me to give out information to potential enemies. But they could walk the bloody plank for all I cared. It was my ship. I could do whatever the fuck I liked.

The man shrugged, clearly unimpressed. "Come talk to me when you have entire cities drafting odes to your prowess."

"That's enough, Bast. No need to brag. We did catch the captain by surprise after all, and we showed up uninvited. Let's not get thrown overboard by the . . . human kraken." Caly looked Hades over. I had to admit, with his tentacle-like shadows, he did look a bit like some sort of sea god.

"He's the god of the underworld. Shadow daddy, if you like. We call him Hades."

"Cas, I need to know if we're killing them or letting them be," Hades warned. "Until you explicitly say they're safe, I'm going to keep inching closer to tossing them over the side of this boat."

I cleared my throat. "It's a ship, you uncultured swine."

"We mean you no harm," Caly offered. "It was simply a joke. I never expected all this."

"I did warn you," Bronn said, sheathing his weapon and moving until he was standing beside her. "As a rule, captains don't appreciate uninvited guests on their ships. Wouldn't you agree, Drake?"

Another man scowled, but didn't answer.

"So why are you here, No Beard? If not to kill me in my sleep and make off with my ship?"

"The *Lorelei* just docked at port. I heard you'd returned

and wanted to see for myself. You were gone for a long time, Caspian. Too long."

"There were a few . . . hiccups getting back home after we investigated the hellmouth. But my mate and I are here now."

"For good?" she pressed.

I had to shake my head. The truth was, I didn't know how long we had before we'd move on. As much as I wanted to stay with my crew, I wouldn't leave Dahlia. Not now, not ever. When it was time to move on, I'd be at her side, no questions asked. I would always be Captain Hook, but from the moment I met Dahlia, my purpose had shifted. I was hers. I had the mate marks to prove it. Which meant my days of pillaging and plundering were in the past, unless she was the one on the receiving end of said plundering. Still, I couldn't leave my men without a captain.

"Say, No Beard, would you do me a favor?"

"Perhaps."

"I'm going to be traveling with my mate indefinitely. Of course I'll pop back to Ravenndel from time to time, but as much as it surprises me to admit this, I believe a pirate's life isn't the life for me any longer."

Caly's glittering gaze roamed over me. "You never cease to surprise me."

"Really? I find him predictable as fuck," Hades muttered.

Tor and Kai's soft chuckles filled the night. I glared at the trio, but then focused back on Caly, feeling in my gut that this was something I needed to do. The last of the tethers keeping me tied to this life.

"Watch my crew for me? Give them a home if they need one? They're good lads, but they need a firm hand. Otherwise they get a little lost."

"Say no more, Caspian. I'm quite good with lost boys."

Bronn grunted. "What's that supposed to mean?"

She smiled. "It's good to see you well, Hook. Ravenndel wasn't the same without you."

"Of course it wasn't. What is Neverland without Captain Hook?"

"Quiet," Bronn answered with a smirk.

Everyone on deck laughed. Except me, the buggers.

A soft gasp from the door to my cabin called my attention away from No Beard and her crew. Dahlia stood bathed in moonlight, her hair gleaming in the light. She wore nothing but a robe, pulled tightly closed.

Glancing from me to her mates, then Captain No Beard and her crew, my girl cocked her head. "Why didn't you tell me we were having a party? Who the heck are all these people? And where are your pants?"

I laughed and gestured for her to come join me. "Dahlia, my darling, I have someone I'd like to introduce you to."

TOR

IT WAS rare for me to be tense and wound tightly when I was home with my family, but since the moment we all arrived to celebrate my sister Astrid's birthday two days ago, my stress levels hadn't decreased. I'd worked myself up over the prospect of showing my new form to my parents and those I loved weeks prior to our arrival, but that had gone better than I'd expected. As Dahlia had predicted, my family didn't care what I looked like on the outside. They were just relieved and happy to have me home.

It was my twin that was the source of the tension now.

We'd barely exchanged two words since our reunion at Blackwood. Alek was nursing hurt feelings, and I . . . wasn't the best at admitting I'd been wrong. Though I stand by my actions and my reasons for them, I hated that I hurt my brother. It wasn't easy to apologize when you knew, given the choices again, you'd behave exactly the same.

"Oh, come on, this is ridiculous. You," Sunday said, snatching baby Eden from my arms, "sit here. And you," she muttered before grabbing my brother by his elbow and ushering him to a seat, "sit here. The two of you need to figure this out because I can't stand seeing you at odds. Also, it's not good for Eden to see her daddy and her uncle fighting."

Dahlia's cool hand slid over the back of my neck as she leaned down to press her lips against mine. "You can do this. You need it."

I let out a grunt that was somewhere between affirmation and acknowledgment. I'd known this moment was coming the second I'd returned home; I couldn't avoid it forever. Though truth be told, I would much rather be outside running drills in the snow naked or tearing my toenails out with a pair of pliers than have this conversation.

But with the way Dahlia had urged me to see this through, I had to at least try.

Once the women moved to the far side of the room and it was just the two of us by the crackling fire, I blew out a heavy breath and met his stony gaze.

"Alek, I'm sor—"

"Don't apologize. You don't mean it. You'd do the same thing all over again if need be. Just like I would for Sunny."

I opened and closed my mouth, not sure what I was

supposed to say to that. "Well, yes, but I never wanted to hurt you."

Alek sighed. "It wasn't your words that hurt me, brother. It was that you cut me out. Even when my world was falling apart and I barely remembered my name, you were there by my side, riding it out with me. When it was my turn to be there for you and show you the same unconditional support, you cast me aside like so much rubbish. We are two halves of a whole. There is no experience in either of our lives that we haven't gone through together. Until you pushed me away and didn't give me a choice."

His words made my chest ache and my eyes burn. "Alek."

"I get it. I swear I do. I'm not mad at you, Tor, I'm just . . . sad. I missed you."

Fuck. I was not going to cry in front of him. "I missed you too, brother. More than you know."

"Promise me, next time we're facing down a foe we do it together?" He stood, holding out a hand for me.

I took his offered palm and let him pull me to my feet and into a hug. "Together or not at all."

"There, was that so hard?" Sunday asked, Eden bouncing on her hip.

"Shut up and give me my niece back. I wasn't done with my cuddle."

Dahlia's face went soft and sweet.

"Something on your mind, Kærasta?" I teased.

"Hey, that's my name," Sunday protested with a smile.

"Only when I say it, *Kærasta*."

"Ohhh, a swoony Viking-off. I'm here for it."

"What's that I heard about a Viking-off?" Our father's accented voice boomed from behind us as he stood in the entryway with my mother in his arms.

"Go on, Nord. Show your boys how it's done."

He smirked, leaned down, and kissed her deeply before looking into her eyes and saying, "Anything for you, Kærasta."

Watching my parents giggle and flirt was a bit like glimpsing into my future with Dahlia. Their love was as pure and deep as it had been since they met, and it only grew stronger with each passing day. I idly rubbed the ring on my finger as Dahlia came to join me on the oversized armchair.

"Well, beauty, who said it best?"

"Oh, you, definitely you."

Pride washed through me. "Damn straight, Kærasta."

Nuzzling into my side, she pressed a kiss to my shoulder before murmuring, "You know what else I really enjoyed tonight?"

"What's that?"

"Seeing you with a baby in your arms. You were so sweet and gentle. It was a side of you I didn't realize was going to turn me on so much."

I palmed her arse and gave it a healthy squeeze. "Is that so?"

"Mmhmm. You always take such good care of me. It shouldn't have come as such a surprise, but you with a baby. Uff da. It does things to me."

"Does it?"

I had to adjust myself before she made things much harder to hide. The way she pressed up against me, her sweet voice, the scent of her. Fuck. And now she was aroused simply because she saw me with a baby?

"What happened to being afraid of my giant-headed Viking babies?" I teased.

"I'm a fast healer. And it might be worth it."

"Oh, really?"

She nodded.

"Well, in that case, I think you should come with me. I have an urgent matter to discuss with you in my bedroom."

Grinning, I picked her up and tossed her over my shoulder.

"Good night. My mate is tired and needs me to tuck her in," I called as we left.

"Don't do anything I wouldn't do," Alek called.

"That doesn't leave much off the table," Sunday countered.

"Children," my mother said with mock exasperation.

"Oh, come on," my father said, the smile evident in his voice, "they learned from the best."

Desperate not to hear anything further from him that might kill my arousal, I picked up speed and took the stairs two at a time.

Dahlia squealed in delight as I made my way to my room. By the time I stood her on her feet with the bed inches away, her smile was wicked and she was already working her sweater over her head. "We should probably call for the others. I think they should be involved in this too. Kai and Hades will want their chance. I'm less sure where Cas stands on the idea."

"Our chance for what?" Kai asked as he strode inside the room.

"Yeah, baby doll. What?" The way her eyes flashed at the question Hades asked was intoxicating.

"The chance to put a baby in me first," Dahlia breathed.

Shock hit me hard. I hadn't realized we were talking about right now. "But you can't. Your tattoo."

Kai ran a hand over the back of his neck. "I broke the spell before we left Blackwood."

"You mean all this time it was a possibility?" Hades asked.

Dahlia nodded.

"Why didn't you say anything?"

"Well, shit sort of hit the fan, and then I got my period in Ravenndel, so it seemed like a non-issue."

"So why now?" I pressed.

"Seems like the time is finally right."

Hades sent his shadows out, curling them around her waist before they tugged her to him. "Ravenndel was a while ago, baby. You know this means we stand a good chance of being successful, right?"

She nodded.

"So how do we decide which one of us gets the honor?" I asked.

"Um . . ." She bit her lip, her eyes unfocused as she thought. "Maybe the same way we decided who got to take me home that night at the pub?"

"A whisper-off? Excellent," Caspian said, late to the party but no less excited. "I excel at those."

"Careful, pirate. If I recall correctly, I won that night."

"Only because I wasn't there," Kai chided.

"Please. I could beat you all with my hands tied behind my back," Hades scoffed.

"Not how a whisper-off works," Caspian said.

Dahlia laughed. "I don't even care who wins. I'm just excited to see how this plays out."

"So what do you say, boys? Shall we wager on it? Winner gets to knock her up?" Caspian asked.

"Aye, but you're playing a losing game."

"Hell yes," Hades said, eyes blazing as he began to unbutton his shirt.

463

I tore my shirt clean off my body in one rough yank. "Lie back on the bed, Kærasta. Close your eyes and listen to us."

KAI

"ALL RIGHT, love. How are we doing this? No touching like the last time?" Hook said, already naked and ready to go.

Dahlia was on the bed, her beautiful body on display for us. "You each get one line. I'm going to close my eyes like Tor said, and I'll call out the name of the one who makes me react the strongest."

"What kind of reaction are we talking about, gem? Physical, or . . ." I trailed my fingers up the inside of her thigh, loving the goosebumps that broke out across her skin.

"Fanny flutters."

"Best you spread those legs for us, baby doll. So we can see what we're doing to you."

"Cheater," Caspian snarled. "We haven't started yet."

Dahlia moaned and brought her knees up as she spread her legs wide and showed us her already glistening pussy.

"After you," I said, offering the first go-round to Caspian. "Since you're so confident the rest of us are cheaters."

"Wait!" Dahlia squeaked. "I have an idea. It's not fair to make you come up with seductive lines. I want you all to say the same thing."

Without any of us having a chance to ask, she floated the line in our thoughts. I grinned.

"Of course. A classic."

Hook cleared his throat and leaned close to her ear. "Are you listening to me, darling?"

She nodded, eyes closed tightly.

"Good. Now shut the fuck up and take that dick like a good girl."

Dahlia let out a little whimper and squirmed, her face flushed with arousal.

Tor went next, replacing Caspian at her side as he leaned in close. Where Cas's words had been like rough velvet, Tor's held a bit of a growl.

He inhaled deeply, as though savoring her scent. "Mmmm, shut the fuck up and take that dick like a good girl."

"Oh fuck," she whispered.

"My turn. Sit down and watch how it's done," Hades said, striding forward as he adjusted himself inside his trousers. "I know you're a good girl, baby doll. I've watched you take me. Now shut the fuck up and take that dick like a good girl so I can leave my baby inside you."

"Fucking cheater," Caspian muttered.

Hades winked. "What can I say? I never did play by the rules very well."

"That's okay," my dragon crooned. *"Neither do I."*

Pushing my way forward, I bent over the bed until one of my fists was planted by her shoulder and my lips were right by her ear. She shivered as my breath fanned over her heated skin.

Taking her by the throat with my free hand, I gave a light squeeze and managed to growl even as I whispered, "Shut the fuck up and take *my* dick like a good girl."

"Kai," Dahlia breathed, her eyes popping open to meet mine.

"That wasn't the line," Tor protested.

"All of you are fucking cheaters," Caspian said, flinging his hands into the air. "I don't know why I even bother."

"It's fine. I'll get her next time. I'm not worried. We've got forever on our side." Hades worked open his fly, a smirk in his voice. "Better get to business, Kai. Our girl is ready and waiting."

I moved to the end of the bed, leisurely stripping while Dahlia panted for me. Once my trousers and shirt were on the floor, I took myself in one hand and released my wings, knowing what the sight did to my wee mate.

"Show off," Hook grumbled.

"It doesn't matter. Look at how fucking perfect our mate is. Have you ever seen anything more beautiful?" Tor asked.

"No," Hook admitted readily.

"Not in any realm," Hades added.

Dahlia blushed at their words, but her eyes were still locked on me and what I was doing.

"Are ye ready, gem?"

She nodded, then a worried look crossed her face.

"What is it?" I asked.

"You promise it's not going to be an egg, right?"

I chuckled, the sound rolling around the room like gentle thunder as I took her by the ankles and tugged her down the bed.

"I promise, gem. Now do as you were told, and take my dick until you're screaming my name. But be warned, mate, I'm not stopping until my baby's in you."

"Yes, dragon daddy."

"That's my good girl."

Hey fuckers, it's me, Asshole. You didn't really think I'd

LET THESE BROADS WRAP THINGS UP WITHOUT ALLOWING ME TO SAY GOODBYE, DID YOU? THAT'S RIGHT. BIG DOG ENERGY ALL DAY, BABY.

YOU CAN DOWNLOAD YOUR COPY OF MY BONUS SCENE AT: WWW. THEMATEGAMES.COM/VILLAINBONUS
OR YOU CAN DOWNLOAD IT ON AUDIO AND LISTEN TO IT AT: WWW. THEMATEGAMES.COM/VILLAINAUDIOBONUS

THE MATE GAMES UNIVERSE
BY K. LORAINE & MEG ANNE

WAR

OBSESSION

REJECTION

POSSESSION

TEMPTATION

PESTILENCE

PROMISED TO THE NIGHT (PREQUEL NOVELLA)

DEAL WITH THE DEMON

CLAIMED BY THE SHIFTERS

CAPTIVE OF THE NIGHT

LOST TO THE MOON

DEATH

HAUNTING BEAUTY

HUNTED BEAST

HATEFUL PRINCE

HEARTLESS VILLAIN

APOCALYPSE

Coming 2025

More by Meg & Kim

Twisted Cross Ranch

A dark contemporary cowboy reverse harem

Sinner's Secret

Corruptor's Claim

Deadly Debt

Also by Meg Anne

Brotherhood of the Guardians/Novasgard Vikings

Undercover Magic *(Nord & Lina)*

A Sexy & Suspenseful Fated Mates PNR

Hint of Danger

Face of Danger

World of Danger

Promise of Danger

Call of Danger

Bound by Danger (Quinn & Finley)

The Chosen Universe

The Chosen

A Fated Mates High Fantasy Romance

Mother of Shadows

Reign of Ash

Crown of Embers

Queen of Light

The Chosen Boxset #1

The Chosen Boxset #2

THE KEEPERS

A Guardian/Ward High Fantasy Romance

The Dreamer (A Keeper's Prequel)

The Keepers Legacy

The Keepers Retribution

The Keepers Vow

The Keepers Boxset

THE FORSAKEN

A Rejected Mates/Enemies-To-Lovers Romantasy

Prisoner of Steel & Shadow

Queen of Whispers & Mist

Court of Death & Dreams

STANDALONES

My Soul To Take: A Forbidden Love Meets Fated Mates PNR

Also by K. Loraine

THE BLACKTHORNE VAMPIRES

THE BLOOD TRILOGY

(CASHEL & OLIVIA)

BLOOD CAPTIVE

BLOOD TRAITOR

BLOOD HEIR

BLACKTHORNE BLOODLINES

(LUCAS & BRIAR)

MIDNIGHT PRINCE

MIDNIGHT HUNGER

THE WATCHER SERIES

WAKING THE WATCHER

DENYING THE WATCHER

RELEASING THE WATCHER

THE SIREN COVEN

ETERNAL DESIRE (SHIFTER RELUCTANT MATES)

CURSED HEART (HATE TO LOVERS)

BROKEN SWORD (MMF MENAGE ARTHURIAN)

~

STANDALONES

Cursed (MFM Sleeping Beauty Retelling)

~

REVERSE HAREM STANDALONES

Their Vampire Princess (A Reverse Harem Romance)

All the Queen's Men (A Fae Reverse Harem Romance)

ABOUT MEG ANNE

USA Today and international bestselling paranormal and fantasy romance author Meg Anne has always had stories running on a loop in her head. They started off as daydreams about how the evil queen (aka Mom) had her slaving away doing chores, and more recently shifted into creating backgrounds about the people stuck beside her during rush hour. The stories have always been there; they were just waiting for her to tell them.

Like any true SoCal native, Meg enjoys staying inside curled up with a good book and her fur babies . . . or maybe that's just her. You can convince Meg to buy just about anything if it's covered in glitter or rhinestones, or make her laugh by sharing your favorite bad joke. She also accepts bribes in the form of baked goods and Mexican food.

Meg is best known for her leading men #MenbyMeg, her inevitable cliffhangers, and making her readers laugh out loud, all of which started with the bestselling Chosen series.

About K. Loraine

USA Today Bestselling author Kim Loraine writes steamy contemporary and sexy paranormal romance. **You'll find her paranormal romances written under the name K. Loraine and her contemporaries as Kim Loraine.** Don't worry, you'll get the same level of swoon-worthy heroes, sassy heroines, and an eventual HEA.

When not writing, she's busy herding cats (raising kids), trying to keep her house sort of clean, and dreaming up ways for fictional couples to meet.

Made in the USA
Columbia, SC
02 January 2025

51000198R00293